T0262612

Her Knight
at the
Museum

Her Knight
at the
Museum

BRYN DONOVAN

BERKLEY ROMANCE

NEW YORK

BERKLEY ROMANCE
Published by Berkley
An imprint of Penguin Random House LLC
penguinrandomhouse.com

Copyright © 2024 by Bryn Donovan
Penguin Random House values and supports copyright. Copyright fuels creativity,
encourages diverse voices, promotes free speech, and creates a vibrant culture. Thank you for
buying an authorized edition of this book and for complying with copyright laws by not
reproducing, scanning, or distributing any part of it in any form without permission. You are
supporting writers and allowing Penguin Random House to continue to publish books for
every reader. Please note that no part of this book may be used or reproduced in any manner
for the purpose of training artificial intelligence technologies or systems.

BERKLEY and the BERKLEY & B colophon are registered trademarks of
Penguin Random House LLC.

Book design by George Towne

Library of Congress Cataloging-in-Publication Data

Names: Donovan, Bryn, author.
Title: Her knight at the museum / Bryn Donovan.
Description: First edition. | New York : Berkley Romance, 2024.
Identifiers: LCCN 2024011496 (print) | LCCN 2024011497 (ebook) |
ISBN 9780593816592 (trade paperback) | ISBN 9780593816608 (ebook)
Subjects: LCGFT: Romance fiction. | Novels.
Classification: LCC PS3604.O5664 H47 2024 (print) | LCC PS3604.O5664 (ebook) |
DDC 813/.6—dc23/eng/20240405
LC record available at https://lccn.loc.gov/2024011496
LC ebook record available at https://lccn.loc.gov/2024011497

First Edition: November 2024

Printed in the United States of America
1st Printing

For Gill Donovan, my knight in shining armor,
and Bingley, our very loud beagle mix

Her Knight
at the
Museum

One

Emily unwound the cloth from the head of the stone sculpture and found herself face-to-face with the knight.

A spark of awareness, as though she'd met the intimate gaze of a stranger, made her catch her breath. There was something about his unguarded expression—the half-parted lips, the searching look in his eyes—that was more human than any statue she'd ever seen before.

"Hello, handsome," she murmured. "Welcome to Chicago."

Tingles between her legs surprised her. How long had it been since she'd felt *that*? Not since she'd found out Tom, her now ex-husband, had been cheating on her. No, even longer than that, if she was honest.

As a museum conservator, she didn't usually have that kind of reaction to old objects. It would've been really distracting as she worked to restore them to their former glory. But the face of this statue, even with some white streaks of sulfation, was already pretty glorious. His hair flowed loose to his shoulders; typical for a nobleman in the early 1400s. The mustache and short beard wouldn't have been strictly fashionable at court in his time, but they suited him.

She'd already removed the layers of protective wrapping, and she'd told her coworkers in Objects Conservation that she'd let them know as soon as she revealed the actual sculpture. He was their newest acquisition, and even for a huge museum like the Art Institute, he was an exciting one. She had a strange urge to close the door to the photography room and keep him to herself for a while.

But of course, she wasn't going to renege on her promise. She had a six-month contract at the museum, but when Jason had hired her, he'd told her it could turn into a permanent position, which she desperately wanted. It wasn't as though there were tons of opportunities for art conservators.

She stepped off the stool and took a moment to use the hem of her shirt to clean a smudge off her glasses. With a project like him, she wanted her vision to be crystal clear. Then she went to the door. In the main office area, Terrence Russell, a tall Black man with glasses who'd worked there for fifteen years, sat hunched over his computer, the coffee she'd brought him in hand.

Because of Terrence's seniority, Emily had interviewed with him, too, and she'd liked him immediately. He was married to a law professor at the University of Chicago, and he had a small studio in Hyde Park where he made sculptures out of wire.

Emily had jumped at the chance to do the morning caffeine run; little things like that were important when you were trying to fit in. Laurie MacGriogair wasn't at her desk, and Emily tried not to be relieved by that fact.

"Terrence, do you want to come see the knight sculpture?"

"Abso*lute*ly," he said, getting to his feet.

"Um, I want to, too," Laurie said. Emily looked over to where the fortysomething redhead stood at the supply closet. She sounded annoyed that she hadn't been invited.

"Sorry, didn't see you there."

Terrence and Laurie made their way to the black, windowless room where conservators took the first official photographs of a new acquisition. Emily got on the stool again to pull back more of the unbleached cotton wrappings, revealing the top half of the breastplate of the armor.

"He's so *big*!" she exclaimed to her coworkers. What would the knight think of her saying that—if he'd actually been a knight? He'd love it. She was sure of it.

Laurie shrugged. "It's nothing compared to the Buddha I worked on last year."

"He's big for late medieval England," Emily clarified, although Laurie probably knew that was what she meant.

Jason Yun, their boss, wandered in. He was wearing one of his frequent tailored suits, and his hair, more black than silver, was tousled as usual. He didn't say hello or good morning, which made Emily nervous, but as he scrutinized the sculpture, she thought she saw pleasure in his keen dark eyes.

"It's good to finally see it again," he said.

Jason was the Curator of Applied Arts and Design, so ordinarily, he would've been Emily's *boss's* boss. But the Director of Conservation was on maternity leave, so for the time being, the conservators reported to Jason. Unlike most curators, Jason actually had conservation experience: he'd been a part-time assistant while getting his PhD.

Laurie squinted at the face of the sculpture. "I would've guessed he was a fake."

"He's definitely real," Emily blurted out.

Laurie opened her mouth to speak, but not before Jason said, "Emily spotted a fake at the Getty Villa."

Terrence turned to her. "Seriously? What was it?"

"An ivory statuette of the Virgin Mary," Emily said, feeling both proud and shy. She'd told Jason about this in her interview, and a former coworker she'd used as a reference had confirmed it. She suspected it was one of the reasons she'd gotten this job.

"How did you know it was a fake?" Terrence asked.

"Um, it had a flat background, so it originally would've been attached to some kind of plaque, but on the back, there weren't any signs of points of attachment."

But as she'd told Jason, she'd recognized it as a fake on sight, and she couldn't even say exactly why. She just hadn't gotten that feeling of history from it—an invisible but undeniable sense, like a vibration.

She definitely got some kind of vibration from this knight.

Jason circled the statue, looking at it from all angles, his hands clasped behind his back. "The documentation goes back to the 1460s, though we have no idea who the artist was."

Artist? Devil, more like!

Emily froze and whipped around to gaze at the sculpture's face. Her heartbeat kicked into a higher gear. She was half sure he'd *said* that.

But of course he hadn't. He was a big hunk of carved limestone. A *remarkable* big hunk of carved limestone, but still.

She gave an uneasy laugh and said, "He almost looks real." Laurie took a sip of coffee, then grimaced down at the cup.

"For the period, it's an unusually realistic style," Jason acknowledged.

"It's so *iconic*," Terrence said, amused. "Classic knight in shining armor."

Emily went back to unwrapping him, her fingers grazing his bare neck.

"Did you wash your hands?" Laurie asked.

"Of course. Just a minute ago." Many people thought that art conservators always wore gloves whenever they touched a valuable object. Often they did, both to protect a fragile work from the oils and dirt on their hands and, in some cases, to protect themselves from toxic materials like arsenic and lead. But for this piece, a thorough hand-washing was sufficient.

It was too bad that Laurie didn't trust her to do it. How had Emily gotten off on such a bad foot with this woman? It bothered her, and not just professionally. Her mother was always telling her, *Not everybody is going to like you, and that's okay.* But it wasn't. When someone didn't like Emily, she tended to obsess about it.

She'll come around, she thought with grim determination.

Pulling more of the cloths aside, she revealed the rest of his torso. She straightened again to study it.

"Even the armor is so detailed," she said, tracing the air just above his breastplate. "I would guess he's from 1420, 1430. The ornamentation reminds me of Edmund Mortimer's armor." It was going to be a perfect example for the presentation she was putting together for the museum's next symposium—a daylong event where scholars and experts in art history gave presentations. She was calling hers *Dating Medieval Sculpture.*

She turned to Jason. "Was this guy famous, too? Or from some rich family?"

He shrugged. "We don't know anything about the subject."

Laurie stepped up the stool to take a closer look at the sculpture's face—and Emily's possessiveness flared. She wanted to say, *Get away from him. He's mine.*

Laurie turned to look down at her. "Do you know how to treat sulfation?"

"Oh, yeah," Emily said. "I've dealt with it lots of times."

Okay, maybe not *lots* of times, but she'd worked on a limestone Syrian effigy and an adorable statuette of a chubby sleeping Cupid in creamy marble. The Getty Villa, a palatial estate on the Malibu coast, had been her dream job . . . and she'd left it so that Tom could pursue *his* dream.

For a long time, Emily had believed that she'd ruined her own life, and being only a temporary employee at this museum was unsettling. But if she could prove herself and get a permanent job here, close to her parents, she'd have fewer regrets. At the very least, she was grateful for the fresh start.

Laura said, "I'm just asking because you had to ask Terrence for help on that terra-cotta."

"I knew what to do." She didn't quite manage to keep the irritation out of her voice that time. "I just couldn't remember where the adhesive was."

Emily looked back at the sculpture as if silently asking him, *Can you believe what I have to deal with?* Maybe she was hoping he'd stick up for her, since neither Terrence nor Jason ever did.

Jason said, "Start with the photos, the condition assessment report, and the treatment proposal, and tell me how much you can get done in time for the show."

They were already in the middle of setting up an exhibition of late medieval weapons, armor, and war-related art from every continent—a process that took months. These would be among the last pieces to be installed.

"It's going to be great next to the armor," Terrence said.

The museum had purchased a suit of armor from the same region—Essex, England—and the same era. Laurie had unwrapped it a few days ago. It was almost completely intact, only missing one of the circular plates at the shoulder, which was why it had commanded such a jaw-dropping price.

Emily had dutifully oohed and aahed over the armor, but she'd secretly found it ominous. Some kind of symbol was etched on the side of the helmet, obscured with a layer of grit and grime, and the eye slits suggested a malevolent glare. It was the opposite of her new limestone friend: an anonymous sculptor's dream of a chivalrous knight, radiating nobility and humanity.

"I don't have time to do much to the armor," Laurie said. "I just finished the shotel." Emily had to admit to herself that Laurie had done a fantastic job on the slim sword from Ethiopia, with its elegant, cruel curve designed to reach around a shield and stab an enemy in the lungs or the heart. They'd opted to sharpen the blade for visual effect.

"Just get the helmet as cleaned up as you can while preserving the patina," Jason said. "They want to install it soon with a sword from the collection in its hand. If you don't have time for any work on it before the ball, that's fine."

The museum was holding its annual Masterpiece Ball gala, a black-tie event in the Modern Wing's Griffin Court that would raise millions of dollars. The entertainment would include a sneak peek tour of the new medieval exhibition, led by Jason himself, before the show was open to the public.

"Hey, Jason, any way you could get your favorite employees some tickets to that ball?" Terrence asked, teasing.

Jason smiled. "Sorry, guys. I'm lucky *I'm* getting to go."

He said he'd leave Emily to it. Terrence and Laurie followed him out the door, but at the threshold, Laurie turned back.

"Hey, Em, thanks for doing the coffee run. Next time don't get me French roast, though."

"Oh." Emily blinked. "You said black coffee."

"Right. But for French roast, they basically burn the coffee beans." She laughed. "No offense, but it's really bitter."

Emily joked, "You say that like it's a bad thing." Laurie didn't smile, because of course she didn't. Emily added, "I'll get you the breakfast blend."

"Yeah, instead of the Starbucks, try Café Libre. That's where Terrence and I both go when we do the coffee run."

"Great. I'll check it out." Where the hell was Café Libre?

After Laurie left, Emily allowed her frozen smile to melt. Every new job, she knew, had a way of making even the most competent person feel like a dumbass, but Laurie seemed to be on a mission to reinforce that feeling, reaching around Emily's defenses to jab her whenever she could.

Oh well. At least Emily had an exciting project ahead of her.

She walked back toward him—

"Emily! Is this a good time?"

Rose Novak entered the room without waiting for a reply and closed the door behind her.

Emily had met her on her first day of work. Rose had been in the office because she was putting together a stop-motion video of Terrence's reconstruction of a stained glass window from Bruges. She'd asked Emily to lunch, and they'd had a great conversation. Still, Emily had been surprised when Rose had invited her to lunch again the very next week. Emily had returned the favor, so she supposed they were friends now.

Rose's curvy figure was swathed in a flowing blue dress. At thirty-three, she was a year younger than Emily, but she always looked a little old-fashioned for a social media manager. A silver pentagram pendant hung around her neck, and she'd tied back her curly light brown hair.

"Hey, Rose," Emily said. "Here he is."

Rose's eyes widened and she walked over to him. "*Wow.* It's gorgeous. Even if it does have some white stuff on it."

Emily nodded. "I'm going to at least get it all off his face before the exhibit."

A faint buzzing sound made Rose look down at her phone. She studied the screen, and then her whole face lit up in a bright smile.

"What is it?" Emily asked.

"My brother. He just got a raise."

"Oh, that's great!"

At their first lunch, Rose had told her all about her brother's struggles with drug addiction, including a short prison sentence that Rose felt he hadn't deserved. Emily had been expecting polite chitchat, not wrenching personal disclosures, but she admired Rose for being so open and honest. Emily wasn't great at polite chitchat, anyway.

"Sorry, hang on just a sec, okay?" Rose texted him back. Then her eyes misted over, and she waved a hand near them. "I'm just so glad he's doing better."

"He's lucky to have a sister to look out for him."

"Thanks." Rose sniffled and looked around the room. "Actually, can we do a little video?"

Emily cringed. "I don't know." Photos made her feel self-conscious enough.

"It'll get a lot more engagement," Rose said hopefully, but when Emily shook her head, she relented. "Okay, just the picture."

"Maybe it should just be of him." Emily had meant to wash her hair that morning, but she'd stayed in bed too long; her beagle mix, Andy War-Howl, had been especially cuddly.

"Come on, don't be shy." Rose made a little shooing motion. Clearly, there was no way to get out of this.

"Let me take off my glasses first." She didn't wear contact lenses often because they made her eyes dry. In the lab, where she often handled solvents, she never wanted to risk absentmindedly rubbing her eyes.

After she'd set the glasses down on the table, Emily stood next to him, her shoulder brushing his arm.

"Now smile!" Rose said.

"Hey, don't tease him. He can't smile." It was a joke, but she imagined the knight feeling hurt by the command.

Rose laughed and took a few pictures. "Perfect." She lowered the phone.

Emily said, "If you have any filters or whatever to make me look better, feel free."

"Please, you're beautiful—but yeah, I'll gloss it up a bit. Can I ask you a couple of interview questions?"

"Okay, sure."

Rose touched the screen. "I'm recording, but it's just for my own notes. What are your thoughts about this *Medieval Might* exhibit?"

"Oh, it's the best one I've ever worked on. So many people think of that whole period as the *Dark Ages*." Like a dork, she made air quotes. Opting out of the video had been a good idea. "Like in his time"—she waved a hand toward the sculpture—"they were already making beautiful clocks and eyeglasses. And a scientist named Occam came up with Occam's razor."

"The simplest explanation is usually correct," Rose said, nodding. "Okay, and what do you love about being an art conservator?"

"Um . . ." To her horror, Emily drew a blank. "Geez, that should be an easy one, right?" She looked up at the knight again. "Well, I've always wanted to do a big one like this. But on any project, I get this sense of the history, and everything it's been through . . . It's almost like time travel. I don't know how to explain it, but it's magical." She laughed. "Is that too weird?"

"No, it's perfect!" Rose lowered the phone. "That should do it. How's your week going?"

Emily scrunched up her face.

"That good, huh?" Rose asked. "What's wrong?"

"It's nothing," Emily said, and Rose regarded her expectantly. "I have an aunt in Pittsburgh who's giving me a hard time about getting married again fast, so I can have babies." The truth was, Emily *did* want babies . . . but even more than that, she wanted to avoid another relationship disaster. And that meant not rushing into anything.

"You have a fur baby," Rose pointed out brightly.

"That's what I told her! Though Tom said he wanted Andy back once he gets settled."

"So, never, then," Rose quipped, and they both laughed.

"I told him he'd already *be* settled if he wasn't a cheating liar."

Emily had found out last Thanksgiving while she'd been at her parents' house in the Chicago suburbs. He'd stayed in California, claiming he was too busy at work.

The other woman's boyfriend had messaged Emily on social media. Emily had ignored him, figuring he was some kind of scammer or troll, until he'd followed up with screenshots of Tom's texts to the woman. When she'd recognized some of the same flirty and dirty phrases he'd used with her, though not recently, she'd felt as though she couldn't breathe.

She'd called Tom while sitting in her childhood bedroom, staring at her old My Chemical Romance, Fall Out Boy, and Panic! At the Disco posters, shaking with anger. She'd rehearsed her answers for when he'd say, *She means nothing to me.*

But he hadn't said that.

I'm sorry, he'd moaned like a child. *I should've divorced you first.*

She'd never suspected a thing. Not even once.

Rose sat down in the empty chair by the far wall. "How are *you* getting settled in? Here at work?"

"Okay." Emily moved closer to her and said in a lower tone, "Laurie still doesn't like me."

"Is she still being all critical? I could try doing a spell to help."

Yikes. Like a hex? Emily gave a strained giggle. "Um, no thanks. No curses necessary."

"Oh, I never hurt people," Rose said quickly. "Sometimes I just keep them from doing bad things. Like I could do a Fiery Wall of Protection spell. It'll protect you from her being mean."

"Okay, that doesn't sound so bad." It didn't matter, anyway. It wasn't like she actually believed in magic.

Rose said, "You know . . . you may think this is weird, but since you were talking about symbolism before, maybe you'll get it."

Emily blinked. "What?"

"I brought you something." Rose reached into her pocket and pulled out a lumpy, polished bright green stone. She held it out to Emily. "It's malachite."

"Uh . . . wow. Thank you." Emily took it and weighed it in her palm. Was she supposed to understand the significance of this? What should she say? No one had ever given her a rock before. "I love the swirly rings." She traced the surface with a finger.

If you want to touch a stone, touch me.

Emily stiffened.

She could've *sworn* she heard that coming from the sculpture. An accented, baritone voice, delivering a cheesy pickup line.

Cheesy, but effective. She would've touched him if Rose hadn't been there. Touch him where? Where did he *want* her to touch him?

This was ridiculous. She was lonely. And her imagination was getting the better of her. *Dating medieval sculpture, indeed.*

Two

he can hear me!

    This woman, this Emily—a pretty variation of *Emelye*, often used in his time—could sense Griffin was more than an object. He was almost sure of it.

Every time she looked his way, his heart leaped . . . or so it seemed. How he could feel such things while being made of stone, he didn't know. Hundreds of years ago, Mordrain—his friend from childhood, turned foul enchanter—had turned him into a statue. A statue that could think, hear, see, feel, yearn, and grieve; the most hellish torment that had ever been devised.

When Rose had first mentioned doing a spell against the red-haired woman named Laurie, Griffin had recoiled, wondering if she was in league with demons, like the conjuror who had damned him. Even if Laurie was as nasty as ditch water, she didn't deserve to be cursed. But as Rose spoke more about it, he'd realized there was no harm in her. In his time, there had been a dame in the village who had dispensed charms, advice, and simple cures, and even the priest hadn't objected to her services.

"Keep it in your pocket," Rose said now of the green stone. "It helps you heal old traumas and break free of the past, which I figured, after a divorce . . ." She shrugged.

Emily said, "No, yeah, I love it."

Yeah meant the same thing as *yea* or *aye* or *yes*, Griffin had learned, but what did *no, yeah* mean? Something between a *nay* and a *yea*, or both at once?

Why had Emily gotten divorced? She had a dog, but no children; had the man failed to render his marital debt? Young wives, it was said, required swiving thrice a week at least, for their health and soundness of mind. Griffin had always supposed that when he did marry, he'd gladly perform the services of Venus as often as his lady wife should desire.

Especially if he had a wife as beautiful as Emily. Her uncovered hair hung loose, but no braids or ornaments could've improved upon the wavy dark brown tresses. What a pleasure it would've been to idly twirl a lock around one finger. She had a pale complexion, touched with powder, and was about thirty years of age, he guessed—the age he'd been before the curse, when he could still speak whenever he liked, roam wherever he wished, and lift his face to the sun.

Behind her eyeglasses were kind, chestnut-brown eyes. He'd seen men wearing eyeglasses, but had he ever seen them on a woman?

How long had it been since he'd seen *any* woman? A long while, which no doubt made her all the fairer in his eyes. For over a century, he'd stood in the foyer of a grand manor. Its last master, Richard Burke III, had died and men had borne the body away. After that, for two years, no one had come. Griffin had marked the time by the changing of the leaves and the snowfall outside the windows.

Emily said to the green stone in her hand, "Don't let me brood about my ex, okay?"

"Nooo, not like that," Rose said in dismay.

Emily's mouth dropped open in surprise. "What?"

"You have to say things positively! If you cast doubt, you ruin the magic. Like if you say, *Don't let me brood*, a small part of the universe is going to hear that as, *Let me brood*."

Emily tilted her head, looking as perplexed as Griffin felt by this logic, but then she said, "Okay, how about this?" She addressed the stone again. "Let me break free of the past."

"That's good!" The two women shared a smile.

Emily thanked Rose again, and they exchanged parting words. Maybe it was a shame that Rose wasn't a mighty sorceress, even one who consorted with the Devil himself, that she might save Griffin. But no, she still would've been no help, because she'd never know Griffin existed, and neither would anyone else.

Emily locked the door behind Rose and walked back to face him.

"Well," she said, in that voice he already loved, sweet but slightly scratchy. "It looks like you and I will be spending a lot of time together."

He would be grateful for this. As long as she graced him with her presence and attention, he would heed her every word and gesture, to give him good things to remember later.

She pushed up her eyeglasses on her nose. Perhaps her vision was weak from long hours of study, for his lady was not only fair, but knowledgeable and wise. She'd already compared his armor to Edmund Mortimer's, and Griffin's armor had been commissioned from the same shop. Whatever else one might have said of Sir Edmund, he had fine tastes.

"First things first," she said. "Let's get the rest of these rags off you."

When the men had come to the country house and wrapped him in cloths, he'd welcomed even their impersonal touch. He longed for carnal pleasures, yes, but also for a friendly pat on the shoulder or a brotherly embrace. In life, he'd scarcely noticed such things.

Then they'd bound his face, as though he were a corpse and, it seemed, closed him into a coffin. Terror had seized him, and for a long, dark hour or more, he lay in mute despair. But he never heard the sound of gravediggers' spades, nor felt a lowering into the ground; instead, he was placed somewhere higher, and he moved forward. Then he supposed he was in a wooden shipping box, like a merchant might use for Venetian glass or wine.

If his lady's hands brushed him again as she unwrapped him, he didn't feel it through his armor. Still, as they neared his codpiece, he imagined the caress of a lover, a sublime joy forever out of his reach. *Christ*. He half wondered that his ache for it didn't crack the stone.

Once she finished, she stood back and gazed at him. "I'm going to take photos for my assessment report. But I need to fix the light first."

She dragged the stool to the center of the room. Her shirt was green and her trousers black. Once upon a time, his green shield had been emblazoned with the sable griffin, his namesake, half eagle, half lion. So had his banners in battle and the painted panels in his dining hall. Had Griffin not been cursed, and had he taken a wife, she would've dressed in green and black with him on Yuletide, Midsummer's Eve, and all the feasts.

But this woman's clothing signified nothing, other than the fact that she was wealthy; bright fabrics like the emerald hue of her shirt were expensive, and her shoes were made of the spotted skin of the leopard, exceedingly rare. They revealed her naked ankles, and he could well imagine kissing her there, or even giving her a gentle bite to make her squeal.

She stepped onto the stool, reached up, and adjusted the angle of one of the metal cones hanging from the ceiling. Her movement pulled her green shirt taut over her small, delectable breasts.

"I don't usually talk to sculptures," she added. "Just so you know."

Demoiselle, please do not stop speaking to me.

She darted another astonished look at him, and his heart seemed to leap again.

He'd been able to communicate with a handful of people over the centuries . . . but not like this, in waking life. Only in their dreams. Unable to move, often staring at the same scene for years on end, he had reached with all his soul to those around him. Perhaps no living man or woman could ever be still enough, or would ever have time enough, to develop such a skill. However, one night, after countless attempts to touch other people's minds, he'd walked right into a serving woman's slumber. She'd recognized him at once. An aging widow, somewhat lonely herself, she'd welcomed his company.

He'd befriended many others over the centuries. Most recently, he'd known the owners of his statue: Richard Burke, his son, and then the grandson, who'd become his closest friend of all. One night, Griffin had gone to visit the third Richard in his dreams and had been unable to find him, and he'd known the old man had died. The sorrow had hollowed him out.

None of them, of course, had ever believed Griffin truly existed. Each person had assumed that their imagination had turned a statue into a make-believe friend.

From the side table, Emily pulled blue rags out of a box—no, they were gloves; she put them on and they fit her small hands like a second skin. Then she picked up a black book and a pen—he'd seen those. As she came back toward him, she opened the book and clicked the pen.

"Let's take a closer look at you." She drew near and looked over his right arm, the one that had been holding his helmet for centuries.

"There *must* have been a repair here at some point," she murmured. He could see why she would say that. The helmet rested on his hip, but his arm jutted out from his body; in an ordinary statue, that thinner part would've been vulnerable. In his time, at the chapel in Colchester, there had stood a statue of St. George slaying the dragon, but George's upraised sword arm had broken off, making it look like the dragon had devoured it and was about to finish off the rest of him.

Emily's fingers delicately traced his shoulder, then his wrist. If only he could've taken off his gauntlet and her glove, to feel her touch on his bare skin. She was so close that he could smell a light, floral perfume on her, the scent of springtime and new life.

"I don't see any repairs, though," she said in wonder and stepped back to scribble something in the black book.

She looked over every inch of him, front and back, sometimes standing on the stool. He guessed it took the better part of an hour.

"Amazing," she said finally, sitting down at the side table. "There's no pitting or flaking . . . or any kind of real deterioration. But there's some discoloration from soluble salts, and I can see where moss grew on your shoulders, so you must've been outside part of the time."

He had been indeed: first in the clearing in the woods where he'd met his doom, and later in a garden. On some windy days, leaves and twigs had blown into his face, and on some winter nights, icicles had hung from his nose and ears while his insides seemed to shudder from the cold. The birds had been a mixed blessing.

She made some notes, then peered up at him. "What kind of super limestone are you made out of?"

A burst of music distracted her and she touched the screen on her nearby phone. Griffin knew about phones; he had seen Richard Burke III use one, there in the foyer where Griffin had stood, and he'd asked Richard about them in one of Richard's dreams. Richard had used them to talk to people in other towns and, occasionally, to tell innkeepers they could expect him later for dinner.

"Hey! Happy anniversary!" Emily said. She set the phone down and began picking up the discarded wrappings on the floor as she talked. "I was going to call you at lunch."

Another woman's voice filled the room. "Do you want us to call back?" This was different. Griffin hadn't been able to hear the person Richard had been talking to.

"I can talk now," Emily said. "Are you at Mackinac Island yet?"

"We're leaving bright and early tomorrow," the voice of an older man said.

"It should be beautiful, just like today," the woman's voice chimed in. "That reminds me, I saw Sharon at Twin Lakes." Emily frowned and shrugged as though she didn't know who Sharon at Twin Lakes was. "Did you know her daughter had a baby?"

"No." Emily put some of the wrappings, which looked like sheets of bubbles, into a barrel. "Why were you golfing? I thought you were resting that knee before your trip."

The woman clicked her tongue. "It's all better."

"Sure, all better three weeks after surgery," the man said, with what sounded like both fondness and irony.

These were Emily's parents, Griffin supposed. How lucky they all were to have one another and to engage in easy and friendly conversation whenever they liked.

"How's that presentation coming along?" her father asked.

Emily winced. "A little slow."

"I'm sure it's nothing to stress over."

"I don't know." Emily glanced at the door as if to make sure it was closed. "I feel like they're more likely to take me on full-time if I do a good job."

"You'll do great," her mom said. "How are you liking the people there?"

Emily folded one of the long fabric strips she'd unwound from him. "One of the other conservators is nice. He talked to me about fun things to do in town." She set the bundle on the side table.

"You mean he asked you out?"

"Nooo, he's gay. And married. But he told me about the farmers market in Logan Square and things like that." She meant the one called Terrence, Griffin guessed; the one who also wore glasses and had deep brown skin, like the emissary from Ethiopia who had been a guest at the Duke of Burgundy's court.

"Are you getting along okay with your boss?" her father asked.

That would be Jason Yun. Griffin had seen him a few years ago, at the Burke estate when Richard was still alive, and Jason had given his name to the maid who'd answered the door. At first, Griffin had thought that Emily might be married to one of the men, and although it hardly mattered—it wasn't as if Griffin could woo her— he'd been glad to figure out that Emily worked with one and for the other.

"I actually haven't talked to him all that much," Emily told her parents, folding another strip. "He's kind of hard to read. But there's this girl in social media who's really friendly. I don't think we're going to be *best* friends or anything."

What made her say that? The witchcraft, perhaps.

"If you don't get hired there full-time, you can always fall back on your chemistry degree," her father suggested.

Her mom clucked her tongue. "I wish you'd never moved to California."

"Well, I loved the Getty. The Silicon Valley move was the mistake."

"I never understood that," her father said. "They were making an app, right? They couldn't do that from home?"

"I mean, his business partners were up there, and they thought they had to have a fancy office to impress investors. And a launch party and booths at tech conferences." She shook her head. "They did everything except make a working prototype."

Griffin was listening with every fiber of his being. They all spoke with more or less the same accent, which fell strangely on his ears. Perhaps he was merely confused. Inflections and manners of speech had changed so much over the centuries that he always strained to understand people, and for a long while, he hadn't heard any voices at all.

Emily's father said, "I don't know why he was making a dating app, anyway. Those never work."

"They do for some people," Emily said, a dismal note in her voice now. She sat down in the chair, stripped off her gloves, and picked up her phone. "I'm going to sign up on one. I just keep putting it off."

"I think you should do it!" her mother said. "You don't understand, Ed. This is how people meet each other now. They don't go to bars and hook up with strangers."

"It worked for us."

Emily said, "I don't want to hear that story again."

Her father chuckled. "Well, if you're going to shop online for a boyfriend, find someone with a good, steady job. Like insurance."

"Or accounting," her mom added. "You don't want to get carried away by a handsome face and a lot of talk."

"Are you saying I'm not a handsome face?" her father joked.

"Now, honey. Not everyone can be the whole package."

"You guys are adorable," Emily said, a wistful look in her eyes. "It's no wonder you've been married forty years."

"You just need to find the right person," her mom said.

Emily glanced up at Griffin, as if she knew he was listening. "I should get back to work. But call me tomorrow when you get to the Grand Hotel!"

After they said their goodbyes, Emily sighed. In the short silence, he tried to communicate.

My lady, 'tis no stone that stands before you but a man.

She stiffened slightly. Had she heard him? He didn't want to frighten her away, and sending thoughts in this way was difficult, but he couldn't stop trying to make himself known . . . not when she was the first person who had ever seemed to sense him.

"I keep wanting to talk to a statue," she said. "I think that means I *really* need to set up a dating profile."

He had no guesses as to what that might be. She took in a deep breath, for all the world like a squire about to go into battle.

"I'm going to look for men my father would like," she told Griffin. "The ones who've lived in Chicago their whole lives and have dinner with their parents every Sunday."

Was this new country called *Chicago*, then? He would've gladly had dinner with *her* parents every Sunday. As lonely as he was, he would've had dinner with almost anyone every Sunday, given the opportunity, but her parents sounded particularly agreeable.

She tapped her phone as she spoke. "Let's see. I'm a woman, I'm thirty-four, I want to date men, long-term dating . . . and now they want six pictures of me." She grimaced. "This is actually the worst part. I deleted about a hundred of them last month since Tom was in them."

After about a minute of tapping the phone, she said, "Okay, maybe this one. It's from a year and a half ago, though . . ." She looked up and showed him the screen, adding playfully, "What do you think? Too much skin?"

In the image, she wore a black dress that left her arms and décolletage bare, with only thin straps over her shoulders to hold it up. If Griffin had been able to breathe, he would've forgotten to in that moment. Had her former husband put that joyful sparkle in her eyes? Having done it once, how could he not have become devoted to doing it again and again?

Emily lowered the phone and studied the image. "I was about eight pounds lighter then, so maybe it's false advertising." She shook her head. "It's like putting yourself up for sale on Amazon. 'Divorced museum nerd! Free shipping!' You know what? I'm going to do the compatibility quiz first."

She sat down in the chair and touched the screen a few more times. Then she said, seemingly reading out loud, "'What do you hope a partner will like about you?' They've got like thirty traits to choose from," she added to Griffin. "*Spontaneous* . . . that's what guys are looking for, right? I used to be." She wrinkled her nose. "I think. I barely even remember the person I was before Tom. *Empathetic* . . . that means understanding, right? All right, I'm going with *kind*, *educated*, and *empathetic*." She gave Griffin a rueful smile. "I may as well just write *boring*, huh?"

An understanding nature and a kind heart seemed to Griffin to be two of the best qualities one could ask for in a wife, and while many men didn't believe a woman should be educated, the sentiment was hardly universal. Griffin himself was a learned man; after centuries of solitude, he couldn't think of anything he'd enjoy more than discussing history and poetry with a lovely lady. Well, he could think of *some* things he'd enjoy more . . . but still, it would be delightful.

As far as he could fathom, she was returning a letter filled with questions from someone who could introduce her to suitors. A trusted priest, maybe, or a well-connected aunt. She fell silent for a few minutes, not reading other questions aloud, to his disappointment, though he was hardly surprised.

But then she read, "'What is your opinion on cheating?'" She jabbed the screen. "'Cheating is never acceptable.' That one was easy . . . last one. 'Besides love, what are the three things you're hoping for in a romantic partner?'"

He loved how she included him in the conversation, even if he couldn't reply. She'd called him *he* instead of *it* to the others, and that had warmed his heart.

"'Someone I can trust' . . . yes." She touched the screen again.

You can trust me. He couldn't help but send the thought to her. She rewarded him with another glance in his direction.

"'Someone who values family' . . . I totally do, but that could get taken the wrong way, you know? 'Someone I can be intimate with regularly.'"

She looked up at him again. "Actually, you're the perfect person to talk to. Like a therapist, but free."

What was a therapist? Griffin attempted to answer. *My lady, whatever you tell me, I shall not judge, and I cannot but keep your confidence.*

"When I found out about Tom's affair, I felt . . . repulsive," she told him softly. "Like this disgusting, farting lump. For weeks I couldn't stop thinking about them kissing and, you know, doing everything else . . . and I would imagine them lying around in bed afterward, making fun of me."

Griffin longed to take her into his arms and murmur reassuring words. What a scabrous plague-sore this Tom had been, and what a shame Griffin would never have the pleasure of thrashing him within an inch of his life.

"I'm feeling better about myself lately, though." She looked back down at the phone. "That's a yes on 'Someone to be intimate with.' Now I need to pick one more . . . 'Someone who makes life exciting'? Hard no. 'Someone who provides me with security' . . . oh boy."

She set the phone down, steepled her fingers, and pressed her lips against them, considering. "I don't need someone to be rich, you know? And companies lay people off all the time these days.

But I do need them to at least be okay with the concept of a job. Even if it's not the *perfect* job." She paused. "I'm picking security." She picked up the phone again and pressed the screen. "And *save*. I'll finish it tonight. And who knows, maybe I'll meet a decent guy. But more likely, I'll just get a bunch of messages from creeps."

She glanced up at him again. "Don't look at me like that."

If Griffin could've laughed, he would've. He couldn't look at anyone in any kind of way.

"I know I sound very unromantic," she told him. "I'll have you know I wasn't always that way. In fact, when I was a kid, I read fantasy novels and King Arthur stories. About guys like *you*."

Griffin's spirits lifted. He, too, loved King Arthur stories. With any luck, she was comparing him to Gawain or Lancelot. No, not Lancelot, given her recent experience with infidelity.

"When I was a teenager, I posted all this really bad emo poetry on Tumblr . . . and when I was in college I fell in love with art history, and I'd be holed up in the library learning about medieval guilds and the Pre-Raphaelites. I was like the most romantic person ever."

She pulled another pair of blue gloves out of the box. "I don't know what happened. Life, I guess." She put them on, stretching them taut over each finger, sealing them off from contact.

"Reality isn't like the stories, you know? Or like romantic art." She smiled sadly. "There's no such thing as a real knight in shining armor."

He couldn't stand it. His soul cried out to her with all its might. *For Christ's love, my lady. I am here.*

She froze like a deer at the sight of a hunter. Her eyes widened and she pressed her hand to her chest.

Oh, she'd definitely heard him that time. Every word.

She asked, "Am I losing my mind?"

If he'd had a heart, it would've beaten loudly enough to echo off the black walls. She walked over to him. He could scarcely hear the light footfalls of her leopard-skin shoes on the floor.

Her chest rose and fell with a shaky breath. He strained to hear her voice, hardly more than a whisper.

"Why do I keep feeling like you're *talking* to me?"

God in Heaven. Longing shuddered through him.

Please see me, he begged in his thoughts. *Please touch me.*

Slowly, she removed the glove, then raised her bare hand to hover close to his cheek.

Aye, my lady, please . . .

Then she lowered it, shaking her head. She turned and left, extinguishing the lights before she closed the door.

Griffin stood in complete blackness and despair.

Maybe she would refuse to work on his statue now. Maybe he'd chased away his first chance in centuries for a true friendship, one in which the other person knew he was real.

No. It couldn't be. She'd said she had a kind heart and an understanding nature, and he believed it. He would reach her the other way, and she would be kind enough to hear him out, and she would understand him.

Come eventide, he would venture out in his mind among souls in slumber, like walking among the stars . . . though truly, each was more like a ball of fine silver thread, pulsing with light. He would search for her and hope to find her dreaming, and if he did, he would let himself flow into those dreams, becoming part of the twinkling filaments.

His loneliness mixed with something far less familiar and possibly more devastating: hope.

Three

Emily pulled the comforter around her, turned to her side, and drifted off to sleep . . .

Tall shelves filled with leather-bound books, in a grove of even taller trees, surrounded her. She was searching for one book in particular . . . She'd loved it, once. What was the title again?

A man emerged from between the stacks of books. His wavy blond hair flowed past his broad shoulders, and his mustache and beard were closely cropped. The bright green velvet doublet, with its full sleeves and pleated hem, barely covered his crotch, and the black hose accentuated suave narrow hips and powerful thighs. It made Emily think of a football player's uniform, although the only padding was muscle.

His black boots, scuffed and worn, made almost no sound as he approached—warily, as though she might turn into a bird and fly away.

"It's you," she breathed.

He made a deep bow. When he raised his head again, holding her in a steady gaze, he finally spoke.

"Lady Emily." His voice was low and resonant.

"Who are you?"

A rueful smile crossed his face. "Forgive me, my lady. It has been so long since I've spoken to such a kind and lovely demoiselle." Her face warmed in a blush as she took a step closer. "I am Sir Griffin de Beauford, who was oft called Sir Griffin the Proud, son of William de Beauford, at your service."

"Emily Porter." She tilted her head. "But you're a sculpture."

He nodded slightly, as if expecting this. "Once I was the living man you see. For hundreds of years have I been imprisoned in the form of stone."

What? "That's not possible."

He gave a bitter laugh. "Would that it were not. I can feel but not move, and hear but not speak, except in dreams."

Oh. "I'm dreaming now," she realized aloud. That was why she was standing in a library surrounded by giant trees, wearing a flowing white gown.

"Aye, my lady. 'Tis the only way I may speak to others, for none can hear my thoughts . . . although, meseems that you came very close."

"I thought I was losing my mind," she murmured. "You told me to touch you."

"More truth to say I begged."

Her chest ached at the longing in his voice. She took his hand.

He startled as though she'd delivered a static shock. Then he bent down and pressed his lips to the tops of her fingers.

Her heart skipped and she gave a nervous giggle. "Um. Okay."

He released her hand, studying her face. "I thought of doing that many times this day, but I hope I have not offended you."

"I—no, why?"

He shrugged. "A lady may laugh for courtesy's sake and yet be dismayed."

Huh. Pretty insightful for a medieval guy. "You didn't offend me. Although, we do barely know each other."

"Aye, but you have stared at me much today."

She laughed. "That's true."

The sculpture hadn't been an exact likeness. Although more realistic than most from its era, it had still reflected that prevailing style. She'd marveled at its skill, but it hadn't done him justice. His broad face was so expressive, so alive. Nothing had prepared her for the allure of his full lips or the warmth in his blue eyes.

"I didn't think you would be so blond," she said.

"Are you displeased, my lady?"

"Hardly. You're—very handsome."

"Aye, or so I was," he said matter-of-factly. "But I've so long stood unmoving and unloved, I judge myself more monster than man."

This was just a dream. So why should anything he said wrench at her heart? "Come on." She bumped his shoulder with hers. "You seem perfect."

"I am far from that." The timbre of his voice dipped lower. "But such fair words are even more welcome from one whose beauty slays me utterly."

"*Wow.* Um. I guess knights really did have courtly manners. Some of them, anyway." She shook her head and took a few steps away from him. "Although, obviously, you're not real."

"So I have often been told." His smile looked slightly forced. "Yet there is no reason why we may not have pleasant discourse together, as I've done with many in their dreams."

"You go into other people's dreams, too?"

"Aye. I spoke thus with Richard Burke the Third for most of his life, and his father and his grandfather, too."

"Richard Burke, the estate owner?"

"The very same, demoiselle." He cleared his throat, and his eyes looked glossy. "He was a worthy gentleman and a dear friend."

"I'm so sorry for your loss." He'd lost his best friend . . . maybe his only friend? Without even thinking about it, she drew nearer to him again. "My God, you must be so lonely."

"Aye, lady, more than I can say. But your fair company is a blessing beyond hope."

She melted a little inside. "I like your company, too. You're like my childhood vision of a knight in shining armor. Or a Prince Charming, I guess, given this whole tunic thing. And it totally makes sense that you would show up in my subconscious, after I was setting up the dating app, and talking about King Arthur—" *Aha!* She snapped her fingers. "That's the book I was looking for!" The one she'd checked out four times from the public library as a nerdy fourth grader.

His face lit up. "I, too, loved these tales of bravery and honor. My father had three books about Lancelot, the Holy Grail, and the tragedy of Arthur, written out and illuminated by an artisan in Rouen." Emily didn't expect this type of detail in a dream, but given all her studies, her subconscious had plenty to draw on.

"Those must've been beautiful. Can you read French?"

"Aye, my lady, French and Latin, for I am a gentleman."

"Of course," Emily said with a hint of irony. "You were from around 1425, right?"

Griffin hugged his elbows, looking away. "'Twas the year of our Lord 1428 that I was damned into this earthly hell."

She shuddered. "I can't imagine anything worse!"

"No more can I, and I have had ample time to consider the matter."

Even if this was made up, her own brain's version of Netflix, his story broke her heart.

She asked gently, "How did it happen?"

He grimaced. "I will not tell the whole lamentable tale, which would prove a poor entertainment and do me no honor besides. An evil and powerful conjuror cursed me to this state." He took in a ragged breath and let it out. "He was a man I once loved like a brother."

"Oh no. Why would a friend do that to you?"

"I defeated him in a grand tournament in London."

"Oh." Emily frowned. "Was he badly injured?"

"Nay, but the injury to his pride proved mortal." He sighed. "'Twas the biggest crowd I had ever seen in my life, with knights from distant realms: Córdoba and Granada, Moldavia, and even Saracens from Damascus."

"Sara . . . ? Oh, right. We call Saracens Muslims now." She took a seat on the fallen log not far from the fire.

"Muslims," Griffin repeated under his breath, as if to commit it to memory. In a fluid motion, he sat down next to her.

"I did not intend to fight that day," he said. "I had just returned again from France, another bloody battle won, and I was sick to death of war."

Emily screwed up her face. "I'll bet."

"The games were exceedingly gladsome to watch, for none were grievously hurt, and Mordrain won one joust and then another. I thought to myself that mayhap it was pleasant to him, to be the champion himself instead of the friend of one."

"You were usually the champion?"

He looked away, staring at the fire. "Already I regret telling this tale. I fear you will not think well of me by its end."

"Whatever it was, you were punished too much for it," she said softly. "Even if it's bad, I'll try to understand, okay?"

He gave a tight nod. "Late in the day, my father arrived and learned I was not in the lists. He became enraged. Why should any respect me, he asked, if I didn't show them my power? He said folk would talk forever of my cowardice."

"Would they?"

"Nay," he said shortly. "But it sounded like truth to me at the time, for he had always told me a man was loved for his riches and his might. I came against Mordrain when he was much winded from a long day of battle. It was not the first time I had defeated him in a tournament. And this time it was in front of . . ." He swallowed. "In front of a lady he loved."

"And he turned you into stone right there? Is that why you were wearing your armor?" If that happened in front of a huge crowd, wouldn't there be a written record of it somewhere?

No, there wouldn't, because this was a dream, she reminded herself.

"Nay. A seven-night later, Mordrain challenged me to meet him in a clearing and do battle. I believed he would gather many witnesses—though truth be told, he had few friends."

Absently, Griffin picked up a twig, worrying it with his thumb. "I had no plan but to make amends, for my conscience was pricked with remorse. He alone was there, armored for battle . . . I dismounted and made a show of casting aside my sword, thinking to make peace. I took off my helmet . . . and he cursed me to this torment worse than hell."

Emily inched closer. "But I don't understand," she murmured. "Did he . . . have a magic wand? Like in *Harry Potter*?"

Griffin said tightly, "He had a staff. One I had not seen before."

"So more like *The Lord of the Rings*."

"I do not know that lord."

As grim as the story was, Emily's lips twitched at that. "Did you know he was a sorcerer?"

"He studied with one, who most believed to be a mad hermit. But I sorely underestimated Mordrain's power."

"How did he do it?"

"He raised his staff and spoke words in some ancient tongue." A bleak, wintry look came into his eyes. "I could not move then, though I was still flesh."

Emily's shoulders hunched up toward her ears. She'd had nightmares like that.

Griffin tossed the twig in his hand into the fire. "Then he told me he had murdered the sorcerer who had taught him, to steal his greatest treasure: the staff of the great Merlin, stolen from his grave on Bardsey Isle."

"Whoa," Emily breathed. "I thought Merlin was just a myth." What was she saying? This was *all* a myth.

"I wish it were so," he said heavily. "He said I had been too fond of ladies' kisses, and that now even if a lady kissed me, I would be stone. He placed four onyx stones carved with strange symbols around my feet, north and south, and east and west. Then, turning his face away, he uttered more words in a foreign tongue. I felt myself turn."

His voice sounded hollow. Coldness slithered up Emily's spine.

"Behind me, I heard my stallion gallop away." A frown etched his brow. "I hope he was found by someone who cared for him well."

Emily touched her hand to her heart. What a sweet man he was to still be worried about his horse.

"I bet he was," she said softly. "What happened to him? Mordrain?"

Griffin shook his head. "'Twas too much magic, mayhap, for a mortal man . . . or else the staff itself despaired of such a master. It caught fire and burned Mordrain with it down to ash, all in a moment. Nothing was left but blackened armor . . . and so also burned my hope to undo the curse."

At least Mordrain hadn't been able to turn anyone else to stone. But that probably wasn't much comfort to Griffin, who had suffered so much.

Impulsively, Emily wrapped her arms around him.

He stiffened as though in shock, then returned the embrace, pulling her close against him and burying his head in her neck. His body against hers was still big and hard, but supple, undeniably human. She could feel his heart pounding in his chest.

When she pulled back, he released her immediately. She took his hand again.

"Did anyone find you?" she asked tentatively.

"Aye, peasants came across me on the morrow. They took Mordrain's armor and my sword, and no doubt sold it."

"They didn't move you, though?"

"Nay, the stone was not easy to move. But later a yeoman and his draft horses and his four strapping sons rolled me over logs bit by bit, over the course of a summer, to his cottage's garden, where I stood guard over the carrots and cabbages."

"I've never even believed in spells, but there must be a way to fix it." A horrible thought crossed her mind. "If it was undone, would you be alive? Or would you . . . turn into a skeleton or something since it's been hundreds of years?"

"Even death is a relief for which I dare not hope."

She squeezed his hand. "That's . . . that's the saddest thing I've ever heard." Her throat tightened.

His blue eyes filled with concern. "Grant pardon, sweet lady, for burdening you with my sorrow. We should speak of more pleasant things."

He stood up and looked around them. "I've seen many wondrous things in dreams, both terrible and fair, but I've never seen a library spring up thus in a greenwood. 'Tis a beautiful sight."

"Not as beautiful as you are," she said lightly, getting to her feet. Was she flirting? Well, why not? "It's really too bad you're not real."

He drew ever so slightly nearer to her. "By the Holy Rood, I swear I am."

By the Holy Rood? Had she ever heard that expression before?

She must've read it somewhere. She was taking this too seriously.

"Why were you called Sir Griffin the Proud?" she asked him. "I mean, as opposed to Sir Griffin the Handsome, or Sir Griffin the Panty Dropper?"

A look of confusion came into his eyes at the last name, but then he shook his head slightly, dismissing it.

"I was first called Griffin the Proud by an enemy, and then by everyone, even myself." He pursed his lips thoughtfully. "In truth, I had great cause for pride. I was rich, the son of an earl, the heir to a castle and another vast estate, and the most powerful fighter in the land."

"Well, they certainly couldn't call you Griffin the Humble," she teased.

He shrugged. "I have always spoken my thoughts plainly, for good or ill."

"It's for good," she reassured him. "When I was married to Tom, my ex-husband, I'd practically have to beg him to tell me what was on his mind." She gave a huff of disgust. "Though I guess what was on his mind for a while was another woman."

Griffin frowned. "He dallied with a wanton wench."

Despite the painful subject, she gave a short laugh. "Oh, it's way worse than that. They're in love."

He turned her hand in his, bent his head, and pressed his lips to her palm.

The sensation of her hand in his, the brush of his lips, and the tickle of his breath gave her a very real-feeling shiver of delight. It was more romantic—more *sensual*—than she would've expected.

He raised his head and met her eyes, his gaze filled with naked sincerity. "You are well rid of your husband, for he was not only a contemptible villain, but a Jack-fool besides."

She ducked her head. "You *literally* just met me."

"You were kind to your friend the cunning woman, and you're kind to me. Mayhap 'tis your sympathetic nature that allowed you to hear my thoughts when no one else ever could." His gaze traveled over her. "Beauty sometimes masks a foul soul, but yours reflects the loveliness within."

"You know," she breathed, "you're kind of making me swoon here."

"Am I?" His voice was a low rumble. He drew closer, his face inches from hers. "I am exceedingly glad to hear it, for I am drawn to you like a pilgrim to a holy well, with a heart full of yearning and lips desiring to drink."

Gently, he pulled her up against him, focusing on her mouth. He felt *so good*. So warm and vital. Her dream slid from day to night, and a bonfire blazed up close by, though fortunately out of the range of the cases of books. A log crackled and flung up two sparks that rose and took their places in the night sky overhead, glowing orange in the midst of all the pale and brilliant stars.

"I'm shaking," she said.

He caressed her cheek. "But not, I think, from fear."

"No," she whispered. *Definitely not.*

"Can you feel my heart beating?" he murmured. She nodded. "Even in life, it scarce beat as hard as it does now, for pure joy."

He cupped her face in his hands and captured her mouth in a kiss. *Oh God.* She felt a faint trembling in his body, too, and had a sense that he was holding himself in check, trying to be gentle, but his mouth on hers was firm and assured. Without breaking away, he dragged the pad of his thumb along the underside of her lip. She whimpered right into his mouth.

He delved into her. To her shock, and pure delight, he tasted sweet and spicy, like . . . cinnamon? His passion sent a rush of liquid heat through her, overriding conscious thought. He buried his fingers in her hair and then tightened them, sending starbursts of sensation across her skull and somehow making her lips feel even more sensitive. His kiss deepened. He demanded more, and she accepted it, invited it, wide open and willing.

Maybe she should offer her whole body up to him in the same way, letting him take anything and everything he wanted. She stood on her toes to better meet his mouth—dangerous, when her legs felt so weak.

His large, strong hands slid down to cup and squeeze her ass. Hmmm, *that* wasn't so genteel and gallant . . . and she loved it, arching her back, pushing herself against his palms. Her tight, aching breasts thrust against his solid chest.

But when he reached down and grabbed a big handful of her gown and pulled it up, baring her hip, caution returned to her in a rush. There was definitely nothing underneath the gown. She put a hand on his before he could hike it up any further, and he froze.

"Hey," she said, "maybe we shouldn't . . . I don't know."

He released the fabric in his hand, searching her gaze. "I cry you mercy if I have offended your modesty."

She gave a nervous laugh. "You're not, um, offending. I guess if I wanted to, I could just open my eyes and wake up."

Sorrow settled on his features. *Oh no.* She hadn't meant to make him even sadder.

"Demoiselle, do you want to wake up?"

"No," she said softly. "I mean, I'm . . ." No, she shouldn't tell him about the wetness between her legs. In medieval England, ladies at court probably hadn't discussed those things. She definitely wouldn't have brought it up in real life, either, with a man she'd just met . . . not that she'd ever met anyone like Griffin.

The corner of his mouth, still temptingly close to hers, quirked up in a knowing smile. "'Tis naught but a dream, my lady. No harm shall be done if you take your pleasure as you will."

"But will you go into other people's dreams?" She shook her head. Stupid question. He was a figment of her imagination. A big, gorgeous, really charming figment.

"I can only go into the dreams of those I have seen while they were awake."

"Why?"

He laughed. "My sweet bird, I know not how I do even this. Though had I not learned, I would be myself no more, but some wretched demon writhing in his hopelessness and rage." Her heart twisted at the thought. He'd survived for centuries on nothing but scraps of human companionship, the kind she took for granted.

He took her hand and looked deep into her eyes. "Only you have seen the man within the stone. In the sight of God, I shall visit no other lady as long as I may visit you."

If he'd been real, she wouldn't have believed him. Tom had promised in his wedding vows to be faithful, too.

"What about Rose?" she asked.

"I would gladly befriend her, but I need only your company."

"You can visit her if you want," Emily grumbled. He needed more friends. An unpleasant thought came to her mind. "But I wish you wouldn't visit Laurie."

He laughed again. She loved the sound of his laugh: genuine, free, and good-natured. "The one who is so sour, she'd turn cream to buttermilk?"

Emily raised her eyebrows. "That's a pretty good burn. Anyway, she's married and has two kids."

He took her into his arms again, kissing the curve of her ear and then the lobe in a way that made her squirm. "We must speak of her ill-tempered ways no more, or my king will no longer be ready to enter the court."

King? . . . Oh my God. That was one way to refer to a dick.

Would he be wearing a codpiece? Emily dared to reach under his velvet doublet. Not exactly, but his hose had some kind of pouch there. His *king* felt big and hard, more than ready to enter the court.

As she palmed it, he made a low sound in the back of his throat that sent more heat pooling between her thighs. She stroked his length, and it twitched hard under her palm.

"Christ Jesus," he rasped, his eyes half-closed. She felt a touch of awe at the sight of his rapt expression. It was only because he'd needed this so badly, she told herself. But no, this was her dream. She was the one who needed it.

And maybe it was all part of the fantasy, but she couldn't help but feel that her heart was beating harder not only from lust, but also from a more profound, magical connection.

Before she could talk herself out of it, she pulled away and stripped off the gown.

He straightened and rewarded her with the most erotic gaze she had ever seen in her life, his eyes hot with desire. It burned away her lingering self-doubts in an instant. He fanned his warm palm across the side of one of her breasts and then lowered his leonine head to nuzzle against it. The rough stubble of his jaw abraded her sensitive flesh, sending tingles to her just-kissed lips and all the way down to her toes. He took a deep inhale, and Emily recalled giving her cleavage a light spritz of perfume that morning. A growl came from the back of his throat. Apparently, he liked it.

His tongue darted across her hard nipple, and her back arched involuntarily. He took her nipple into his mouth and sucked. A moan escaped her. He caressed and feasted upon her breasts, his fervor just barely checked, it seemed, by intense concentration on her enjoyment. After a minute, he lifted his head again to give her a tender, ardent kiss that almost brought tears to her eyes.

For a man who hadn't touched a woman in centuries, Griffin

didn't seem to be in much of a hurry. She appreciated that. A lot. But this dream had gone on so long already, and sooner or later, it was going to end.

"Please," she breathed, pulling at the bottom of his velvet doublet. It looked like it would be difficult to take off.

He stepped back, yanked it over his head with a loud rip of fabric, and tossed it aside.

His fine linen shirt, open at the neckline, revealed a magnificent expanse of shoulder and collarbone. Emily couldn't resist leaning forward to lick and nip him there, and she relished his sensual groan.

"Take everything off," she blurted out.

Really? Maybe it was only fair, since she was standing there completely naked, but hearing herself issue a command still shocked her.

The corner of his mouth lifted in an enigmatic smile. He removed his boots and remaining garments at once.

Orange firelight flickered on his bare body. The cliché "Greek god" came to mind, and she'd studied enough sculptures and bas-reliefs to know that description wasn't exactly right. He looked every bit as powerful but better fed, thicker in a way she liked. No wonder it felt so good to be held by him. The play of shadows emphasized the strong planes of his hairy chest and the intriguing lines that cut a V from his hips downward. His thick, slightly curved cock stood at full attention.

"Good Lord." Emily sighed.

"Do I please you, *mon trésor?*"

Oooh. Well, he'd said he knew French. He made it unbearably sexy with his smooth, deep voice and the darkening lust in his eyes.

His hands grazed along the sides of her body before coming to rest on her hips. "I am glad of it, for your beauty would put Venus herself to shame."

Emily shook her head. "I'm actually pretty ordinary," she whispered.

His handsome features reflected genuine confusion. His gaze swept across her exposed body. "Why would you say so?"

"I'm not—"

He cut her off with another fervent kiss. "I swear to God and all His angels, you are the most perfect thing I have ever seen." His voice cracked on the last word.

And then he knelt in front of her and gazed up at her.

Help. She might swoon for real. Well, he was a knight. He'd probably dealt with a swooning woman or two in his day. In his own bedroom, no doubt. But the way he was looking at her threatened to dismantle every defense she'd ever put up around her mind and heart.

He nudged one of her thighs, urging her to a wider stance. Emily obeyed, her legs trembling again. He stroked his hand between them and, finding her slick with desire, made a low sound of approval. His face was only a few inches away. He could probably smell as well as feel her arousal.

"Aye, you are a goddess," he murmured, grasping her hip with his free hand. His fingers dipped into her, and his thumb grazed across her needy clit, coaxing a soft cry from her lips. "And at your temple I shall worship."

She set her hands on his beautiful, broad shoulders for support. He watched her as he touched her, seemingly entranced by her every tiny reaction. Her eyes closed when he pressed into her harder. He rolled his thumb over her swollen bud, sending currents like electricity through her body, enough to fry her brain.

"And at your altar, I will offerings make." In his seductive baritone, it sounded like the filthiest thing Emily had ever heard. He set his mouth over her clit and sucked on it.

"Oh God." Hardly knowing what she was doing, she grabbed a fistful of his thick golden hair. The bonfire roared, its flames leaping dangerously high. "Yes. Griffin, *please.*" His grip on her hip tightened. She was so close—

Something smacked her in the face.

She jerked away.

Her dog's tail flopped in her face again, and she opened her eyes. She was lying in her bed, alone.

No, no, NO!

She carried Andy War-Howl out in the hallway, plopped him down on the floor, and shut the door. He gave a resigned whimper. She flopped back on the bed, squeezed her eyes shut, and willed herself back into the dream. The streetlight shining through the window didn't usually bother her, but she pulled a pillow over her face to block it out. *Come on—*

Nothing. *Ugh!* She tossed the pillow aside, though she could've screamed into it from pure frustration.

In her current state, she had no chance of drifting off again. A heavy ache between her legs begged for a satisfaction she could not have—an orgasm with a knight who was gallant and sinfully skilled in equal measure. The part of her brain in charge of dreams deserved Oscars all around. It had never invented anything so elaborate, or so sexy, before.

His deep voice reverberated in her head. *And at your temple I shall worship.* Good Lord, but he said pretty things. And while she would've expected medieval sex education to be somewhat lacking, he definitely knew his way around down there.

She shucked off her pajama pants and snatched her vibrator from the drawer in her nightstand. In about four seconds, it stopped working.

"Oh God," she groaned. It needed charging. She tossed it aside and reached down there to do it old-school. Her knight proved to be a very efficient fantasy. Within a minute, her climax brought her relief.

It would've been so, so much better in the dream, though. She thought again of the way he'd tasted: like mulled wine spices. She didn't know what she'd been expecting when she kissed a real medieval knight, but it wasn't that.

But he *wasn't* a real knight. In a dream, he could've just as easily tasted like wasabi, and then he could've mounted a giant land jellyfish and blobbed away.

So why did all those details feel so convincing?

She grabbed her laptop from a shelf and wrote down as many of them as she could remember. When she finished, she got up and went into her kitchen to make a pot of coffee, choosing the mug from Barcelona. The only foreign city she'd ever visited had struck her as terribly romantic—and the Agbar Tower, depicted on the souvenir, was decidedly phallic.

Had Griffin lived in a castle? Was it on a mug somewhere?

Why did he feel like a real person to her?

She was lonely. That was all. Her sex-starved id had concocted a dirty fantasy.

It had been a lot more than that, though. He'd touched her heart.

It was just a dream, you ridiculous turnip.

But what if it wasn't?

Four

Alone in the empty black room, Griffin ruminated on his past with Mordrain.

For countless years, inasmuch as he could, he'd pushed away thoughts of his friend turned monster. But after telling Emily about the curse, memories crowded his mind.

Mordrain's father's modest demesne had bordered the de Beaufords' expansive Essex estate, and Griffin and Mordrain had grown up almost as brothers. Together, they had hunted pheasants, foraged for mushrooms, and played quoits, tossing rope rings around stakes in the ground. With Griffin's father's chess set, they'd started many games and had finished somewhat fewer. Mordrain had been cleverer, planning several moves ahead. Griffin, although he loved handling the pieces of finely carved walrus ivory, would quickly grow bored sitting still. He'd find excuses not to finish, robbing Mordrain of victory.

Once, in their twelfth year, they attempted to spy on the harlots in the back room of the public bathhouse. Mordrain stood on

Griffin's shoulders to peer into a knothole, but the bathhouse owner rounded the corner and shouted at them, and Mordrain tumbled to the ground. The man regaled them with curses as they fled, and only at the village well did they stop, out of breath both from running and from laughing.

Let us go to the hermit's cave, Mordrain suggested.

'Tis too far away, Griffin said. *And he is a moonsick old man.*

Everyone thinks he is mad, but he's not, Mordrain said stoutly. *He can make people fall ill, and control storms and battles. He's going to teach me everything.*

Griffin had scoffed. *You win a battle with a sharp sword and a good horse, not with magic.*

In the end, they resolved to ride out to the River Blackwater and set willow traps for eels. It was October when they would be ribboning their way toward the Sargasso Sea. Griffin lent Mordrain his sister's pony, for unlike Griffin, he possessed no steed of his own. The sunshine limned the yellow birch leaves and the horse's manes. They talked about the glory they would find someday in battles and tournaments, and the fair ladies they'd woo.

When they'd ridden back in the evening, they'd come across two girls from the village on their palfreys. One girl had said to another, *There's Griffin with his little pet jackdaw*, and they had both giggled. Mordrain often wore a badge of his family's crest, with the black bird on the white ground, as though it were the king's own insignia rather than one of a lowly house. He was shorter and smaller than Griffin, and on Alyse's pony, he looked shorter still. *Pay them no heed*, Griffin had said to Mordrain after they'd passed the girls, but he had enjoyed their admiring looks.

Perhaps he should have said more than that. Still, they had enjoyed many merry times together. Griffin had even gone with Mordrain and his parents to the May fair in London, where they'd watched acrobats and archery tournaments, and had eaten fried cakes topped with honey and spiced almonds. How could he have guessed that their friendship would come to such a bitter end?

The door to the black room opened and his lady Emily ventured in, sending all other thoughts flying away like a murmuration of starlings. She shut the door behind her. She looked lovely as ever, but pale, with shadows beneath her eyes.

She came right over to his statue and whispered, "You're not real, right? You can't be."

In all the time that Griffin had been going into people's dreams, never once had they spoken to him about it in statue form. At most, they'd given him an amused, private shake of the head.

But never before had he been naked with a beautiful woman in her dream, let alone teased and tasted her at the place of her delight. His contact with the living had been so limited that he hadn't visited many unmarried women in their slumbers. Of these, a few had not aroused his desires. Another one, an agreeable companion, had told him she had no use for amorous embraces, and with yet another, he'd gotten no further than a kiss before she'd declared that such a dream was a sin.

As close as Emily had been to *the crest of her pleasure*, he knew that she hadn't meant to wake up. In vain he'd waited for her to sleep and dream again, ready to take her if she were willing, as a bridegroom took a bride.

Even though their time had been cut short, being with her had brought him more pleasure than he'd known in all the time he'd been cursed. What was more, her kindness had begun to heal the grievous wounds of his soul.

"I can't feel you in my head," she murmured. "Not like last night."

I am here.

She jumped.

Yes! She could still hear him.

"I couldn't get back to sleep after the dream," she said softly. Inwardly, Griffin frowned. He had intended to entertain her dreams, not disturb her rest. "If you were real, and what you told me was true . . . it would be so terrible. I couldn't stop thinking about you being stuck here alone."

The door burst open, and Laurie peered in. "Are you going to be done with photos today? I'm waiting to do pictures of the armor."

Emily cast a wry glance in Griffin's direction before telling Laurie, "They move him tomorrow."

"Okay. But you might want to confirm that with them." She shut the door.

"Don't worry," Emily said to Griffin. "They'll just move you out of this photo studio to the other room off the main lab so I can do a little restoration. And then in a few weeks, they'll move you for the exhibit, and you'll see thousands of people. That'll last for about four months." Although the exhibit would hardly be dignified, he had to admit that it would afford him more entertainment than he'd had since . . . well, since he'd been alive. He would see so many faces, and hear so many conversations, giving his mind new things to mull over. "Then I'll finish restoring you, which is going to take several more months." Griffin liked the sound of the last part especially.

"Are you really in there?" she asked more softly. "Because if you are, I feel a little shy about last night."

Why, sweeting? You were glorious.

"Oh God, I think I really am going crazy," she whispered. Then she raised her hand and caressed his cheek.

Something in his soul welled up at her silken touch. It was more pleasurable and intense even than her touch or her kiss in her dream, because it was real. Though she felt only stone, he felt her living warmth. If only he could have lived in the world as she did, discussing whatever they liked at any hour, sweeping her up into his arms for no reason at all. His longing for her expanded within him, a sweet agony almost too much to bear.

He cast his adoration toward her. *Gentle lady. You undo me.*

She gasped and drew her hand back as though it had been burned.

His cheeks were wet. Rain? A leak in the ceiling . . . No. Moisture touched his face and nowhere else.

His statue was weeping. *He* was weeping.

She backed away from him, her eyes wide, as if she regarded a devil from Hell.

"This isn't happening," she said, a tremble in her voice.

He tried to open his mouth and speak aloud. If he could produce tears, then why not words?

They wouldn't come. He attempted to lift a hand to reach out to her, but it didn't budge. *Do not be afraid*, his soul implored her.

She ran to the door. His heart lurched. He'd wanted her too much, and now she was abandoning him—

She closed the door silently and locked it. Then she turned around and got out her phone.

After a few moments, she said, "Rose? I'm in the photo studio. Can you come here?" A pause, and Emily looked up at Griffin. "Cancel it. Get over here *right now*."

Praise God. Although it took a lot of energy to reach her waking mind, much more than strolling into a dream, he sent his thoughts to her anyway.

Thank you for not being afraid.

She stared up at him again. "Yeah, I'm not scared exactly, but I'm a little freaked out." A small smile touched her tempting lips. "And excited. Has this ever happened before?"

Nay, my lady, never. 'Tis your doing.

A few minutes later, someone knocked on the door. Emily

opened it a crack and peered out, opened it wider to admit a slightly out of breath Rose, and then slammed the door again behind her.

"What's going on? Did you murder someone? Did you deface a Monet?"

"I don't want anyone else to hear about this!" Emily glanced at Griffin again. "Except him."

"Hmm, I don't know," Rose joked, following her gaze. "Can Sir Limestone here be trusted?"

"Don't call him that! He's been through enough!"

Rose blinked. "*Okaayy.*"

"I'm going to tell you something, and I want you to keep an open mind."

"But I'm usually so judgmental," Rose deadpanned.

"And you can't tell anyone. *Anyone.*"

"I promise, I won't!"

Emily pointed at Griffin. "Hurry up, touch his cheeks!"

Her eyes wide, Rose walked over to Griffin, saying, "I thought you were supposed to wash your hands—"

"Just do it! Sorry, sorry. Please!"

Rose obeyed. Griffin felt vulnerable at the touch. He didn't know why or how he'd wept, now after all this time.

Rose withdrew her hands immediately, holding them up in the air. "It's wet."

"Okay," Emily said on an exhale. "I thought I was losing my mind. He's crying."

Rose peered at her. "I know there have been some Virgin Mary statues who cried, but they were hoaxes. There was this whole podcast about it."

Emily gave a strained laugh. "This guy is *not* the Virgin Mary." At Rose's bemused expression, she added, "We should sit down." They both settled themselves in the two chairs in the room, and Emily took a deep breath.

"Yesterday I felt like this sculpture was talking to me. Like in my head."

Rose looked at Griffin and back to Emily. "Has this happened to you before?"

"No!"

"Do you . . . hear voices at other times?"

"I'm not crazy," Emily blurted out. "Sorry, mentally ill. Except I have some depression and anxiety."

"Who doesn't?" Rose quipped.

"He's definitely the only piece of artwork that's ever communicated with me telepathically."

"What did he say?"

"He said, *I am here.* And he wanted me to touch him."

"Well," Rose said cheerfully, "you're going to be touching him a lot, so that works out great."

Griffin smiled to himself at this. Emily believed he was real, and while she might not be able to convince her friend of it, the fact that she was trying meant more to him than she would ever know.

"That's just the beginning," Emily said. "I had a dream about him last night. Except he wasn't a statue. He was a real guy."

Rose's eyebrows lifted. "A real knight in shining armor?"

"He was wearing fancy medieval clothes. He told me he was from 1428."

"Your subconscious is trying to research an acquisition." Rose shook her head. "You've been working too hard. You should be dreaming about fun stuff."

"Part of it was *very* fun." A blush of pink tinged Emily's cheeks.

Rose's features lit up with delight. "You had a sex dream about a statue?"

"Shhh!" Emily cast a nervous glance at the locked door.

More quietly, her blue eyes dancing, Rose said, "I have to ask.

Was he rock-hard?" Emily briefly covered her face with her hands. "I'll take that as a yes."

If Griffin had been able to, he would've laughed out loud. It wasn't often that ladies made such ribald jokes. As far as he knew, anyway. Perhaps all ladies spoke freely and merrily of such things among themselves.

"We didn't . . . *He* went down . . ." Emily gestured toward her thighs.

"*Ohhh*," Rose said. "Did they even know how to do that back then? Of course they did," she said, answering her own question. "They didn't have much else to do for fun."

"He was *really* good at it."

An unfamiliar-of-late feeling surged through Griffin: pride. The thing he'd once been known for, and a mortal sin, some said, but it was his, and he wouldn't relinquish it.

His fair lady only told half the story, for she didn't speak of her own incomparable skill at kissing. Her passion and her mouth's tender yielding beneath his own . . . It had almost made him come undone.

"And he was so charming," Emily went on. "He had the most amazing way of talking. He said things like *sweet lady* and *demoiselle*."

"Awww," Rose cooed. "This sounds like the best dream."

Emily said seriously, "I think the sculpture is a real person."

Rose tilted her head. "How does that work?" A courteous question, Griffin thought, considering.

"He said his name was Griffin de Beauford, son of William de Beauford, sometimes called Griffin the Proud. And some guy got mad at him and magically turned him into stone . . . I wrote down all the details. And he can still hear, and see, and feel, but he can't move or talk or anything."

"He said he had been like that for centuries?" Rose cringed. "That would be awful. But you can't really believe—"

"And just now, when I touched his cheek, the statue cried!" Emily's voice took on a slightly frantic edge. "How do you explain that?"

Rose touched a finger to her lips, pondering the question.

"There are two possibilities here. Either it's some kind of weird moisture or condensation on the sculpture that just happened to coincide with you touching its cheek, or . . ."

"Or what?"

"Or this is a man who was turned into stone, who can visit you in dreams. I know which one I'm rooting for."

Rose was not, Griffin deemed, a sensible woman. Given his situation, he appreciated that about her.

Rose asked, "Could you find out anything about him?"

"What do you mean?"

Her friend threw her hands up in the air. "What's the first thing you do when you meet a new guy?"

"You're right. I should Google him."

She should do *what* to him?

Emily took out her phone and began tapping.

"All I can find is some French guy," she grumbled after a moment. "A guard for Louis the Sixteenth."

Rose hovered over her shoulder. "Try spelling it G-R-Y-F-F-O-N."

Clearly, they were looking at a census or historical record, but would they be able to find him? He knew of at least four different ways to write his name. He tried sending the correct spelling to Emily.

Emily froze and looked up at him. "Oh! It's G-R-I-F-F-I-N," she repeated, typing it in.

"Did he, um . . . tell you that?" Rose asked, almost in a whisper.

"Yes. Look!" She pointed. "Griffin de Beauford, born 1398."

Rose scooted her chair closer to look over her shoulder. Emily touched the screen again, and after a moment, she gasped.

"Son of William de Beauford. Oh my God."

"What year does it say he died?" Rose demanded.

"It doesn't say. There's a question mark." She sounded a little breathless, and she pressed a hand to her chest. "What if it's real? I'm going to pass out."

Rose leaned in closer. "Can you find anything else?"

Emily tapped some more. "A death notice for the dad. 1438. His daughter Alyse inherited the estates."

Griffin was not truly surprised, yet it pleased him to think of his little sister, a grand lady in her own hall. Had she ever wed?

"I didn't know daughters could inherit land then," Rose mused.

In the absence of sons, they usually did. A lord with no male heir might sometimes draw up documents to bequeath his lands to a nephew, in order to preserve the family name, but Griffin's father had not been fond of Griffin's male cousins, both of whom had managed to avoid going to war.

"It mentions Griffin." Emily's voice trembled. *"Declared dead in absentia."*

Rose held up her hands in a definitive gesture. "This is the coolest thing I've ever heard of in my entire life. Maybe any of my lives."

Emily covered her mouth with her hands. She'd gone white as wax.

"Are you all right? You look like you've seen a ghost," Rose chirped.

"I take it back. This can't be happening," Emily said. "I probably, somehow, read about his family online years ago. I go down all kinds of rabbit holes with research." She shook her head. "I mean, can you imagine me writing the condition report? 'Stains from weather and pollution. Little to no degradation of limestone. Human soul trapped inside.'"

It's true, Griffin said.

Emily looked up at him. "I feel like it is." Then she turned back to Rose. "But it's impossible! Right?"

Rose shrugged. "Honestly, I believe in way weirder shit than this."

A short burst of music emanated from her, and Rose pulled out her own phone. "Oh! I've got a livestream in ten minutes." Stuffing the tablet back in her pocket, she said, "I'll text you later, okay?" She rushed out of the room, slamming the door behind her.

Emily walked over to him. "Griffin," she said quietly. "Were you born in 1398?"

Aye, on the Assumption.

"Why can you talk to me when I'm awake, if you can't do it with anyone else?"

I do not know. He could only be grateful for it. It seemed to be taking less effort than it had before.

She looked up into his face. "I believe you."

His throat tightened. In just three words, she acknowledged his suffering, his humanity, as no one had ever done.

"Are you still in there?" she asked.

Aye. Grant pardon. I know not what to say.

She placed her hand on his cheek again. "There must be some way to un-stonify you."

Please God, do not kindle my hopes. It was too late for him, and he'd made his peace with despair. But no, that was a lie. Part of him could never accept his mute and motionless fate.

"Of course, if I *did* manage to make you a real boy again, you'd probably just run away with some Renaissance Faire wench." Maybe she sensed his confusion, because she added crossly, "Oh, they're very hot. With the bodices and the boobs and the steins . . . but this whole idea is crazy, anyway."

She narrowed her eyes in thought. "You said the sorcerer said a magic spell after he froze you, and that's when you turned into a statue. What did he say? Do you remember the exact words?"

Of course he did. The gloating rhymes had rung in his ears for centuries, tormenting him. He shared them with her now.

As still you are, so shall you ever be:
A man of stone, doomed for eternity.
Though you took pride in praise, and kisses, too,
No flattery or kiss shall this undo.

"That does sound really final," she said and paced a few steps. Then she stopped and snapped her fingers. "Wait! It's really *un*-final! Remember what Rose said about magic? That if you cast any doubt, you ruin it?"

Griffin did remember. Having nothing else to do, he repeated overheard conversations in his head several times, imagining what he would've said if he'd been able. He quoted Rose now.

If you say, "Don't let me brood," a small part of the universe is going to hear that as, "Let me brood."

"Exactly!" Emily said. "So if you say, *Don't let fine words or a kiss break the spell*, maybe the universe hears, *Let fine words or a kiss break the spell!*" She finished on a triumphant note, but then her shoulders sagged. "This is completely ridiculous. But I mean . . . it's worth a try, right?"

It sounded like he'd get another kiss out of it, so yes. Indeed, he considered it worth countless tries.

"I know this is very Frog Prince," Emily said. "But I'm going to give it a go."

With an air of determination that charmed him to his core, she grabbed the stool and plunked it down in front of him. She stepped up on it.

"All right," she breathed, leaning closer. Then she pulled back. "Hang on." She went to the door, peered out, and then locked it and walked back to him. She got back on the stool so they were again face-to-face.

"This is *very* against conservator rules, by the way," she murmured.

Then she snapped her fingers. "Wait! The spell also talked about flattery." Griffin felt a stab of impatience. She pursed her lips, so close to Griffin's now, in thought. Then her gaze met his, her brown eyes filled with sincerity.

Softly, she said, "You are the sweetest and most gallant man I've ever met . . . which is why I'd be amazed if you were real."

She did him too much honor. After a breathy laugh she added, still quietly, "Do you think I should hold Rose's magic rock? I've got it in my pocket."

Aye, sweet bird, if you wish. It can do no harm.

She cupped his cheek with her hand and pressed her lips against his. The sensation was pure bliss, and it was agony to not be able to return it. Then she pulled back, stepped off the stool, and regarded him closely.

Then she gave a wry smile. "Okay, nothing's happening."

But something was happening.

Griffin was crumbling from the inside. In mute horror, he felt himself not coming alive but coming apart.

No, this was for the best. How many times had he wished and prayed for death to release him? He knew not what awaited him on that far shore. Sweet oblivion? Heaven, whatever that might be? Not damnation, he knew. He'd suffered enough.

Why, then, should he not embrace this end? Only because of the lady who stood before him, who had brought new light and hope into his grotesque existence.

She turned and walked away. Regret and longing pierced him as the stone of his body disintegrated. But if she were nothing more than a lovely angel of death, still he should give thanks.

"Gramercy, sweet Emily."

She startled. With a loud gasp, she whipped back around to stare at him, her eyes huge and mouth wide open. Could she see that he was dying?

"You . . ." She trembled, her face white. "You talked! You're . . ."

It took Griffin a moment to understand. He had spoken aloud. She'd heard him, not in her mind, but as any living person might.

Shock went through him like a lance, knocking him to his knees. The steel greaves of his armor crashed against the hard floor. His helm, which he had carried for so many centuries, fell out of his hand and rolled aside.

I can move!

Emily approached him, saying in a soft high voice, "Oh my God, oh my God, oh my God."

Am I dreaming?

He leaned back, balling his hands into fists at his sides, and roared at the top of his lungs.

His voice. Reverberating off the walls!

A man's voice from the next room demanded, "What the hell was that?"

He shouted, "This is no dream!"

"Nooo, quiet," Emily pleaded, kneeling to face him.

Griffin's heart filled to overflowing. He gripped her hands and bent his head to kiss one and then the other. They were small in his, shaking and cold. But his own hands were warm. Warm!

"My dearest lady. My sweet angel of deliverance." His throat tightened as tears came, unbidden but not unexpected, and he welcomed them. "My Emily." His voice broke on her blessed name.

"How is this happening?" she asked, her voice balanced between joy and terror.

He took her face in his hands and kissed her. As wondrous as their kisses had been in dreams, they couldn't compare to this one in waking life. The taste of her overwhelmed him. Bliss coursed through every fiber of his body, a liquor more fiery than any ever brewed. It gave him strength along with joy.

"'Tis all your doing." He gazed into her eyes. "You are the queen of my heart, and all the days of my life I will do you service where you will command me." He bent and pressed his forehead against her hands clasped in his, feeling the vow bind his soul and rejoicing in the rightness of it.

"Griffin, you can't . . ." She trailed off as he raised his head. Tears gathered in her eyes.

"My lady, I can do whatever I wish," he said gently, smiling. She shouldn't be kneeling on the hard floor. He stood, helping her to her feet along with him. She frowned and picked up his helm.

"I can kneel if I will, or stand if I will," he marveled. He was not a piece of furniture, bound to remain wherever he was placed. "I am a man!" He ended on a shout, stretching his arms wide. His lungs rejoiced to take in air. Every muscle in his body itched to be in motion.

"Shhh, I don't want anyone—"

"I'm alive!" Wild joy rose in him. He could see the world again!

"Wait!" Emily squeaked as he ran for the door.

Five

Emily chased after Griffin, carrying his helmet, as he bolted out of the photography room and into the office—making Terrence, at his worktable, jump and drop a piece of ruby glass. It shattered into a few pieces on the floor.

Terrence put his hands on his head. "Fuck!"

Emily cowered.

"Your pardon, good sir!" Griffin called out. Then he froze. Emily followed his gaze. The Essex suit of armor that Laurie was going to restore stood near the entrance to the photography room.

Griffin asked warily, "Whose dark armaments are these?"

"Those would be *our* dark armaments," Terrence said, crossing his arms. "Do you have a visitor badge?" Laurie wasn't at her desk, thank God.

Griffin shook his head. "It reminded me of something. But all is well." Then he laughed. "More than well!" After a quick glance around him, Griffin ran for the doors to the museum offices.

With a helpless whimper, Emily hurried after Griffin, grabbing her purse off her desk with her free hand as she passed. How was a man in a full suit of armor so fast? She shifted the purse to her shoulder and clutched the helmet to her midsection as she jogged after him. He barreled down the stairs, clanking. *Oh God*—what if he tripped and fell? It had been so long since he'd moved.

He had no trouble, jumping down the last two stairs like a child. "Huzzah!"

"Griffin!"

He held up a finger, as though to say he'd only be a moment, and dashed down the length of the gallery like a bull in a china shop— if instead of china, the shop was filled with Greek and Roman marble sculptures of gods, goddesses, and great men from the first century A.D. He ran into a brass pole holding up a velvet rope around a marble statue of Cronus, and Emily gasped as it clattered to the floor, taking down a second pole with it.

Oh, shit. Her heart pounded as she ran after him, less from the effort than from the shock of it all.

Well, she *had* promised Laurie that he'd be out of the photography room.

Griffin paused in front of a large window in the middle of the gallery, his steel-plate armor shining brightly in the sun. Her purse strap fell from her shoulder to her forearm, and her purse banged against her thighs as she caught up with him. Below, in the formal garden, colorful flowers bloomed at the bases of trees with white blossoms that, at every strong breeze, rained petals onto the grass.

He turned to her and shouted, "I'm free!"

He threw his arms wide, and Emily let out a shriek as she put out her free hand to protect a marble statue of a toga-draped Athena. Griffin's gauntleted hand came within a fraction of an inch of smacking the goddess in the face. He was resplendent, joyous, and a museum conservator's worst nightmare.

A woman with her two children stared at him. The boy smiled

in delight, while the girl, maybe five or six, frowned and asked, "Who's that, Mommy?"

"That's what I'd like to know," Terrence said, striding down the gallery toward them. Emily pulled her purse back onto her shoulder, thinking, *Just act normal.*

Griffin spun to look at him, his face still lit up in a smile. "Again, grant pardon, good sir, but I am overcome with joy at being alive."

"Good for you." Terrence's voice dripped with irony, and he looked to Emily for an explanation.

What could she say? That she was really, *really* good at restoring sculptures?

"He's, uh, practicing for the Renaissance Faire," Emily said. It popped into her head because she'd just been talking about it. Her breath was shaky. She'd always been a terrible liar.

Griffin said to Terrence, "I am Griffin de Beauford, called by many Griffin the Proud, and now that I am able, I'm honored to meet you."

"Terrence." His eyes narrowed. "I didn't see you come in."

"You get so focused on your work!" Emily blurted out, sounding inane to her own ears. "We, uh, I have to go. There's an emergency." She handed Griffin's helmet to him and then grabbed his free hand. That would keep him from stretching his arms out again and possibly knocking something over.

"What emergency?" Terrence looked Griffin up and down. "Does he have to go save a fair maiden?"

Griffin laughed. "Nay, for as you can see, 'tis this fair maiden who has saved me!"

Oh God. She had to get him out of here.

Emily tugged at Griffin's hand. "Come on."

To her relief, he obeyed, though he raised a hand and called back over his shoulder to Terrence, "I bid you good day, sir."

She needed to get him to a private place where she could have a minute to *think*, to process all this, to talk to him without being disturbed. But after a few more steps, he stopped, pulling Emily closer to him.

She completely forgot she was in a rush. How amazing to see his human face, not in a dream, but in the light of an ordinary morning.

His eyes, summer-sky blue, were narrow but fringed with longer-than-average lashes. He had fine lines at the corners of his eyes and near his mouth, as if he'd smiled and laughed often before the curse. He looked the same as he did in her dream, with his straight nose and a full and sensuous mouth, but the most striking thing about him was his open, unguarded expressions and manner of speaking. It was as if it had never occurred to him to lie or to even tamp down his feelings. And right now, his gaze was filled with grave devotion.

"Gentle and beautiful lady," he murmured, "grant me one more kiss, I beseech you, for this may be but a brief reprieve from my doom."

She hadn't even thought of that. "I don't think that's going to happen. I think you're really alive."

A gleam came into his eye that could only be described as wicked. "I will truly know so, if I may have that kiss."

Emily laid her hand on his cheek and he kissed her again. The museum around them, her office, her wonder and alarm at his transformation, all blurred into nothing.

His armored grip around her waist and breastplate against her chest were startling new sensations; caught between steel and more steel, she felt soft and fragile, and he groaned into the kiss, urging her lips to part.

He's really here. She'd been having a hard time processing that, but the way he kissed her filled her soul with the truth. She felt giddy with it, a wild thrill because magic was real . . . and because everything about his kiss was magic, too, warm and vital.

When he pulled away and she opened her eyes again, several people had gathered to stare at them.

"Wow," one teenaged girl breathed to another.

"This museum is getting so cheesy," a white-haired lady muttered, shaking her head.

Emily ducked, her face flaming. "We should go."

"As you wish." He spoke loudly, his baritone voice carrying, as if to make up for all the centuries he'd been silent. As they walked, his armor clinked softly, but there was joy and energy in his every step that matched the happiness of her heart. He nodded toward one of the headless Roman sculptures they passed. "I am fortunate that my head stayed on my shoulders!"

Emily shuddered at the implications of this. "What would've happened then?"

"It matters not," Griffin said, with an expansive wave of his hand. "I'm alive!" His voice rose to almost a shout again.

But then he stopped dead in his tracks at a bronze Rodin—a figure of a muscular man in a contorted position with a downcast head. His face went white.

"Hey." Emily looked from the statue to him. "What's wrong?"

A line etched between his brows. "What is this place?"

"It's, um, it's a museum."

"I do not know the word." He swallowed. "And are there other tortured souls such as myself?"

"No!" Emily's heart went out to him. The Rodin was especially expressive, and it was exactly life-sized. She could see why it had given him that idea.

"These are just ordinary statues," she explained. "For this one, the artist made a mold and poured melted bronze in, and then the bronze hardened."

"'Truly?" He turned to her, distracted by this new information. "Like bakers use molds for the breads for Candlemas?"

"Um, maybe?" What he would've called Candlemas, February second, had turned into a celebration of a weather-predicting rodent. She gestured at the Rodin. "We have the mold the artist used. It's just a sculpture."

He nodded with a wry chuckle. "Forgive my foolishness."

"Oh no, I get it!" She squeezed his hand. "Come on. I'm taking you home."

He raised his eyebrows as they turned the corner. Then he looked down at the helmet tucked under his arm and jiggled it. "It feels good to carry it under my left arm instead of my right."

Her mouth dropped open. "I'll bet."

A wave of vertigo swept over her. What if *none* of this was happening? What if she was having some kind of psychotic break? Maybe she was walking alone, imagining that people around them were stopping to stare at Griffin in his armor.

But no, there were warning signs before psychotic breaks. Okay, thinking she could hear a statue's thoughts might count as a warning sign . . . but overall, she was sane. Worried about her job and her future, yes, and pissed at her ex—but really, what could be more normal than that?

She could just be dreaming again, though. Her footsteps slowed. *Wake up, wake up.* Nothing changed.

Griffin gave her a questioning look. "My lady, are you well?"

"I—yes. I think I'm a little in shock."

He nodded, but his eyes glinted with joy. "'Tis a most miraculous thing."

She guided him down a wide-open hall leading to a side exit to the street. His gaze traveled everywhere, scrutinizing the floating stairway and the trees and cars outside the two-story-high windows.

Then he tugged at her hand and pointed. "My name?"

She looked up at the sign. "Griffin Court, that's right." She laughed. "It's a coincidence." Or was it? She'd thought that in the past year, she'd wised up and learned how the world worked, but apparently, she had no idea. He gazed up at the glass ceiling and the bright blue sky and clouds beyond it, his face suffused with happiness.

"I'm starting to believe that you're really here," she said.

"As am I, my lady. Though I still know not where I am. Is a museum a palace?"

Unexpected joy bubbled inside her like champagne. "No. They collect a lot of beautiful paintings and sculptures, and people visit to look at them."

"Like a cathedral," Griffin said promptly.

"Uh, not really. People are here to see the artwork."

"As I said. The bright colors of the windows and the altarpieces delighted us, especially in the winter when all was brown."

Huh. That made sense. In his time, no one had screens filled with an endless supply of bright images.

She shook her head. "Just think of all the things I can learn from you."

He gave a hearty laugh. "Meseems it will be I who learns from you."

He showed no signs of slowing down as they approached the glass doors that led outside, and Emily rushed ahead to open one before he walked right through it. He looked it up and down, marveling, as he stepped outside. Then he strode forward, stretching his arms out to either side again as if to accept the adulation of the entire city of Chicago.

What would she say to her coworkers when she returned? She'd have to think of something. No one could blame her for a giant statue gone missing . . . could they? It wasn't as if she could've shoved it into her purse.

Then he gasped, thunderstruck, staring up at the buildings on the other side of Millennium Park.

"Are those towers?"

A smile slid across her face. She couldn't imagine what the city must look like to a man of his time.

"They are. Look, some of them are even taller." She nudged him and pointed down the street, to the other side of Michigan Avenue, where they loomed shoulder to shoulder. He stared at them in rapt astonishment.

"We call them skyscrapers," she supplied.

"Ha! An apt name!" He waved his arm in a gesture that encompassed the whole city block. "Did *men* build all these?"

"Yes. Probably a few women, too. A woman designed that one—the curvy one?" She pointed to the Vista Tower, her favorite building in Chicago: three columns, the tallest standing 101 stories high, of glass in varying shades of aqua.

He turned to her in wonder. "And people live in them? Up there in the sky?"

She nodded happily. "And work in them."

A mild breeze touched their faces, and Griffin peered down the street. "We're near the ocean," he murmured with pleasure, looking toward the blue expanse beyond.

"It's a lake," Emily corrected him, and when he turned to her, shocked, she laughed. "Lake Michigan. It's very big. But we're going this way. You can stay at my place." She inclined her head in the opposite direction, toward her train stop.

He touched his hand to his chest. "That is very kind . . ." He trailed off, peering down the sidewalk, at a woman jogging in their direction. Her braids were pulled up into a high ponytail, and she was silently lip-synching to whatever song she was listening to.

Griffin raised a hand to her, calling out, "My lady, are you in distress?"

She stopped as she reached them and took out one of her earbuds, squinting up at him. "What?"

"Who chases you?" As he stood even straighter, his gaze swept their surroundings. He reached for a sword at his hip, then glowered at the realization that it wasn't there. Emily clapped a hand over her mouth. God, if he didn't look sexy, standing there ready to fight off whatever threat might come along.

As the woman gave his costume a once-over, he added stoutly, "If I may be of service, I will."

She laughed. "You're cute! That's good!" With a smile at Emily, she put her earbud back in. "Have a great day!" She jogged off again, leaving Griffin bewildered.

"Some people just like to run," Emily explained as they continued down Monroe. "For exercise."

"Does life not offer exercise enough?"

"Not really—"

"Who is that?" he hissed, grabbing her hand and staring across the street with fresh alarm. "That *face*?"

She knew what he was talking about even before she followed his gaze to Crown Fountain. A fifty-foot-high screen displayed a video of a woman's face, blinking. For a medieval man who'd been cursed by evil magic, it had to be terrifying.

"It's not real," she told him, squeezing his hand. "It's like a big painting, but it moves. Come on, I'll show you." She looked for traffic, then hustled across the street with him. The sounds of young voices and laughter reached their ears.

"It's a fountain," she explained. "See the pool, where the children are running around? And if we're lucky—there! Look!"

The woman on the screen pursed her lips and a stream of water emerged. Children ran under the stream, screaming with delight, and Griffin burst into laughter.

"I have never seen such a grand folly! Are these the children of the noble families of Chicago?"

"The . . . *No*. Anyone can come to this fountain."

He turned to her in surprise. "Even the peasants?"

Reflexively, she looked around her to see if anyone had overheard him. "Don't call anyone peasants, okay?" She tugged on his hand, urging him to walk again.

He waved a hand at the passing traffic. "These coaches. How do they move so fast?"

"They're called cars, and . . . I don't know how to explain that."

"Are they armored for war?"

"What? Oh no. We just make them out of steel."

They reached the corner of Michigan Avenue and he took in a deep breath, scanning the skyline again. "Chicago is a country filled with marvels."

Emily's heart swelled with pride. Although she loved all four seasons, he was seeing the city at its best, in late spring. Along the clean streets and sidewalks, planters and raised flower beds overflowed with yellow pansies, periwinkle hydrangeas, and other colorful plants and flowers, and some of the country's most brilliantly designed buildings gleamed in the sun.

"I'm so glad you think so," she said. "It's a city, not a country. A city with almost two and a half million people. More than that, actually."

His head inclined back and his mouth parted with astonishment as he took this in. A young man in a polo and khaki shorts, walking in their direction, side-eyed him.

"Good day to you, sir!" Griffin called out to him.

The guy snorted and mumbled something under his breath.

Griffin's smile evaporated. He straightened and strode after the guy. "You do me a discourtesy, sirrah."

Oh no. As Emily trotted after Griffin, the young man took a step back. "The hell?"

"You have answered my goodwill with disrespect. If it is a quarrel you seek—"

"All right, good morning, okay?" The guy held up his hands. "Jesus."

Griffin nodded in the guy's direction as he hustled away.

Emily grabbed Griffin's gauntleted hand and pulled him in the opposite direction. "Don't you dare start any fights."

Griffin blinked. "My lady, it was he who spoke to me in an uncivil manner."

Oh, boy. *He started it* had probably been a reasonable defense in his time.

"Listen, most people in Chicago are friendly. But if someone's rude, you have to just let it go." Off his blank look, she added, with a grand wave of her hand, "Um, pay it no heed." She felt ridiculous saying that, but when comprehension crossed his features, she mentally patted herself on the back.

He frowned. "Do all men now suffer fools to answer fair words with foul ones?"

"No," she admitted. "People get in stupid fights all the time. But it's what uncouth, vulgar people do. And drunks."

Amazement dawned on his face. "I wonder that the nobility allows themselves to be spoken to in a churlish manner."

"We don't have nobility here. Per se," she added. The very rich had way more power than any bygone duke or earl. "But if a stranger is rude, yeah, the . . . noble thing to do is ignore it. Besides, some people have guns." She hated to have to tell him about this, but he really needed to know. "They're a weapon that can kill you very easily, just by moving a finger."

His face fell. "Yes, I've heard of these, from the TV."

Oh. "You've watched TV?"

"I could see but little of the pictures, from where I stood inside the front door, but I could hear."

"Okay. Wow. So you know some things."

He shrugged. "All too little, I fear. I greatly enjoyed the plays, but I could not make sense of all the news of the world."

"I'll bet. Well, if you fight someone, even if you don't get shot, you could get arrested."

He blanched at that. "To have only a cell's breadth for pacing 'twould be little better than being trapped in stone. I would sooner die than be a prisoner again."

"Speaking of getting locked up . . ." She took his hand, continuing with him down the sidewalk. "You probably shouldn't tell anyone you used to be a statue. Or that you're from the 1400s."

"Why should I not?"

"Because no one will believe you, and they'll think you're . . . They'll think you're mad. And they have these prisons for mad people."

"Like the lunatics at Bedlam, chained in their filth."

"Well, it wouldn't be *that* bad, but . . . yeah, I don't know if they can put you in one against your will, but I'd rather not tempt fate."

He nodded gravely. "I will pretend to be a man of this time."

It wasn't going to be easy. He carried himself with his head held high and his shoulders back, he kept gaping at things, and he had that booming voice and that rich accent, a bit different from any British accent she'd heard before. And of course, he was wearing a full suit of armor that glinted in the sun. Even on the sidewalks of Chicago, filled with people with different styles, languages, and backgrounds, he didn't exactly blend. She couldn't take him shopping immediately, and they couldn't lug all that armor home on the train. Everyone stopped to stare as he passed.

"To be sure, though," Griffin said, "your friend Terrence knows that I was once stone."

"I'm pretty sure he doesn't. Because that's not a thing that happens." What *had* Terrence made of it all? *Ugh*. And Griffin had inadvertently caused him to drop and smash a piece from a stained glass window about two hundred years older than Griffin. Would she be fired for having an unruly guest at the office?

Lost in thought, Emily stopped at the crosswalk, but Griffin strode a few more steps right into the traffic.

Six

No! Emily's heart lurched. A car squealed to a stop as two screams ripped through the air—hers and the driver's.

Griffin's eyes widened, staring at the bumper touching his shins and then up at the woman behind the wheel, who clutched her chest in relief, staring back at him. She punched the horn, a brief scolding blast that made Griffin jump.

"Come back!" Emily hollered to him, gesturing frantically. With a relieved shake of his head, he jogged back over to her side.

"Oh God, I'm so sorry." Her heart was still pounding. "See that light up there, with the red hand?" She pointed. "That means we can't cross yet."

He gave a solemn nod. The walk sign changed, and he shot Emily a questioning look that made her give a shaky laugh. "See, that's a person walking. That means we can go."

They crossed the intersection and walked under the tracks for the "L." The rumble of the approaching elevated train made Griffin look up. As the sound grew louder, he grabbed her by the waist and hustled her to the other side.

"It's okay! Look!" She pointed up. "It's a train. It's taking lots of people where they want to go."

He watched as it disappeared. "It moves so fast."

She slipped out of his hold to face him. "*You* were on a van and a private jet to get to this country. The jet was even faster."

"What is a jet?"

"Um, an airplane? It's like a . . . big steel carriage in the sky."

"I've heard of them." His face looked, well, stony. "I was wrapped in cloths and could not see."

Her heart ached for him all over again. She gave him a tight hug. Because of his suit of armor, it was kind of like hugging a truck, but his smile made it worth it.

"I'll show you later on a map where you are," she said. Keen interest came into his eyes. "You're pretty far away from home."

"Am I?" He gazed at her as if, on the crowded sidewalk next to a busy street, they were the only two people in the world. "Or have I finally arrived?"

He had to stop saying things like that. And *looking* at her like that.

She gulped. "Well. I hope you like it here."

They passed the historic Palmer House Hotel on the other side of the street, its grand entrance protected by a bronze canopy and lit up with a hundred lights. A slim blond bride in a white gown with elbow-length sleeves and a full skirt stepped out, smiling and looking up and down the street.

Griffin stared at her, and Emily ignored a twinge of misgiving. When the woman disappeared back into the hotel's opulent lobby, Griffin turned back to Emily.

"Her manner of dress was almost like that of a noblewoman of my time."

"She's a bride. A lot of women dress like that on their wedding day."

"Truly?" he asked as they walked on again. "Though not oft in white, I daresay."

Was he slut-shaming modern women? No, not at all, she realized. "Most brides wear white these days. But in your time, they wore bright colors, right?"

"Aye, mostly blue, for constancy, but sometimes red or gold or green, or Tyrian purple. If I myself had wed, my bride would've worn green, the color of my house." He looked wistful at that, but then asked, "How do you know so much about my time?"

She felt a hint of smugness. "It's my job." Who would've guessed that all those studies would pay off in a conversation with a man from the 1400s?

He glanced back at the hotel again. "Did you wear such a white gown, my lady, when you were wed?"

"Yes." She swallowed. "But I don't want to talk about it."

"Then nor do I, sweet bird," he said, so gently that it made gratitude well up inside her.

It wasn't all the money that both she and Tom and her parents had spent on the wedding—although it had been a lot, which sickened her now—or all her meticulous plans and Pinterest boards for the event. It was the hope and happiness she'd felt on her wedding day, and all her delirious plans for a happy ever after, that pained her whenever she thought about it now.

"Anyway," she said, turning the corner to walk to the Red Line stop, "we're going to get on a train ourselves now."

"Like the . . ." He pointed back at the "L," and she nodded.

He cleared his throat. "'Tis a fine day, and if it pleases you, my lady, I prefer to walk."

Awww. The train had to be daunting to someone used to walking and riding horses.

"Sorry, but it would take hours to walk there. Which I don't think you'd enjoy in that armor." He inclined his head, acknowledging that point. "And I need to go back to work."

Reality hit her. She needed to get Griffin settled. Who knew what he would do with himself in the long term, but in the short term, he needed clothes, food, a place to sleep, and probably, a lot of discussion about all he'd been through and about the modern world.

She was not going back to work today.

"Actually, forget that. I'll text my boss. But I take the train home every day. It'll be fine."

He nodded. She pulled up her Outlook app and sent an email to Jason with the subject line, **Personal Emergency**, since that was what she'd said to Terrence. The email itself was vague: *unavoidable, time-sensitive matter, so sorry.*

She flinched inwardly as she hit *send*. It was the first time in her life she'd left work without warning, and it sounded, well, suspicious. But what else could she say? She couldn't claim illness or a family emergency, when Terrence had seen her running through the galleries after a jubilant knight.

They reached the Monroe station. "This way," she said, leading him down the stairs.

An old man sat at the bottom, holding a sign that read, *Homeless. Anything Helps.* Emily reached in the front pocket of her purse, where she kept dollar bills just for this reason, and deposited a couple of them in his plastic bucket.

"Thank you. God bless you," the man said.

"You, too."

Griffin nodded at the man, and as he followed Emily out to the platform, he murmured, "You are generous and kind, my lady, but this I already knew."

She shrugged. "I don't give every time, but I do at least once a day."

Griffin looked up at the arched ceiling above. "We are under the streets of the city?"

"That's right."

He noticed a man staring at him and raised his hand with a smile. "Good day, sir."

"How ya doin'," the guy responded with an amiable nod.

Should she tell Griffin that he didn't need to say hello to strangers? There was nothing wrong with saying good morning, though. After the terrible isolation he'd endured, of course he wanted to connect with people. He was a grown man; he could figure out for himself how he wanted to interact with the world. Besides, other people on the platform were smiling at him.

They boarded the train and Emily slid into a seat. Griffin adjusted himself with some difficulty into the seat next to her, his leg clanking when it bumped into a steel pole. The train moved forward, and Griffin gripped the pole with one hand and the seat with the other as it accelerated; he was staring at the columns flying past the windows. He closed his eyes, and his face had gone pale.

Emily leaned close to him to murmur, "Are you all right? Do you feel sick?" He might be more susceptible to motion sickness, for all she knew. The man in the seat across from them stood up and walked halfway down the car to another seat.

"Ah . . ." His brow creased as if considering the question. "Nay, my lady."

He was just scared. Of course. Nothing in his experience had prepared him for hurtling down a tunnel like this. The train slowed for the next stop, and he opened his eyes.

"Have we arrived?" he asked hopefully.

Emily pressed her lips together to hide a smile. "No, we've got several stops like this to go."

He watched a couple of people get off the train. "I see." When the train moved forward again, he kept his eyes open. "What propels it forward, when there are no horses?"

"Something called electricity. It's complicated."

He managed a smile. "You do this every day, my lady? What an exciting way to travel."

On public transit, it was very bad when things got exciting. She considered herself fortunate that her rides had always been merely boring and dreary. Outside the windows, the tunnel walls gave way to sunlight.

"Ha!" Griffin exclaimed aloud. "We emerge from the earth again." Apparently feeling braver, he leaned nearer to her to look out the window at the brick apartment buildings they passed.

Seeing him experience this like they were on a thrilling Disney ride somehow made it seem not so boring, after all. He made her feel . . . well, *alive*, more so than before.

Emily took out her phone to check for a response from her boss and found several texts from Rose.

EMILY
Someone just asked me about a
stunt thing??
For the medieval exhibit?
With a KNIGHT IN SHINING
ARMOR
DO YOU KNOW ANYTHING
ABOUT THIS
?!?!?

In spite of her worry, Emily laughed. Griffin was peering at the screen, and she moved it so he could see.

"Messages from Rose," she explained. "They just came ten minutes ago." While he processed that, she texted back.

I kissed him.

Griffin gave her a pleased sidelong glance. Rose's response appeared on the screen.

AND?!?!

Emily texted back.

It worked.

After a few seconds' pause, in which Emily could almost see Rose's mouth hanging open, little dots bounced on the screen, indicating she was replying.

OMG OMG OMG
Where are you now?

Emily answered, **I'm taking him to my place.**

"What is . . . O-M-G?" Griffin asked.

"Hey, knight in shining armor. What's your name?"

Emily and Griffin both looked over at the young woman sitting a couple of seats away. She had short black hair and big brown eyes with lush false eyelashes. A teasing smile played at her full lips. Griffin looked over to her and returned her smile with a roguish one of his own. Emily found herself casually scooching just a fraction of an inch closer to him.

"Griffin de Beauford, my lady. I am honored to meet you."

He'd said the exact same thing to Terrence, so why should Emily mind? But surely, she wasn't imagining the way he'd perked up when he laid eyes on this stranger?

"I'm Melissa. You know, I've seen some wild things on the Red Line, but this is the first time I've seen a knight."

"Then we both have cause for astonishment, my lady, for this is the first time I've ridden a train."

"So I noticed," Melissa said with a laugh. She was flirting with Griffin as if Emily wasn't right there. "Maybe we could grab a coffee sometime." Not only flirting, but *asking him out*.

Griffin said, "Gramercy, my lady, but no. I am going with Lady Emily to her home, for she has kindly invited me to stay the night." One of the other passengers, a beefy white man with a buzz cut, smirked.

Melissa said good-naturedly, "Well, all right, then." Not appearing the least bit put out, she returned her attention to her phone.

Emily's face burned. Did Griffin know the woman had more than coffee in mind? And was he expecting more than food and shelter once they got to Emily's apartment? Given their very hot shared dream, he might have been. She wasn't the least bit nervous that he might get pushy if she said no, but it could be awkward.

Real sex was out of the question. Their whole situation was all so . . . well, shocking didn't even cover it. They needed time to adjust. Maybe they'd get involved, and maybe they wouldn't.

Maybe he'd quickly lose interest in her. He'd been alive for less than an hour, and already a pretty woman had hit on him. Emily didn't even have the right to object. Griffin didn't *belong* to her. He wasn't a stray she'd adopted, like Andy War-Howl.

Yes, she had a huge, *huge* crush-to-end-all-crushes on him. Who wouldn't? And yes, he returned that crush . . . but that was because she was the first woman he'd kissed in hundreds of years, and because he was grateful. Gratitude was a terrible foundation for a relationship. It wouldn't last.

Besides, it wouldn't be fair to take advantage of Griffin's situation.

She'd had too much power over him. And at least for the short term, she still did.

He needed so much, and he'd been through so much. She could help him. No matter what happened, it would be an amazing experience to help a medieval man find his way in the modern world. And he would be a wonderful friend.

She looked down at her phone again, angling it now so Griffin couldn't see it. He seemed transfixed by the passing scenery, anyway.

Rose had texted, **Can I come over??**

As starved as Griffin was for human connection, he'd probably enjoy talking to Rose. Nobody other than her parents had even been to her apartment, which suddenly struck her as a little sad. Still, she hesitated, searching her brain for a reason to delay the visit.

Griffin sucked in a breath. Emily looked up to see him staring at the train barreling toward them on the adjacent set of tracks.

She put a hand on his steel-bound arm. "It's fine. They just pass each other." He visibly exhaled as the Purple Line rushed right past them.

Her friend sent another text. **Or do you want to keep him all to yourself?**

Maybe Emily did. Who *wouldn't* want her very own knight in shining armor?

He couldn't stay in the armor, though.

A lovely vision appeared in her mind: him wandering around in her apartment nude.

With an inward shake of her head, she texted to Rose, **I was just thinking where I could get him some clothes.**

I can steal a few things from my brother, Rose suggested. **He's about his size.**

Well, that decided that. Her desire for one-on-one time with this swoony man wasn't more important than meeting his basic needs.

That would be great! She texted the address.

Rose asked, **When should I come by? I don't want to interrupt anything.** ☺

Emily glanced over at Griffin again to find his gaze intent on her. His expression of astonishment had burned away to something more serious, something that made her insides quake.

He was thinking about certain other basic needs, and she could hardly blame him. But for her, it was too dangerous. She wasn't freewheeling like Melissa over there. Especially not where this walking miracle of a man was concerned. He was the kind of person everyone fell in love with, and maybe—probably—she was the kind no one stayed in love with for long.

Emily answered Rose. **You won't interrupt anything.**

Seven

She is my one true love, Griffin thought as he followed Emily off the train.

He wouldn't say it yet. There must be a great difference between a lady returning a man's ardor and affection in a dream and doing so in real life. But even awake, she'd returned his kiss with a passion like fire; so hot, his lips still were close to burned.

What drew them together was more than lust—though after all he'd been through, he would have welcomed that alone, with a glad heart and a glad everything else. They were destined for one another. What else could explain the fact that she alone had sensed the man within the stone, and that she, against all odds, had managed to set him free?

Should he ask her this day to be his wife? It would be hasty but not unseemly. His own father had visited his mother but twice before their wedding day. No less than the good King Henry V, God rest his soul, had proposed to Catherine of Valois upon their very first meeting.

But his sweet Emily must still be exceedingly astonished at his coming to life. He should school himself to patience, that virtue which, in his previous life, he never would've claimed to possess. Surely tonight, or tomorrow, she would turn to him for such delights as they had already enjoyed in her dreams, and more. In a seven-night or so, the time would be right to speak of that rarest of things, a marriage based on true love.

Emily led him down another smooth, hard path, this one less crowded. Even in the armor, his limbs delighted in movement, and he couldn't resist taking a few running steps.

"I'm walking! I'm walking down the street!"

Two young women strolling hand in hand, one with hair cropped short as a nun's, cast bemused looks at him as they passed. He'd gotten a little ahead of Emily, and he stopped to wait for her. It wasn't as if he knew where they were going.

Besides, he wanted to be at her side. Always.

She was smiling, and he could not keep a grin from his own face, but he said, "Forgive me, lady. I shall endeavor to refrain from such rejoicing. But you cannot imagine what a thing it is, to be alive, to go where you will, to look at what you will."

"You rejoice all you want!" she declared as she drew up to him again.

He gazed at the blue expanse above them, filled with fat white clouds. "This was always my favorite kind of sky."

She looked up. "Really? Not sunset or sunrise?"

"Ha! I will see them both again," he realized aloud. Neither had been visible from the foyer at the Burke estate. "So many things I will do again! Has a man ever been so glad of heart?" He pointed up at the sky. "This, this is one thing that has not changed." As they walked on, he added, "Nor have the stars at night, I hope."

She scrunched up her face. "I'm afraid you can't see much of them in the city."

Strange. "Why is that, my lady?"

"The lights we have at night are too bright."

He wasn't sure he understood this, but he shrugged. "No matter. What need have I for stars when I can behold the light of your eyes?"

"We, um . . ." Why did she look away, and why did her smile fade? Had he so misread her affections? Nay, this must be her womanly modesty, for which she had no use in dreams.

Stopping abruptly, she said, "This is my building. Come on." She pointed to a three-story structure of ruddy brick with two half towers, standing cheek to jowl to a similar one of gray stone.

"You live in a grand house," he said.

"Nope. I only live in a small part of it."

They walked up the six steps to the entrance and went inside, and then she led him down a hallway with a few doors. She stopped at one, and a terrible beastly sound came from the other side. Griffin straightened, and Emily shot him an apologetic look.

"That's just my dog." She drew a key out of her leather bag and turned it in the lock, clearly unafraid of the fearsome hound within. "He's got a really loud howl."

A howl or a roar? Thank God he was wearing his armor. Though the beast no doubt adored Emily, for she could likely tame a dragon with her charms, he might feel very differently about a stranger. They entered, Emily closing the door behind them, and Griffin braced himself.

The ruckus ceased and a hound only as tall as Emily's knee trotted up to them, his nails clicking on the wooden floor, his tail wagging enthusiastically.

This was the creature who'd raised such a dreadful alarm? With his fur of white and black and brown, and his speckled front legs and nose, he was a jolly, handsome dog, if a bit overfed. He put his paws up on Griffin's knees in greeting.

"Get down, you silly potato," Emily chided.

Griffin would have to ask her later what a potato was. "Hail, good fellow," he said, scratching behind the floppy ears. The hound gazed up at him with warm brown eyes. Griffin asked Emily, "I believe you said his name is Andy?"

"Yeah. Short for Andy War-Howl."

"He is well named, for that howl puts many a battle cry to shame."

"Yeah, and it's actually—never mind, I'll tell you later." She pulled a long strap from a hook by the door and attached it to his collar. "He's been inside all day, so he needs to go out and—you know." She led Andy toward the door. "Just make yourself at home, and we'll be right back."

Griffin was somewhat in need of a piss, himself, but it was not yet an urgent matter. He looked around the tidy room with a bay of large windows, white walls, and a bare wooden floor. So this was where his lady lived! A small table near the door held a tray filled with silver and copper coins, along with a fine necklace of black pearls. It must have cost a fortune, for they were all the same size.

Next to a low table sat an armchair and a sofa such as his friend Richard Burke III had used, not only as seating but oft as a bed. Near the windows, two chairs flanked a round dining table. A sleek black TV hung on one wall, and against another stood many shelves lined with brightly colored objects. He walked straight to them and picked one up.

"Books," he said aloud, stupidly. A hundred of them at least. Emily *was* wealthy, then. His own father had owned only four. Why didn't such a rich woman have an estate of her own?

He wasn't going to ask. In this new world, he'd need to choose his questions carefully. If he asked every single one in his mind, he'd sound like a fool, and his pride couldn't bear that.

The book covers were thin as sheepskin. He opened the one in his hand; the lettering was strange but astonishingly regular. The forms of the letters were different, and so were many of the spellings; only with great difficulty could he make out the words. Frustration and shame pricked at him. *I am still an educated man*, he told himself. The language had changed, but he would change, too. He carefully returned the precious object to its place on the shelf.

Emily returned and unclipped the leash from the hound, who bounded up to greet him happily again.

"Andy, get down!" Emily chided him and then said to Griffin, "You probably think it's strange that I have a dog in the apartment."

"I am sure he keeps the kitchen free from vermin."

"There aren't any vermin in my kitchen!"

"Well done, Andy," Griffin said, giving the dog another pat on the head. "There was a dog at the Burke estate for a time. A tiny thing with big ears, who would sometimes stare at me or sit at my feet." The memory tugged at his heart. "You will laugh, but I believed he knew I was real."

"I bet he did." She was far from laughing; her eyes welled up with tears.

Her sympathy pierced Griffin's heart, and his own throat tightened. After living for nigh an eternity with no one to care about him, her unshed tears sparkling in her eyes were more precious than diamonds to him, because they were on his behalf . . . and yet, he didn't want her to suffer any distress. He closed the space between them and gently wrapped his arms around her.

"How glad I am, and how grateful, I shall never be able to say, but let us not grieve what has been."

He wished he could better feel her body next to his. As if thinking the same thing, she stepped back and said, "You should take off your armor." She held up a palm, clarifying, "I mean, it can't be comfortable . . . What do you have on under there? A gambeson?"

There was a word he hadn't heard anyone speak in centuries: the quilted jacket that could be worn under armor, or even on its own for some protection from an unexpected dagger. "Aye, a gambeson over a linen tunic and hose."

She bestowed another smile on him, brighter than the noonday sun. "You can't wear that every day. Rose is coming over later with some modern clothes for you that'll hopefully fit, and we'll get you some more."

He gazed down at the armor with a pang of misgiving. "Can you aid me in taking it off? I am loath to make you my squire, but I have never done it alone."

"Oh!" To his relief, she didn't appear to be in the least insulted by the suggestion. Surprised maybe, but if he wasn't mistaken, also delighted. "I'll do my best."

He held up his hands. "I'll remove my gauntlets first." After he set them on the low table, he held up his hands in front of him and studied the fine blond hairs dusting the backs of them, the folds around the knuckles, the visible vein tracing a short path from the wrist. His hands. His flesh.

She said cheerfully, "I'm at your command."

The innocent words gave him a less-than-innocent thrill. He lifted an arm. "Undo the buckles on the sides, if you will, my lady."

"Oh, right." She drew near enough to him that he could smell the light sweet scent of her clean hair. He gazed at the curve of her cheek and her ear, near enough to kiss, and his heart pounded so hard in his chest, he wondered it did not echo within the steel.

"Oh my God, this is so cool," she murmured as her nimble fingers unfastened the buckles. Soon she had the breastplate off, and she held it in both hands, admiring it. "I can't get over how gorgeous this is close up. Is the trim here brass?"

"Aye, but gilded with pure gold."

"*Wow.* You know, if we could get someone to authenticate this, you could sell it for a *fortune.*"

A flash of anger took him by surprise, and he stiffened.

She meant no disrespect. While she might know what a gambeson was, she likely didn't know what a suit of armor meant to a fighting man—a nobleman.

"I will never sell it," he told her gently.

"But it's just . . ." Maybe something in his eyes warned her off. "No, I understand." From the tone of her voice, he doubted that she did.

No matter. No man and woman, even from the same era, understood everything about each other. She couldn't force him to sell it and wouldn't try.

Together, they removed more of the armor. When she knelt to help him remove one of the greaves from his lower leg, wicked thoughts chased all others from his mind. After so long, Griffin still remembered with perfect clarity what it was like to be stroked by a lady or taken into her mouth. His soldier perked up, eager for action. Griffin swallowed, grateful for the cover the padded tunic provided.

"There," she said, getting to her feet again and looking at the pieces of armor around them. Andy stepped on one, and she gave a little shriek. "We can move all this to the coat closet for now. I'll figure out how to keep it preserved."

Together, they gathered up the pieces. Emily carefully arranged the pieces with coats and blankets between them so they didn't touch one another. Even an excellent squire wouldn't have stored them with so much care.

"Thank you, my lady," he said when she was finished. "Now will you please guide me to the privy chamber?"

"The privy . . . ? *Ohhh.*" She covered her mouth with her hand. Her cheeks flushed pink, an agreeable sight, to be sure, but why was she so embarrassed? He was no longer stone and had the same needs as anyone.

She squared her shoulders. "Come with me. I'll show you how the bathroom works."

He followed her to a tiled room with a huge tub for bathing. Her cheeks flushed again when she explained the use of soft white paper in a roll, and—to his complete astonishment—how the toilet worked.

"God's bones," he exclaimed, and then winced. He knew better than to use such a foul curse in the presence of a lady.

She laughed, unbothered, and showed him the bath, along with shampoo, deodorant, toothpaste, and a toothbrush—she had a spare she could give to him. The soap he was familiar with, though hers had a different scent than the cakes that came from Castile. He asked about the bottle of thick ruby liquid, labeled *Japanese Cherry Blossom Shower Gel* and *Bath and Body Works*. She explained that was also soap, but that many people thought the scent was more appropriate for ladies.

Then she demonstrated the shower.

He held his hand out under the warm stream of indoor rain. "As hot or as cold as you like?" he asked, marveling.

"That's right. How often did you take baths, before?"

"Every Saturday night, but less when at war. How often do you?"

"I usually take a shower like this, not a bath." She leaned over and turned the metal knob, and the shower stopped. "But every morning."

"I do not wonder, when it is so easy and doesn't burden the servants."

"I don't even have servants," she explained. "Most people don't."

That seemed highly inconvenient. He looked up at the shower again. "I have an extraordinary desire to try it."

And he had an even stronger desire to ask her to join him. What a delight it would be if she did, revealing her lovely body as she had in the dream. The hot water would turn her skin pink and run in rivulets over her breasts and belly . . .

"I'll leave you alone." She patted his arm. "Are you hungry? I can figure out something for lunch."

"I do feel a gnawing in my belly." And a yearning in every other part, but he must not press her, especially when he was a guest in her house.

"What do you usually like to eat?"

He laughed and shook his head. "My lady, it is not for me to make requests. You have already done me kindness upon kindness by allowing me to stay here. I do not believe I have even thanked you, but I do so, with all my heart."

Adorably, she looked abashed, dropping her gaze. "Well, you have to stay *somewhere*."

"I shall soon find a means to make my fortune again, for I do not object to labor as long as it still befits my dignity."

He'd expected her to look impressed. Instead, worry flitted through her eyes. "We'll figure it out eventually."

She closed the door. Griffin stripped off his clothes, used the toilet, and then found himself staring in the mirror. It was brighter than any he'd ever seen before.

It was even brighter than the mirror in the hall at Windsor Castle, which Griffin and others had marveled at, once upon a time. He'd been a guest for the Michaelmas feast—a rare honor bestowed upon him because of his triumph against every challenger at the royal joust. Mordrain had been eliminated in the first round: knocked clean off his horse and onto his arse, to uproarious laughter.

At the end of the day, he'd clapped his hand on Mordrain's shoulder and said, *At least you are friends with a champion*. He'd felt certain that Mordrain basked in his reflected glory. After the royal feast, Griffin had regaled his friend with every detail, so that Mordrain might feel as though he'd been there. He'd described the king's dignified toast, the colorful tapestries on the walls, the boar's head and the fine white bread, the ladies' sumptuous gowns and flirtatious remarks, the servants' livery, and their alacrity in keeping all the silver cups filled with fine claret.

Mordrain had responded politely, though he'd been subdued. Griffin, smiling all the while, had been watering the bitter root of envy that had found purchase in Mordrain. Oh, and he'd watered it many times before that, and many times after. He'd talked endlessly about the manor his father had already left in his hands and the improvements he intended to make, when Mordrain's father had only one manor, hardly more than a cottage. He'd teased Mordrain for spending time with the hermit. When Mordrain had told Griffin that he himself would be a great sorcerer, Griffin had laughed in his face.

Resentment had grown into hatred within his friend like an ugly vine, choking his soul, until it demanded to be sated with the most twisted and extreme revenge. How could Griffin have not known? How was it possible that he'd been so deluded and witless?

Griffin saw the line etched between his brows. The mirror reflected every pore of his face, every crisp light brown hair on his chest. It was *too* real.

Maybe he was deluded even now. Maybe none of this was real at all. He'd survived for so long on the knife-edge of madness. He'd walked in others' dreams. What if this was a fantasy of his own?

Panic rose in him. If he woke up and found himself stone again . . . he would be able to do nothing. He would not even be able to turn to a rope or friendly dagger to set himself free.

In the other room, Emily talked in a high-pitched voice to her dog, interrupting his frantic thoughts.

Emily. In her dream, she'd said she'd imagined him, her romantic ideal. But never, not even after hundreds of years of torment, could he have conjured up a vision like her. She was too lovely, within and without, and too singular and surprising. His heart quieted into contentment again.

Eight

Griffin turned on the shower and stepped into it, remembering to draw the curtain closed so water didn't splash on the floor. As the hot water hit his bare skin, he groaned in pure pleasure. He picked up the soap, which produced an extraordinary amount of lather when he rubbed it in his hands, washed every part of him, then stood under the cascade for a long time, as though it could rinse away the loneliness and desperation of hundreds of years.

Finally, he turned the water off, got out, and dried himself with a towel before wrapping it around his waist. He walked out and found Emily standing in the kitchen, with Andy prancing at her feet. When she looked up at him, her eyes widened.

"Having washed, I did not wish to don unwashed clothes," he explained.

"Right!" she said brightly. "Well, Rose should be here soon. She told them she was going home sick." She turned her gaze away. "We should cover you up. You're going to get too cold."

"My lady, 'tis the merry month of May, and the sun—"

"This apartment is *very* drafty."

She hurried down the hallway. The dog looked after her, then hopped onto the sofa, curling up into a cozy ball. Emily returned some moments later with a large blanket in her arms. "Here, we'll just . . ."

She wrapped it firmly around his torso while trying not to get too close to him, holding her arms out at full length. The blanket was fuzzy and softer than wool, pleasant on his skin. When she flipped one end of the blanket over his shoulder, like a toga, a different feeling hit him square in the chest. It had something to do with being taken care of, after all his time of isolation and desperation.

Something chirped behind her.

"I made us lunch," she said. She turned to open a little cupboard and took out a plate. The savory aroma filled Griffin's senses. "It's just leftovers. Chicken breasts stuffed with cheese and mushrooms." She transferred it to two plates that already held vegetables. "If you don't like it, I'll figure out something else."

"Of a surety, I will like it." His stomach was grumbling. "Might I trouble you, too, for a draught of water?"

"Oh, of course." She pulled a large glass from one cupboard and then opened another, which released a cold wave of air, and deposited what sounded like rocks into the cup. She then filled the glass with a spout like the one in the bathroom and handed it to him.

"Thank you, my lady." The glass was exceedingly cold. Small blocks of ice floated on the surface of the water, as though in a thawing lake.

She smiled. "Has anyone ever told you that you have the best manners? Here, sit down." She handed him the plate as well, and when she joined him at the table, she deposited a knife and fork next to his plate as well as her own.

"Oh!" she exclaimed. "Do you even know how to use these?"

An uncomfortable heat rose on the back of his neck. "I have seen others use them, and I believe I can." He would do his best, anyway. She had just complimented his manners, and besides, he was a nobleman, of the house of Beauford. He could not disgrace himself at the table.

"I can help you if you need to."

That pricked at his pride. "Nay, 'tis well enough," he said vaguely.

Mimicking her actions, he stabbed the chicken breast with a fork, sliced off a piece with the knife, brought it to his mouth. The flavors of the chicken, with the cheese, mushrooms, and herbs, nearly made him fall out of his chair. It had never been like this before when he'd satiated his hunger. Back then, he'd been nearly sleepwalking through life, scarcely aware of his own senses and taking everything for granted. He let out an appreciative growl.

"You like it," she said, pleased.

"Kings never dined so well." He raised the cup to his lips and took a drink. The cold filled his mouth and he swallowed down gulp after gulp.

"Good. I thought about ordering something that Chicago's famous for, like deep-dish pizza or hot dogs, but they might seem strange to you."

"You take pride in your city," Griffin noted. He should focus on civilized conversation, so as not to wolf down the first meal he'd eaten in centuries. "Were you born here, my lady?"

"I was. Well, the suburbs—one of the towns not too far from the city," she explained. "My parents are still here. But then I moved to California—very far away. I got a job in Los Angeles I *loved*. The Getty Villa . . . It's a beautiful huge house, like a castle, off the coast of Malibu, overlooking the ocean, and it has the most amazing collection." She sighed. "But then I moved again because my ex-husband started a business."

"This business was far away from the villa?" He was trying to follow.

"Exactly. I cried like a baby when we were packing up our stuff," she said.

If he were to meet this Tom, would Emily's new rule about not starting fights still apply? Would it not be right and fitting to give the man a sound beating? Most likely he would never cross paths with the vile worm, and maybe that was for the best.

Still, his heart ached for Emily's sorrow. She had been punished for being a devoted wife. Wordlessly, he set down his fork and took her hand. She gave it a squeeze.

"In my heart, I knew it was a terrible idea," she confessed. "When I married him and moved to San Jose, I basically ruined my own life."

"I am so sorry, my lady."

She gave a rueful smile. "I think I've been pretty lonely. I'm not close to the friends I had growing up here, which is totally my fault. And I feel like a failure, slinking back to Chicago."

"Meseems the failure is only on his side. 'Tis good your family is near. And Rose, I think, is a good friend to you."

He could not yet say that his own company was a boon, as needful as he was of many things. Before he asked her to be his wife, he would find some way to provide for her every comfort. Perhaps there was less use these days for an excellent horseman, but he was intelligent and uncommonly strong besides. How difficult could it be?

"I like Rose a lot," Emily said. "I've only known her a couple of months, but she's easy to get to know. She has no filter." Immediately, she added, "Which means she says whatever she's thinking."

Andy sounded a throaty howl and someone knocked.

Emily hopped up. "That's probably her." Griffin got to his feet and followed her to the door. She opened the door to Rose, who carried a large brown bag in her arms. "Hey! Come on in."

"Thanks!" Rose said as she stepped inside. "So I brought—"

Then she laid eyes on Griffin. She squeaked, dropped the bag, and covered her mouth with her hand, staring at him—oblivious to Andy, who propped his front paws on her leg hoping for a cuddle.

Griffin inclined his head. "Demoiselle, I am Griffin de Beauford, at your service."

She wrapped her arms around Griffin in a tight hug. "Welcome to the twenty-first century! It's kind of a shitshow. But sometimes it's amazing." She drew back. "You doing okay so far?"

Griffin caught a tight expression on Emily's features. *Jealousy.* Warmth spread in his chest.

Smiling at Rose, he said, "I would be lost, like a sailor in a vast sea, were it not for my lady Emily, a bright star to guide my way."

Rose turned to Emily. "Oh my Goddess." Emily's cheeks had again turned pink as an apothecary's rose. She gestured for Rose to sit and did the same.

"Thank you *so much* for coming," Emily said. "I know it's kind of far from your place."

"Thanks for letting me! It's not *that* far." She added to Griffin, "You guys will have to come to Pilsen sometime."

Emily nodded. "I love the Mexican museum there."

"Aye, my lady, thank you," Griffin said to Rose, his spirits soaring. He'd only come to life that day, and already, he was getting friendly invitations! "In what direction is Pilsen from Chicago?"

"Oh, it's part of Chicago," Rose said, and then shook her head. "I can't believe I'm talking to you! Best fake sick day ever."

Emily frowned. "I told Jason it was a family emergency. Do you think I'm going to get fired?"

"Of course not!"

"But Terrence saw me leave with Griffin when he was in his armor. I told him that he was a Renaissance Faire actor."

"*Ohh.* That's awkward," Rose acknowledged. "If Jason asks later, say Griffin's your cousin."

That could be an inconvenient lie, Griffin thought. In his time, at least, the Church had forbade the marrying of cousins.

"A cousin once removed," he suggested.

"Yeah, I guess," Emily said doubtfully. "But what am I going to tell them about the missing statue?"

"Oh *shit.*" Rose covered her mouth with her hand. "They're going to think they have an art theft on their hands. Like, a *major* art theft."

"Exactly." His lady looked paler than usual. "Jason's going to be *freaking out.* What if he thinks I'm part of it?"

Griffin's heart dropped. In all the wonder of being alive, he hadn't considered what trouble it might cause her.

"You must tell Jason the truth," he told Emily. "I will come with you and explain it all."

"No!" both ladies said together. Emily added, "If I say the sculpture turned into a person, I'm going to look *more* suspicious."

Sorrow, more familiar to Griffin than the sound of his own voice, filled his soul. "I must tell him it was I who stole it."

Such a theft would be answered with more than a fine or a flogging. He'd lose an ear, or both, or a hand . . . or his life. He'd suffer any of these without hesitation to save Emily, who had already saved him from a far worse punishment. But God help him, he wanted desperately to live.

Rose peered at him. "How would you say you did it?"

"I would say I . . ." His mind went blank as a field covered with a fresh snow.

Emily said gently, "Besides, they'd ask you where it is now."

"And it isn't anywhere," Rose said firmly. "So there's literally no evidence pointing to anyone."

This all made sense. Griffin's fear, a dark tide, ebbed. "And indeed, how could my lady Emily have stolen it, in the sight of so many others and the light of day?"

"Right. That would be impossible," Emily said, sounding as though she were trying to reassure herself. "I'm just going to say I don't know where it went."

Griffin nodded. "And as you said before, we will tell everyone that I am a man of this time."

Rose snapped her fingers. "Speaking of that . . ." She pulled clothes out of the bag. "Here. I've got shoes in here, too, but try these on first."

Griffin took the sturdy blue breeches and a soft shirt that bore the image of an eagle gripping a sword in its talons.

"Whose blazon is this?" It was not seemly to wear the emblem of another man.

Rose looked at him blankly.

"Coat of arms," Emily told her. "What's the design?"

"Ohhh," Rose said. "It represents some musicians."

"Anyone can wear it," Emily reassured Griffin.

He shrugged and pulled the blanket off his shoulder. Emily darted forward.

"Oh! Why don't you, um, go into the bedroom to change?"

"Very well, my lady."

Griffin walked down the hallway, with its smooth white walls, to the room with the biggest bed he'd ever seen in his life. As he stripped, he wondered: had her husband pleased her in the bedchamber?

Jesus, that I might hold her naked in my arms. Though he would not get her with child before they were wed, he would fulfill her desires along with his own, as soon as she permitted it.

How long would that be?

He got dressed, then looked down at the odd ensemble. He was not a vain man, and yet . . . No, in truth, he *was* vain and had always been so, but as a drinking song of his time had once put it, beggars could not be choosers.

Could Emily respect a beggar, though, who wore another man's strange castoffs? Would she not see him as a peasant, even if he wasn't supposed to use the word? He had to, at least, stop gaping at everything like a country clodpole.

He plucked at the short sleeves of the shirt. There was nothing else for it; he had to wear something. He returned to the ladies, attempting to hold his head high.

When Emily's gaze landed on him, her mouth parted. She said, a little breathlessly, "Wow, look at you, all modern."

Perhaps it was not as bad as he'd thought.

Rose dug into her purse. "I want a picture."

A little frown appeared between Emily's brows. "Actually . . . can you get me with him first? With my phone?"

Rose brightened. "Sure."

Emily handed it to her, explaining to Griffin, "It'll make a picture of the two of us. Like a painting, but it won't take any time."

Rose said, "You've got like fifty un-listened-to voicemails on here."

"I know. I get a ton of spam." She moved closer to Griffin and told him, "Smile!"

Rose had commanded that before, but this time, he could obey. He did so gladly, putting his arm around her as she faced Rose.

"Beautiful," Rose said as she handed Emily's phone back to her.

"I am grateful for the clothes," Griffin said, and then he couldn't stop himself. "Though I fear they do not flatter me overmuch."

"Oh, please," Emily said. "You look better than anyone has ever looked in an old Slayer T-shirt. I'm going to have to fight women off with a stick."

"You claim me, then, as your lover?" He couldn't help it. Her words had him grinning. "And woe betide any demoiselle who disputes it?"

Emily took a deep breath. "Griffin, we need to talk."

"Are we not talking, my lady, even now?" he asked lightly.

But Rose gave him a worried look, as though Emily had made a serious pronouncement. "I should go."

"Lunch tomorrow?" Emily asked her. "I'll come by your office."

"Yeah, that sounds good."

When Rose left, Emily sat down on the sofa. "Griffin, come sit."

"As you wish, my lady." He sat close to her, the better to listen, his thigh touching hers.

"You know I like you a lot, right?"

He laughed. "Aye, 'tis clear as day."

"I guess it's not arrogant if it's true," she said, her voice wry. "But I'm not your, um, lover. You and I are just friends."

Griffin tilted his head. He'd deemed her honest, yet this was plainly false.

"Do all friends now kiss one another as you have kissed me?" He lowered his voice, though there were none to hear. "Do you let your friends strip you bare and kiss your sweet—"

"That was a dream!"

His body had roused at the memory. "Aye, it was. Although our last kiss was not."

She hesitated, biting her lip. He considered his next words carefully.

"I thought your fondness for me overflowed the banks of friendship. Did I misjudge so greatly?"

"No," she admitted. Happiness flooded back into his soul at that one simple word. "You're kind, and I love talking to you, and you make me feel . . ." She trailed off, shaking her head.

"Then why should we not enjoy ourselves as lovers do?" A

horrible thought occurred to him. "Did you send that letter asking for other suitors?"

She screwed up her face. *"What?"*

He hated his confusion. "You answered someone's questions about what kind of husband you would prefer . . ."

"Oh. The dating app. No, I'm not going to do that . . . for now, at least."

Griffin exhaled in relief. Surely, this meant his courting would not be in vain.

He said, "Think then, sweet lady, on how I have been imprisoned. Hundreds of years in the form of stone. So many days yearning for a woman's touch!"

She stiffened like a cat that didn't want to be stroked. "So you think I *owe* you?"

"No, I . . ." *God's teeth.* He hadn't meant that. A man's desperation did not mean a lady's obligation. He'd explained this very thing to a young soldier once.

But that young soldier had been without an amorous touch for weeks, not centuries.

"Here's the thing," she said. "You're super horny, and I get that. If I didn't already know you were such a gentleman, I'd be nervous about having you here."

The meaning of the word *horny* was clear enough. He could well imagine his lust as a horned, heavy-balled bull, snorting and snuffing after a cow in the first blush of spring.

"I'm very glad you trust me, my lady, and well you may," he said slowly. "But I am not merely—horny. You cannot but know my heart's true devotion."

Her face softened. "Griffin, you think you really like me, but I'm practically the only person you know! You're going to meet all kinds of other people, and once you do . . . you'll probably feel differently."

"The merry maiden on the train did not tempt me, and I daresay she would tempt many a man. And Lady Rose is lovely, wise, and kind, yet my regard for her is as for a sister."

"That's only two women. And you just came alive *today*."

He took her hand, and when she did not pull away, he lowered his head to kiss it. "Do you not believe in fate?"

Her breath caught. "What do you mean?"

He stroked his thumb alongside hers. "Is it not strange that I should come so far to you, from another place and another time, and that our two souls should be in such sympathy?"

She looked down at their joined hands. "I used to believe in fate. I met my ex-husband on the night of a meteor shower. How romantic is that?" Griffin must've had a bewildered expression on his face, because she explained, "A meteor shower is when it looks like there are a lot of falling stars. There's a big one every August."

"Ah. I know of what you speak, but how could it turn one's thoughts to romance?" It was her turn to look confused. "Those represent the tears of St. Lawrence, who was roasted to death over hot coals." In his time, they had celebrated his feast day with solemn songs—and, more pleasantly, with partridges and pheasants cooked on spits. "The falling stars are a reminder that we, too, can expect to suffer."

Her brow creased and she muttered, "Well, that explains a lot." She met his eyes again. "The point is, I was so sure it was meant to be, and then it didn't work. No matter how hard I tried."

The sadness in her voice tugged at Griffin's heart. What kind of man could have found such a sweet lady wanting? Maybe this Tom had been fate's fool, destined to spurn her so that Griffin might win her, now that the wheel of fortune had finally spun to his favor.

"Look, first things first," she said. "You've got to learn all about this world. It's going to take some time."

Griffin nodded. "And whilst I do so, you may learn of me, and judge if I am constant and true."

Emily closed her eyes and shook her head. "No, you need to stop talking like that."

"Talking in what way, my dove?"

She squirmed. "You know . . ."

"Pray tell me," he insisted, with mock innocence. "For lo these many centuries have I wondered why ladies once called me Griffin Silvertongue."

She gave an incredulous laugh. "You're making that up!"

"You impugn my honor," he teased. In truth, it had been only one lady on a certain Twelfth Night, and he'd known exactly what she was talking about. "Moreover, you insult my skill."

"I do *not*—you're impossible," she declared, disentangling from him and standing up. He reminded her of a lady pushing away a plate of sweets.

Gazing up at her, he said, "I will not ask to share your bedchamber, but I pray that with time, I will be welcomed there."

For all Griffin's foolish mistakes, he'd never been a fool when it came to understanding ladies. It was desire that quickened her breath and put that spark in her eyes.

He was sure of it. And it gave him more than enough reason to hope.

Nine

Emily opened her eyes early the next morning and felt around for her glasses on the nightstand.

God, that was a wild dream.

No. It had really happened. Hadn't it?

Andy stirred at the bottom of the bed as she got up but closed his eyes again. She tiptoed out to the living room.

There Griffin was, sprawled out on his back under the spare comforter, his full lips slightly parted. One of his arms lay across his midsection, and the other was flung up near his head. For several moments, she just stared at him.

He'd kept her up until past one a.m. Not in the sexy way, but in the intellectually curious way—which, she had to admit, was pretty sexy to her, too. She'd shown him a map of Chicago, and he'd asked how many leagues lay between her apartment and the museum. Almost three, she'd learned after Googling. One question had led to another, and she'd found herself attempting to explain almost six hundred years of European and American history.

The comforter she'd given Griffin, its corner torn from Andy chewing on it as a puppy, was only pulled up to his ribs. She admired that well-defined vertical line between his pecs and the whorls of golden-brown chest hair. That would be such a nice chest to lay her head on. Or to run her hands up as she straddled him. *Mmm.* Was she crazy to make him sleep on the sofa?

God, I'm such a creep. She looked away—and noticed the clothes neatly folded on the coffee table: not just his T-shirt but also his jeans, socks, and underwear.

Oh, right. Sleeping in the nude. Pretty much everyone in his time had done that.

She was going to leave him alone today. Yesterday, she'd claimed a personal emergency, and it seemed too suspicious to claim that said emergency was ongoing, especially when they'd soon discover a sculpture was missing. At least it was Friday; after this, she'd be able to spend time with Griffin, uninterrupted. But in the meantime, he'd have no way to get hold of her. Should she get him a phone?

She went back to her bedroom and Googled, *Can you still buy burner phones?* On Amazon, she found a basic phone with prepaid service that would arrive at the apartment in the next day or two. A flip phone—though still very futuristic, if you were a medieval knight. After a few minutes of consideration, she also ordered boxer briefs and socks from Target with same-day shipping.

With an irrepressible smile on her face, she went to the kitchen to make a pot of coffee. She'd probably need even more than usual, although the absolute thrill and strangeness of his presence had her buzzing. If his presence was possible, what else was possible? Everything? She turned to grab a mug—and jumped. Griffin stood in the doorway, wearing his jeans, shirtless and barefoot. She laughed at herself.

"Good morrow, my lady," he said. "I fear I must be like a specter to you."

"No! I just didn't hear you." Somehow, his very presence filled the room with energy. Whenever she was with him, the air between them seemed to sparkle. "Did you get some rest?"

"In truth, I hardly slept more than does the nightingale."

Her shoulders drooped. "I told you too much at once."

"Nay, had you not cried me mercy, I would still be asking you questions, for I have so many my head is like a bee bole."

"A what?"

"A bee bole?" he repeated. "The hole in a garden wall that shelters the bees?"

"I'll have to look that up." She came over and took his hand. Couldn't she go five minutes without touching him? But she just wanted to reassure him. "You were probably thinking about all the horrible things that have happened in the past six hundred years."

"Aye, but I thought much on the good things, too." He liked to focus on the positive, Emily thought. It wasn't exactly her strong suit. "I also lay awake listening to the sounds outside. A few times I went to the window to gaze out, for the lights make the nighttime bright." His mouth tightened in a rueful expression. "But there is something I must confess."

"What?" Emily asked warily. She withdrew her hand and moved to pour herself a cup of coffee.

"In the wee hours, I wished to be sure you were real, so I crept like a thief to your bedroom door that stood ajar, to look upon your peaceful form and hear your soft breathing."

Ohhh. She smiled. "I'm glad I wasn't snoring. I was literally doing the same thing to you ten minutes ago, so no worries."

Andy trotted into the kitchen, yawning, and she fed him and then took him outside. After they came back in, she pointed out things that Griffin could eat that wouldn't need heating up, since that seemed safest. The ice cream particularly fascinated him.

"May I try it now?" he asked, peering into the container.

"Um, sure." She grabbed a spoon out of the drawer, scooped out a bite, and held it up to him. "Here."

A little tingle went through her as he ate the ice cream from the spoon in her hand. It would've been so natural to kiss him next.

He stiffened and his eyes widened.

"You don't like it?" she asked.

"'Tis like nothing I have ever known! Cold as snow, sweeter than honey, and filled with nutmeats and heavenly delights."

She grinned. "Rocky Road's the best."

After she'd gotten dressed and put on some makeup, she came back into the living room, where he was perusing her bookshelves again. She explained the building passcode and gave him her keys in case he wanted to walk around the neighborhood.

"You can just make yourself at home," she said, then immediately felt a sense of unease. She should warn him about some things. "Um, but the jars in the cabinet in the bathroom . . . those are medicine, so just leave them alone." What else? "Oh! And these holes in the wall." She pointed to the electrical socket above the baseboard. "*Do not* touch them or stick anything in there, or it could kill you."

His eyes went wide. "Why do you have them in your house?"

"Um, because they power everything? It's kind of like fire, right? You need it, but you have to be careful with it." He nodded soberly, side-eyeing the electrical socket. "And the stove . . ." She tapped the edge of it with two fingers. "I'll show you later how to use this, but in the meantime, don't touch it, okay?"

She paused to take a breath. "I'm just worried about you," she admitted. "I don't know what I'd do if something happened to you."

His eyes misted over. Oh no. Had she scared him?

"I'm sure you'll be fine," she hurried to add, but he held up a hand and stopped her with a small smile.

"It has been so long since someone cared for my health, let alone a kind and lovely lady . . ." He cleared his throat. "Meseems my very soul must expand, to make room for such a gift."

Emily felt like she might melt into a puddle. Impulsively, she hugged him. His strong arms wrapped around her, holding her tight.

"You always deserved to have people care about you," she said. Maybe that was obvious, but something told her he probably needed to hear it.

When she pulled back, his gaze was on her lips.

If they kissed again, they weren't going to stop. And he was in no state to be making big decisions like that.

"Um, I haven't shown you the TV remote yet!" she said brightly, snatching it up from the coffee table. "So here's the button to turn it on." The distraction worked: he stared from the remote in her hand to the screen, currently on the local morning news show. "And here's how you change—"

"At the Art Institute of Chicago," the anchorman said, "news of a shocking—and mystifying—art theft. WGN's Charmaine Adams joins us live from the museum with details."

"Oh my God," Emily breathed. Her knees felt rubbery, and she let herself fall back on the sofa. Griffin sat down next to her.

A reporter stood on the front steps of the museum, a crowd of curious onlookers behind her. Emily struggled to focus on what she was saying.

". . . a recent acquisition and had not even been put on display. Now, this is a life-sized limestone sculpture, so it was first assumed it had been moved by museum staff."

She clamped a hand over her mouth.

Of course it was on the news. Why was she surprised? *Oh no.* Her parents. She scrambled for her phone and found texts from her dad, from after ten o'clock last night.

**We left you two voicemails.
We're watching the news about
the theft!
Wasn't that the sculpture you
were working on?**

"Shit, shit, shit," Emily said out loud, aware of Griffin's concerned gaze. Her phone vibrated with another text, making her jump.

**Did you see this on the front
page?**

He sent a link to a *Chicago Tribune* story:

$2M KNIGHT SCULPTURE REPORTED STOLEN
FROM ART INSTITUTE OF CHICAGO

"Oh no," she moaned. She dropped the phone and bent over, holding her head in her hands, vaguely aware of Griffin standing up.

The reporter's voice said, ". . . while all public areas of the museum are open today, these offices will remain closed as the FBI searches for clues regarding this remarkable heist. Authorities are left to wonder who would—and *could*—carry out such a daring crime."

She lifted her head and switched off the TV. At least no one had said her name yet. Had they? She needed to read the *Tribune* article . . . but she was scared to. Her parents would've told her if her name was in there. Right? She felt bad as it was. They were on their romantic getaway on Mackinac Island, and they shouldn't have to worry about something like this.

Griffin returned from the kitchen with a glass of water. "Drink, my lady. You have had a shock."

"Thank you." She took it from him and had a sip.

Griffin knelt down next to her, his face as grave as she'd ever seen it. "Forgive me, *mon trésor*, but I must know. What is the penalty for such a theft?"

"Oh God, I don't know." She tried to think about the question rationally. "A guy got arrested for stealing a couple of Matisses, a few months ago, and he got a suspended sentence. He didn't actually go to prison," she added.

"He wasn't punished at all?" Griffin got to his feet.

"I wouldn't say *that*. Getting arrested is really bad." It still made her sick to think about. "It would be the end of my life as I know it."

Griffin froze, his face drained of color. "So it *would* mean the gallows."

"No! Oh geez, no. No one is *ever* executed for theft." He closed his eyes briefly and gave an exhale of relief. Leave it to a medieval guy to really put things in perspective.

She felt horrible for scaring him. For his sake as much as her own, she needed to get it together. She didn't want him home alone all day freaking out about this—or, even worse, feeling *guilty* about it.

"They don't have *any way* to accuse me of stealing it." She stood up and took his hands. "It was just strange to see everyone talking about it. But nothing bad's going to happen to me." As she said it, she almost believed it.

"I am much relieved to hear it." He gave a rueful smile. "But there will be gossip about you, and for that I am truly sorry."

"Let them talk," she said, and felt an unfamiliar recklessness. She'd always worried about what people thought of her, but the hell with them. She'd saved Griffin.

He lowered his head to kiss her joined hands. "You are very brave."

It was probably the first time anyone had ever said that to her. She hated to leave him.

"Am I even supposed to go to work today?" she wondered aloud. "I mean, my office is a crime scene. God, this is so surreal."

She let go of Griffin's hands to pick up her phone again. Mentally bracing herself, she opened her work Outlook. An email from Jason bore the vague subject line: Current Events and Work Tomorrow.

"I have a message from my boss," she told Griffin, then clicked and read aloud.

"'Hi, everyone. By now you are all no doubt aware of the disappearance of the new medieval sculpture. Because there is still a possibility that it has been misplaced within the museum, and because this is an active investigation, I strongly urge you not to share details about this to anyone other than law enforcement officials. Please refer any media requests to our public relations team.' Sounds good to me," Emily commented dryly to Griffin, then kept reading.

"'Report to the administrative offices at 300 and 310, where temporary work spaces have been assigned to you. IT is in the process of setting up temporary laptops. FBI agents will want to speak to everyone. Please know that I will personally assume everyone is innocent until proven guilty.'"

"I am heartened to hear that," Griffin interjected.

Emily looked up at him. "Yeah, me, too." Griffin took a seat on the arm of the sofa, looking over her shoulder as she scanned the rest of the email.

"He says the loss of such a valuable piece is very upsetting to everyone at the museum . . . He feels hopeful that it'll be recovered . . . and that we need to focus on the administrative parts of our job and be as professional as we can."

She closed the Outlook app and sucked in a breath as she noticed the time. "I should get going."

Now was not the morning to be late to work. Jumping to her feet, she stuffed the phone in her purse.

"I want you to have a wonderful day today, okay?" she said to Griffin, who got to his feet again as well. "Enjoy yourself. You deserve it."

She stood on tiptoe and kissed him on the cheek. That was all right, wasn't it? People even kissed their brothers on the cheek . . . but the way he stared down at her breasts when she pulled back was anything but brotherly.

"Bye," she whispered and dashed out the door.

Once she was settled on the train, she read a dozen messages from Rose, which oscillated between commentary on the ten p.m. evening news and declarations of astonishment that anyone could have done such a thing—in case the police or the FBI ever read Emily's text messages, she supposed. She wished she could believe Rose was being paranoid, but she wasn't. She was being smart. Emily first texted her parents—**I know, so weird, I have no idea what happened, I'll call you tonight**—and then Rose, agreeing that the theft was wild.

Then she Googled jail sentences for art theft. The maximum sentence was ten years, but even the Frenchman who'd stolen two *billion* dollars' worth of art, from over two hundred museums, had only served six. Most first-time offenders didn't go to jail at all.

She wasn't even going to get arrested, she reminded herself again. Would she lose her job, though? Museums were pretty careful about having good reasons to fire employees, if only to avoid lawsuits, but these were extreme circumstances.

Once she'd gotten to her stop and had walked up to Michigan Avenue, the sight of police cars lining the side street near the museum greeted her. Crowds of people milled around on the front steps. Many people had selfie sticks or friends to record them.

A slightly hysterical laugh escaped Emily's lips. This was

horrible . . . but also hilarious. No one noticed her as she made her way to the side entrance.

She found the temporary office space, and her badge worked on the security reader at the door. The area had a small conference room, six cubicles, and a snack vending machine with nothing in it. Laurie already sat at one of the cubicles, even though she had two sons in grade school and usually arrived later. She was wearing a dress and heels instead of her usual jeans. Terrence sat in the space across from her.

Laurie looked up from her desk and asked in a flat tone, "Where were you yesterday?"

She thought Emily had stolen it. Emily was sure of it. After all, Emily was the new person, the temp worker, and it had been her project. While she stood there, purse in hand, Laurie added, "Terrence said you left with a friend who was wearing a suit of armor." She and Terrence exchanged dubious glances.

"I had a personal emergency," Emily said, fully aware of how ridiculous this sounded. The cubicle next to Terrence's appeared unclaimed, so she sat down in the brand-new office chair and set her purse on the bare desk.

"They're doing an inventory in the labs to see if anything else is missing," Laurie said, glaring at Emily's purse as though she wanted to search it. "And they're looking at all the security camera footage."

Why hadn't Emily thought of that before? They had a security camera at the entrance to the offices, and in all the galleries . . .

"Is there a security camera in the photo room?" she asked. She'd never noticed one, but she'd never looked for one, either. Her breath became shaky again. What if they had footage of Griffin coming to life? Would the government whisk him away to some secret location? Would she lose him?

"No. Because it only opens to that office, and there aren't any windows."

"Right," Emily said. There would be no empirical evidence of a centuries-old sculpture becoming a human being.

Jason strode into the office with two people behind him: a white man with a ruddy face in a blue button-down shirt and dress pants, and a woman with a tawny complexion who wore a black pantsuit, her hair pulled back in a neat bun.

"Good morning, everyone," Jason said. "I know it's an upsetting day for all of us. These agents are trying to learn all they can about the statue's disappearance, and they're here to ask a few questions." He seemed unruffled, which was odd. This was, from a museum's standpoint, a major catastrophe. Why was he so calm?

"Of course," he added, "you're not legally obligated to answer any."

The agents' smiles vanished, and they both swiveled their heads in Jason's direction. Emily hadn't expected that from her boss, either.

"But I'm sure they don't have anything to hide," the man said, affecting a good-natured tone.

"I'm sure they don't." Jason glanced at his watch. "If you need anything else from me, please don't hesitate to call." He strolled out.

The agents walked over to Terrence, the closest employee to them, at his worktable.

"Terrence Russell, right?" the woman asked, smiling. "We won't bother you for long. Do you want to go get a cup of coffee?"

"Oh, no thanks," Terrence said with a shake of the head. "I'm not answering any questions."

Emily straightened in her seat. *Really?* Laurie looked as surprised as Emily felt.

"Mr. Russell, you're not under any suspicion here," the male agent said. "We're just trying to collect a few facts."

Terrence said pleasantly, "I don't waive my Fifth Amendment rights."

"I know what your boss said, but it doesn't look good for you if you refuse to talk."

"You just said he wasn't under suspicion," Emily blurted out.

The woman held up her hands in a placating gesture. "We just want to put together a timeline. It'll rule you all out as suspects."

"Of course," Laurie said. She'd turned all the way around in her chair. "That totally makes sense."

The woman smiled warmly. "We appreciate that. We know that in your jobs you care a lot about artwork. The museum spent close to two million dollars to acquire this piece. You might be able to help us find it again."

Her partner added, "If none of you were involved, this is your chance to clear your names."

Terrence folded his arms across his chest. "I'm going with my husband's advice here. He's a professor at the University of Chicago Law School."

Ha! Emily had almost forgotten that. A smile tugged at her lips, but she concealed it as the female agent turned to her.

"Emily Porter, right?"

"That's right."

The woman smiled. "Can you tell me what you do here at the museum?"

"Sure." That seemed innocuous enough. "I'm an art conservator. I help preserve and restore sculptures and objects . . . I specialize in stone and ceramics."

"That sounds fascinating. I've visited this museum a bunch of times, but I never even thought about that."

Then the woman cast a quick glance toward her partner. It was less than a second, but Emily caught it. *See, let me handle this*, the look said.

"Let's go get a cup of coffee and talk," the male officer suggested.

What would happen if she went with them and just told them the truth?

Well, she knew what *wouldn't* happen. They wouldn't say, *Oh, well, that explains everything*, and close their police report.

And they certainly wouldn't leave Griffin alone. No matter what, she needed to keep authorities away from Griffin.

Terrence, and his husband, had the right idea.

"Yeah, I'm sorry," she said. "I'm not going to answer any questions, either."

The female agent shrugged. "I know you don't have anything to hide. You won't have to testify if you weren't even there."

"Sorry," Emily said for the second time, still not meaning it. "I'm going to get to work." She opened the loaner laptop.

The male agent said, "If either of you change your minds, here's my card." He set one on her desk and then on Terrence's.

Laurie gave an incredulous huff and then told the agents, "I'm the one who noticed it was missing, and I'm happy to talk to you."

The man smiled. "We appreciate that. Laurie MacGriogair, right?"

"That's right. There's a great café not too far from here."

"Sounds good to me," the female agent said.

As Laurie left with them, Emily's head felt like it was being squeezed. Laurie wouldn't say anything bad about Terrence, whom she liked, but who knew what she'd say about *her*? In the short time Emily had been there, she'd had a few moments of awkwardness and confusion, like one always did at a new job. Laurie had noticed every single one. Could any of those be cast as evidence that Emily was just there to steal things?

Terrence sat down at his computer, which put him almost elbow to elbow with Emily. He clicked a few keys, but she doubted he was really focusing on his email.

"I can't even get my email," she muttered to him.

"The IT guy's coming back. They called him to do something at the lab." Go through all their data, Emily supposed.

"I know you didn't steal it," she couldn't help but say.

He gave her a sharp look. "How do you know that?"

Good question. "You seem honest to me."

He pursed his lips. "Well, I don't know *what* to think of you."

That hurt. Laurie had basically hated her from day one, but she'd wanted Terrence to like her.

"I'm not a thief," she said. They were both still talking quietly. There were cameras in this office, but she doubted there were microphones. "Even if I'm the most likely suspect."

"I wouldn't be so sure." Bitterness filled his voice. "For a while, I was the only one in the lab."

"I'm sorry," she said miserably. "Do you want me to talk to them, after all? I can tell them what good work you do, and—"

"Absolutely not. You're acting very suspicious."

"Suspicious how?" she demanded, knowing she should probably just leave him alone.

"All I know is, this man in plate armor who looks a *hell* of a lot like the statue comes running out of the room. And then the sculpture is gone."

Goose pimples raised on Emily's skin. "What are you suggesting?" *Say it. The statue came to life.*

"It was a diversion that got me out of the office. Other people could've taken it then."

"You think I helped some friends steal it? Joke's on you. I don't have any friends." But she did. As Griffin had pointed out, Rose was a good friend. When someone helped you bring a statue to life, that was a bonding experience. "Besides, if I was going to distract you, don't you think there would be easier ways to do it?"

He shrugged. "It got out that door somehow."

"Then why isn't it on the security footage?"

He narrowed his eyes. "How do you know it isn't?"

She couldn't shake this dangerous urge to make him at least suggest what had really happened.

"Why didn't you see my friend go into the photo room?" she asked. "Even if you were really focused on the Bruges window, don't you think you would've noticed a guy clanking around in a suit of armor?"

The chirp of a swiping badge at the door distracted her, and a man wearing an employee badge walked in. "Emily Porter?"

She nodded.

"I'm supposed to get you set up on Outlook."

She vacated her office chair and stepped out into the hallway to play with her phone. If only she could text Griffin. It was so odd not to be able to reach out to a person in the middle of the day. Maybe that was a hypocritical thing for her to think, considering how terrible she was at keeping up with her phone messages.

Leaning against the wall, she checked her voicemails now and saw a new one from Tom.

Ugh. What did *he* want? She listened to the message.

"Hey, Em, I hope everything's good with you. Listen, we're going to be in Chicago to meet with one of our potential investors, and I wanted to set up a time to pick up Andy. I miss him a lot, and Tori really loves him, I mean, she loves beagles, so . . . yeah."

Tori loved Andy? His casual words landed like a backhand, when she thought she was past being hurt by Tom.

No. Just no. They couldn't have Andy. Not now. Tom had waited too long, and he had a hell of a lot of nerve reminding her that he'd had sex with Tori *in their bed.* He probably wouldn't have bothered to try to get Andy now if it weren't for his stupid girlfriend.

Well, Tori wasn't stupid; infuriatingly, she was smart, judging from her LinkedIn profile, which Emily had looked up at one point. And now, because God forbid Tom work a regular job—oh no, he was too special and brilliant for that—he had some kind of new start-up with her.

"Hope it goes better than the last one," she muttered, hoping with all her heart that it would tank. Just an epic, Hulu-documentary-miniseries level of failure.

She shoved the phone in her back pocket and put her hands on the top of her head—then quickly brought them down again, because the position reminded her of someone about to be arrested. As the likely prime suspect in an art theft, with a medieval knight for a brand-new roommate, she felt too discombobulated to explain to her ex-husband that she wasn't giving him the dog back, after all. She needed time to put together some well-crafted arguments.

"Emily?" She looked up to see the IT guy leaning his head out the door. "You should be all set."

When she came back into the office, Laurie still wasn't sitting at her cubicle. What was Laurie telling them about her? Would the FBI get a warrant and search her apartment?

If they did, they'd find the fifteenth-century suit of armor, in mint condition, in her coat closet. She'd rather not have them get a close look at the flawless craftsmanship and the real gold trim. It was the kind of piece one expected to see in a museum, or at the very least, in a very rich man's private collection. If the authorities asked her where it had come from, what would she say?

Maybe she could put it into storage . . . No. That was an even worse idea. If she rented a storage space, it would be searched immediately.

She sat back down at her new cubicle and logged onto her email. Maybe she should talk to Griffin again about selling the armor. It didn't have any documentation, but it would still be worth a lot, and he should have his own money in case . . . well, in case he stopped being crazy about her. It pained her to think about that, but she needed to be realistic.

Of course, she didn't want to be caught selling it herself. But if Griffin was, somehow, the official seller, and nobody was looking for the armor, who would know?

She shook her head at herself. He'd told her he was never giving it up. After all he'd been through, she wasn't going to press him to sell the only thing he owned—and the only thing that connected him to his former life.

Laurie finally returned with the agents, saying, "I hope you arrest the thief soon."

Ten

Emily spent the next hour finishing her condition assessment report on Griffin as a statue. Someone would probably want it, even if she'd never worked on anything so pointless in her life.

At noon, she went to Rose's office and found her at her desk. She was wearing a pink maxi dress and was engrossed in texting someone.

"Hi," Emily said. "Still want to go to lunch?" Two of the young women she worked with gave Emily curious looks. Maybe they knew she worked in Objects Conservation.

"Yes, definitely," Rose said. "Hang on, I'm just texting my brother." In a few moments, she finished typing and picked up her purse.

"Did you get a chance to tell him thank you for me?" Emily asked.

"I did! He was happy to help."

Emily still intended to take Griffin clothes shopping. Rose's brother's sneakers were a bit too large, and the jeans were about an inch too short. Those were things he really needed to try on.

As they walked out of the office, Emily said, "I like your dress."

"Oh, thanks! On Fridays I wear pink," Rose quipped.

"That's a *Mean Girls* reference, right?" Emily had never actually seen the movie.

"No, it's a witch thing. Friday is dedicated to the goddesses Venus and Freya, and pink is their color, and it's a day for self-love and romance. You know, just basic correspondences." Emily definitely did *not* know, but Rose gave a wave of her hand as they headed down the stairs. "But tell me about the FBI agents."

Emily explained how she'd followed Terrence's example and clammed up. "You'll be fine," Rose reassured her. "You guys are right not to talk. I think my brother should've tried that." She darted a look at Emily. "My brother's one of the smartest guys I know. But when he was an addict, he did dumb things."

That was so sad. "I'm so sorry. It must've been hard on you, too."

"But he's three hundred days sober today. He texted me."

"That's fantastic!"

As they went down the stairs, Rose said, "So I was listening to this podcast about the theft."

It took Emily a moment to process this. "*How?* It wasn't in the news until last night!"

"People have police scanners, you know. Anyway, the going theory is that it was the Chicago mob."

"*Is* there still a Chicago mob?"

Rose shrugged. "There sure was when I was growing up in Cicero, but I think a lot of those guys are dead?"

"As long as they're not talking about me." Emily froze, stopping again. "You didn't put up that one post, did you? With me and his statue?"

"No . . ." Rose cringed, drawing up her hands near her body like a T. rex. "Okay, I forgot to un-schedule it. So it was up this morning, but for five minutes, tops. I deleted it."

Oh God. Emily's throat tightened.

"I'm so, so sorry," Rose said. "We had this big meeting about how to answer questions about the theft, and public statements, and I . . . but it wasn't up for long, seriously!"

Emily took a deep breath and let it out. Not many people could've seen it, could they? People didn't obsessively check the AIC social media accounts. It was a museum, not a celebrity.

"Oh, and you weren't wearing your glasses," Rose added. "People might not recognize you, anyway."

That was some consolation. She didn't want Rose to feel bad, after all she'd done to help. "I'm sure it's fine. I'm lucky you saw it so soon."

"Not really. Most of the time I'm awake, I'm online. But I have to be, right?" Her face hadn't yet rearranged itself from a pained grimace. "There's one other thing you should know."

"What?"

"There's a video of Griffin running around and then kissing you."

Emily's hands flew to her suddenly hot cheeks. "How?"

"What do you mean, how? A gorgeous knight in shining armor, running and shouting through the museum? Yeah, people are going to take out their phones."

"I wish social media didn't exist." Emily winced. "Uh . . . sorry."

"Eh, I've thought it before, too. Do you want me to send you the link?"

"No!"

"You're a stronger woman than me," Rose said wryly. "Come on." She gestured with her head, urging Emily to keep walking down the stairs.

"Are we going to the food trucks again?"

"If that's okay. I'm addicted to those tacos."

Emily nodded.

"How's Griffin doing? What did you do last night?"

How *was* Griffin doing? "I tried to explain America and Europe to him."

"Wow. Can you explain them to me next?" Rose joked. "Is he freaked out by women working and stuff?"

"Not at all, actually. He knew two women who ran breweries."

"Seriously? That's so badass." A sly smile played at Rose's lips. "So where did he sleep?"

"On the sofa," Emily said firmly and explained her conversation with Griffin.

"I don't know," Rose said. "I see what you're saying, but you're obviously into him. You get starry eyes every time you look at him."

Emily clicked her tongue. "I do not."

"Cartoon-level starry eyes," Rose insisted. "And it seems like he's even crazier about you."

"That's what I thought about Tom."

Rose cast her a sidelong glance. "Are you really comparing a literal knight to your dirtbag tech-bro ex?"

"No? I don't know." They exited through the glass doors and headed toward the food trucks.

"You could just have a fling," Rose said in a lower voice as they got in line. "Aren't you curious about how a guy from his era does it?"

"*Rose!*" Emily laughed despite herself.

But then her friend frowned. "There's no chance he has some kind of medieval STD or anything, is there?"

A cold wave of horror washed over Emily. "I never even thought about diseases." How could she have been so stupid? "He has no vaccines! And I took him on the *train*!" Who knew what his immune system was like?

Rose grabbed her arm. "*Breathe.* He's probably going to be okay."

"But how am I going to get him shots?" Emily fretted. "He doesn't even have an ID."

"Yeah, about the ID . . ." Rose pursed her lips. "I know a guy."

Despite her worry, Emily had to smile. *I know a guy* was such a Chicago thing to say, particularly when it came to shady things.

"He's a friend of my brother's, actually," Rose added, "but I know him, too."

"If he can help, that would be amazing." The back of Emily's neck prickled. Since when did she casually break the law? But Griffin couldn't be undocumented forever. He would be a great member of society if people would give him a chance.

"But I need to get shots in him, fast," Emily thought out loud.

Rose frowned. "I know there's a few free clinics in town. I'm not sure whether they ask for ID."

"Right. I'll look that up." A more horrible thought popped into her head. "Oh my God, what if he has the *plague*?"

"Not everyone from the Middle Ages has the plague, Emily," Rose chided. They'd reached the front of the line, and she turned and ordered her chicken taco with extra avocado. "What are you getting?"

"Um, same," Emily said, in the middle of typing *timing of plague outbreaks Europe* into her phone. "Thanks." She let Rose pay for both, since she'd paid last time. "Here we go . . . big outbreak in 1400, when he was a little kid, and the next outbreak wasn't until 1438. It's probably okay."

"He doesn't look plaguey," Rose said helpfully, taking the tacos and handing one to Emily. They both went to sit on the nearby short wall.

Rose murmured, "I think that guy over there is staring at us."

"What guy?"

Rose studied the paper plate in her lap. "Ten o'clock. White guy, white button-down shirt and jeans."

Emily spotted him. He looked to be maybe forty, trim, and he was sipping a coffee.

"I think he's staring at *you*," Emily said.

"How can you tell? We're sitting right next to each other." Rose snuck another glance. "He's good-looking."

Emily agreed. He also looked, well, stable. Like someone with common sense. Not exciting, maybe, but the kind of guy that she'd envisioned when she started to set up a dating profile.

Griffin was the exact opposite of that. He didn't even know enough about the world for common sense to be an option. And he was *very* exciting. But trustworthy? No, because he didn't know enough about the world for that, either.

To Griffin right now, everything was amazing. The TV remote. Her. But before long, it would just be a TV remote, and she would just be her ordinary self.

She asked Rose, "Why don't you go say hello?"

Her friend recoiled. "Oh no. I'm too shy."

"You are not! But I get it," Emily admitted. "I could never go up to a guy on the street and just start talking."

"No, you just meet them at work and take them home to live with you." They both laughed.

What would she and Griffin do if she got fired? Or even if she didn't manage to snag a full-time position, which seemed like a distant dream now? What would he do, in the long term, regardless?

Well, that was something for Future Them to figure out.

The sun was going down by the time Emily walked up to her apartment building that evening. Griffin strode toward her down the sidewalk—sending a flutter of excitement along her nerves.

Rose was right. She *was* crazy about him.

"Griffin!" she called out. "Did you go for a walk?"

As he reached her side, he smiled, warmth shining in his blue eyes, and in an instant, all her dire worries released their choke hold on her. A girl could get used to coming home to a smile like that.

"Aye, my lady, I did. Has there ever been a brighter spring day? My only wish was that you could've joined me, for I confess I sorely missed you." He was standing close enough to kiss her, and his gaze hung on her lips. "To see you again is sweeter than words can say."

How was she supposed to keep any kind of emotional distance when he said things like that *all the time*? "I'm glad to see you, too." She put in the passcode for the building.

Griffin opened the door, and it took her a split second to realize he was holding it open for her. "Oh! Thank you." Feeling awkward, she ducked her head and slinked past him—accidentally brushing her shoulder against his chest. Even *more* awkward.

"Um, where did you go?" she asked him.

"I walked north along the vast lake and past several fair beaches," he said, following her in. "Then I came to a large university with vine-covered buildings, and a hall of glass right by the shore."

Emily blinked. "You walked to *Northwestern*?"

He shrugged. "There and back again cannot be more than three leagues."

She couldn't argue with him, mainly because she'd already forgotten how long a league was, but the distance to Northwestern's campus had to be . . . five miles? Andy howled as they neared her front door, and they exchanged a glance and laughed.

"I need to get him outside. Do you want to come with me?"

"I first must visit the priv—the bathroom," he corrected himself.

Andy was sniffing at the shrubs in front of the building when Griffin came out to join them and said, "You must tell me of your day and all that has passed."

Emily grimaced. "The FBI was there. Like . . . constables? Or a sheriff and his men?"

His face fell. "But no one was arrested?"

"No. They were just asking questions, which I didn't answer." Maybe, by keeping him from getting worried about the investigation, she'd keep herself from freaking out, too. She made herself smile. "And hey, at least it's Friday! I don't work on Saturdays and Sundays. It's called a weekend."

He nodded, and she could almost see him filing this new term away in his head. "I like weekends."

As they returned to the apartment and she closed the door behind them, she said, "I have to talk to you about health."

A frown creased his brow. "Are you ill, my lady?"

"No! I'm fine." She bent to unclip Andy's leash. "But . . . there are illnesses that a lot of people get in our time, including one that you never had. It's killed millions of people."

His face was grave. "A new plague. I did not know."

"But there are medicines that will make you less likely to get sick, and *much* less likely to die if you do. They put medicine in a needle and prick you with it, and it goes into your body." He nodded, seeming to follow this. "Would you object to going with me and getting them tomorrow morning?" After some digging around on her lunch break, she'd found that one of the free clinics on the West Side had stopped asking for IDs around the time of the first big COVID outbreak, so she was hoping for the best.

"I would be grateful to do so."

"Okay, great," she said. "Are you thirsty?"

"Aye, but sit, and I will bring it to you."

Oh. She sat down on the couch and Andy hopped up next to her. That part of the conversation had gone perfectly well, but she still felt anxious about what was to come. In a minute, Griffin brought two glasses of ice water and handed one to her.

"Thank you," she said, beaming up at him.

He nodded and sat down in the chair opposite her, studying her. "There is something more that you would speak of, sweet bird."

It wasn't a question. There were a lot of things he didn't understand, but when it came to picking up on her feelings, his comprehension was off the charts.

"Yes. You know, there are some diseases you get from sleeping with people. So I have to ask about the women you've slept with."

"In truth, I have only slept with men." He took a long drink of water.

Wait, *what*? "Really?"

He nodded. "On campaigns, for even the son of an earl does not have a tent to himself."

"Oh . . . I'm . . . not sure we're talking about the same thing." She gave a little laugh. She needed to be more specific. "I'm talking about when you put your, um . . ." What words had they used in his time? "Your manly part? Prick?"

"Prick, yes," he said, nodding. Why was she speaking of this now?

"Right," she said. "When you put that in a woman's . . ." She gestured vaguely toward her crotch. "Or in someone's, you know . . ." She cleared her throat, determined not to be a prude. "In someone's back, uh, side . . . ?"

Understanding dawned on his face. "Ah. I am not likely to do such things with a man, for I have been tempted only rarely, and the Church says it is an even graver sin."

"Well, it's not," she said sharply. "A few people still think it is, but it isn't."

He shrugged. "Very well. Neither have I done those things with a lady."

She set her glass down on the coffee table. "Griffin, are you telling me . . . you're a *virgin*?"

Eleven

Never had Griffin been in such a frank conversation with a lady, not even when he used to visit a shepherdess in her dreams. He hadn't importuned her, although she'd been as jolly as a colt, for she'd been a man's willing wife, but she'd amused him greatly in their conversations by hinting at the triumphs and travails of her marriage bed.

Emily did not, as he'd believed, possess much in the way of feminine modesty. He didn't fault her for it. With God's grace, she would soon be his wife, and what use then would they have for minced words? It made him feel closer to that blessed state already that she could speak to him of such things, with such candor.

Was he a virgin? He opened his mouth to answer, then shut it again.

"What?" she prompted him.

"It may not be pleasant to hear of ladies who have come before you, though there are none before you in my heart."

To his relief, she giggled. "Well, you know *I'm* not a virgin, right?"

"I did guess, for you have been wed."

"I was with a few guys before I was wed, too. Which isn't un-usual these days!" She gave him a warning look. Did she think he would judge her for consorting with other men? Not likely, when every fiber of his being strained with eagerness to be the next.

"'Twas not unheard of in my time as well." He couldn't help the smile that tugged at his lips. With all her admirable studies, she must've known there had never been an age when only chaste and pious saints walked the earth.

And though she was his angel of deliverance, he was glad she was no saint. He allowed his gaze to travel down her body. A saint shouldn't have hips that flared like that, or thighs so shapely, or a sweet, scratchy voice that roused both his highest ideals and his basest desires.

"Christ forgive me," he said, "but knowing you are so hot of blood enflames my own ardor even higher."

"I'm not *that*, um, hot of blood, I'm average . . . although with you . . ." She trailed off, stroking the tassel on the throw pillow next to her on the sofa. "So you're *not* a virgin?"

He lifted a shoulder in a shrug. "I do not know that I deserve to be called one, for many a time have I spent myself in the mouth or hands of a playful lady."

A vision came to his mind of Emily taking him into her mouth in such a way, right then on the sofa, kneeling between his feet where he sat like a king on the throne. Her sweet lips wrapped around his girth, her wet brown eyes lifting to meet his . . . *Christ Jesus.* His imagination, which had become more vivid to sustain him through hellish years, was now a curse. And his lady might think it would debase her to thus be used.

"But you never did more than that?" Emily pressed.

"As in our dream, oft I have slipped my greedy fingers into a silk purse to steal the pleasure there."

Her mouth fell open. "That's, uh, certainly an interesting way to put it."

Since she had no objections to honest speech, he might as well make a clean confession of it. He made himself more comfortable, setting his feet on the coffee table. "And betimes my tongue has delved into it and has tasted that pearl that brings a lady exceeding joy."

Emily's eyes widened and she put the pillow on her lap. She gave a shaky laugh. "Honestly, I could tell you'd had some practice."

He felt the smile spread across his face again. "I cannot regret it, for it pleases me that I have pleased you, and I would do so again, as many times as you would allow." His body yearned for her. *Soon.*

"How, um . . . How long had it been since you'd done these things with a lady? When you were first cursed?"

Too long. "It had been four months."

"And you hadn't had any problems with your health since then?"

He understood the question perfectly. "Nay, none of the ailments that might come from such vice."

"But you've never actually . . ." She made a circle of her finger and thumb and inserted the finger of her other hand.

He laughed out loud. He hadn't seen anyone make that gesture since he had been a boy among other boys, and he'd never expected to see it from a lady.

"Nay, my gardener has never assayed the walled garden."

It was Emily's turn to laugh. "Did you just call your dick a gardener?" He must've looked confused, because she said, "That's what we call . . ." She gestured toward *his* crotch this time, which he liked even better. "A prick. A few people still say prick. Or cock, which I like better. I think it's, uh, more sexy." Her cheeks flushed.

"What does that mean? Sexy?" He didn't ask about the definition of every unfamiliar word. Doing so would've driven her mad. But something told him this one was important.

"Um . . . appealing? In a way that inspires lust."

Ah. "Like you, my lady. You are sexy."

"I . . ." Her eyes sparkled. "Thank you. But . . . what were we talking about?"

"Your favorite word for my prick is *cock*," he reminded her. "There is some sense to that, for often it has risen early in the morning."

She burst out laughing, and he laughed with her.

"I can't believe you're technically a virgin," she marveled. "Was it a religious thing?"

He shook his head. "Nay, you give me too much credit. The Church had more rules than I could remember, and some I did recall and did not heed. But to get a child on a maid is a serious matter. I would be bound to take her for a wife, so she would know no shame and so the child might have a father."

She rewarded him with a loving gaze. "That's very honorable of you. Why didn't you get married? There must've been a lot of willing ladies."

He'd asked himself this same thing many times over the centuries. "I did not think then that I was ready to marry. Nor did I think that I had met the lady destined to be my wife." He couldn't resist giving her a meaningful look. She averted her gaze, but not before he read her emotions. Worry, but there was pleasure there, too.

"You know . . ." She toyed with the tassel on the pillow again. "People can do that now without having a baby."

"By withdrawing?" He shook his head. "I have heard it does not always work, and that in the heat of passion it can be difficult to retreat."

"That's not what I meant. There's medicine that women take to keep them from getting pregnant. Getting with child."

He frowned. "I have heard of ladies using pennyroyal, tansy, and rue, to wash out the planted seed, but such herbs may do the lady grievous harm."

"No, the medicine prevents a . . . seed from getting planted in the first place. I take it every morning."

He set his feet on the floor again and sat up straight. His mind reeled. "And it has made you barren, my lady?"

"No! If I stopped taking it, I could probably get pregnant. I think I'd like to someday." She frowned. "When I was with Tom, I thought I wasn't ready. But maybe part of me knew things weren't right between us."

This was a lot to consider. "In my time, a lady could not choose to not bear children, unless she went into a nunnery."

"Well, we get to choose now," she said, a little defensively.

He had not meant to cause offense. He was only trying to comprehend this extraordinary change. Deliberately, he moved from his chair to a place next to her on the couch.

"My sweet cinnamon, you know the tale of Sir Gawain and Dame Ragnelle, do you not?"

"I don't think . . . Did you call me *cinnamon*?"

"I did, my lady. Because you are enticing and sweet."

The small smile at her lips made her even more so. "Kind of like we say *honey*."

"Aye, we would say that, too."

"Except cinnamon is more spicy."

"Does it not please you? There are other names of love. *My fair bird, my dove, my sweeting, my treasure, queen of my heart . . .*"

She drew up her knees and wrapped her arms around them. "I like cinnamon. I like *all* of those." How beautiful she looked sitting next to him, in her black shirt of some fabric as fine as silk. "Speaking of cinnamon . . . when I first kissed you in the dream, that's what you tasted like to me. Isn't that strange?"

He smiled. "Not strange at all, for I would rinse my mouth in the morning with water and white wine, steeped with cinnamon, fennel seeds, and cloves."

Emily's mouth fell open. "Medieval mouthwash." Then she shook her head. "I forgot what you were saying. Something about Gawain and Dame somebody."

"Ah. It is a story about what women want most." He noted the skeptical twist of her lips and felt obliged to explain. "Gawain wed Dame Ragnelle, who was hideous to behold. She was often called the Loathly Lady."

She snapped her fingers. "I did read this once, but I forget how it goes. Loathly Lady—that's horrible."

"Aye, but Gawain treated her with perfect courtesy." Someday he would tell her the whole tale, for she would be moved by Sir Gawain's honor. "On their wedding night, he entered the bedchamber and found a beautiful bride. He learned that she was cursed to be hideous for twelve hours every day. She told him that according to this curse, her husband could choose whether he wanted a lovely wife in the daytime, or at night."

She nodded. "Right. I can't remember which one he picked."

"He told her that she should be the one to choose." Griffin smiled. "And with that, the curse was lifted, and she was always beautiful."

"So that's what women want most?" Emily asked. "Beauty?"

"Nay, not at all. *Sovereynté*. Women want the power over their own bodies and their own lives."

A smile spread across her face. "I like this story."

He reached out and took her hand between both of his own, stroking the tender place between her forefinger and thumb. "This medicine you speak of is a miracle. You and I could partake in every earthly delight and never fear the consequences."

She stared at him, transfixed.

"Are you imagining it now, my lady?" he asked in a lower tone. "Amorous embraces between us, and all the ways our bodies might meet?" He was, and his breath came faster at the images in his mind. Never, in the Before Times, as he'd started calling them in his mind, had his yearning been so strong.

"You . . . you have to stop saying things like that. We're not doing that yet."

"Not until I am invited," he said promptly, and a smug voice inside him added, *'Twill not be long*.

He had not known that cocksure feeling for so long that it startled him. Before, his pride had led to his doom . . .

But it was also a part of him. He could not help but welcome it, for with it he was whole. Perhaps, if he kept it in check, it would do no harm.

T he next morning, Griffin was woken up from his sleep on the sofa by a sudden weight on his chest. He opened his eyes as Andy planted his front paws on his shoulders, his tongue lolling cheerfully.

"Good morrow to you, too, Master Andy," Griffin said, scratching behind one of the dog's velvety ears. He rolled his head to one side and then back to work out a kink. It was glorious. Every day was like the first day of his life. Would his wonder ever diminish?

A banging sound led him into the kitchen. Emily, wearing a soft *T-shirt*—he'd learned that word yesterday—and loose-fitting pants, crouched in front of an open cupboard of pots and pans. Just the sight of her filled him with tenderness. Her hair was mussed and her sweet feet were bare. What would happen if he got up, picked her up in his arms, and sat down again with her on his lap? Even cuddling her would be bliss.

"Good morning," she said, smiling as she stood up, a copper kettle in hand.

Morning, not morrow, he noted. "Good morning to you, my lady."

"I know you don't like coffee." He'd tried it the day before and had, to his regret, spit it out: it was bitter as wormwood. "But I thought you might like to try tea. You're British, after all."

As she filled a kettle with water, he said, "It does not seem right for you to serve me."

"Tea is easy. But I'll show you how to do it." She peered at him. "Aren't you used to people serving you?"

"Aye, by men, women, and children, too, in every matter of thing." He leaned against the doorframe. "But they were servants, and you are my beloved."

"I . . ." She looked up at the ceiling briefly, as though for help from heaven. "Come over here. I'll show you what I'm doing."

He needed no second invitation to stand at her side.

"All right, I'm setting it on this circle on the stove, okay? And then I reach back here . . . and turn this knob all the way to where it says 'high.' That means, um . . . high heat." She looked up at him. "Oh my God," she murmured helplessly.

"What troubles your mind, my dove?"

"Um, nothing." She darted away from him—indeed like a graceful dove flying to the far rafter of a barn—and took a box out of another cabinet. "I'm showing you the easy way, with tea bags. You take the tea bag out of the paper packet, like this." She demonstrated.

He drew closer to inspect the tea bag. "Dried herbs?"

She beamed at him. "Kind of!" She put the bag in the cup on the counter, with a string hanging on the outside of it. "Dried leaves grown in China."

"I know of that country! The land from whence the Venetians brought silk and spices and jade, and the horns of unicorns."

Her lips curved upward at his last words. "Unicorn horns?"

He nodded. "For goblets that would render any poison useless, and the treatment of the gout. And to give an old man new vigor in the bedchamber, or so 'twas said."

"Okay, but unicorns aren't *real*."

It was his turn to be puzzled. "I am sure they are, for there were many accounts of them. In the East, for in Christendom, they had faded away," he added sadly.

"And do you think griffins are real? The animal on your coat of arms?"

"They were in my time, my lady. They also lived in the East and in the Byzantine lands." He laughed and leaned back against the kitchen counter. "Do you believe I'd have an imaginary beast upon my shield?"

She gave him a small smile. "Well, I'm clearly no expert on what's real."

The kettle let out a shrill whistle, and she picked it up off the stove. "Okay, we pour the hot water in the cup with the bag, and in a few minutes we take the bag out—Andy!"

Griffin turned to see the dog running into the kitchen, tossing his head proudly, with something pink in his mouth. It had straps, like a little harness.

Emily snatched it out of his mouth. "My new bra!" she admonished the dog, who had the grace to lower his gaze. She cast a flustered look at Griffin. "He *loves* these. He knocks over the hamper to get them. I don't know what his deal is."

Griffin peered at the item in her hand. "What is it for?"

"Oh." Her cheeks flushed. "I wear one every day under my clothes. Like . . ." She briefly held it up against her chest, then pulled it away again. "Anyway."

"I see. And the padding is for extra protection?" She looked away, even more chagrined.

He hadn't meant to embarrass her further. Before she could answer, he quickly added, "I understand. We wore padded codpieces on campaign, and at tournament, too, for even though the armor covered us in full, one could still be sorely injured by all the jostling and battering."

That got her attention. "Did *everyone* wear them in battle?"

"I would guess so, though I had neither the time nor the wish to inspect them all."

She laughed, her embarrassment gone. "Fair point."

"There is one such codpiece among my old clothes, should you like to examine it."

"Yes! I've always been told that padded ones didn't come until much later. It would be *amazing* to see your codpiece." Abruptly, she looked away, rubbing the back of her neck. "For academic reasons, I mean."

He inclined his head, trying to meet her gaze. "What do you mean, *mon trésor*?"

She went over to the steaming cup of tea and took out the bag. "I'm giving a . . . scholarly lecture, about clothing and hairstyles and things in sculptures from your time. Could I maybe ask you some questions later?"

"I am ever at your service." His voice came out husky.

"That's—generous of you."

When she invited him into her bedchamber, he would show her the true meaning of generosity.

She pressed her lips together and ducked her head. It was not only he who felt this way. Never had his soul sparked against another like steel and flint.

"Careful, it's hot." She handed him the steaming mug and startled when their hands touched. "Give it a minute. Let's go sit down."

She grabbed some coffee for herself, and they sat at the table. Andy settled beneath her feet.

Griffin sniffed the tea, then took a cautious sip. It had a brighter flavor than he'd expected. He took another drink.

"'Tis very good!"

She laughed. "It became a very big thing in England, centuries ago, and it still is. Lots of us like it here, too."

He nodded and drained most of the cup. "What are you teaching people, sweet bird, about clothing in sculptures?"

"How to use them to estimate the date of a sculpture when there's not much provenance. In other words, when there aren't many papers that prove how old it is, or who owned it. Your provenance went all the way back to the 1460s, which was one of the reasons you were worth so much."

Something about her words hurt. He distracted himself by reaching a hand out to Andy, who came over for a scratch behind the ears.

She noticed the change in his demeanor at once. "What's wrong?"

It came to him slowly, and he did not speak until he was sure he had it right. "The stone was not me. It was a thing. But I was not a thing."

She reached over and took his hand. "I didn't mean it that way." She gave a small, sympathetic smile. "You know, as soon as I met you in my dream, I started to call it *your statue*. I thought of it as a separate thing from you. Does that make sense?"

He nodded, appreciating her attempt to be kind. Why should his heart be troubled when he had been delivered from despair? But the shadows of his past stretched long, and he could not seem to keep from speaking of them.

"For centuries, I wished I had left the night after the tournament and stolen off to some far country . . . perhaps Malta, where the sun shines brighter, or so 'tis said." He sighed. "Or if my fate were inescapable, I would've hanged myself from some lonely tree."

"Oh my God." His lady's face had gone white as chalk, and when he looked up, her lovely eyes glistened with unshed tears.

Something in his chest swelled at her compassion. He lowered his head and kissed the inside of her wrist, the delicate place where the life he valued most ran close to the surface. She took in a quick breath and he felt her tremble.

Her gaze hung on him. "You don't feel that way now, right?" she whispered. "Wishing you had died instead?"

"I have wished so for centuries," he said. "But here with you, I am glad to have survived."

"Oh, Griffin. Can I give you a hug?" *An embrace*, he translated mentally. "I don't want to do anything else, but . . ."

He gathered her close, bowing his head to her neck. She held him tightly. The warm clean scent of her hair and her soft breasts pressed against his chest filled his senses. *Ah God, that I might know this embrace every day of my life.* She trembled in his arms, and it was almost more than he could stand. His body, ever stupidly hopeful, stirred in arousal, and he made no move to hide it or step away.

No, she was the one to do that. "It's good for you to talk about these things," she said, a little breathlessly. "You can always talk to me. It'll make you feel better."

His flare of irritation surprised him. "My dove, you know well there is one thing that would ease my body and soul as nothing else would do."

"I don't think that's how overcoming trauma works," she said gently.

Trauma. Word upon word he didn't know. It taxed his brain. He'd been a diligent scholar in Latin, if not the quickest one, but learning as a lad had not seemed so difficult as learning now.

"Trauma is, uh, damage. Suffering," she supplied. She translated many words now without his asking. It showed both wisdom and kindness, and she'd already shown him such sweet sympathy. A man could appreciate good fortune while desiring more.

But he was squandering this good fortune with his ill humor. He'd been a stone statue for lifetimes. He could wait a few days longer to taste her lips and her luscious queint again. It wouldn't be more than a few days, would it?

He smiled and willed his happiness to return. "I would rather not speak of any such trauma again, nor even think of it."

She didn't return his smile. "Don't you think it's better to deal with those feelings, though?"

He laughed. "Nay, I do not." He should make short work of such grievous tales, or better yet, keep them to himself. His lady, for all her sweet sympathy, loved the way he lightened her heart. He had nothing to offer her but laughter and the devotions of his body, and so far, despite the sublime dream they had shared, she'd refused the latter. He could at least offer high spirits, merry tales, and song. It made him a jester, maybe, which pricked at his pride . . . but then again, had he not done the same for his men, more than once, to dispel their fears before a great battle? Emily faced no such trial, but in matters of courtly love, even humble service was honor.

It would be no hardship to conceal his past sorrows. Better yet, he could cast them into the River Lethe and let those waters of forgetfulness bear them away.

"'Tis morning, and we have a fine day ahead of us," he said, still smiling. "Shall we not make the most of it?"

Twelve

After such a heavy conversation, Emily wished she didn't have to take Griffin to the clinic. But when she led him to the parking lot behind her building, he was completely distracted.

"You own this carriage?" He circled it, admiring it from all angles. "And you drive it yourself?"

It was the first time anyone had been impressed by her seven-year-old Honda. "That's right," she said, heading for the passenger side. "I've been driving cars since I was sixteen." His eyebrows shot up, as if she'd casually mentioned she could fly like a bird.

She opened the door for him, which made her smile to herself. Hey, she could be chivalrous, too. "Here, get in." Once he was in the passenger seat, she showed him how to put his seat belt on.

As she pulled out of the parking space, he asked, "Are there no roads that reach from here to the museum?"

"There are . . ." It took her a moment to understand the question. "Oh! I usually take the train to work because it costs a lot of money to park. To leave your car anywhere near the museum."

He nodded slowly, processing this. "If you lived close by, you could walk."

She laughed. "I could. But I can't afford the rents in that neighborhood, either."

A half hour later, Emily pulled into a parking space at the free clinic and said to Griffin next to her, "Okay, this is it."

With any luck, what she'd read on online forums was true: the clinic wasn't checking IDs. But they were supposed to, and that put her on edge.

They ventured inside. The windowless waiting room had worn carpet. On three sides, people sat in chairs, hunched over their phones.

"Sign in here," the woman behind the reception desk said. They both approached the counter, where the woman was watching CNN at low volume.

Griffin looked doubtfully at the pen. He whispered to Emily, "Where is the ink?"

She suppressed a giggle. "I'll sign it for you." Not only was he not used to operating a ballpoint pen, but his handwriting might be hard for a modern person to decipher. As she signed his name, she wondered, what *would* his handwriting look like? Cultured and genteel, or—

"In Chicago, the FBI continues to investigate a dramatic and mysterious theft." The newscaster's words seized Emily's attention, and she and Griffin both looked up at the TV screen. "As we reported earlier, a one-ton limestone sculpture disappeared from the Art Institute in broad daylight. Today, we have an interview with an expert on the famous Gardner Museum theft, who explains why he thinks this had to have been an inside job."

Emily instinctively turned her face from the receptionist, then stepped away from the desk. Griffin moved to her side and touched his fingertips to the back of her arm. He leaned down to murmur in her ear, "Let them blather. Words are not proofs."

Shakily, she touched his hand. She'd been the one reassuring him before. Now, he was doing the same thing for her, and doing a good job of it, too.

He gestured for her to sit in a lone empty chair between an old man in a stained T-shirt and a pale woman bouncing a fussy, flush-faced toddler on her lap. Emily paused, not liking to leave Griffin standing there alone, and then worried that her hesitation might be misconstrued as snobbery. She took a seat. Griffin leaned on the only part of the wall available for leaning, near the door.

The place made Emily feel foolish for worrying so much about her job. Unlike a lot of people, she had her parents to fall back on, and she had a college degree; she was never going to be in real trouble. Although, she did have Griffin to worry about now, too. Hopefully, she hadn't made things worse, exposing him to something by bringing him to a crowded waiting room.

Two people carried on a conversation in Spanish. Griffin cocked his head in their direction and then said to Emily, "I did not know Spaniards visited this city."

The two people stopped and peered at him suspiciously. *Oh God.*

"Lots of people in this city speak Spanish," she told Griffin. "And Polish and Chinese and a bunch of other languages. People have moved here from all over the world." She felt the tension in the room dissipate just a bit. Or at least, she hoped she did.

Griffin smiled broadly. "'Twas always thus in great cities. London was much the same."

That was a good thing to say, but still, she wished he'd speak a little more quietly. He did not have an inside voice. He had a lord-at-the-head-of-his-great-hall voice.

"There, the Spanish were physicians," he continued. "The Venetians were merchants; the Flemish were weavers; the Greeks, fearsome soldiers of fortune; and I believe most of the clockmakers were Dutch."

"*Buddy*," a middle-aged man said wearily. Emily understood the meaning completely: *Give it a rest.*

Griffin frowned slightly, probably searching his memory for the word *buddy* and coming up with nothing. Modern conversations had to be so exhausting for him. And yet he plunged into them, eager in every situation for human connection.

The young man sitting closest to Griffin shuddered.

Griffin turned to him, concern creasing his brow. "How long have you had the chills, good sir?"

The guy startled, gave him a suspicious look, and muttered something that could have been *four days*, but could've just as easily been *fuck off.*

The man had been shivering since they'd come in, Emily realized now, though she hadn't paid much attention to it. She'd been busy minding her own business. But at what point did minding one's own business become indifference?

But that was just how things were. People mostly walked around in their own little bubbles. Griffin probably understood now that no one was in the mood to talk.

Unfortunately, the dour silence had her straining to hear the television again. Were they still talking about the so-called theft? Had they mentioned *her*?

Griffin took a step into the room and addressed them all. "'Tis exceedingly dull to wait here, is it not? Perhaps someone would like to sing a song to help us pass the time."

Oh no. Emily leaned forward and said in an undertone, "Griffin, no one wants to sing."

He gave her a guileless look. "But there is no better way to set aside one's worries." Was that why he was doing this? To take her mind off the investigation? "It always lifted our spirits at camp, when I was at war."

"You're a veteran?" the old man next to Emily asked.

"Yes, he is," she said quickly.

"And sailors at sea are well-known for their singing," Griffin continued, "and even strangers at an inn on a cold winter's night will lift their hearts with song."

Everyone stared at him.

He smiled. "I anticipated that I might be the first, for once one person has sung, others oft feel emboldened to do the same."

Should she just tell him to shut up? But that would be mean . . . and even as she was squirming in secondhand embarrassment, part of her was dying to know what he would do next.

"Most of the songs I know are in French, which you may or may not know," he said, "but if you do not, I am happy to tell you the meaning afterward. This one I learned from Jack Grey, as fine a fellow as you would ever meet, in the days before a fearsome battle."

He took another step into the center of the room, as if it were his own theater in the round, and sang.

Emily's mouth dropped open.

His strong, resonant baritone filled the room. The melody was distinctly of another time. His stance was relaxed, perfectly at ease. He was enjoying himself.

And he wasn't the only one. Nobody was staring at a phone now—except for one young woman, who'd begun recording him. He met Emily's eyes more than once, singing the song with conviction.

A volunteer stepped into the room. Her eyes widened, and then she gestured silently toward the mother with the toddler. The mother sighed and stood up to walk into the office, casting a reluctant glance back at Griffin.

When he finished, several people in the room applauded. One man said, "Dude, that was awesome."

"What did you say?" an elderly woman asked him. "In English."

"Ah yes, good dame."

Emily felt a flutter in her chest. It was a love song. She was sure of it.

"'Tis a song about a mule who was once a blacksmith's daughter," he said.

A *what*, now?

"I know what you will guess," he said to the little group. "That the mule is a symbol of an unwilling maid." Griffin's sidelong gaze met hers, and amusement curled his lips upward. She let out a little huff of indignation. "But 'tis not so. The man brings the mule to the blacksmith, but the mule speaks and says she is the blacksmith's daughter."

It wasn't exactly the swoonworthy translation Emily had been expecting. And he'd *known* she would interpret it as a love song. She shook her head, a smile playing at her lips.

She had to learn not to underestimate Griffin just because he was confused by the modern world. He knew French and Latin. He spoke eloquently without effort. The night they'd stayed up late to talk about history, he'd made astute connections and asked insightful questions. Incredibly, all on his own, he'd figured out how to enter people's dreams.

He wasn't only a gallant medieval smokeshow. He was, well, *smart*. And that was a little unnerving.

An old man peered at him. "He didn't notice his daughter was a mule?"

"Nay, my good sir. She only became a mule after meeting a priest in secret." He tilted his head thoughtfully. "In truth, 'tis a strange song, now that I explain it."

The older lady said, "I thought it was going to be a love song."

His gaze locked on Emily and his congenial smile gave way to a more serious expression. "As to that, I can sing a love song, if you wish."

The waiting room went perfectly still. Emily searched for a light quip in response, anything to break the tension, and came up with nothing.

"This is also in French," he said quietly, his heated gaze never leaving her. "The meaning is . . . Sweet, lovely lady, only you have sovereignty over my heart." He frowned, concentrating on the translation. "And I have humbly cherished you . . . but my joy will come to an end if you do not take some pity on me."

Emily's heart pounded. He glanced briefly at the ceiling, clearly still thinking about the meaning of the French words in English, and when he met her gaze again, his eyes burned with fierce intensity.

"You bind and torment my heart, and grant me no relief, and yet I desire nothing but to be in your power."

Everyone was staring at her now.

She'd kept telling herself he wanted sex because he'd been stone for hundreds of years. It was more than that. He wanted *her*.

But he'd said that from the beginning. She just hadn't believed it.

He began to sing again. His voice was strong and fine as before, but each word was filled with longing. She had to look down at the floor. But he was too beautiful, too moving to look away from for long. Even as the French lyrics washed over her, his earlier words echoed in her mind. *You cannot but know my heart's true devotion.* He'd been right. His feelings were too much to deny.

When he finished, a moment of silence hung in the room.

"That was beautiful," she said quietly. Several others quickly assented, and a few applauded. Griffin gave a gallant bow of acknowledgment.

"I know a song," the elderly man piped up.

Griffin turned to him, a broad smile crossing his face. "Then sing it, good sir!"

The romantic moment had passed. He was back to being jovial, the life of the party—even in a situation that was very far from being a party.

The old man launched into "Uptown Funk." Emily didn't know what she'd been expecting, but it hadn't been that.

The young man broke in loudly. "Wait, wait. Let me start first."

This earned him a glower. Undeterred, the young man began wordlessly singing the bass line, and the glower gave way to a broad smile. On the right beat, the old man started again.

When they came to the line about being too hot, most of the room joined in. Not Griffin, but he was beaming and tapping his toe along with the song. A few people clapped in time, and Emily couldn't resist providing some backup vocals at the appropriate place.

The door to the office opened just as they shout-sang a line in unison. The nurse jumped a step backward, her eyes wide, and the song dissolved into a round of laughter.

"You're a rowdy bunch," she said, a delighted smile on her face.

The patients laughed and met one another's eyes, like people who'd been in on a prank . . . or who had achieved some kind of group victory.

And they had. They'd come together to triumph over boredom and isolation. And it was only because of Griffin. Emily beamed at him, and he smiled back.

She'd never met anyone like him, for reasons that went far beyond the fact that he was from a different century. He'd suffered so much, but he could make joy out of nothing.

The nurse said, "Griffin de Beauford?"

"Yea, lady, I am he," Griffin said, still grinning.

"You can come on back."

"Can I come with him?" Emily asked. "I sometimes need to translate for him."

The nurse held up her hand to Emily like a traffic cop. She asked Griffin, "Do you want her to come with you, or would you prefer to be seen alone?"

Griffin said, "I would have her by my side always." A couple of *awws* came from the others.

Once they were in a patient room, the nurse said, "I'm Katrina. How are you feeling today, Mr. Beauford?"

"As well as I have ever felt, Lady Katrina."

"Just Katrina is fine. What brings you in today?"

"He's never been to a doctor in his life," Emily explained. "No shots, no tests, no anything. So we want to get him a checkup, vaccines . . . anything you can do."

The nurse pursed her lips for a moment, regarding Griffin. "Do you mind telling me where you're from?"

"From a part of England that no one ever visits, my lady."

Emily's pulse kicked up a notch. "He lives in Chicago now, though." Would that be enough to get him treatment? Maybe the woman would demand a driver's license, after all, and they'd be screwed.

Katrina said, "Hang on a minute." She walked out to the hallway and called out, "Travis? Can you take my next one? This one's going to take a while."

Yes. Emily let out a sigh of relief.

Katrina took Griffin's pulse and blood pressure. His eyes widened at the cuff, and Emily said quickly, "It's going to stop getting tighter in a minute."

Katrina asked him, "Do you use drugs?"

"No," he answered. Had he understood the question? Emily wasn't sure, but it didn't matter since he'd answered correctly.

The cuff eased. "Do you drink?"

"Aye, of course, lest I die of thirst."

"She means alcohol," Emily interjected. "Like ale and wine?"

He turned back to the nurse, beaming. "That is very kind. I should be glad to raise a cup with you."

Katrina blinked. "I'm not giving you alcohol. I'm just asking about your health."

"Ah." He looked mildly disappointed. Emily made a mental note to buy the guy a beer soon.

The nurse asked for his consent to draw his blood for tests, and patiently explained this after Griffin asked her to clarify. They arranged to have the results texted to Emily's phone since he didn't have one. Then she administered several vaccines.

Finally, she said, "Well, Mr. Beauford, you should get test results in a few days, but as far as I can tell, you are in perfect health."

"Thank you, my lady. I hope you are in excellent health as well."

Katrina flashed a smile that made her look twenty years younger.

It would take him a little time to stop saying *my lady*, Emily supposed. Especially because she hadn't corrected him on it. She didn't really want to. Every time he said it, something inside her melted . . . especially when he said it to her. And apparently, she wasn't the only one.

Emily was glad to step out of the clinic and into the bright spring day again. No doubt most people who went to the clinic felt the same way.

"Do we not owe a payment to the good nurse?" Griffin asked.

"No, it's for people who don't have the money to pay. Like people who just came here from other countries, and people who don't have homes."

"People like me."

His subdued tone made something twist inside her. "You have a home," she said firmly. "With me. As long as you want it."

He took her hand in his, bent low, and kissed it—sending a delicious shiver through her whole body. "And for that, my heart's queen, I give you thanks beyond measure."

What if he wanted to stay with her forever? That would probably be *amazing*.

He wouldn't want to. And that was what she was afraid of: the inevitable abandonment and heartbreak when he found someone better.

They might as well enjoy themselves in the meantime, though.

"Come on, let's go have some fun," she said.

He opened his mouth to say something, hesitated, and then asked, "What is fun?"

The question made something sparkle inside her. She squeezed his hand.

"Fun is the same as . . . pleasant times. Doing things that make you smile or laugh. Does that make sense?"

His smile came back now, reaching his eyes. "Merrymaking."

"That's it."

"Aye, lady. Let's have fun every day."

Nobody could have fun every day. Although, with Griffin, a person might come pretty close.

"I like the sound of that," she told him. "Let's try."

Thirteen

As he rode in the car, Griffin admired Emily's profile. She wore a blue cap with a partial brim, only over her face, and she'd pulled her dark brown hair back in a band, exposing the curve of her neck and the delicate shell of her ear. A gold and sapphire earring sparkled in the lobe.

"Are you staring at me?" she teased.

"Heaven forfend, my lady," he said lightly, but averted his gaze to look out his own window. They passed shops with signs, some with words he didn't know: *Zen Leaf, Donuts, Pizza, Walgreens, Thai.* And what was a Shake Shack? A brothel, most assuredly, like London's infamous Rocking Horse Inn.

"When was this city built?" he asked. Recalling how new the whole present country was, he added, "Perhaps two hundred years ago?"

"That's a good guess. Probably not quite that old, though. These tall buildings are a lot newer, of course. The name Chicago comes from a Native American word for wild leeks that grew here."

"Do they still? They make a fine winter soup." His mouth watered suddenly at the thought of it: leeks simmered with salted ham, onions, and dried mushrooms, in a broth made golden by saffron.

"I doubt it. But we can get them at the market, any time of year."

As he pondered how that might be possible, they reached streets filled with more cars. A man in a bright yellow-green jacket held up a hand, signaling her to stop, and a throng of people crossed the street.

"Such crowds," he murmured to Emily.

"It's like this on every game day. On the weekends, anyway."

She parked in a small lot on a narrow street. "The stadium's about four blocks from here," she told him as they walked to the corner—under the tracks of the "L," but Griffin had made his peace with that now. Sturdy girders supported the cars, and it had been decades, Emily had explained, since any of them had fallen on anyone's head.

They turned onto a larger street lined with festive pubs, many with terraces where friends ate, drank, and made merry. Many wore bright blue shirts, and even more wore blue caps like the one that looked so jaunty on his lady. Emily was about to step into a puddle, and Griffin swiftly took her hand to pull her around it.

She made a sound that was something like *Ope.* "Thank you," she added.

He kept her hand in his, since she showed no objection to it. "Why do so many wear blue?"

She stopped to face him. "Our team is the Chicago Cubs, and we're all wearing blue to show that we want them to win. There are two teams, and men take turns trying to hit a ball with a bat—like a club?"

He nodded. "Yea, I know what a bat is. The peasants—I mean, those fine persons who were not noble—carried them to fight off thieves."

She grinned at the way he corrected himself. "Okay, well, one team tries to hit a ball with a bat, and the other team tries to catch the ball after they hit it, and the one who hit the ball runs to a . . . a plate?" She gestured with her hands as she talked. "Oh, but the men want to catch the ball before it bounces. But if it does bounce first, they throw it to the man who's already standing on the plate."

Griffin's confusion must have shown on his face, because she laughed and started walking again. He matched her pace. "After you watch for a while, you'll understand."

He nodded. "Will any take offense that I am not wearing blue?"

"No, no one will mind," she reassured him.

"I only ask because in my time, such matters were oft of grave consequence. I knew a baroness who fell deeply out of favor with Queen Catherine for wearing black to her coronation."

Her head whipped around to look at him. "Queen Catherine who?"

"Catherine of the house of Valois, King Henry's bride."

"Wow. Did you go? Where was it?"

"Westminster Abbey, my lady, and aye, I did."

Her eyes were wide. "What did *you* wear?"

He smiled at her curiosity. "I wore a tunic of green brocade from Burgundy, patterned with golden leaves."

Emily gave a low whistle. "You must've looked amazing."

Griffin felt a pang of wistfulness. The beautiful Catherine had been carried on a gilded litter through the crowded streets, which had been draped in cloths of gold. He would never again dress that way or attend an event of such grandeur.

"Of course, you always look amazing," Emily added, and his regrets melted away like the last bit of ice in a springtime stream. "I would *love* to tour Westminster Abbey someday."

"As would I, sweet bird, for when I was there, the towers were not yet complete."

Emily screwed up her face. "If I'm remembering right, they

didn't finish the towers until about three hundred years after your era."

"Truly? The builders must've been extraordinarily idle."

She laughed. "I'll show you a picture on my phone when we sit down. Did they have a romantic wedding? Were they in love?"

The question hummed between them. Her hand was still in his, and Griffin stroked his thumb along her fingers, which fluttered in response.

"That I cannot say, for they wed at Troyes to seal the peace there," he said honestly. "But I have no doubt that King Henry was dazzled by his bride on that day. She was such a beautiful young queen."

Emily's lips tightened in sudden displeasure.

Jealousy was a sin, he'd often heard, and he knew better than anyone that it was dangerous besides. He wouldn't have tried to make her feel that way for the wide world. Yet it spurred another familiar, sinful emotion—pride—which he supposed he could enjoy in a very small dose.

Griffin added, "Although Catherine was fair, her beauty would dim next to yours. One may think the full moon is bright if one has never seen the noonday sun." He gazed over at her. "And if you were a bride, in a gown of silk, a coronet set upon your hair . . . I would think Guinevere had stepped out of legends and into real life."

She ducked her head and covered her mouth with her hand. When she took it away again, her cheeks were flushed pink. "If Henry flattered Catherine half as much as you flatter me, she was a lucky woman."

It had not been flattery, but simple truth. He would've said so, but his words had already made her bashful. A woman with a stroller passed them, and he took the opportunity to change the subject. "Even the babes wear blue caps."

She gave him a thoughtful look. "Do you want one? A cap, I mean."

"In truth, my lady, I would love one." He was a fool, maybe, but after all the grim and brutal trials he'd been through, his heart still lifted as though he were a child at the May fair, getting a wooden sword or a clay horse to take home.

"Okay, let's do it," she said, and beckoned him into the open doors of a nearby shop called Sports World.

It must've been where everyone purchased their hats and caps, for there were a hundred or more different kinds of each, as well as stockings, toys, pennants, and other items whose uses were a mystery to him. It took him more time, maybe, than it should have, to decide upon a hat with the head of a bear cub upon it. After she paid for it and removed the tags and they stepped out onto the street again, she gave it to him to try on.

"What do you think, my lady?"

She clapped her hands. "You look so good! My big Cubs fan!" Her upturned face seemed to be almost begging for a kiss. He doubted she would object, but he'd told himself that he'd wait for her to kiss him first. He was doubting that plan now. How much longer would that be?

As they walked on, the scent of grilled meats wafted through the breeze, giving him an idea. "Are there any deer in Chicago?" He was a fine hunter. With a bow and arrows, he could at least keep her supplied in venison while he sought a steady occupation. He could set traps for rabbits, too.

She looked over at him, surprised. "Not many in the city, I don't think. But there are tons of them in the suburbs, where my parents live."

This city, with the wide expanses of rock-hard streets and walkways and towering buildings, sometimes awed him and sometimes disturbed him. "Do you ever wish there were more woods and meadows?"

"There are some beautiful parks. But sometimes I wish I had a garden like my parents, so I could grow flowers and tomatoes and things."

"Why then do you live in the city?" She'd explained to him before that many people lived far out in the country and took the train or drove into the city for work.

She shrugged. "When I was a kid in the suburbs, I always imagined living in the city. I guess I thought it would be, I don't know, exciting and romantic. And hey, I was right." She gave a tentative smile, and his heart beat harder. "But it would be nice to be able to pop in and see my parents whenever. And like you say, to have more nature around. Plus it's cheaper. I could rent a bigger place . . . maybe even one with a fenced yard for Andy."

At the end of the street, a crossroads teemed with crowds, and a round amphitheater rose above them. A red sign declared it **WRIGLEY FIELD—HOME OF THE CHICAGO CUBS**. Griffin stopped in his tracks to stare up at it.

"'Tis enormous," he wondered aloud, and then laughed. "Ever am I feeling like a peasant from the country visiting London for the first time, for I am always amazed."

"It *is* huge." They got into a line of people waiting to enter, and when they reached the woman at the gate, Emily produced her phone, that device that accomplished all things.

Once inside, Emily reached out to hold his hand again. "Welcome to the Friendly Confines."

When she led him to their seats, he had to bite his tongue to keep from commenting on the crowds. There were nearly as many people, he would've guessed, as in the whole of London—or at least, London in his time.

Ivy-covered walls surrounded a great green grassy field, a welcome sight. All around him, people were in high spirits. Two men laughed about their wagers. A child stood in her seat and danced to loud music that seemed to emit from the sky. He'd always loved merry crowds such as this, at tournaments and fairs.

"How often do they have these games?" he asked as they sat down.

"Uh, I'm not sure. Hang on." She pulled out her phone and typed into it. "One hundred and sixty-two a year. Only half of them are here. For the other half, they travel to other cities."

He couldn't help but shake his head in wonder. This huge gathering was a regular occurrence.

"Okay, this guy's my favorite! And he's up first to bat."

The man at bat did not even attempt to hit the ball on the first few times it came his way. Curiously, Emily clapped the first time he ignored it, as though he'd done something praiseworthy, but remained silent the second two times. Then he hit the ball with a mighty crack and the bat split into two as he released it and sprinted for one of the plates. Griffin cheered. But a man in the field grabbed the ball and threw it to the man who stood on the plate, and the batter trotted away with stoic rejection. Emily clicked her tongue with disappointment.

He said, "It surprises me that you are fond of such sport, for I had thought all your love was for art and books."

"You thought I was too much of a nerd?"

Griffin smiled, for it was clearly a jest.

"Well, that's understandable. But my parents are huge Cubs fans. Especially my dad. When they won the World Series, my dad was sobbing. It was the only time I ever saw him cry, except when my grandma died."

Griffin took her hand. "Tell me more of your parents, if you like." He had not given her family or her childhood much thought, which struck him now as a strange oversight. She was not Venus, emerged from a shell.

Her father was a chemist, she said. Her mother taught classes about politics and the government at a place called Harper College.

Sometimes in high school, Emily had done her homework at the coffeehouse there while her mother taught. Emily had been good friends with a couple of girls but hadn't been particularly popular or sought after by the boys; she'd been shy, her skin prone to something called breakouts, and she'd been engrossed in her studies.

Griffin asked her a couple of questions, but for the most part, he remained silent, listening intently. After a while, cheers distracted them and they looked down to see the ball sailing into the stands.

"Home run!" Emily exclaimed, jumping to her feet. Griffin stood, too, applauding, as the Cubs player rounded the bases. "Look, there's the replay." Emily pointed. On the big screen, they saw the man hit it. She yelled, "Wooo!"

Griffin joined her. "Huzzah!" She darted an amused glance at him. No one else had said *huzzah*, he realized. Still clapping, he imitated her instead. "Wooo!"

"That was so great!" she said as they sat down. "I almost made you miss it because I was talking."

"Even the pleasure of the sport does not match the pleasure of hearing your voice."

She smiled and ducked her head. "Are you ever going to stop saying things like that?"

Things like how sweet she was, and how alluring? "I have not the slightest intention of stopping, my cinnamon, unless it causes you displeasure."

"Well, it definitely doesn't," she murmured. "And you know, I think I said this before, but you're a really good listener."

He laughed. "In truth, I was not known as such in my own time." Then he sobered. "When I was stone, it was a blessing to hear someone talk. It entertained me and gave me new things to ponder. And meseems I grew accustomed to not interrupting."

"I hope I'm a good listener for you, too." She gave him one of her quick hugs. "What was *your* childhood like? Your family? I only know a little about your dad, and I think you had a sister, Alyse, right?" He nodded, his heart twisting with regret. "Were you the only two children?"

"Aye. Through no fault of my mother's," he added quickly. "When she was with child, she ate no juniper berries in her meat pies and stayed abed much of the time. But there were two miscarriages, one stillbirth, and one babe who did not live the day."

"Oh, wow," Emily said, her voice filled with sympathy. "People still have miscarriages all the time, but I know fewer babies survived in your time."

Griffin nodded, frowning. "The girl child who lived just one day . . . I was seven years old and loved her at first sight, and though they told me she'd gone to live with Christ in heaven, it broke my heart."

"I'm so sorry." Emily squeezed his hand. "You must've been such a sweet little boy."

That dragged a smile out of him. "I was a hellion much of the time."

"An adorable hellion, I bet. What was your mother like?"

"She died in the birthing of my sister, the one who lived. When I was ten." Emily's eyes grew watery. It both distressed and comforted him. "But I remember everything about my mother. She was plump and fair of hair and indulged us much with stories. Betimes she was too melancholic . . ." He paused. He was trying to unlearn his older way of speaking, as much as he could, but it was hard, and even more so now that he spoke of family. "Sometimes she was sad and would shut herself up in her chamber, and my father grew impatient of those spells."

"Who could blame her?" Emily said indignantly. "She went through a lot."

"Aye . . . but as a boy, I would fear I was a cause of her sorrow."

"Oh no." Emily squeezed his hand again. "She must've adored you. Of course that wasn't true."

"It wasn't," he agreed. He'd figured that out for himself, after many years of mulling it over. "It was her nature. And other times, she was filled with joy, and you wanted to be close to her, the way you want to revel in the rays of the sun."

"You get that from her. That joy. And that charisma." He didn't recognize the last word, but affection shone in her eyes.

"You found a record of my sister inheriting the estate," he said. He'd been meaning to ask her about this. "Do you know anything else about her? If she wed, or bore children, or lived a long life?"

Emily shook her head, the corner of her mouth turned down in sympathy. "I can try to look some more. What was she like?"

His throat tightened. For centuries, he'd tried to push his grief about her out of his mind, and for the most part, he'd succeeded. He'd had to. Trapped in stone, with no present comfort, the grief would've destroyed him. Always when he'd been under the curse, he'd felt the constant threat of turning into something not human, some kind of evil spirit.

Now, it was safe to think of them. But it hurt.

"Alyse was much taken with Mordrain, the man who had me cursed." Emily's eyes went wide. "My father opposed the match, for Mordrain was from a new house, less grand in honor. Mordrain had been my friend since we were boys, and I oft thought of speaking up for their union."

Despite the bright sunshine and the colorful crowd surrounding them, dread chilled him. Emily would learn more about his short-comings now. But she deserved to know.

"When I was trapped in stone, I would imagine—for days on end, meseems—of giving the most noble speeches to my father about love." He gave a short, humorless laugh. "But I did no such thing when I had the chance. If I quarreled with my father, he was cold with me for days . . . and I half thought that, because of the greater dignity of our house, he might be right."

"We don't think as much about the dignity of houses now," Emily said gently. "But most people thought that way in your time, right? And I can understand why you wouldn't want to fight with your father, especially when you already lost your mother."

"You are right, my lady." He hadn't considered this before.

"He never should've gotten *that* angry with you," Emily said. "Parents are supposed to make their children feel they're loved no matter what."

"Truly? I have never heard that said." He very much liked the idea of it, though. If he and Emily were ever blessed with children, he would think on that.

She shook her head. "You need to stop feeling guilty."

Perhaps she was right. Still, having carried it with him for so long, he was reluctant to let go of it.

"The last time I spoke with Alyse, she was angry with me for fighting Mordrain in the tournament."

"Alyse was the lady you mentioned before," Emily realized aloud. "The lady Mordrain loved, who saw him lose."

"Aye," Griffin said heavily. "I was not ready to speak of her." Emily squeezed his hand, sympathy glistening in her eyes.

He explained, "After that tournament, Mordrain had told her he could no longer love her, when she had a foul brother like me." It pained him to talk about all this, but it was a relief, too, like an infected wound lanced and cleansed. "I wish I'd gotten to say goodbye to her."

She wrapped her other hand around their joined ones. "She wished that, too, I'm sure."

He'd always imagined Alyse being angry with him for disappearing. But maybe Emily was right.

"All families fight," she said. "And with your father against the match, it sounds like Mordrain might've just been giving up on your sister, anyway."

In all Griffin's musings, he'd never thought of that.

"I'm sure Alyse loved you very much," she went on to say. It was true. She had. "And you saved her. Can you imagine what might've happened if she'd married Mordrain? All husbands and wives fight, and he was straight-up *evil*. Who knows what kinds of curses he might've used on her?"

He'd never thought of that, either. And what she said might have very likely come to pass.

The tension in the back of his shoulders loosened. Maybe there had been a glimmer of good in the most contemptible evil of the curse. But of course, Emily herself was another glimmer of good.

"You ease my heart greatly," he said. "Thank you." His chest still ached, but it was a clean ache now, free from self-loathing and regret . . . and tinged with hope.

Maybe he would meet Alyse again in Heaven. No, he certainly would. There was no question that she would be there, and no loving God would exact an eternal punishment upon him for his petty sins after all he'd been through already. He felt sure of that, as sure as the afternoon sunshine warming his skin.

He looked around them, his heart lighter. "A day like this . . . I cannot tell you what a joy it is."

She smiled. "What do you like about it?"

"The blue sky above, the breeze, a new sport, a crowd of people in high spirits. The scents of ale and delicious food, and the cries of the sellers. The field and the green growing ivy on the walls, the songs of birds and their quick flights, searching for crumbs—" She laughed, and he broke off. "What is it, my lady?"

Her face radiated happiness. "You notice all the good things. And I take so many of them for granted, just like everybody does— oh!" she squealed and pointed.

He looked that way and saw both of their faces, enormous, on the big screen. *God's bones!* Why . . . ?

Emily grabbed his face and leaned in.

She wanted a kiss!

Griffin lowered his head and pressed his mouth to hers, wrapping his arms around her, stroking her back as he drank in her sweetness. Vaguely, he was aware of cheering around them. He deepened the kiss, though it couldn't match the depth of his passion for her. A kiss would never be enough, but it was so good . . .

Someone behind them called out, "Woooo, yeah!" She pulled back and broke off the kiss, staring at him with a dazed look in her eyes. Then she gave a shaky laugh.

"That was a little much for the Kiss Cam."

"The what?" he asked stupidly.

She pointed again at the big screen across the field. It showed an elderly man leaning in to give his wife a sweet kiss. A scattering of *awwws* rippled across the crowd.

"Everyone was watching us kiss," he realized aloud. "This whole crowd." But of course they had been. He'd seen their faces on the screen. When Emily had grabbed his face, all other thoughts had gone out of his head.

She laughed. "That's right. You're famous! Oh, he's up again." She pointed at the field, where the man who'd broken his bat before approached the plate again.

This time, after letting one pitch by him, he sent the ball sailing through the air and watched its trajectory even as he dropped the bat and started to run. It went beyond the field and into the far stands.

Emily jumped to her feet, cheering, and so did everyone around her. Griffin stood up and cheered, too, as the man ran around the bases, the joy of victory evident in his every movement. He threw down his helmet as he reached home plate, punctuating his triumph, and one teammate grabbed his hand and slapped him on the back, and then another. Griffin's spirits rose to see it.

"Yes!" he roared out over the stands, still clapping, loud enough that the people around him, whose cheers were subsiding, turned to him with approving grins.

As they sat down again, Emily said, "You liked that!"

"Aye, my lady, I did. It reminds me of the grand melee at a tournament, when one's side has triumphed on the field."

She sucked in a breath. "That's it. Why didn't I think of this before?"

He blinked. "What is it?"

"I'm so stupid! It's right by my parents' house!"

"You are most assuredly not stupid, my sweet. But what—"

"Okay, in my defense, I only went there twice as a kid. I haven't been there in *years*."

Griffin bit back exasperation. "My lady, if you would be so good as to—"

"Medieval Legends!"

"What?"

"It's this place, this big place, where people go have dinner and watch tournaments! Men dress up as knights . . . They're actually very good, they're on horseback, and the horses are amazing . . . and they fight with swords!"

God in heaven. Such a tournament existed, even now? An eager thrill coursed through him.

"Tell me more," he said.

"No one really gets hurt. Or at least, not seriously."

"Sparring," he said. Even better. He'd had enough of glory bought with blood.

"They make it look real. I think it takes a lot of training. But you're already an expert sword fighter! You may know more about it than anyone alive!"

True enough, but never in these modern times had it seemed like a benefit. "You think I should join this company of knights?"

She nodded. "And hundreds of people go. They have shows a few times every week."

Griffin's hopes soared. "Where are these tournaments?" Surely, these knights were held in great esteem.

"They're close to where my parents live. It's too far from my apartment to drive you every day, but maybe you could take the train and a bus . . ." She frowned. "Actually, that might take hours."

He shrugged. "I have nothing else to do. Your ways of travel are so easy and smooth, and you have so many books. I could read the whole time." He'd already spent some hours looking at her books, and he'd found that as he persevered, he became more accustomed to the wording and the strange print. He wanted more time with them.

"Well, that's true." She gave a dismissive wave of her hand. "Whatever, we could figure it out. We're getting that fake ID from Rose in a couple of days." She'd explained this to him before; a false document of a false life, which rankled him, but it was necessary. "They have auditions. Tryouts."

He nodded. "The sooner I may assay, the better. The world shall have service for my skills, and I shall pay you back all that I owe."

The faint frown appeared at her brow again. "It may not pay a *lot*, okay?"

"No matter." He knew he would never again have the income of an earl's son, but that of a knight for hire would do very well. That paid enough to have a home, a fine horse, handsome clothes, and a cellar full of ale. Truly, what more could a man want?

"But if you're going to live with me, it would still help a lot with rent," she added.

Would it? His lady was not, praise God, in great need of money. The sapphire earrings she wore today were not her only jewels, and even more astoundingly, she had a closet filled with clothing and shoes, more than he'd ever seen in one place at once. It would've put even a queen's wardrobe to shame. She'd asked him about selling his armor, but she could've as easily sold a dozen of her shirts and dresses for a handsome sum and still have more than enough to wear.

Still, he hoped that soon they would be a married man and wife. Of course they would face all the expenses and travails of the world together, and sample all its joys.

"Anyway, I can't think of a better way for you to make friends," she went on to say.

His spirits lifted even further at the thought. He would surely meet some fine comrades among this company of knights.

"Yea, I will pursue this course with a glad heart."

Emily beamed at him and whipped out her phone from her pocket. "I'm going to find out when the next audition is." Scarcely a minute passed before she said, "Okay, here it is!" It never ceased to amaze him how quickly she could do that.

"They're coming right up! I think they're going to love you— oh!" As cheers rose around them, her attention turned to the field. "That's it! We won!"

She pulled him to his feet along with her. Music swelled and she swayed with the beat, clapping her hands. Along with the rest of the crowd, she burst into a song about the Cubs.

"We sing this every time we win," she paused to shout to Griffin. "It's my favorite thing!"

"So 'tis not so strange, after all, to sing," he noted. He'd noted more resistance at first than he'd expected, at the house of the doctors.

She laughed. "I guess not!" It gladdened his heart so much that he might've been singing of his own future victories. Their two souls struck a chord of harmony, his baritone strength to her sweet soprano, and so it must always and ever be.

Fourteen

he next morning, while Griffin was still asleep on the sofa, Emily closed her bedroom door, opened her laptop, and watched a national news program from the night before. She used her earbuds so Griffin wouldn't happen to hear it, even if he woke up. He felt things so deeply, and after all he'd been through, she didn't want to keep reminding him that his coming back to life was causing a lot of trouble.

"It's being called the most impossible art theft in history," the news anchor said. He reviewed the reasons why, including the fact that nothing had been captured on any of the security cameras.

Then he interviewed a former FBI agent from the Art Crimes division, asking, "Would there be any way to sell such a large, high-profile item?"

"This was clearly a bespoke job on behalf of a multimillionaire client. For instance, we've seen a lot of Chinese billionaires funding the theft, or one might say, the recovery, of Chinese art and artifacts, and many works of art also find their way to Saudi Arabia."

"But we're talking about a knight in shining armor," the anchor pointed out. "An iconic symbol of Western civilization. Is there any chance this was politically motivated?"

Emily's phone rang, and her mom's name flashed on the screen. She snapped the laptop shut and, with a sinking feeling, picked up.

"Hi, Mom."

"It's about time," her mom said.

"We've just been worried about you," her father added. Clearly, they'd put her on speaker.

"Sorry, it's been so crazy—"

"Emily, you need to talk to a lawyer," her father interjected.

"No," she said, although the thought had crossed her mind once or twice. "I'm not in any trouble." *Yet*, her anxious inner voice added.

"My friend Karen's new husband is a lawyer," her mom said. "He just got that alderman acquitted of tax evasion."

Emily shook her head, trying to follow this. "Is that a good thing?"

"The point is, *he's* good," her dad said. "And he'll set up a free Zoom with you."

"I mean . . ." *Ugh.* It couldn't hurt. "Okay. Thanks."

"Good. We'll send you his email."

A new knot of worry tightened in her stomach. "*You* guys know I didn't do anything wrong, right?"

"Honey!" her mother exclaimed. "What a thing to ask!" Her scandalized tone soothed Emily's nerves.

When she got off the phone, Griffin was emerging from the bathroom with a towel wrapped around his waist. His gaze landed on her and a big smile transformed his face.

"I am still amazed at this shower. The hot water never ceases, and to feel it run over my skin is more soothing than almost anything I can name."

She imagined running her palms over his dripping body, though she doubted either of them would find it soothing. The wet ends of his hair clung to his broad shoulders. Was he naturally lacking in modesty, or was he finding opportunities to walk around her apartment half-naked to tempt her? If it was the latter, it was working.

"I'm glad you like it," she said as he strolled to the end table where she'd folded his clothes. "Are you ready to go shopping?"

She'd decided to take him downtown to Marshall Field's, now Macy's. Emily hadn't visited the stately department store since high school, even though it was only a couple of blocks from her work, but she had fond memories of it, and they were having a sale. Granted, Griffin might've been just as impressed by a Target, but having him here was making her realize just how much she loved her hometown. She wanted to show it off.

The night before, she'd exchanged a few texts with Rose about Medieval Legends tryouts and the Cubs game. She'd even sent a selfie of her and Griffin in the bleachers, which Griffin had spent a solid ten minutes admiring. Emily had wound up inviting Rose along on the shopping trip. So after Emily and Griffin drove downtown and parked in a nearby garage, they waited for Rose under the famous ornate clock on the corner of the building.

"It's made out of cast bronze," she told Griffin. "When I was a kid, I was so fascinated when my dad told me how the air turned it green."

"'Tis impressive," he said, gazing up at it.

"Let me show you the store windows." She took his hand and guided him over to one, where mannequins in shorts and tank tops gathered around a purple barbecue grill. "During the holidays, they put up displays of toys, and winter wonderland forests, and all kinds of things . . . It was one of my favorite parts of Christmas."

He gazed at her, his eyes filled with affection. "I hope I may see them with you next Christmastide."

She ducked her head, smiling. How amazing would that be?

With Tom, she'd only spent one Christmas in Chicago, and he'd refused to go downtown the night she suggested it, saying it was too cold. She'd love to show Griffin all kinds of Christmas traditions. And before that, Halloween . . . Would he like pumpkin spice lattes? He did like cinnamon . . .

Her heart squeezed. Who knew what the future would bring? She might not always be his tour guide to the modern world.

"And who is that man, up there, with the lute?" He pointed upward.

She looked up at the giant, colorful mural. "Oh! That's a guitar, but it's like a lute. His name's Muddy Waters."

Griffin frowned. "'Tis a vile thing to call a man."

"Oh no, I think he might've picked it himself? He was a very famous singer in Chicago, before I was born." Maybe she should take Griffin to a blues bar sometime. She could just imagine him living it up at Rosa's or Buddy Guy's.

"Ah." He gazed up at the man's face again. "I am sorry I could not hear him sing."

"Oh, you can! We can listen to him later."

He gave her an incredulous look, and then understanding dawned in his eyes. "His music is on your phone."

She grinned at him. "That's right! Everything's on my phone."

Far down the sidewalk, Rose was walking toward them, and Emily waved. Her friend wore a paisley maxi dress, and as she came closer, Emily saw a crystal point pendant hung from her neck. She looked even more witchy than usual.

"Hey there!" Rose said. "How was the clinic yesterday?"

Griffin smiled at Rose. "It was fun."

"Not the answer I was expecting," Rose admitted cheerfully.

"He got all his shots," Emily said, which sounded more like something she'd say about Andy War-Howl. "They didn't ask for an ID."

"Thank Goddess. But I actually have one of those for you guys." Her voice was filled with pride. She dug around in her fringed purse.

"Already? How? That's so fast!"

"I told him it was a rush order." Rose held up a card so they could both see it. "Looks pretty good, huh?"

The photo Emily had taken of Griffin, against a blank wall as directed, now had an aqua blue background. Even when Emily squinted, it looked like a perfectly valid Illinois driver's license, with the faint image of Abraham Lincoln and the state seal in the background.

"I'm impressed," she marveled. "How did they do that?"

"All I know is they make them in England."

"I am loath to carry a false document," Griffin said.

Rose rolled her eyes. "Well, you're going to need it."

Emily added, "She could've gotten in trouble, getting that for you."

Understanding and regret came into his eyes. "Indeed, my lady Rose, I am most grateful. If I can repay you, though it be with my life, I will."

"Let's not get carried away," Rose said.

Emily asked, "Seriously, how much do I owe you?"

Rose waved off her concern. "He owed me a favor."

They entered the store, and Griffin gazed up at the multiple floors lined with stately pillars, topped with a skylight.

Rose said, "Hey, before we shop, there's something I should tell you. But I want you to stay calm."

"Too late."

"Tonight one of the *biggest* true crime podcasts is doing an episode about the theft. Which is surprising because they usually only do murder."

Somehow, she'd been expecting something worse. "Can we stop saying theft? There was no theft." She added to Griffin, "A podcast is like someone speaking to a big crowd. But over phones and computers."

He nodded thoughtfully. "I am sorry to hear of this podcast."

Emily rolled her eyes. "There's already been a bunch of them about it." It was nothing compared to the national news.

"They've got three million listeners," Rose said. "All over the world."

That *was* a lot. "But as long as they don't talk about me, personally—"

"That's what I'm trying to tell you." Rose's voice was measured. "This episode is all about you."

"*What?*" She was loud enough that a couple of passing shoppers looked over in surprise.

"They're going over you as a suspect. How you haven't been in Chicago long. How you left your museum job in Los Angeles suddenly."

Heat rose on the back of her neck. "That's ridiculous! I left because I followed my ex to Silicon Valley! I'm only guilty of stupidity, not theft." Even as she said it, she had the nagging sense that she should've expected this all along.

"It wasn't stupidity," Griffin said. "You trusted him."

"Yeah, I won't make that mistake again," Emily quipped. When he didn't smile, she added, "Kidding."

"Did you know that some handmade valentines went missing from the Getty Villa?" Rose asked. "They discovered they were missing about a month after you left. They were surrealist."

"My whole life is surrealist," Emily grumbled. "No, I never heard about that. I've never even worked in paper conservation! Plus, I'm not an art thief."

"You don't have to tell *me*," Rose soothed crossly. "I just thought you should know. I think you should temporarily deactivate your Facebook. And your LinkedIn."

Emily nodded and took a deep breath. "That's very smart. I'm never on there, anyway."

As she pulled up the Facebook app, Rose said, "Do you have any other accounts under other names? TikTok? YouTube? Some kind of artsy OnlyFans?"

"Ha-ha," Emily said at the last one. "No." She'd deleted Instagram after discovering she was completely unable to keep herself from using it to stalk Tom and Tori.

She had to reset her passwords, but after a few minutes, she'd deactivated both. "There. Hatches battened down."

"It won't be forever," Rose assured her. "Everyone will move on to the next crime. I mean, people do weird murders every day."

"Well, that's looking on the bright side," she grumbled.

They took an escalator up. "Stairs that move," Griffin murmured, almost to himself. Rose and Emily exchanged an amused glance. It took Emily's mind off the supposed art theft and the podcast. The hell with them all, anyway. She hadn't done anything wrong.

Once they stepped off the escalator, Griffin surveyed the display of dress shirts and ties and the tables and racks beyond.

"You probably want more casual clothes than this," Emily suggested, leading him to another section.

He stopped at shelves of polo shirts. "So many bright colors. I like them."

Emily eyed the display dubiously. They did come in many hues, including fuchsia, canary yellow, lime green, and one with pastel stripes like an Easter egg. She opened her mouth to suggest that he go with one of the more understated colors. Most of the men she knew gravitated toward black and gray. Then she closed it again. It *was* spring, after all, and the man knew what he liked. In his time, bright colors meant wealth and gaiety. The good life.

She suggested a size to try and spotted the dressing room. "You can go in there"—she pointed—"and use one of the little closets to try them on."

Griffin nodded, his eyes bright with enthusiasm. He started grabbing shirts.

"I guess if I hadn't been clothes shopping for six hundred years, I'd be pretty excited, too," Emily murmured to Rose.

Then the price tag caught her eye. *Yikes.* Well, they were a famous brand name. She didn't see any signs to suggest they were part of the Memorial Day sale.

"Hey, Griffin?" she called after him as he headed toward the dressing room. He stopped and turned around. She took a few steps over to him and said in a lower tone, "Let's only get a couple of these, okay? They're really expensive. And we'll also find cheaper ones." She'd need to get other things for him, too. For one thing, now that he had a driver's license, he'd need a wallet.

He nodded, looked down at the shirts thoughtfully, and then returned all of them to the table except for the emerald green and the black ones. "The colors of my coat of arms," he said to Emily.

"I like it. You know what, while you're at it, let's grab you some pairs of jeans, too. Those are on sale." She guided him to the display and picked out several, then asked him if he minded coming out and showing her.

Once he was out of earshot, Emily said dubiously to Rose, "I guess we'll see what he looks like as a prep."

"Lots of people wear polo shirts," Rose said, leaning against one of the faux Corinthian columns. "Good job holding those I-went-to-art-school attitudes in check."

"Ha-ha."

In a lower voice, Rose asked, "So did he get all his tests? Like for STDs?"

"We'll get the results soon, but as far as STDs go, he's very low risk. He hadn't been with anyone for months. Plus with sex, he has . . ." *Limited experience*, she'd been about to say, but that wasn't exactly correct. She whispered, "He's a virgin."

"He has an aversion to sex? But—"

"A virgin," Emily said more loudly.

"Oh!" Rose's mouth dropped open. *"Seriously?"*

"I know."

"But I thought he wanted to . . . ?"

"He does. Very badly."

Rose nodded. "And what about you?"

Emily sighed. "Same."

Griffin emerged from the dressing room in a green polo, spotted them, and walked over.

"Okay, you look amazing," Emily admitted. The combination of his shoulder-length hair and beard with the conservative style was, well, hot. "And if this one fits, the black one will, too." She scanned the floor and saw a half-off rack of long-sleeved shirts. "Let's go over there and see if they have anything in blue."

"Why blue, my heart?"

"It'll go with your eyes." As she said this, she was distracted by them. They were a warm blue, like the sky on a sunny day, with a ring of gold around the iris. "Though they look amazing no matter what color you're wearing."

He smiled. "I would very much like a blue shirt," he said in a low voice, "especially if it is pleasing to you, my lady." The tone of his voice made her feel fluttery all over.

"Oh my Goddess," Rose muttered, pressing her palm to her heart.

Emily found a chambray shirt for him to try, and then paused. "Did you have clothes with buttons?" That had hung up her research on her presentation, *Dating Medieval Sculpture*. She knew buttons had been invented in the West in the 1200s, but it had been hard for her to tell how soon they'd become widespread.

He grinned. "Aye, I did."

She made a mental note of it. God, she'd barely started on the section about men's shirts and tunics, and the symposium was coming up fast.

As Rose and Emily waited, Rose mused, "So he's got a driver's license, *and* he's losing his V card."

"I didn't say that."

Rose's eyes widened in a *give-me-a-break* look.

"I don't want to get too involved."

"It's a little late for that, since you brought him to life."

"That's just it! He thinks he's into me, but he's just, like, imprinted on me."

Rose's face screwed up in skepticism. "He's a man, not a baby duck."

"Exactly! He's a red-blooded male, and once he meets lots of women, he's not going to be that into me."

"Why would you think that?"

Because it was common sense?

"I'm not one of those people with a bunch of charisma or anything." One of those people with tons of charm who always knew the right thing to say, who instantly made everyone happy to be around them. She'd known a few of those people. Tom's girlfriend, she'd gathered, was one of them. On his Instagram, he'd talked about her joie de vivre, which had been enough to make her want to vomit. And Griffin was one of those people. Wouldn't it make sense for him to pair up with another of the same?

"*Charisma?*" Rose made the face of someone who smelled literal bullshit. "You're perfect for him. You know all about the Middle Ages, which not many people do! And you're gorgeous," she added, exactly as a best friend would. "At the very least, you'd have an amazing new experience, and you're *wasting* it."

She was right. Even if it ended badly, Emily could take heartbreak. She'd survived before, hadn't she?

Still, her conscience nagged at her. "You don't think I'd be taking advantage of him?"

"When he's been crazy about you the whole time?" Rose rolled her eyes. "He can make his own decisions. He's a big boy."

"My lady." Emily looked up to see Griffin walking toward them in the blue button-down shirt, the sleeves rolled up to expose his muscled forearms. "What do you think?"

He had a natural confidence in his stride. If he hadn't been from medieval times, she would've called it swagger. And he almost always had a slight smile on his face, as he did now, surveying his surroundings with approval. She hoped he never lost that joy in living, and not just because it tended to rub off on her. Maybe, with a little time, she'd have joie de vivre, too.

Emily beamed at Griffin. "Let's get it."

Fifteen

When Griffin stepped out of the department store along with the two ladies, Emily turned to him and said, "What would you like to do now?"

What were his choices? He sneaked another glance at her breasts. She was wearing a top that stretched over them in a most beguiling way, and he'd figured out now that she wore one of those padded undergarments, like the one Andy had dashed through the apartment with, that made them stand up proudly. She hadn't been wearing it that morning, and her breasts had been slight, soft curves beneath the soft shirt she'd slept in. Christ Jesus, he loved the way they looked, either way.

Rose caught him looking, and the corner of her mouth quirked upward. "Actually, I need to head back. But you two have a good time."

Emily hugged her, and then Rose embraced Griffin, too, saying, "Good to see you, big guy." It was apparently common to do so, with meetings and partings, and it pleased him. He was hungry for the touch of friends. He was going to make more of them. Emily wanted to make more friends, too, in this city; maybe they could do it together.

As Rose was walking away, Griffin asked Emily, "Would you

like to go on a walk, my lady?" He could've gladly wandered for hours, observing the people and the buildings that seemed to have been built by those who, like the builders of the Tower of Babel, hoped to reach up to heaven itself, and as far as Griffin could tell, had come very close.

"That's a great idea! It's such a beautiful day."

"It will rain," he felt obliged to say, "but I do not mind, if you do not."

She scrunched up her face. "It's supposed to be sunny today."

"But the air feels lighter, and look, the birds are taking shelter." He pointed to the sparrows chirping in the nearby tree.

"Hmm, we'll see," she said doubtfully. "Anyway, I'd love to take you to the Riverwalk."

"Very well," Griffin said, for courtesy's sake, though he could not imagine it would be pleasant to walk along the banks of a river in the city. Maybe the citizens of Chicago were inured to the stench. At least it wasn't a hot day.

As they passed down city streets, Emily told him about other places in Chicago he needed to see, including Lincoln Park, the University of Chicago, a boat ride where they talked about the architecture, and several other vast museums.

She went on to say, "And then there's the Shedd . . . They have these huge glass tanks full of water, where you can see fish, and octopi, and pretty much everything that lives in the ocean. Plus sea lions. Do you know what those are?"

He nodded. "They have the tail of a fish and the head of a lion." He'd seen one on the shield of a knight from Spain.

"Um, no . . . Do you know what seals are? Not the wax things, but the animal?"

"Yea, and in Orkney, they sometimes turn into women." She gave him a skeptical look, and he assured her, "I heard all about it from a wise sea captain. This museum is called the shed? Despite its great size?"

"It's called the Shedd Aquarium. A man named Shedd started it. We'll go soon, okay? But look." She gestured ahead of them. "We're at the river."

As she led him down a broad, curving set of stairs, he realized aloud, "I don't even smell it."

"Smell what?" She tilted her head. "You thought the river would stink!"

"Yea, my lady," he admitted. "The stench of the Thames in London was nigh enough to knock a man flat, and even London Town was but a little village compared to your Chicago . . . but now I see how pleasant this is."

Couples and families wandered along the paved bank. Some people sat at metal tables in metal chairs, drinking coffee, wine, or ale, chatting and laughing. A man and a woman paddled by in the narrowest of boats, while another, larger boat sped in the other direction. The sunlight glinted on the little waves in its wake.

"Isn't it nice?" she asked, then pointed to a counter beneath a sign that read **TINY TAPP**. "I'm going to buy a bottle of water. Do you want one?"

"Aye, thank you." The walk had made him thirsty, too, and even if the river didn't smell, he supposed it might not be fresh enough for drinking.

As they stood in line, his gaze fell on a rack of colorful printed papers, gathered in bundles. Books with soft covers, he realized, when he picked one up. With some effort, he made out the letters. *Hollywood's Handsomest Bachelors!*

"Do you know these men?" he asked.

"Um, not personally? But they're very rich and famous." She gave him a flirty smile. "Not as handsome as you are, though."

His gaze trailed down her tempting form, his blood heating. It was she, above all, that he thirsted for.

"Can I help you?" the young lady behind the counter asked them, a touch of impatience in her voice.

"Oh! Sorry," Emily said. "Two bottled waters." Griffin set the booklet back into the rack, carefully so as not to damage it.

The lady retrieved them and set them down on the counter. "That'll be seven dollars and seventy-three cents."

Griffin waited for Emily to haggle, but she only dug into her purse. She was too gentle, he realized, to even argue.

"We will pay five dollars," he told the lady firmly, "and no more."

The young lady looked from him to Emily. "So you only want one?"

Emily's mouth formed a silent O of understanding. "We don't bargain for things," she told Griffin.

"What, never?" he asked, dumbfounded. The man in line behind them gave a loud sigh.

"With a few things, but not food," Emily said, and turned back to the young lady. "Go ahead and ring it up." She even put an extra dollar in a jar on the counter. Then she handed Griffin his bottle, which was astonishingly light.

As they walked back to the water's edge, Griffin said, "'Tis very strange to pay any price a seller demands."

"I didn't even think about that," she admitted. "There's a lot I don't know about your time. The things I do know are mostly related to art."

She pulled out her phone to tap and stare at it. "Tomorrow afternoon," she murmured to herself.

"What's tomorrow afternoon, sweet bird?"

"I have a meeting. Um . . . it's a work thing." No doubt she felt it would be too tedious to explain. "Hang on just a minute, okay? I'm going to reserve a conference room."

Griffin took a long swig from the bottle, draining half its contents, and then squeezed it experimentally. It was made of some remarkably flexible glass. He watched a large boat go by, then looked down at the water. Even the butchers weren't throwing their entrails into it, it seemed. There was something strange about it, though . . .

When Emily put her phone away again, he asked, "Why does the river not flow to the sea? I mean, to the great lake?"

"Oh, that's right!" She spun to face him triumphantly. "You are looking at the only river in the world that flows backward."

He gave a huff of surprise. "The world is full of wonders."

"Oh, it's not a natural wonder. It used to be a lot dirtier, just like you were expecting, and the lake is our drinking water, so we *forced* it to flow backward."

Shocked, he cast another look down at the waters below. "Was this a sorcerer, or some Heracles, who could change the course of a river?"

"Nope. Just a bunch of engineers and workers. And on St. Patrick's Day . . ." She paused. "Have you heard of St. Patrick?"

Griffin's spirits brightened even further. It always cheered his heart when she spoke of familiar things. "Aye, as a youth he was enslaved by Irish raiders, but later he returned to convert them all to Christendom." He took another long drink.

She lifted her eyebrows. "Well, St. Patrick's Day is the only feast day we celebrate in a big way in this country."

He was surely misunderstanding her. "There are sixty holy days a year. You cannot tell me you work on all these days, when you should be enjoying the customs and foods, and holding observances, both solemn and lighthearted."

"Unfortunately, we *do* work on most of those days. We only have, I don't know, a dozen holidays?"

"But without the various feast days, does not every week feel the same?"

She gave a wry laugh. "Well, kind of." Then she squeezed his arm. "But not since *you're* here."

He smiled at that. "How do you celebrate St. Patrick's feast day?" They might as well speak of the few celebrations she was allowed. "Do you put a shamrock in the bottom of a glass of ale and drink a toast to the saint?"

Her mouth fell open. "Close! A lot of people drink green beer." Before he could ask how green beer was made, or whether it tasted like grass, she added, "But that's not the best part." She bounced on her toes. "We also turn this whole river green."

For a moment, he stared at her like a clodpole . . . and then he realized what was happening. She was trying to fool him!

He roared with laughter and, on an impulse, he picked her up and swung her around. She gave a startled, "Oh!"

He set her down on her feet and wagged his finger at her. "That was an excellent jest, sweeting. I almost believed you."

People at nearby tables had turned to stare at them both. She laughed, sounding a little breathless. "I'm not jesting!"

Griffin looked to the other people watching them in case they could confirm or deny this. "The whole river? Then why is it not still green?"

She shrugged. "I don't know. The dye doesn't last more than a day."

"We must come back to the river on St. Patrick's Day," he told her, "so that I may see this wonder for myself."

"Sure. Along with a couple million of our closest friends."

Griffin shook his head. "I cannot believe you recognize no other saint's days. Not even St. George's Day, when we all paraded on horseback in our armor?"

She cocked her head. "You did? Why?"

"Out of respect to St. George . . . but in truth, 'twas to show off."

"I'll bet you were a resplendent sight," she said with a sparkle in her eyes. *Resplendent*—that was a word from his time, and he guessed she'd used it on purpose for his sake, which touched his heart.

"That is the second time on this walk you have called me handsome," he pointed out, lifting his chin.

"Oh, *I'm* sorry," she teased. "Are you tired of hearing it?"

"If you said it a hundred times, I would not tire of it." He touched his fingertip to her nose. "Which I think you know."

She beamed at him. "I might've guessed." She took his hand and they walked on.

He'd drank all the water in his bottle, and he squeezed it again. "Do we keep these?"

"What? Oh no, we can just throw them away."

"Very good." He threw it—and it smacked a man right in the face as he sped past.

Griffin froze. Emily gave a shocked yelp.

The man yelled, "Hey!" and glided unnaturally back to them.

"You have wheels on your boots," Griffin realized aloud in wonder.

"Did you just throw *trash* at me?" he demanded.

Shame enveloped him. It could not have caused an injury other than to the man's dignity, but that was serious enough.

"My good sir." He sketched an apologetic bow. "'Twas never my intention to strike anyone, though there is no excuse for my carelessness. I most humbly apologize."

He scowled at him. "You shouldn't be throwing trash, anyway."

"He's not from this country," Emily said quickly. She scuttled to retrieve the bottle on the sidewalk.

Somehow, Griffin had misunderstood her. "You are right," he told the man, "and I will never do it again."

"You better not," he grumbled, and then turned and glided away in his wheeled boots.

Emily walked a short distance away from him and deposited

both of their empty bottles in a barrel. Clearly, that was what she'd meant for him to do.

He'd ruined Emily's afternoon. Once he'd been a gentleman, a nobleman, one who knew how to behave at every opportunity. Could she still respect him, when his ignorance made him foolish? Should he ask her about it?

She returned to his side, laughing. "I'll try to be more specific." She slipped her hand in his. "That was totally my fault."

His embarrassment vanished at her touch and at the merriment sparkling in her brown eyes. There was no reason to bother her with his worries. As always, he reminded himself to take things lightly.

A few tiny raindrops fell, and she gasped. "It's raining! You were right!"

This assuaged his pride. "I do know some things, my lady."

The rain was no more than a sprinkle, and they walked as much as possible under store canopies as they headed back the way they'd come. When they got to one window he'd wondered about before, displaying stacks of little brown balls and blocks, he couldn't help but ask what they were.

"Oh yes! It's chocolate," she said. "There was some of it mixed in the ice cream the other day? It tastes like *heaven*. Do you want to get some?"

The ice cream had been delicious, but still, this confection didn't look like anything he wanted to put in his mouth. "Nay, thank you, my lady, for your presence is sweet enough."

Pink rose in her cheeks. They walked on a few steps, and then she snapped her fingers. "Oh my gosh, we do celebrate another saint's day! St. Valentine's Day! Except we just call it Valentine's Day, so I forgot."

"Ah." He felt a smile tugging at his lips. "In my time, that day had become a celebration of courtly love."

Surprise and then delight illuminated her features. "Really?"

"Aye, there were contests of romantic poetry, and dancing, and professions of love."

She squeezed his hand and told him of their St. Valentine's Day traditions. They exchanged letters with poems or affectionate jokes, enjoyed lavish dinners, and gave each other gifts. The men, in particular, gave the ladies chocolates.

Surely, he would enjoy all these celebrations with her . . . although being here was cause enough for celebration.

Sixteen

Griffin enjoyed the ride home, his view alternating between her behind the wheel and the everlasting lake dotted with white boats. When they went into Emily's apartment, Andy was frantic to get out, and Griffin accompanied them both down the sidewalk.

Andy let out his howling version of hello as a young woman crossed the street to approach them. She wore high-waisted, faded blue jeans and a knitted . . . *something*, not unlike Emily's bra.

It was not the first time since Griffin had come to life that he'd seen a young lady walking around in public with her midriff naked to the world. No one minded now, although a woman who'd done so in his time would've been put in the stocks for public lewdness.

"Good afternoon, my lady," Griffin greeted her. "What ho?"

She narrowed her eyes. "*What* did you call me?"

"He means, *What's up*," Emily said quickly. "He's British."

The young woman gave Griffin a wary sidelong glance. "There were a couple of guys around here asking about you."

"Who?" Emily demanded.

The young woman shrugged. "I don't know. They described you and asked me if I knew you, and I said no, but said I'd seen you around. And then they sat in a car for about two hours, like it was a stakeout. I guess they finally got bored and left. They asked if I'd seen you, too," she added to Griffin. "But I hadn't."

Emily wrapped her arms around her middle. "Well, if anyone else asks, could you still say you haven't seen him?"

The young woman looked up and down the block. One couple pushed a stroller, and on the other side of the street, a man strolled with a brown sack clutched in one hand. "It's not like you're doing a great job of hiding him. But I won't tell anyone if you tell me something." The young woman took a step closer to Emily and asked in a low tone, "Did you take that statue?"

Emily drew back. "No!—How do you even know where I work?"

"I saw a TikTok about all the suspects."

Some of the color drained from Emily's face. "Well, I didn't take anything."

The neighbor gave a huff of disbelief. "Be for real."

This foolish cod was calling Emily a liar to her face. Griffin reminded himself that the girl was too young to know better.

"Excuse us," he said, putting his hand on Emily's shoulder, "but we do not intend to tarry." Nor did he intend to let a gossip ruin Emily's day.

"That's right," Emily agreed immediately. "No tarrying." They turned away and headed back inside.

"I like how you put that," she murmured to him. "'We do not intend to tarry.'" Before they went inside, she stopped, stood on her tiptoes, and kissed him on the cheek. More innocent than the kiss at Wrigley Field, yet his whole mind and body seemed to focus on it, driving him to distraction.

As they got onto the elevator, he imagined her fingers gripping his hair as he kissed her, or her nails digging into his shoulders as he brought her to ecstasy. A couple of the ladies he'd known had done this, as he employed his tongue. Would she be the kind to leave marks? She was so polite and genteel, but perhaps he could make her forget that she was. Unlike the scars he bore from battle, he would wear a scratch or a bite mark from Emily with pride.

How long must he wait?

It had been only days since he'd met Emily. Men had waited longer for a woman, God knew. But it had been *centuries* since he'd been in a lady's bed.

As they got off the elevator on her floor, Emily said, "What are you thinking about?"

He had little talent for lying, and less taste for lying to her. He cleared his throat. "Grant pardon, but I would fain not say."

She gave him a compassionate look and squeezed his hand. "Those guys looking for us were probably just podcasters, or maybe journalists." He'd already forgotten about them, when they had brought her distress. "I know it's weird to have people asking about us, but I'm sure it'll all blow over in a day or two." The tone of her voice suggested she was sure of no such thing.

Back inside the apartment, while Emily opened a can of dog food, Andy grabbed a stuffed duck toy from the corner of the room and brought it up to Griffin. With some difficulty, Griffin wrested it from his mouth, then sent it flying down the hallway. The dog joyfully scampered after it and grabbed it, making it squeak.

"Hey bud, come have dinner," Emily called to him, setting a bowl on the kitchen floor. Andy trotted back and tucked into his meal, and Emily took a seat on the sofa.

Griffin sat next to her, smiling. "He takes much pleasure in his play."

"He does." Emily inched closer to him and gave him a meaning-ful look. "So, I've been thinking that maybe I should also take some, um, pleasure in my play."

"What do you mean?" She'd explained to him earlier how people sometimes ran on the streets for health and for fun; maybe she was thinking of doing the same.

"I mean . . ." She took a deep breath. "I was thinking of going into my bedroom."

He wasn't following her train of thought, but no matter. "If you are weary, my lady, by all means, take your rest." He gestured toward her chamber.

"No. In fact, I have a *lot* of energy . . ." She dropped her head. "Ugh, why am I so bad at this?"

"So bad at what, my lady?"

"Probably because I was with him for so long," she said, as if to herself. She turned back to Griffin and her eyes were wide, vulnerable.

"Griffin, do you still want to be lovers?"

The question stunned him like a blow. Did she really need to ask?

Pleasure in play . . . the bedroom . . . When had he become so thick-skulled?

He took her lovely face in his hands and kissed her as gently as he could manage. He felt her slight tremble, strengthening his will to go slowly, though the savage beast in him, made mad from centuries of isolation, wanted to devour her in a demanding kiss, wanted to strip her naked and bend her right over the back of the sofa and drive into her—he who respected her more than any knight ever respected a queen, he who had never swived a lady in his life.

She put her hands on his upper arms, stroking them. Every inch of his body was tense and hard. She filled his senses: the scent of her floral perfume and her sun-warmed skin and hair, the touch of her hands, the taste of her. He deepened the kiss, urging her mouth wider under his, and she yielded easily; her head tilting back in sweet acquiescence to his invasion.

He stroked her soft cheek, smoothed her hair back, his hand touching her ear. Then he broke off the kiss and dipped his head to taste that graceful curve where her neck met her shoulder. She squirmed in pleasure.

He whispered next to her ear, "I want to strip you bare as Diana in her sacred grove." He kissed her neck again, and then let her feel the scrape of his teeth there. The needy sound that came from her was all the encouragement he required.

He drew back long enough to pull her T-shirt over her head. She let him do it, raising her arms, and then stripped off her bra almost before he could blink. She could not want this as badly as he did, but still, her eagerness delighted him. Her breasts were the perfect size to cradle in his palms. They were exquisite, with nipples the pink of a Lenten rose, tightened to hard points. Her lips were plump and cherry red from kissing, and he pulled her close to kiss them again.

He stroked her bare back. Were his hands too hard and rough against such smooth, soft skin? No, he wasn't going to think over-much. This was truly happening, an actual dream come to life, and he was going to savor every moment.

But then she paused and drew back from him, looking over her shoulder.

"We shouldn't do this in front of Andy," she murmured.

Griffin looked over at the dog, whose eyes were wide with curiosity. "You are right. He is but an innocent hound."

He picked Emily up as he got to his feet.

She let out a startled squeak. "Oh my God." She wrapped her arms around his neck tightly as he carried her to the bedroom. "Don't drop me."

He gave a low laugh. "You should rather fear I shall never let you go."

"I'm too heavy for you to do this," she protested as he carried her through the threshold of her bedchamber and kicked the door shut behind them.

"That is a strange thing to say, sweet bird, whilst I do it," he teased. He sat her on the bed and stared down at her as she half reclined, propped up on both elbows.

"Take off your jeans now," he said. It would be quicker for her to do it than for him to make an attempt. "And your . . ." She wore some flimsy thing beneath them, made of satin and lace; he had seen them in the clothes to be washed. Sudden irritation, and impatience, made his voice rough. "Take off everything."

Her eyes widened. "Since when are you so bossy?" Her rapid, shaky breath made her breasts rise and fall. Something dark and powerful swelled up in him, exulting in the effect he had on her, making him feel like a lord again . . . nay, more than that; a king.

He sat on the bed next to her and placed his palm flat on her torso, between her breasts and her belly. Even there, he could feel her pulse, the movement of her ribs. Christ Jesus, he wanted to touch every inch of her body; the small of her back, the curves of her arse, the arches of her feet. He wanted to know it as well as he knew his own.

"*Bossy.* I do not know that word, my lady," he confessed as he studied her face, watching her reaction. Her eyes looked darker, the pupils larger, and they glistened. "But I do know that it is something you like."

"Bossy means you're telling me what to do."

He smoothed his hand lower, exploring the contour of her stomach and feeling it quiver. She lay back flat on the bed, making it easier for him to explore.

"Mmm." He glided his hand down into her jeans. "And do you object?" She hadn't obeyed him yet.

He swept his hand slowly from one hip bone to another, dying to know whether, if he reached down any further, he'd find her wet with desire. She rocked slightly, as if encouraging him to do it, but he wouldn't, not until she complied.

"It's just that . . . you don't *usually* boss me around."

His finger brushed across something, the lacy edge of her undergarment. "I was the son of an earl," he reminded her in a low tone as he stroked one finger slowly along that edge. "I was the leader of an army in France. I am no stranger to giving commands."

She reached out to caress his thigh through his own jeans. "This is my bedroom, not a battlefield."

"Aye, in truth, they are as unalike as two things might be," he conceded, somehow managing a casual tone despite his enraptured state. "And yet both have maneuvers . . ." With his thumb, he drew a little circle on the silky fabric of her undergarment. "And advances . . ." He unbuttoned the jeans with a hard tug. "And retreats."

He withdrew his hand. Her brow knitted slightly in uncertainty. Aye, she was his, more than she knew. He leaned down and dragged his tongue along the soft flesh right above the waistband of the jeans. Her little whimper heated his blood. But he would go slowly, driving her frustration upward. He had lived for centuries, and still, he had all the time in the world. Right in the subtle hollow of the top of her hip bone, he bit her. She let out a squeal, followed by a giggle.

He looked up at her. *Oh God.* The mischievous smile that played at her lips, her hair spread on her naked shoulders—his prick was so hard, it might have been limestone still.

"Take off all your clothes this moment," he said.

She smiled and opened her mouth to make a jest—but then, when she met his gaze, the words on her glistening lips faded away. She unzipped her jeans, and as she lifted her hips to pull them off, she demurely averted her eyes, her long eyelashes almost sweeping her flushed cheeks. He hadn't expected her shyness, and it made him feel a sudden tenderness and protectiveness—even as he, per-versely, wanted to undo it, wanted to make her forget herself and beg him to do wanton acts to her like a shameless Jezebel and cry out his name.

Christ, he was going to have to rein in his thoughts, or he would shame himself like an overeager lad. But what youth had ever been so eager as he?

She kicked her feet free of the jeans and the little undergarment, and he caught a glimpse of her queint: rosy, glistening, and wet.

He swallowed hard, his mouth suddenly dry. Her body was in every way ready for him. She was as he'd wanted her, like a nymph lying in a fair meadow. He took the vision of her in all at once: her smooth bare arms, her breasts rising with her short breaths, the flare of her hips, her mound of dark curling maidenhair, and her rounded, inviting thighs.

"What's wrong?"

Wrong? Startled, he looked up. Her eyes were filled with uncer-tainty.

"Sweeting, nothing is wrong," he rushed to say. "You must forgive me if I am struck dumb, for you are exceedingly sexy."

She laughed, surprised out of her moment of worry. "You re-membered that word."

"Aye, my lady, how could I not, when I spend so many hours with you?" He leaned over and kissed her on the mouth. "You are the sexiest woman I have ever seen in my life."

"Hmmm." She smoothed her palm up the side of his body, the caress a delicious fresh torment. "You probably don't remember the others."

When he'd been trapped in stone, he'd remembered them all. Who knew how many hours, how many days, he'd spent reliving those memories, moment by moment . . . including moments that had never happened? He dropped his head again to kiss her belly and then nuzzle his cheek against it. The little wiggle she made amused him; he'd hardly gotten started.

"In truth, their names, their faces, all vanish entirely from my memory . . ." He trailed a few kisses higher, in the direction of one of her pert breasts. "The way the morning mist burns away in the splendor of the dazzling sun." He stroked the outer curve of her breast, gazing up at her.

"You . . . really say the nicest things," she said softly.

"I am glad you think so." He dragged his thumb along the hardened nipple. "But as I am no bard, I cannot find the words worthy of your beauty." His voice pitched lower. "And meseems there are better uses for my tongue."

He cupped the breast to bring it to his mouth, intending to begin gently, but as soon as his lips touched that irresistible firm nipple, he took all of it and more into his mouth. As he sucked and nibbled there, he reached down to press his palm between her legs. Emily moaned and rocked. He kept his hand firmly in place, grinding the heel of it against her most sensitive place as he lavished attention on her breast, and then the other, so as not to neglect it. Her gasps turned into little cries, sweeter than any birdsong to his ears. She gripped his shoulder with one hand, the other one half covering her face.

She was close, and he focused on his task, exulting in it. He knew enough about a woman's body to know that a pause now would be either artless or wicked. He'd already teased her a little when he wanted nothing more than to bring her pleasure.

He'd spoken nothing but the plain truth of the women he'd known before her, but did she still think of her former husband? He'd been the last one to pleasure her thus, if he understood things aright.

She moaned Griffin's name.

He smiled darkly to himself. Nay, she had no thought of that villainous wretch. She bucked under him.

"Oh God," she cried out, as though he'd transported her closer to Heaven.

Yes! He took hold of her cheek, belatedly aware that his hand was still drenched with her pleasure, and she was still gasping when he claimed her mouth in a deep kiss. She glided her fingers lightly down the side of his body, almost unconsciously, maybe, but it could've just as easily been calculated to drive him mad. Now that he'd brought her to climax, the beast in him roared for his own satisfaction.

He broke off the kiss. *"Mon trésor.* I must have you." His voice came out rough.

"Yes," she breathed. She gave a tiny smile and plucked at the hem of his T-shirt.

He got up on his knees on the bed and took it off. Her gaze was fixed on him. He stood up to shuck off the jeans and boxer briefs.

"Wow," she murmured. "You look even more amazing than you did in my dream."

He moved back onto the bed and stretched out over her, propping himself up on his forearms so as not to crush her. She spread her legs wider to accommodate him.

He knew at least the basics of this. As a boy, he'd blundered upon his uncle servicing a plump widow of their acquaintance, and there had been certain lewd sketches that had been passed among the squires. Years after that, at war, he'd seen a fellow soldier with a strumpet, up against a wall. But it was one thing to watch or hear of a deed, and another to do it. He'd felt like a king, carrying her to her bed, like the ruler of the world . . . Now, even as he was ready to claim her, he felt like an untried youth.

"You know I have not done this before," he murmured.

Her eyes sparkled. There was no apprehension in them, nor judgment, nor pity.

"Thank you for letting me be first," she whispered. He hardly knew what to say to that. The honor, and the gratitude, was surely all on his side. "I'll help you, okay?"

The pride in him revolted at that, but he pushed it away and nodded. Only a fool would refuse help when he didn't know exactly what he was doing.

She reached down and wrapped her hand firmly around his hard length. Griffin sucked in a breath. Her hand was small and soft but so sure. She guided him to her entrance, the tip of his prick against her hot, luscious queint. He didn't need any urging to glide into her.

Her sleek heat surrounded him, clasping him tightly.

"God in Heaven," he whispered, as she moaned again. No, he was in Heaven . . . becoming one with her.

"Good?" she asked in his ear, petting his hair.

He nodded but could not answer. It felt something like the first time a woman had sucked his cock, but he and that jolly brewster had meant nothing to each other. Still, he'd much regretted making her gag with a rude thrust, and being new at this more sacred act, with his beloved Emily, he had to take care, listening to her voice and the language of her body, in order to learn how to best please her. He drew back and stroked in again, as slowly as he could, but with her encouraging hand on his arse, he sheathed himself nearly to the hilt.

"Yes." She moaned. "That's perfect."

He thrust again, and again, reveling in the sensation. Her hips rose to meet his, matching his rhythm, and the sounds of her gasps and little cries entranced him.

Her eyes were closed, leaving her vulnerable to his awestruck gaze. She tilted her head back on the pillow; her brow knitted briefly, as though the pleasure of that particular stroke required extra concentration. She threaded her fingers through his hair, then gripped it lightly. He was hers . . . and she was his, more with every glorious stroke. He wanted it to last forever.

But it might not have been more than a couple of minutes before his control began to slip. He couldn't help but move faster. The light scent of her perfume mingled with that of her blatant arousal. Her soft voice said something else, but he couldn't make it out.

"My love," he said hoarsely. "I'm going to—"

"Do it. Inside me."

Her breathless command pulled him toward the shore and the depths beyond. Emily's embrace tightened as he exulted in the plunge. Ecstasy overtook him. *Yes.* A wordless shout tore from his lips—joined by a sudden loud cry from hers, and her body squeezed around him as his seed pulsed into her.

Griffin brought his mouth down on hers, clumsy in his passion and his haste, but she steadied him with her hand on his cheek and returned his kiss with tenderness. Then he bowed his head to her shoulder, breathing hard. For long centuries, he'd lamented never having done this, but he had long stopped imagining doing it with someone he adored.

He pulled out of her, reminding himself that his seed would find no purchase. It was strange not to worry about a babe arriving before they were ready to receive one. He lay next to her on his side, propped up on one elbow so he could keep looking down at her lovely face, flushed with satisfaction.

She was his lover—but he'd heard that word used in much more trifling assignations. A nobleman in a marriage of state quickly gone cold, slaking his desire with a series of indulged ladies. A yeoman and a widow keeping each other company.

He needed better words for Emily. She was so precious to him. But even without that possibility, they belonged to each other.

She leaned over and kissed his chest, below the collarbone. Her easy familiarity pleased him. She whispered, "You liked it, right?"

"Need you ask, my dove?" He gave a wondering laugh. "Never in my life have I known such bliss."

She graced him with a loving smile. "I'm glad."

A roaring howl came from the other side of the bedroom door.

"Oh my God," she said with a laugh that made her body shake under him, and then she called out, "Andy, shut up!"

The dog's baying ended, replaced by a few disgruntled woofs. She shook her head.

More quietly, she told him, "I was about to say that *you*"—she punctuated it with a gentle kiss on the cheek—"were amazing."

Her praise was worth more than gold, but he could not quite accept it. He cleared his throat.

"I did not last as long as I had hoped, but I confess I lasted longer than I feared I might."

She laughed, a sound of pure merriment, with no mocking in it as far as he could tell. "What? It was perfect. Plus . . . sweetheart, you were a *virgin*."

Sweet heart—his soul warmed at that. An easy-to-understand endearment, not unlike those of his time, though he had never heard it before. And it was the first time she'd used such a love-name with him. He must've done so a hundred times with her, in a short time, but until this moment, he hadn't realized how much he'd yearned to hear her respond in kind.

He'd missed something else she'd said, but she continued, amused. "You did *not* do that like it was your first time." He chose to believe her, because it flattered his pride. "Not to mention you'd been turned to stone for *centuries*. I was fully prepared for you to, um, get too excited for it to even happen."

"It might've been much worse," he agreed.

She shrugged. "We would've just tried again later."

He hadn't considered that. Somehow, he'd imagined this as something one won or lost.

If she would give him more chances, that meant her heart had already made at least some commitment to him, whether she'd admit it or not.

He turned to her. "And I was not too fast, at the end?"

She smiled. "No. You're not going to break me. You can go slow or fast or rough . . . whatever you like."

That was indeed a satisfactory answer. He adjusted them both so that he lay on his back, her head resting on his shoulder. He pulled the blankets up over them both, for he could not have his sweetheart go cold. Surely, she felt it, too; how right they were together. He would be with her for many years. There was plenty of time for swiving, whether in the morning, noon, or night.

She said, "When you say those romantic things, it, um . . . heats my blood." He smiled; she was deliberately using his phrase. "I guess you could say I have a chivalry kink."

The gist of this, at least, was clear enough. "'Tis no effort to speak of your beauty and all your qualities, nor of my devotion, for they fill my senses." With the tip of his finger, he traced a star shape on her shoulder, and then another. "And I'll do it often, if such words make you wet as with morning dew."

Her jaw dropped. "I don't know if that's poetic or just dirty." Andy scratched at the door. "Mmm. I should let him in."

"Aye," he said, though part of him didn't want her to move. "The poor hound can hardly bear to be away from his sweet mistress's side, and who can blame him?"

"Aww." She hopped up and went over to the door, affording him a very agreeable view of her bare back and round dimpled arse. It was almost worth her absence from his side. Opening the door, she said, "Come on in, buddy."

Andy bounded into the room—floppy ears flying—onto the bed, and onto Griffin's chest.

"Aghgh!" Griffin pushed the hound off and avoiding getting licked in the face.

"Andy!" Emily admonished him, laughing. "Settle down there, bud." She returned to the bed, sitting with her knees up and pulling the covers up around her, and Andy made a few turns in place before curling up at her feet.

She looked over at Griffin's chest. "He didn't scratch you, did he?"

"If he did, it is no matter."

She frowned. "Do you mind my asking how you got this?" She touched the jagged scar on his chest, purple and shiny. "You have one under your arm, too . . . You didn't have them in my dream."

"Did I not?" he asked, stalling.

"If you don't want to talk about it, forget I asked."

"They are both from swords. I received this one"—he touched the scar on his chest—"in a surprise attack on the camp in Brittany."

Emily's shoulders lifted in a shudder. "That sounds terrifying."

It had been. Images flitted through his mind—burned bodies, men's screams. His lady did not need such details. "'Twas soon after our battle at Verneuil-sur-Avre."

"Where you were fighting the French," she said, half a question.

"The French and the Scots, with the Burgundians on our side."

"Is that where you got the one here?" She indicated the place under her own arm.

"Nay, that was at a great battle at Avranches . . . Do you know the place?" She shook her head. "On the border between Normandy and Brittany. I was wearing my armor, but under the arm, and in other places, there are gaps."

She nodded slowly. "Did you lose the battle?"

"Nay, my heart. We were outnumbered many times over, yet we prevailed . . . but two of my brothers-in-arms were cut down by arrows." A heavy feeling settled on him. "The lands we won were lost again, and what was it all for? I benefited from the victories, in reputation and favor, but so many died, and the common soldiers, even if they lived, gained little." His self-reproach overwhelmed him.

Her eyes were filled with understanding. She picked up one of his hands and kissed it. "You were doing what was expected of you."

Everyone had said it was right and good, the will of God, even. But the other side had believed that, too, and they could not have both been in the right.

Griffin snorted. "We should've all stayed home in our beds."

In the interminable hell of his frozen existence, he'd come to that conclusion many times. As if to emphasize it now, he pulled Emily down next to him again. Andy readjusted himself, finding a cozy spot between her legs and his.

"It's easy for me to forget that you were in battles like that," she said.

"I would like to forget myself."

She took in a breath as if to say something, but then she didn't speak.

Griffin, attuned to her every gesture in this moment of closeness, touched her hair. "What would you say, sweeting?"

"I just . . . Since you didn't even like going to war, are you *sure* you don't want to think about selling your armor?"

He stiffened. Had he not been clear on this matter? Had she seduced him in order to persuade him?

No. She wasn't conniving, and he'd been eager all along. But his blood was simmering.

"I know I asked before," Emily said in response to his silence. "But even if we couldn't get it authenticated, it would be worth a lot of money."

"I know," he said shortly. *God's bones.* Did she think he didn't know the value of a fine suit of armor?

"And it's not just that. I . . ." She trailed off, seeing his expression. "You know what? It's fine. Forget I asked."

"If I fight in these tournaments for sport, will I not need armor?"

"You would use theirs. Yours is too fancy for them. It's too fancy to wear at all, honestly."

That gave him a moment's pause. What was the value of a suit of armor that one never wore?

No. It was unthinkable.

"When I was turned to stone, I lost any mote of power or respect that a man might have. And now, even my own noble name means nothing." Bitterness flowed through his veins as he said it. He'd thought that he cared nothing about such matters. He'd thought just to be alive was blessing enough.

She leaned over and kissed him on the cheek. "I know."

That should have lightened his mood, but he found he could not smile. "I will spar at those tournaments or find some other worthy labor. But I will not sell my armor."

Seventeen

Emily stared after him as he walked out of the bedroom. He went into the bathroom, closed the door firmly, and in a few moments, she could hear the shower running.

There was nothing wrong with taking a shower after sex. So why did she feel like he was washing every trace of her off him? Maybe she should go join him in there and try to smooth over hard feelings. No—she'd give him space.

If he hadn't just talked about how awful and pointless war was, she never would've brought up the armor again. It was just that she kept imagining the FBI barging into her place with a warrant and finding a priceless, knight-related artifact she had no business owning. Wouldn't that be enough evidence to arrest her on?

She hadn't wanted to alarm Griffin, so she hadn't explained that. But she should.

Heaving a sigh, she got up and pulled on her jeans, skipping the panties, because after Griffin had excited her the way he had, they honestly needed to go into the laundry. She didn't feel like putting her bra back on, either, so she tossed it back in the underwear drawer where Andy couldn't play with it and grabbed a big comfy sweatshirt instead. In the hallway, Andy put his paws on her, whining.

"You need to go outside, don't you, buddy? Come on." He followed her to the front door where she leashed him up and took him down the hallway toward the front door.

The woman who lived in the corner unit walked toward them. Emily braced herself right before Andy let out one of his trademark howls, making her jump.

"*Maldito perro*," she muttered.

Emily held up a hand. "I'm sorry he's so loud. He's actually really nice."

The woman gave her as wide a berth as the narrow hallway would allow, with a critical glance at Emily's bare feet. Emily didn't often wish she'd lived in Griffin's time, but at least back then, no one would've judged her too harshly for being shoeless and walking a howling dog.

Although she'd only been planning to take Andy outside the front door, she now decided to walk him to the corner and back. It gave her more time to think about what to say to Griffin. She'd say again how incredible he'd been in bed. More important than that, she'd tell him how much he meant to her. How he'd brought so much magic, so much *life*, to her life.

She needed to tell him how much she admired him, and how even without a famous name, his nobility was obvious.

When she and Andy had almost reached the front door of the building again, Andy transacted his business under a shrub next to the sidewalk. As he bellowed, she pulled a plastic bag out of her front sweatshirt pocket and squatted down to clean up after him.

"Emily?"

The voice sent a jolt of anxiety through her. She jumped to her feet and found herself standing face-to-face with her ex-husband.

Him, and his new girlfriend.

Oh no. She'd completely forgotten to call him back.

"Tom!" she blurted out stupidly as she tied the bag shut.

He looked exactly the same: tall, lean, with artfully messy light brown hair. He wore a black tee, jeans, and chunky high-top sneakers. His girlfriend, her black hair a little longer than when Emily had last seen her, wore a white midi dress with sandals that showed off a fresh pedicure. A delicate gold heart necklace hung around her neck: a gift from Tom, almost certainly. It was a much better ensemble than Emily's jeans, oversize sweatshirt, and bare feet, accessorized by a bag of dog poop.

Andy put his paws up on Tom's knees. Tom said, "Hey, I missed you, too!" and scratched him behind the ears.

Did Andy still miss Tom? Emily had always spent more time with Andy and had been the one who fed and walked him. The dog had seemed confused when he'd found himself in a crate in the front seat of a U-Haul, in a few hotel rooms, and then at their Edgewater apartment. But at the end of every day, he'd seemed happy enough, resting his head on her leg or her shoulder with a contented sigh. And while he'd greeted Tom in a friendly way, he did that with everyone who let him.

"You can't take him," she told Tom. So much for well-crafted arguments.

He exchanged a look with Tori that plainly said, *See? I told you she'd be unreasonable.* To Emily he said, "I said I'd take him once I got settled."

He *had* said that. But she hadn't believed him. He hardly had a good track record for keeping his commitments, after all. And that had been several months ago.

"You took too long," she said. "Now *he's* settled." Tom had abandoned the dog. After abandoning her.

Andy put his paws up on Tori's knee. She giggled and said, "What a handsome boy."

Emily's anger flared. When Andy put his paws back on the sidewalk, Emily wasn't sorry to see faint paw prints on Tori's white dress.

Behind Tori, across the street, a man stood on the sidewalk, holding up his phone in their direction . . . was he *recording* her? Instinctively, Emily held her hand up to her face. This jackass neighbor was probably livestreaming her, the suspected criminal, as she stood barefoot, arguing with her ex and his lovely girlfriend. The ultimate cringe content.

"Can we come inside and talk about it?" Tom asked.

"*Yes*," Emily answered immediately, turning on her heel.

She threw away the plastic bag in the bin near the door, then took a deep breath as she put in the code for the front entrance. Griffin was going to meet Tom. And Griffin was annoyed with her. Adrenaline fired her nerves as they followed her into the building.

Emily asked, "Did you both drive here from San Jose?" She and Tom had talked several times about taking a road trip together sometime: making the perfect playlist, listening to audiobooks, having deep conversations as the miles rolled by. That had been one of the worst things about his affair and the divorce. He'd ruined not only several years of memories but big and small future dreams, too.

"We flew out, but we're renting a car to drive back."

As they neared her apartment door, Andy let out a series of loud *baroos*.

"I thought he would've outgrown that," Tom said.

"Nope!" Emily answered. She stopped at her door and dug for her key.

They went inside—and then Emily stopped short.

Griffin sat on the sofa, stark naked.

Surprise touched his features. He must not have heard them talking in the hall. Andy had probably drowned out everything else.

Griffin glanced around him, then pulled the fringed throw off the back of the couch onto his lap.

"Good afternoon, sir—demoiselle," he said to Tom and Tori. If he was embarrassed, it didn't show; he sounded just like a lord in his own hall.

Not that he had anything to be embarrassed about. The way Tom and Tori were gaping at him made Emily even more aware of his magnificence—his powerful arms, the broad chest with golden-brown hair, the slender hips . . . He secured the throw around them as he stood up.

Andy strained against his leash, and Emily unclipped it. He bounded over to Griffin, who patted his head.

"Forgive me," he added to Tom and Tori with a small smile, "but I knew not we would be receiving guests." Tom's eyebrows raised at the *we*.

Emily's cheeks burned, and she felt on the edge of bursting into nervous laughter. "Griffin, this is Tom, my ex-husband, and his girlfriend, Tori."

The goodwill drained from Griffin's face. "Hey, how's it going," Tom said, dropping his voice about a full octave.

Griffin looked them both up and down, his lip curled with disdain.

Tori ventured, "So, Griffin, what do you do?"

"What do *I* do, *puterelle*? I know well what *you* have done—"

"*Hey*, hey," Emily interrupted, holding up her hands, as Tori drew back in surprise. Emily wasn't sure what *puterelle* meant, but she could guess.

Tom, his face flushed, took a step toward Griffin. "Listen, bro—"

"Do you seek a quarrel, bedswerver?" Griffin asked, turning on him. That was a new one to Emily, too, but the meaning was obvious. "You will find one."

"Hey!" Emily grabbed Griffin's hand and his attention. In an urgent undertone, she said, "Remember what I said? About the law?"

His jaw clenched. "You are right, my heart's queen." Emily felt a rush of gratitude at the endearment. Griffin might've gotten annoyed with her before, but he was on her side. "I cannot bear to return to any prison."

Tom's mouth fell open. "Emily, you're dating an *ex-convict?*"

She rolled her eyes. Griffin had been referring metaphorically to being trapped in stone, but she didn't owe Tom any explanations.

Griffin said to her, "I wonder greatly that you have invited this vile filth, more unwelcome than dung that sticks to the bottom of a boot."

"Hey," Tori objected, and Tom gave her a quick shake of the head, no doubt concerned that Griffin might murder them. Andy hopped up on the couch and curled up into a comfortable ball, oblivious of the tension.

"I did *not* invite them," Emily explained. Things had been fraught enough between her and Griffin without him thinking that. "I don't even want them here."

"Ah." Griffin turned back to Tom and Tori. "Leave at once and never return upon pain of death."

"Wait, not death," Emily said weakly. "They can stay for a few minutes." She hated confrontations like this, but she needed to convince Tom that he and his ex-dog were never, ever getting back together, so that he'd leave them both alone for good.

Tom held up a hand. "We don't want any trouble. I'm just here to pick up Andy." Andy's head popped up at the sound of his name. "We agreed to this before."

"I didn't know you'd go *months* without wanting him back," Emily said. "He kept me company when I was all alone. I'm really attached to him." Her heart pounded harder.

"I'm attached to him, too," Tom said. "And you got to have him all this time." Next to him, Tori looked around at the bookshelves, avoiding eye contact with everyone.

"I got to have him because you didn't want him," Emily protested. "You said it was too hard for you to deal with him while you were moving. But I was moving, too. You never want to deal with the hard parts, only the fun parts."

Griffin, still mostly naked, crossed his arms across his broad chest. She knew that if she told him to throw Tom and Tori out of her apartment, he would happily and efficiently do it. Instead, he was standing still and keeping his mouth shut, and she guessed it wasn't easy.

"Andy's been through a lot already," Emily told Tom. "You shouldn't confuse him again." She glanced back at Andy, who sat on the sofa, looking at her worriedly.

Tom sighed. "Okay, I wasn't going to bring this up. But what's going to happen to him if you get arrested?"

"Arrested?" she repeated with shock—as if she hadn't been obsessively thinking about the same thing.

"She will not be arrested, you plague-sore!" Griffin said.

Tom's face screwed up in bafflement. "What?" At the same time, Tori said mildly, "Ew."

Tom told Emily, "Everyone's saying you had to be involved with the theft. You and maybe your friend Rose."

Her mouth dropped open. "How do you know about Rose?"

"There's this guy making videos about it. His girlfriend knows somebody who works with her." Emily mentally cursed the museum's social media department. "They say you told Rose to tell her brother thank you. Her brother who's the ex-con who works at the moving company?"

"You think I stole something with Rose's *brother*? I don't even know the guy!" Despite her bravado, she felt a little queasy.

Tori asked, "Then why did you thank him?"

"I . . ." Then she remembered. She'd told Rose to thank him for the clothes he gave to Griffin. "That's none of your business."

Tori raised her eyebrows, looking dubious. Emily's temper rose even higher. The last thing she needed was this woman, right under her roof, suspecting her of theft.

She said, "Just because you two are sneaky doesn't mean everyone else is."

Tom's jaw tightened, and Tori's face reddened. Griffin nodded meaningfully in mute support.

"I knew you were going to do this," Tom said. "Make this personal."

Emily scoffed. "How would this not be personal? Look, I'm flattered that you both think I might be a criminal mastermind. And maybe thinking that makes you feel better about how you screwed around behind my back." The whole time, they'd acted as though she'd be too polite to mention Tom's infidelity.

Tom grimaced. "Emily, can we just—"

"If anything ever happened to me, my parents would take Andy. You remember they live out here, right? Not that you ever liked to come home with me." She shot a look at Tori. "For obvious reasons."

Tori folded her lips and looked away. Emily never had the opportunity to tell her off before. Part of her wanted to be classy . . . but making the woman uncomfortable was undeniably satisfying.

She concluded, "Anyway, I'm not getting arrested, I didn't steal a giant stone sculpture, and I won't give up Andy."

Standing at her shoulder, Griffin nodded, looking at her with pride.

Tori shifted from one foot to the other. "Maybe we should adopt a new dog," she suggested quietly to Tom. "One that's just ours. He does have a pretty loud bark . . ."

Tom's shoulders slumped. "I guess." He asked Emily defensively, "Can I at least pet him again?"

"Of course." Although, if Griffin hadn't been there, she might've worried that he'd pick the dog up and leave with him.

Tom went over and stroked Andy's head. Andy's tail thumped and he licked Tom's hand. Tom bent his face down to the dog's and murmured, "Aww, that's a good boy. We had some good times, didn't we?"

Emily swallowed. The day they'd adopted him and brought him home came to her mind, as clear and immediate as if it had happened last week. And how they'd dressed him up as a UPS driver for Halloween in the first year of COVID because they'd ordered so many things online, but he'd wrestled his way out of the dog costume and then destroyed it . . .

"If you had a shred of wisdom or of loyalty, the hound would still be yours," Griffin told Tom quietly. "But far beyond that, so would the love of a beautiful, gracious, and honorable wife." As he said the word *honorable*, he slid Tori a look of cool contempt.

Tom straightened, another flush creeping up his face. "No offense, but you just met her. You have no idea how difficult—"

"Insult my lady at your peril."

Griffin didn't raise his voice, but clearly enunciated every word with a deadly edge, filling the air with tension. Emily had never seen the icy look in his eyes before.

Andy hopped off the couch and trotted off to the bedroom. Emily felt a surge of spiteful happiness at that. Andy seemed no more attached to Tom than to anyone else.

"We should go," Tori told Tom. "We need to check into our hotel."

"Aye, get you gone," Griffin said, still skewering Tom with his glare, "and if ever you return without my lady's leave, you will not find me in such a generous mien."

His baritone voice crackled with authority. It didn't matter that he was standing half-naked in her apartment living room. He could've been addressing his army.

Once Emily had closed the door behind them, she sank onto the sofa, clasping the back of her head with her hands. *"Ugh."*

Griffin sat down next to her, oblivious to the throw slipping off his waist. His nearness and nakedness swung her thoughts back to their time in the bedroom. *God*, he'd made her feel so good, and he'd been so passionate. She'd always been the romantic one, but Griffin had been right there with her in those heights and depths of emotion . . . of love.

Griffin frowned. "So that is the man who hurt you greatly, *mon trésor*, and not so long before." He looked toward the door that Tom had just exited.

Emily nodded. "You know, it's not just that he cheated on me. Although that was horrible. Things were bad for, I don't know, maybe a year before that. It seemed like he was sick of me being so, I don't know, sad and sensitive . . . and I was mad at him for talking me into uprooting my life. We'd have these fights that went on and on . . . It was like we were stuck in a maze and couldn't get out."

"The blame was all on his side," Griffin said stoutly.

"I don't know if that's true . . ." She looked up at him. "But I have to admit, it felt pretty great to have a handsome knight tell him he's an idiot."

"I am happy to do so as often as you like." A brief smile crossed his face, but the look in his eyes was still wistful.

Emily swallowed. She needed him to understand something. "Tom said *I love you* on our third date. I hadn't even thought about love then. But I just said it back, like automatically, because I didn't want to hurt his feelings. Besides, I always wanted to be in love, you know? I loved the whole idea of romance, like flowers and poetry and . . ." she smiled sadly, "knights in shining armor. So I just went along with it, and told myself I was in love. And it turned out to be such a disaster."

He studied her. "Having suffered with such a husband, it may take some time yet to learn that I am trustworthy."

"I know you are. You're the most amazing man I've ever met."

At that, he flashed a smile, and then his face grew serious again. "I would speak to you more about the armor."

"No, let me go first." Her heart ached. "I feel a little anxious about having it in the apartment, with all the suspicion about the statue theft." His brow creased, and she rushed to add, "But nobody's going to come in here and look around. Selling it might draw *more* attention to it. The other thing is, I just think you should have your own money. Because you . . ." She sighed and her shoulders sagged a little. "Because you deserve a comfortable, happy life, even if you get tired of me."

Griffin captured her gaze in his, soulful and vulnerable. "I can tell you plainly that if I lived another thousand years, I would not tire of you."

Her heart gave a dangerous happy leap at that. She ducked her head.

"It's just that we haven't been together long at all . . ." Then she reached out and took both of his hands, adding in a whisper, "But we do feel very right together."

It didn't make any sense. As much adjusting as Griffin still had to do, he shouldn't feel right to *anyone*. And no one should feel quite right to him, either.

Try telling her heart that, though.

He took her hand in both of his and lowered his head to press it to his lips.

When their eyes met again, she asked gently, "What else were you going to tell me about the armor?"

"Ah." He nodded. "To me, the armor does not represent the

wars or the tournaments that, indeed, sullied it with shame and sorrow. Over the past hundreds of years, I have endeavored to think little of those times, so as not to go mad."

Her heart twisted with sympathy. "I wish I'd never asked you about your scars."

"You may ask anything, and I will always answer the best I can," he pledged. "Through the torments of hell itself, my good memories have sustained me . . . and chief among them are the day the armorer fitted me with that beautiful suit, and the day I wore it when I was made a knight, filled with hope for the future and the desire to do good."

Wow. "I can understand that. Though I can't really know what you've been through . . . Honestly, it's amazing that you can still function. You're very strong."

"I have not always felt strong," he admitted. "And now I am in a bright new world, but it is often bewildering, and meseems—" He corrected himself. "It seems to me that as long as I have the armor, I am still myself."

Oh, Griffin. "I would never want to take that away from you," she said softly. "I hope you're having some good days now, too."

A tiny smile twitched at his lips, and it lightened her mood to see it.

"You know that I am," he said. "Although my imagination is powerful, I had not even dreamt of such a pleasure as awaited me in your arms. May I make a thousand new memories of—" He paused, appearing to search his mind. "Sunshine, and roses, and swiving, to fill the space where despair and chaos have been."

"What's swiving?"

He gave an easy laugh that did her soul good to hear. "A word I should not use with a gentle lady."

"Is it . . . what we just did?"

"The very same, sweet bird. I am glad to see you smile. I fear that I have brought you too many frowns and sighs."

She peered at him. "What do you mean? You make me smile all the time."

"But as you say, my very presence has brought suspicion upon your head."

"That's not going to come to anything," she reassured him—and herself.

She was *not* going to Google herself. If she did, she might disappear down rabbit holes for days. It had to blow over. It just had to.

"If I had my old rank and power," he mused, "few would dare to spread such lies about you, with no proofs." He gave an ironic chuckle. "Or mayhap even *with* some proofs."

Emily drew her legs up and wrapped her arms around them, facing him. "I know it's hard not being a nobleman anymore," she said gently.

He grimaced. "It should not rankle me. I am fortunate beyond measure to be alive."

"You can at least start sleeping in a king-size bed," she joked. He looked at her blankly. "My bed. It's what they call king-size. I was thinking you should start sleeping with me in the bedroom. If you want to."

A gleam came into his eyes. "Aye, my lady, I should like that very much indeed. Though I do not think we will only be sleeping."

She felt a twinge of regret. "I'm still sorry I ruined the moment earlier."

He gave a shake of the head and stroked her hair away from her face. He met her gaze with unguarded sincerity. "The joining of your perfect body with mine was to me such a moment of radiance that no trifling disagreement may cast a very long shadow upon it."

The bright happiness she'd felt before returned, at least in part. "I feel the same way, my lord."

His mouth fell open.

She grinned. "That's how a lady would say it in your time, right?"

"Aye, and I like hearing it from you, more than I can say."

She snuggled into him, unwrapping the throw enough to cover him up as well.

What an incredible day. She'd had something she'd almost convinced herself was impossible. *Closure*. And not just because she'd told Tom and Tori what she really thought. It was also because she'd had amazing sex with a virgin knight. He'd been every bit as chivalrous and ardent as in their shared dream. It had been romantic and wonderful.

I'm falling in love with him.

No, I'm not. She didn't even know who he would be once he'd fully adjusted to the modern world. Considering he'd been trapped in limbo for centuries, this was a fleeting, liminal state, like the one between being asleep and being awake.

Eighteen

Griffin woke up from a deep sleep into darkness, and fear shocked his heart. He'd been stone again and lowered into a grave. Mordrain, in his armor, had stood over him, staring down. Though Griffin hadn't been able to see his face, he'd known it was Mordrain from the gilded design etched onto the side of his helmet: the jackdaw, eater of carrion, an ill omen.

Then he felt the softness of Emily's giant bed beneath him and, as his eyes adjusted, made out the outline of her sleeping form. He took in a deep breath and let it out.

The sun had not yet risen from its own bed in the east. He showered and put on his new jeans, a perfect fit, and the green shirt. They pleased him more than he could say. In the living room, he watched the rest of the play on the TV that he'd begun last night. It was a story about a band of heroes named the Avengers, and Emily had told him if he enjoyed it, there were twenty or thirty more very like it.

Emily had told him that much of the fighting and spectacle was mere illusion, but it looked very real, and the actors were wonderfully adept at feigning joy, anger, fear, and sorrow. Of course, this was one reason why actors couldn't be trusted; they made their livelihood as liars, betraying their souls for no more than a shilling. They wandered from town to town like hungry wolves, having no home to call their own, not even as much as a swineherd's hovel or a whore's quarters at a brothel.

There were actual women in this play, rather than youths dressed up to play them, and Griffin could only wonder at what had led such lovely demoiselles to such shameful conduct. Nonetheless, he loved the characters, especially the man who'd been revived after decades of being frozen in ice. They were becoming a band of brothers, like King Arthur's knights or Robin Hood's men. Griffin liked the growing friendships at least as much as the fighting, though that part of the story also gave him a twinge of yearning.

No doubt, he, too, would have a band of brothers, at Medieval Legends. Once again, he would be admired by all. He would ask for Emily's hand in marriage as soon as he was invited to join the glorious company of sparring knights.

"And I thought I was up early! You look nice."

Griffin looked up to see Emily standing there in her T-shirt and the soft loose pants she'd worn for sleeping, fuzzy and printed, improbably enough, with the images of many purple owls reading books.

"Good morning, my cinnamon," he said, switching off the play. "Has the sun risen, or is it only your presence that fills this room with light?"

Smiling, she shook her head. "How'd you get to be so smooth?"

"You are the smooth one, or so I recall." He pretended to look thoughtful, touching his finger to his lips. "Though we should go back to bed so I can make sure."

She laughed. "I'd enjoy that, but I have to go to work."

He would rather not have been left alone, but with the company of endless plays, and so many books, not to mention the agreeable hound, he could hardly complain. "And what work are you doing, my lady, now that your chief task has come to life?"

"Good question." She sat down on the chair of the sofa, next to him. "At least we're back in the conservator labs again. I got an email about it." She shrugged, but he could see anxiety in her eyes.

The room filled with chiming music. "That's probably my parents," Emily said. "They should be back from vacation." She swept the room with a glance. "Where's my phone?"

At least twice a day, she asked that question. She was marvelously careless with the device, considering she relied on it to do a hundred things or more. Griffin stood up, went to the little table by the door, and with a touch of smugness took it out of the tray.

"It was under the sofa," he told her.

"Thank you!"

It had already stopped ringing by the time he handed it to her. She looked at the screen. "Oh, it was Rose."

She pressed a couple of buttons and sat down in the chair. It rang for a moment.

"Emily!" Rose's voice filled the room. "Have you left for work yet?"

"No. I mean, it's six thirty." Emily gave Griffin a quizzical look. "Why?"

"What are you and Griffin doing tonight?"

"Um . . . just hanging out, I guess." Her face flushed.

"So like, Netflix and chill?"

"No . . ." Griffin didn't understand the question, but Emily's tone of voice made it the least convincing *no* he'd heard in centuries. She herself must've realized it, because she laughed. "I mean, yesterday, it was chill and then Netflix."

"Oh my God! Was he—"

"You're on speaker," Emily nearly shouted.

"I need to hear about this later. But I have a favor to ask." Rose's deep inhale was audible over the phone. "Remember that guy at the food trucks?"

"What—the cute guy in the white shirt?"

"After we went shopping yesterday, I went over to the taco truck, and he was in line! We talked for a while and then he asked me out."

"Oh, wow," Emily said. "See, I told you he was looking at you!"

"He admitted it," Rose said cheerfully. "He has the nicest eyes. And the nicest voice."

"What's his name?"

"Aaron Johnston. He works at Sotheby's."

Emily blinked. "Like the art auctions?"

"Yeah. He's a VP of European art, I guess?"

"Wow. That's impressive."

"He's a little older than me, but I don't care about that. And he's a Sagittarius. They're perfect matches with Aquarians."

Griffin hadn't understood all of the conversation, but he perked up at this. Apparently, Rose was well-versed in the science of the stars. He himself knew much of it, from a section in his Book of Hours called *On the Heavenly Spheres*.

"We took our tacos down to the lakefront and sat on a bench to eat them." Rose's voice sounded dreamy. "I thought it was impossible to get a date these days without an app."

"But here in Chicago, you can just buy a taco or kiss a statue," Emily joked, and she and Griffin exchanged a fond glance. "Are you going out with him?"

"Um . . . that's what I need to talk to you about. Can you and Griffin come with me?"

"On a date?" Emily laughed. "I'm no expert, but I don't think you're supposed to bring friends."

Rose's sigh rustled static over the phone. "He asked me out for drinks tonight, and I mean, he seems *so great*. But I just have *really* bad judgment about guys, you know? So I wanted a second opinion. I told him I was going to happy hour with a couple of friends, and he could join us, and he said okay."

"But there wasn't really a happy hour?" Emily guessed.

"No. I asked a couple of my other friends, but one of them's teaching a Pagan Ethics workshop, and the other one has vortex therapy."

From the expression on Emily's face, Griffin gathered that she was nearly as flummoxed by these activities as he was.

"Listen, I know this sounds like you're my backup choice," Rose said. "But you're actually one of my favorite people. But since we haven't been friends that long, I didn't feel comfortable calling you in an emergency. Except now I am."

Emily smiled and touched her hand to her heart. "You're one of my favorite people, too. You can *always* call me in an emergency, okay? You've helped me out with *huge* emergencies!"

"So you and Griffin can come?" Hope and desperation touched her voice. "I'd really like your opinion."

Emily's amused gaze met Griffin's. "Where are we meeting?"

"At Cindy's?"

"*Fancy.* I've only been there once." She turned to Griffin and explained, "It's, um, an elegant tavern at the top of one of those tall buildings. It's practically across the street from the museum."

Griffin thrilled to the idea. Now that he thought of it, he was astounded that he had yet to visit a tavern since his transformation. Often, he'd imagined that if he were free of the curse, that was the first thing he'd do. He could judge whether this Aaron was a worthy gentleman, and perhaps converse with other friendly folk, too. Although Emily filled much of the void within him, he'd always hated being alone, loving the company of friends.

"This will be a rare pleasure, Lady Rose," he called out so she could hear.

"Hang on, though," Emily said. "I'm not going to have time to come back here after work and go downtown again for happy hour."

Griffin had already worked this out in his head. "I will go on the train with you and spend my day perusing the museum."

"That's a great idea," Rose chimed in. "You'd learn about thousands of years of culture. Not just American and European, either."

The corner of Emily's mouth turned down. "That's true. But won't people recognize him from the videos?" Noticing Griffin's bewildered look, she explained, "People have been watching you. Kind of the same way you were watching the *Avengers* movie."

It took him a moment to understand. "People are watching my life? Every moment, like a play?" Horror gripped him. Had they seen him swiving Emily? Or, worse, pissing and shitting?

"Noooo, no," Emily said. "They just saw you in the museum, after you came back to life."

"Ah." He breathed a sigh of relief.

"If he's wearing his regular clothes, I don't think anyone will notice him," Rose said. "Thousands of people visit every day. He can ride the train with you, then go through the main entrance like any tourist."

Emily snapped his fingers. "Plus, he can wear glasses."

"You have a spare pair?" Rose sounded dubious. "But he won't be able to see in them."

"No, I have a pair of clear ones. To protect against blue light on the computer. My mom got them for me, but I never use them since I don't wear my contacts. Hang on." Emily trotted to the bedroom, and he could hear her opening one drawer, and then another.

She returned triumphantly, glasses in hand. "Here!" She thrust them toward Griffin. "Try them on."

Griffin obeyed. They felt strange and modern on his face.

"What does he look like?" Rose called out over the phone. "Clark Kent?"

"Like a fool, I am sure," Griffin called back to her good-naturedly.

"No, you look smart!" Emily said. "They're a little small on your face, but it does change your look."

"I will also wear my cap," Griffin said. He looked very different in it, and he was fond of it.

Emily nodded. "That's a good idea. We'll go."

G riffin rode the train with Emily and a crowd of other passengers, most of them looking sleepy, grim, or both. They weren't looking forward to their labors in the city, but he'd be glad when he had labor to go to. One lady had tattoos, such as one might have gotten to commemorate a pilgrimage to the Holy Land, but they covered the whole of her bare arms, and the butterflies, roses, and skulls might or might not have been symbols of faith. She was working some kind of small tapestry depicting another skull wearing a crown. He complimented her on her handiwork.

She gave him a wary look and muttered, "Thanks."

"It reminds me of the Prince of Portugal," he said.

She peered at him. "What?"

"Peter, the Prince of Portugal? And the Corpse Queen?" There had been an extremely rude drinking song about them, in the Before Times.

The lady put down her needle. "This sounds like my kind of story."

Very well, then. Griffin scanned the train just to make sure no children could hear.

"The prince fell in love with his wife's lady-in-waiting, Inês, but as you can imagine, his father-in-law didn't like that." For Emily's sake, he tried to use the plain, modern manner of speaking, as well as he could. "The father-in-law had her murdered. Peter got revenge and executed the hired killers, ripping out their hearts."

"Holy *crap*," the lady said.

Emily's eyes widened. "Did this really happen?"

"Aye, and it gets worse. When Peter became king, he had her body dug up from the grave, dressed in queenly garments and jewels, and crowned and put upon a throne next to him. Then all the nobles were compelled to pay homage to her by kneeling and kissing the hem of her gown."

The lady's mouth fell open. "That's amazing." But Emily shuddered, and another dame, and a gentleman, too, were screwing up their faces in disgust.

"I will tell a more cheerful tale," he assured them, and launched into the story of Guillaume and Melior. It gave him a soft, warm feeling to recount the story of the werewolf king, and the lovers who lived happily ever after in Sicily, because his mother had told it to him when he was small. He told the story with such flair and wit that the ending brought a smattering of applause from a few listeners.

"I thank you, good sirs and demoiselles," he said, flushed with pride. "What kind of tale will you hear next?"

Grinning, Emily laid a hand on his arm. "Sorry," she said to him and their fellow passengers. "This is our stop."

"You should be an actor," a man said to him.

Griffin flinched. He should be a homeless, traveling buffoon, no better than a thief? Indeed, the two trades often went hand in hand. But the man's smile suggested nothing but goodwill, and Emily beamed at him. It was a joke; one he didn't understand.

Nonetheless, he let out a hearty laugh. "I would not say that, sir! Good day to you."

At the corner of the busy street, Emily gave him directions to the café where she would meet him for lunch, adding that he could ask anyone in a uniform if he got confused. Her coworkers, she said, never ate there. She was going to go in the side entrance as she always did, and he would go in the front and give the ticket she'd printed out to the gatekeeper.

She stood on her toes and gave him an enthusiastic kiss. "Eleven thirty!"

The museum was a marvel beyond Griffin's wildest imaginings. He'd seen a bit of it before, of course, but he'd been distracted by the fact that he was alive.

All the tapestries, statues, and fine objects in a grand palace in his time would've been just another chamber in this vast castle of treasures. Galleries displayed sculptures and riches from the Far East, some a thousand years older or more than he himself was, and objects from this very continent made long before Europeans reached its shores.

When he glanced at the phone Emily had given him, it was eleven twenty, though it seemed that no time had passed at all. The museum had filled up by now, and Griffin smiled to see a throng of children bouncing and giggling down the hall under the watchful eyes of women who he supposed were their nurses.

After he'd greeted Emily at the café and they'd gotten lunch and found a table, he asked her, "How is your work, sweet bird?"

She grimaced. "I don't really have any, so I've been trying to work on my symposium presentation. At least Laurie wasn't there. She was out at the dentist."

"How is your . . ." He paused to find the word. "Your boss, Jason? Has he spoken more of the theft?"

"I haven't seen him yet today. So far, he's hardly seemed upset."

"It surprises me. He was interested in the statue for years."

Emily scrunched up her face in confusion. "What makes you say that?"

"Because he came to the Burke house to look me over and speak with Richard Burke, five or six years ago."

"Seriously? Are you sure it was him?"

"Aye—yes," he corrected himself. "He gave his name to the housemaid."

"That's so *weird*. Jason didn't work for the museum then."

Griffin shrugged. "Did he work for another one?"

"I have no idea, actually. But yeah, he must have."

She asked him about the galleries he'd visited, and he told her about his favorite things—the giant bronze man with the long earlobes, sitting cross-legged, which had made Griffin feel tranquil just to gaze upon; the jade mask; the gold filigree frog.

"You've hardly even seen anything yet!" she exclaimed.

"I could scarcely go faster. There is so much of history I don't know."

"Most people don't know much of it," she said. "But most people aren't as curious about it as you are."

"I can understand why you love your work. You imagine what life must have been like for the people who made the thing or used it."

"Exactly! It's so exciting working on old pieces. Even if they don't come to life," she added with an impish grin.

"It must be an honor to restore and preserve them."

Behind her thick-framed glasses, her eyes shone. "You really understand me. You know that?"

"Because it is a pleasure to do so. What should I see next?"

She bounced a little in her seat. "I want to show you a couple of things myself. As soon as you're done."

Griffin set the rest of his sandwich aside. "I am done now."

She led him in brisk strides down the hall and up a flight of stairs. "I'm going to show you where Andy War-Howl got his name."

He supposed there was a portrait of a lord's dog by the same name. Instead, she led him to a painting of a woman's head, rendered in garish hues of pink, black, and yellow.

"I do not understand," he confessed.

"This woman is Marilyn Monroe, and she was very famous, and so was the artist." She pointed to the little sign next to the work. "Andy Warhol. He did those others, too." She gestured at other ugly paintings around them. "So Andy's named after him, but he's Andy War-Howl. Because he's so loud."

Griffin burst out laughing. "That is very good!" He added, "I hate this painting."

"Yeah, that doesn't surprise me. Let me show you one you might like." As he followed her, she added, "But it's okay if you hate this one, too!"

She led him to a huge painting depicting men, women, children, and even a couple of hounds, enjoying a summer afternoon at the lake. Several others had gathered to gaze at it, too.

"You're right. I like it," Griffin said. He hesitated, then asked more quietly, "But why do the ladies have such enormous arses?"

She let out a little chirp of laughter. "They don't really. There's like a cage under their skirts, holding their skirts out? It's called a bustle. I don't know, it was just the fashion then."

"Ah." He pointed. "One could eat one's dinner off that one."

"Come here, you haven't seen the best part yet." She took his hand and, sidestepping another couple, led him to stand inches away from the painting. "See? It's all made of dots."

Griffin gasped. The more closely he looked, the more the dots ceased to have shape or meaning. "How did he do it? How did he know how?"

"That's a good question. He was ahead of his time."

He turned to her. "Show me more things you love."

She looked charmingly overwhelmed. "Oh, gosh, we need to take a whole day sometime. This afternoon, you should go to the medieval galleries. We have all kinds of paintings and objects and armor from your time."

"Yes, I would like that very much."

"Did you see the Chagall windows before? The big blue ones?" He shook his head. "Well, anyone who visits the museum needs to see those, and they're close to my office."

When they reached the wall of windows, casting rich cobalt light on the floor, Griffin's mouth fell open in awe. His heart lifted.

"What do you think?" Emily asked eagerly.

"It is as if I am looking at Heaven itself."

"That's what I thought the first time I ever saw them, as a kid," Emily said, her voice soft. "The artist is Jewish. He came to America to escape the Nazis." She gave him a questioning look.

"I remember what you told me about them," he said soberly. He gazed at dancing figures, the yellow sun, the lavender bird, the books that had taken flight, all glowing like a bright dream. "And yet this is pure joy."

"It is. And hope."

He'd felt this way when he'd visited the Canterbury cathedral with his father and his sister, who'd been no more than five. The memory of the pilgrimage flooded back to him now. The rosy apples and little venison pies the cook had packed for the journey. Alyse had bragged that she'd helped make them. More likely, she'd chattered with the cook nonstop; she'd been gay as a spring lamb then. The scent of camphor incense in the sanctuary. The bright stained glass windows, entrancing Griffin and Alyse both.

The recollection was more sweet than bitter. The past and the present, usually separated by an unfathomable gulf, felt not so vast now. Pieces of him were coming back together like these pieces of stained glass, arranged into an unbroken pattern.

"Thank you for showing me," he said.

Emily's brown eyes sparkled. "You know, people have been known to kiss here."

"Have they, sweeting?"

"Mm, yes. I would say it's almost a Chicago tradition."

Warmth spread through his chest. "God forbid that I should ever neglect the traditions of this great city."

He gathered her in his arms and, in a moment of inspiration, picked her up off her feet and swung her around. She squealed and then giggled. He set her down and kissed her mid-laugh, and she pressed up against him. In a few moments, he broke away and stepped back, because even if kissing was a tradition here, being in an obvious state of arousal was probably not.

At the very least, he'd made her forget about her worries at work for a while. This was a beautiful place, very like a church. Maybe soon, he would marry her here.

Nineteen

When Emily returned to the lab, Terrence was still busy at his worktable, setting pieces of stained glass into new caning with a rubber mallet. Emily hadn't talked to him yet, other than to say good morning; he seemed intent on his work. She sat down at her computer and opened up a blank slide of her PowerPoint, with a title at the top: **Characteristics of the Medieval Body.**

She made a steeple of her fingers and pressed them to her mouth. *Hmm, let's see. Broad shoulders? Full lips? Thick . . .*

That's enough, you absolute cabbage, she chided herself. When she'd first outlined this presentation, she hadn't imagined this section would be so distracting.

Laurie arrived a few minutes later. After putting on her magnifying visor, she got back to work scraping at the surface of the Essex armor helmet with a surgical scalpel, removing the almost invisible layer of grime without scratching the surface or flaking the original gilding.

The silence in the lab was tense. Emily envied both Terrence and Laurie for having projects to work on, but she was glad she didn't have to work on the armor. Something about the way those malevolent eye slits stared back at Laurie as she worked filled Emily with dread.

Jason stepped into the office and leaned against the doorframe. "I hope you all had a good weekend. And I hope you managed to do something besides watch the news and listen to podcasts."

"I heard you have connections to Chinese billionaires, Jason," Terrence said dryly.

Emily's mouth fell open. "They're saying *that*?"

Jason rolled his eyes. "Yeah, not bad for a kid who grew up in San Bernardino." Emily recalled Jason saying that his father was a high school physics teacher.

Terrence said, "Don't feel bad. Apparently, I have South Side gang connections." He gave a bitter laugh. "Sure I do, if you count our Hyde Park HOA."

Emily drooped in her chair. "This is awful. I'm so sorry." Laurie gave her a sidelong look, and she added, "Sorry you all have to deal with that."

"On the upside," Terrence said, "I sold five sculptures in one weekend."

"Oh, wow. The ones at that Wicker Park gallery?" Emily had looked them up online. They went for a few thousand apiece.

Terrence nodded. "And one big commission. Silver lining." He looked over at Laurie. "How are things going for you?"

"As usual, nobody can spell my last name," she said. "It's the first time I've ever been glad of that."

"I'm still seeing the most about Emily," Terrence said, and added in a dramatic voice, "'Tonight: the medieval masterpiece and the mousy mastermind.'" Emily's horror must've shown on her face, because he added, "Guess you didn't watch that one."

"I've been avoiding it all."

"The board of directors is setting up a reward for the sculpture," Jason said. "Two million dollars. And a share of it for any information that leads to its safe return."

Terrence gave a low whistle. "Makes me wish I knew something."

Laurie said, "Like the FBI agents told me, *someone* knows something." She avoided Emily's gaze.

Jason said, "I know the disappearance and the allegations are a huge distraction, but the medieval weapons exhibit is still moving forward, and we've only got a couple of weeks."

"I'm going to be done with the window by Friday," Terrence said.

Laurie patted the helmet with her gloved hand. "I'm almost to a conservation surface here. I'm just going to go over it with mineral spirits."

Jason walked over to her table to inspect her work. "You did a great job of preserving that patina."

Couldn't Jason feel it? The dark rage coming from the helm?

Emily told herself that her imagination was running wild. It was no wonder, after her experience with Griffin.

Laurie said, "I'm going to figure out what to use to replace some of the gilding here. Now that I can tell it's a bird." She traced her finger in the air above the etched symbol. "I think it's a crow."

It reminded Emily of a medieval illustration she'd seen once, depicting a crow—or was it a jackdaw?—picking at a corpse. Shuddering, she shook off the thought.

She attempted to make her voice casual as she asked Jason, "What would you like me to work on next?"

He said, "You remember what we were saying about the Valtierra altarpiece?" He pointed to the wooden panel, about six foot square, laid out on the large back table. Its ornate frames held scenes

from the Crucifixion and Resurrection, and the central panel depicted St. George slaying the dragon.

Emily nodded. They'd talked about it in a group staff meeting.
"Someone tried to protect it with a coat of beige tempera." They'd
slapped brown paint right over the beautiful bright pigments and
gilding.

"Exactly," he said. "I know we talked about someone from
Frames Conservation doing that one, but they're swamped with the
Friends of Caravaggio exhibit, so we may be giving that one to you.
Put together a plan to reveal some of the original brightness."

He was talking to her like a professional, not a criminal. Emily's
spirits rose.

"Absolutely," she said eagerly. "I think the colors are really important to understanding the piece."

"Right," he said distractedly, and then added, with more interest, "How so?"

"Some people went to church just to see those bright colors. Especially in the winter, when everything else in their world was
brown."

He raised an eyebrow. "Where did you read that?"

"Um . . . I just think that must've been true. Most people couldn't
even afford colorful fabrics . . . you know?"

He tilted his head thoughtfully. "It's a good insight."

Emily basked in the compliment, completely undeserved as it
was. She was living with the world's most charming cheat sheet.

"They *loved* St. George back then," she added. "The St. George
Day festival was a big opportunity for the knights to parade in their
armor and show it off." Now both Terrence and Laurie were staring
at her in surprise.

Jason said, "I think we should add that to the notes. Send that
to me in an email, with cited sources."

"Will do." Surely, she could find a written source about it some-where.

Jason seemed to be trying to put them at ease, which Emily could only take as a good sign. After he left, she spent the rest of the afternoon considering cleaning solutions for polychromed wood.

It was almost enough to take her mind off the worry that Griffin might be recognized by someone, after all . . . and her worries about her upcoming online chat with the lawyer.

Late in the afternoon, Emily went to the small meeting room she'd reserved just for that Zoom. She closed the door firmly be-hind her and wished it would lock.

When she'd been with Griffin on the Riverwalk, she'd told him this meeting was a work thing. Technically, it hadn't been a lie. Be-sides, this meeting was just a precaution, and to set her parents' minds at ease.

She'd half expected a man in a suit with leather-bound books in the background. But Steve, a silver-haired man with glasses, wore a Hawaiian shirt and was sitting on his back deck drinking an iced tea.

"I've got a half hour," he said. "Anything we say here is confi-dential, so just tell me the truth. Karen tells me you were the one, uh, refurbishing the sculpture."

He asked several questions about her work background, how long she'd been working at the museum, and whether she'd ever been arrested or accused of any crime before. "And what have you told law enforcement so far?"

"Nothing."

He pursed his lips thoughtfully. "Good. Tell me exactly what happened the day of the theft."

Oh, boy. Maybe this had been a bad idea.

"Well, a little after ten thirty a.m., my friend Griffin came to visit me at the conservator labs."

"This is the guy in the suit of armor you were making out with," Steve said.

Emily felt the hot flush rise up to the roots of her hair.

"Yeah, they showed the TikTok on Fox News."

Oh no. Griffin was even more famous than she thought. She *never* should've brought him back to the museum.

"How did your friend get into the labs?" Steve asked. "Those are restricted, right?"

"I . . . don't know. I was in the photography room. Maybe someone else swiped him in."

"Maybe you could ask him," Steve suggested. "They said on the news that there was no security camera footage of your friend going in. Does that seem weird to you?"

"It does." *Weirder than you know.* "But I had nothing to do with an art theft."

Steve took a swig of his tea. "Have you known this Griffin long?"

"No, not long at all."

"Where did you meet him?"

"At the museum."

Steve set the glass down. "So he was a visitor there?"

"Yeah, he was . . . there for an exhibition."

"And you would categorize your relationship as, what? Dating?"

"Yeah." She'd better not leave it at that. "My parents don't know this, but he's moved in with me."

Steve's bushy eyebrows rose. "Do you know if this guy has a past?"

A strained laugh escaped her. *He sure does.*

"I mean, has he been involved in anything shady?"

Emily shook her head. "He's probably the most honest person I know."

She expected Steve to look skeptical, but he merely nodded and took another sip of beer. "Okay, million-dollar question: why was he wearing a suit of armor? Because between that detail and the fact that you were the last person to see the sculpture, it looks like . . ." He waved his bottle in the air. "Shenanigans."

"He's, um . . . He's auditioning at Medieval Legends. He was getting used to moving around in armor."

He stared at her for a beat. "The place with the sword fights? Eat baked potatoes with your hands?"

Emily nodded encouragingly.

"So he already auditioned?"

"No. He's going soon."

"Well, I guess it makes a *little* bit of sense," he grumbled doubtfully.

She'd be relieved to have Griffin get that job for so many reasons. He needed to have friends and work of his own, and she figured Medieval Legends was the one place where he could really be himself. And if he worked there, so many things about his story, such as the TikTok video that apparently the whole world had seen, would seem more logical.

Steve asked several other questions. He encouraged her not to discuss the theft over the phone, email, or text, in case something could be taken out of context. If the FBI or the police visited her apartment, she shouldn't let them in without a warrant, and if they asked her to step outside, she should decline. *Gladly*, Emily thought.

He shrugged. "But with a high-profile case like this, the FBI's not going to make an arrest without a confession or real evidence. They don't want to embarrass themselves."

Emily thanked him profusely before they logged off the Zoom, feeling more at peace than she had since the moment she'd turned on the morning news about the supposed theft.

Then she called Griffin, feeling a wave of relief when he picked up and told her he was still in the medieval armor gallery. Once she met him down there, he was telling two boys about the finer points of swords, literally.

Emily and Griffin left the museum, crossed the street, and

stepped into the crowded lobby of the Chicago Athletic Association building, which had been turned into a hotel. She took a moment to appreciate the black-and-white tile floor, the marble staircase, and the smells of grilled meats and garlic wafting from the ground floor restaurant.

She led him into the wooden-paneled elevator and they reached the rooftop bar. Its glass ceiling arched over well-dressed guests, like a greenhouse filled with flowers. Emily had been surprised that Rose had suggested the upscale restaurant for a happy hour, but it was hard to think of a nicer place for one. Rose had already texted Emily to say that she and Aaron were seated on the open terrace beyond, so Emily and Griffin made their way there.

Two different women stared appreciatively after Griffin as they passed. Well, a ball cap and a pair of glasses could only hide so much. The second one, who looked to be about Emily's age, caught his eye.

He inclined his head gallantly. "Good evening, my lady." She raised her eyebrows and gave a delighted smile.

Emily felt a tickle of familiar anxiety. This city was filled with beautiful, interesting, funny women. She had told herself many times that he'd soon realize that when it came to romance, he had almost limitless options . . . that she had good qualities, obviously, but in the end, there was nothing that made her truly special.

The fear didn't have the same choke hold on her that it once had, though. It was hard not to feel special when Griffin was complimenting her all the time.

"Emily! Griffin!" Rose stood and waved from a far table. She was wearing a white dress and what looked like a turquoise pendant necklace, and she'd put her hair up. Emily raised her hand in response, and they went over to join her and the new guy, who also got to his feet.

"My lady Rose," Griffin said warmly, and she gave him a quick hug.

"It's Aaron, right?" Emily asked, holding her hand out to the politely smiling man. He stood maybe five-ten, and he wore a blazer over a T-shirt and jeans; exactly how she'd expect a VP at Sotheby's to look, not that she'd ever seen one. "I'm Emily. I work at the museum with Rose."

"Yes, I think I saw you before. Nice to meet you—"

"I am Griffin de Beauford, a friend to my lady Rose of Pilsen," Griffin said, stepping forward, "and I hope you are courting her with honor and respect."

Rose flushed, and Emily didn't know whether to laugh or cringe.

Aaron didn't miss a beat. "Of course," he said sincerely. Rose was right; he did have a nice voice. "Good to meet you, Griffin." He reached out his hand, looking Griffin in the eye.

Well, that wasn't so bad. Maybe she should've prepared Griffin for socializing, but it wouldn't feel right to tell a grown man how to talk and behave . . . how to fit in. People shouldn't have to try so hard to fit in; especially wonderful people like Griffin.

At least she'd taught him how to shake hands. As he shook Aaron's, his gaze wandered toward the horizon, and he went a little pale. "I did not know we'd ascended so high."

Aaron tilted his head. "Where are you from, Griffin, if you don't mind my asking?"

"A distant island," he replied. Rose shot Emily a wry look.

"What part?" Aaron asked pleasantly. "I'm pretty well traveled. I might've been there before."

Griffin gave him an ironic smile. "Sir, you have not." He peered down at the buildings and the lake below. "I suppose it must be safe."

"It is," Emily reassured him. "Let's sit down." He obeyed, and the rest of them took their seats, too, but Griffin couldn't stop staring out at the spectacular view. Hundreds of lights twinkled below them in the blue twilight.

"Um, can I get you two some drinks?"

Emily turned to see the server looking from her to Griffin. "Yes, I'll have a glass of rosé," she said.

"An ale for me, good woman," Griffin said, "but not bitter, if you please." Emily regretted bringing home the IPA for him, but she'd never been a beer drinker, and Tom had always drunk IPAs. Griffin had told her, politely, that it tasted like bile.

The server's brow knitted, and she pointed to the neglected menu on the table. "We have several ales."

"You might like Dovetail lager," Aaron suggested to Griffin. "It's made here in Chicago."

"I will have that, then."

"Make it two," Aaron said easily. "And let's get some appetizers. Rose—you love avocados. Avocado toast with goat cheese?"

She beamed. "Um, that sounds great."

Aaron told the server, "Two of those, the smoked salmon dip, and one order of the fried potatoes." He glanced around at them. "Anything else?" He flashed a self-deprecating smile. "It's on me, so go nuts." As they shook their heads, he added to the server, "Hey, extra pistachios on the avocado toast, please." She nodded as she retreated.

Griffin had gotten out of his seat again and had wandered closer to the edge of the balcony. She couldn't exactly tell him to sit down, could she? She'd sound like his mom.

"My friends, what is that strange thing?" he asked, looking back at them. "'Tis like a giant raindrop wrought of silver."

Emily gave a ridiculous little gasp. "You didn't see it before!" Major tour guide fail.

Aaron got up and went over to Griffin, gazing down along with him. "That, my friend, is one of the most famous sights in Chicago. It's a steel sculpture. Everyone calls it The Bean."

"I marvel that a thing so large and so smooth could be made of steel."

"It wasn't easy," Aaron said. "We're very proud of it."

Aaron clapped Griffin on the shoulder—and Emily's heart squeezed to see it. Griffin had told her that when he'd been a statue, he'd treasured even the most incidental of human touches. Aaron wasn't acting as though Griffin was odd. She exchanged an approving glance with Rose as Aaron sat down next to her again.

The server returned with the drinks, and Griffin sat down, too. Aaron held up his glass. "May we live all the days of our lives."

"Yes!" Griffin said, a little too loudly. They all clinked glasses. Rose's eyes sparkled.

Okay, that was smooth of Aaron, Emily thought. Maybe she'd steal that toast. He made her feel like they were out with a proper grown-up, which made no sense. She was thirty-four, for God's sake. In Griffin's time, she would've been a matron.

"Rose said she met you at the food trucks by the museum," Emily said to Aaron.

He chuckled. "That's right. It was the first time I ever asked a complete stranger out on a date."

Rose's mouth formed an astonished O. "Really?"

He gave her a sheepish look and a shrug, and then went on, "I follow the Art Institute social media accounts, so I recognized her from a couple of interviews. And she was standing there, so pretty in her Stevie Nicks dress . . ." Rose beamed. "We started talking, and I couldn't help myself." His cheeks and the tips of his ears flushed.

That was adorable. Still, a jarring thought crossed Emily's mind. What if he was married? She was probably being paranoid, after being married to a cheater. But he *looked* married.

She asked, "So have you always been single, or . . . ?"

"No, my wife and I broke up. I mean, I'm divorced," he said, as though admitting something embarrassing. "I have been for a few years now."

Rose gave a nervous laugh. "We don't have to cross-examine him."

"It's fine," Aaron said to her. "It didn't come up the other day." His expression told Emily that he knew exactly what this was: a group interview for the position of being Rose's boyfriend. But so far, she'd have to say he was killing it.

"I'm divorced, too," Emily offered. "Pretty recently."

Griffin's arm went around her shoulders. Warmth spread through her. Maybe part of it was the wine. But being divorced had made her feel like a failure and a cliché, even though she knew, on an intellectual level, how antiquated and ridiculous that was. And Griffin chased away those feelings.

"Sorry to hear," Aaron said.

"I don't know if I am," she quipped. "So you work at Sotheby's? It's a pretty small office here in Chicago, right?"

"It is, but I work for the New York office. I used to be a private art dealer here, and I started working remotely with them during the pandemic. It just stayed that way." He shrugged.

"Are a lot of your old clients here?" Rose asked.

He shook his head. "Most of my clients are international. One of them was texting me the other day about the theft here at the museum. I bet all your coworkers are freaking out about that."

The back of Emily's neck prickled. Before she could stop herself, she darted a look at Griffin, just as his smile faded.

"Well, it's been crazy," she said, picking up her wineglass again. "I mean, it's not the first time anything's been stolen from the museum, of course."

"Is that right?"

"Yeah, in the 1970s three Cézannes were stolen. We got them back, though."

Aaron snapped his fingers. "Oh, yeah, I heard about that. Who stole them?"

"It was someone in packing and shipping."

The server arrived with plates of pistachio-crusted avocado toast, smoked salmon dip with little golden toasts, and fried potatoes drizzled with a garlicky sauce.

"Okay, we're going to need one more of those," Aaron said, pointing at the potatoes, and then asked Rose, "Another glass of wine?" She barely had the chance to nod before he said, "Another glass of the sauvignon blanc." As the server retreated, Aaron added to Griffin, holding up his own glass, "How do you like the lager?"

Griffin smiled. "'Tis fit for a king."

Aaron took another drink himself. "My dad always makes fun of me for drinking craft beer. When I was growing up, he always came home from the tractor factory and had a Michelob."

Rose did a double take. "Wait. You mean Caterpillar?"

Aaron nodded. "I grew up in Peoria." Emily had never been there, even though it was less than three hours south.

"You didn't strike me as a Peoria guy," Rose said.

"Don't be a snob," Aaron teased.

"I'm not!" Rose exclaimed. "My dad worked for Caterpillar, too. But there was a layoff, when I was in third grade, and, um, he died after that."

"Oh no," Emily said, at the same time that Aaron said, "That's awful. I'm so sorry."

"Thanks. That's when we moved to Cicero."

"Does your mom still live there?"

"Um, no." Rose's brow knitted. "She, she died a few years ago."

Emily's heart went out to Rose. It must've been so hard to lose both parents, both too soon. Emily was so lucky that her parents' biggest concerns were knee surgery and becoming grandparents someday.

They didn't even know she was living with a man now. What would they think? He was the opposite of the kind of normal, stable, insurance-selling guy they'd recommended.

"I'm sorry," Aaron said. "Why did you all move to Cicero? Do you have other family here?"

Rose shook her head. "She got a job at a factory, but it closed when they went overseas."

"That's bullshit," Aaron declared. "See, this is why people steal art." Emily had to smile. Not that she approved of art theft, obviously. She was probably more against it than most people. But it was just a joke.

Aaron pursed his lips thoughtfully. "You know, compared to the Cézannes, the sculpture isn't that big of a deal. The museum had just bought it." He shrugged. "It wasn't culturally significant."

Emily sat up a little straighter in her seat. "It was an amazing piece." She should really change the subject, but she couldn't help herself. "If it hadn't gone missing, it would've been one of the most beloved pieces in the collection."

"Really, you think so?" Aaron's voice was curious rather than challenging.

Emily glanced at Griffin again. "It had that certain something that only a few pieces of art do."

"You saw it up close?"

He didn't know, then. Oh, well. Rose would've told him sooner or later, anyway. "I *worked* on it. The detail was incredible. And it had a very clear provenance."

"Oh, yeah, it's still worth a fortune." He shrugged. "Of course, it would've been covered by the museum insurance. And I almost feel like the thieves deserve a big payday."

"Why?" Emily's voice came out at a higher pitch than she'd intended.

"This is the greatest art theft in all of human history. The size of the statue. The fact that it was taken from a major museum in broad daylight. The thieves had to be *brilliant*. The theft is almost a work of art unto itself." He took a bite of fried potato. "It's got to be earmarked for an overseas buyer. I just wonder if they're getting enough for it." He gave a wry smile. "To be honest, my client in Greece was texting me to say he'd pay several million dollars for it."

"Oh my God," Emily murmured.

Griffin frowned and leaned forward. "Have you sold other stolen goods to this friend?"

Good question, Emily couldn't help but think. But also a pretty insulting one. Rose shot a worried look in Aaron's direction.

Something flickered in Aaron's eyes. "Not as far as I know." Emily's hackles went up. But in the next breath, he said, "I always do my due diligence. But even great museums have been known to make questionable acquisitions."

"That's true," Emily admitted. Art authentication wasn't an exact science.

Aaron shrugged. "Enough talk about work. Rose, I want to know more about you."

He asked her questions and listened attentively, making flattering comments here and there. When Rose talked about where she'd gone to college, it prompted Griffin to ask Emily quietly about her own education. She told him about dorm rooms and frat parties; since Aaron seemed completely wrapped up in whatever Rose was saying, Griffin told Emily about Latin tutors and his year at Oxford. But when Rose started talking about more arcane subjects, it got their attention again.

"One of my favorite things is my chrysocolla necklace. It helps you exude your goddess energy," she was explaining to Aaron, gesturing gracefully.

Griffin asked, "And why do you not wear it every day, my lady?"

Rose hesitated, and Aaron said lightly, "I don't know if the world could handle your goddess energy on a regular basis."

Rose's eyes sparkled. "But if you wear it sometimes, it helps you attract the right people."

"Were you wearing it when I met you?"

"I was, actually."

How strange that a short time ago, Emily had rolled her eyes inwardly at Rose's talk about the metaphysical powers of stones. Seeing a stone turn into a person right in front of one's eyes made it hard for a person to remain a skeptic. And Emily had been holding the malachite Rose had given her when she'd kissed Griffin.

A minute later, Rose said, "Emily, do you know where the ladies' room is?"

"Yeah, I'll go with you." Emily had no idea where it was, but she guessed that Rose wanted to talk about Aaron. She didn't have to worry about abandoning Griffin. If Aaron found Griffin's *my lady*-ing and so on strange, he was too polite to say anything about it. Between Aaron's easy social skills and Griffin's outgoing nature, they seemed to get along fine.

As soon as the restroom door closed behind them, Rose turned to her, "He seems good, right? I've had some bad experiences. Like last year with this guy, Jake the Snake." She shook her head.

Emily couldn't help it. "His name was Jake the Snake, and that wasn't a red flag?"

"People called him that because he had five pet snakes."

For Emily, that also might've been a red flag, but Rose was open-minded. It was one of the things Emily had already come to appreciate about her.

"Well, Aaron's no Jake the Snake," she told Rose.

Rose narrowed her eyes in thought. "But does he seem . . . off? Maybe *too* perfect?"

"Is there such a thing?"

"Of course, you don't think so, with your knight in shining armor."

Emily's stomach twisted in a little knot. Rose's date with Aaron was solid—*real*. Her affair, or whatever she should call it, with

Griffin, still felt fragile. She felt like a conservator of it, too; fearful of exposing it to the grime of too much reality.

They stepped back out onto the rooftop. The twilight had given way to black velvet night, the city lights glittering like stolen diamonds. She was in *her* city, the one she'd always loved, on a perfect night with new friends, and the whole summer ahead of her.

As they walked back to their table, Griffin was leaning forward in his seat as he spoke to Aaron, who was on the edge of his seat himself, nodding seriously, and not breaking eye contact with him. What in the world? Maybe the guys were talking about *them*. That would only be fair.

Griffin looked up and met her gaze, and the corners of his lips turned up in a roguish smile.

Maybe this was a dream she'd wake up from, just like she had the first time she'd met him, but before she did, she was going to enjoy every minute of it.

Twenty

As soon as Emily and Griffin got back to the apartment, he started kissing her. She pulled away to tell him she had to take Andy outside and she wanted to take a bath first.

"I will take him," Griffin said. "You bathe."

"Okay."

"When I return, may I watch you bathe?"

Emily laughed. Griffin made her feel so confident, she almost said yes, but she wanted to shave in private. "Maybe next time."

After her bath, she put on her robe, noticing that Andy was dozing at the foot of her bed. When she came out into the living room, she found Griffin sitting on the sofa, bent over a paperback with a rapt expression.

"What are you reading?" she asked. He'd spent a lot of time reading already, but those had been history books.

He held up the red and black cover. A romance novel.

"Oh!" she said. "That's, um, that's a spicy one."

He set it on the coffee table. "It is very good. Do you have more like this?"

She laughed. "Actually, yeah, but they're on my phone."

"I would very much like to read them and learn all I can about bedsport."

She felt a smile spread across her face . . . and a flutter in her belly. "Is that right?" She sat down on the sofa next to him. "Well, I know you love to learn."

"Aye, but I cannot learn from books alone," he said, feigning earnestness. "I am certain that I need a great deal of practice and instruction."

"Hey, that goes both ways. I want to learn more about what *you* like, too."

His gaze traveled over her. "You know what I like. You, naked."

"I'm sure it's a little more complicated than that."

He shrugged. "I am a simple man from a simpler time."

She laughed again, and he did, too. "I'm just saying that when it comes to the bedroom, there are lots of possibilities."

He took her hand and turned it over to stroke the inside of her forearm and wrist lightly with one finger. "What kinds of possibilities, my sweet cinnamon?"

The deep rumble in his voice and the delicate caress made her shiver. "I don't know. I mean, maybe sometime you'd like me to be on top?"

"Can you do that?" he asked with such blatant amazement that she pressed her lips together to stop herself from giggling. She didn't want him to think she was laughing *at* him.

"Aye, of course you can," he added with a faraway expression, clearly imagining it.

"If that would feel too weird to you, though—"

"Nay, I would like that very much." He stared at her intently. "What else, my lady?"

Her cheeks heated. "Well, I could . . . You know how you go

down on me?" She gestured. How had he referred to it? "Tasting the . . ."

"Aye," he said, understanding. "Yes. I love to *go down* on you." He repeated it, she could tell, so he would remember her term for it.

"Well, I could be on top for that, too. Like, kneeling over your face . . . ?"

"We must do this." The hoarse edge to his voice startled her.

She was turning him on. Not just a little. Seriously turning him on.

Oh my God. I'm talking dirty. She'd never thought of herself as someone who did that. Not that she thought it was wrong; she'd just never had the confidence. But now she was doing it accidentally.

And . . . well, it was turning her on, too. Maybe it was no wonder, since she was talking about sex to a very horny knight.

He shifted where he sat, his gaze raking over her. "What else?"

"I mean, obviously I could . . ." Why was she acting like a Sunday school teacher? She'd already taught him that word, after all. "Suck your cock." This time, his astonished expression took her aback. "You *must* know about that."

"Aye, I do, but I knew not that you might perform such a base act."

This was way too much fun. "Base?" she asked innocently. "So you wouldn't want me to do it?"

He gave a choked laugh. "Although I said base, I would feel exalted."

It was all the invitation she needed.

She stood up and let the robe fall to the floor. When she'd been with Tom, she'd liked to get undressed in the dark, but Griffin's desire for her made her feel bold and free.

"You look like Eve in the garden," he murmured.

An image popped into her head: a particular depiction of Eve, from an illuminated German Bible from around his era. She *did* look like that Eve.

During his time, Eve, and other naked women, had usually been depicted with small breasts and a bit of a belly. She'd assumed Griffin was being hyperbolic, with his talk of goddesses and such. But he'd been used to images like that. And somehow, in all her studies, she'd missed a very important concept: Eve and the other ladies had been portrayed in that way because men thought it was *hot*.

In fact, there was *no* kind of body that had not been considered hot. The busty hourglass sculptures of ancient India. The plump nymphs of Peter Paul Rubens—pellucid cellulite and all. The boyish flappers in fashion illustrations from the Jazz Age. Now that she considered it, she just happened to match the late medieval ideal.

And as she stood in front of him, with nothing on her body except his hungry, worshipful gaze, she felt an unfamiliar and glorious sense of beauty and power.

Smiling, she joined him on the sofa again—her knees on either side of his thighs this time, her arms wrapped around him—and bent down to kiss him, her hair falling like a curtain on either side of her face. She reached down to undo his jeans. A low sound came from deep in his throat as he grabbed the back of her head to pull her closer in, forcing her mouth open with his, invading it.

His desire turned her insides to liquid heat. He might have all the courtly words and manners of his time, but he also had its fierceness. His fingers sank into her hair and tightened, pulling on it. If he'd been any other man, his roughness might have scared her. But she trusted him. Griffin would never hurt her.

He broke off the kiss and took hold of her sides, urging her upward a bit to kiss her breasts. She let out a soft, high-pitched *ohh* and her legs trembled beneath her. Feeling unsteady, she gripped his shoulder for support with one hand, and with the other, she stroked his glorious blond hair. He bit her lightly, a sensation right between pain and pleasure that made her gasp.

"Oh God."

She was already aching for him. A glance down confirmed that his cock stood ready, tinged violet-red. She moved to lower herself onto him, but he still held on to her tightly, preventing her. When she met his eyes, questioning, she found them dark with need.

"Take me into your mouth," he said, his voice low and harsh. "As you said before."

Right. She'd somehow forgotten that. He was going to drive her crazy with delaying. But then . . . she could do the same to him, and it would only be fair. Still shaky, she got off the sofa and knelt between his feet, pulling at his hips to urge him to the edge of the seat. He immediately moved, giving her perfect access, half lying back as if lounging indolently on a throne but staring down at her.

In a moment of risqué inspiration, she reached between her thighs to slick her fingers with wetness, then wrapped her hand around his girth. He rewarded her with an amazed groan. She stroked him a couple of times before swirling her tongue around the straining tip.

"Christ Jesus," he hissed.

She took as much of him as she could. He straightened up enough to touch her hair.

Ugh, he'd better not push on her head. Tom had done that—not just once, which would've been forgivable, but a second time after she'd pushed his hand away.

He only gripped her hair again. To her surprise, she liked that tug at her scalp and his intensity behind it. Being on her knees on the bare wooden floor, pleasing him, hearing him panting with pleasure, made the throb between her legs almost unbearable, even as another part of her felt satisfied.

She couldn't tell him, *I love you*. She didn't trust her luck or her judgment enough to believe it . . . or at least, to believe that it would end in anything but heartbreak. But she could show him, in no uncertain terms, how deeply she felt for him.

"Sweet Christ," he uttered on a groan, and then his muscles tensed. "Stop now, or I shall not be able to stop myself."

She lifted her head up, stroking him with her hand again. "Go ahead," she encouraged. "Do it." To make her meaning clear, she licked the tip again. Doing this always turned her on, and this time it was unbearable. She wanted him inside her so badly it almost hurt. But even more than that, she wanted to put him first.

"Nay." He gave a quick shake of his head. His tight expression, somewhere between agony and ecstasy, thrilled her. "Stand up."

She obeyed. "You want to go back to the bedroom?" She wasn't against it.

He shook his head, but then wrapped his arm around her waist, pulling her in that direction . . . What *was* he doing?

The next thing she knew, she was facing the back of the sofa, and his hand was on her back, urging her to bend over.

Oh. My. God. Even though she knew by now he wasn't all genteel words and flourishes, she hadn't expected this. His hands gripped her hips; his foot pushed against the inside of hers, urging her to a wider stance. She complied immediately, dying for him by that point. She felt thrilled that he hadn't taken her up on her earlier offer of coming in her mouth, as sincerely as she'd meant it.

"Look at you," he murmured.

She could only imagine what he was seeing: her brown hair tumbling around her on the sofa cushions and the pale expanse of her bare back as she was bent over for him, waiting and ready. His large, warm palm stroked down her spine, then rounded the curve of her ass. She whimpered and wriggled against him impatiently.

He reached around to cup her and then gave an appreciative growl. "So wet for me."

No kidding! "Griffin, please . . ."

He pressed harder there, moving in circles.

"Oh!" Her pleasure spiraled upward. He shifted behind her, and she begged, "Please don't stop yet." She was close, but she might not get there if he entered her now and took his hand away . . .

His hand stayed right there, circling at her most sensitive place, as he thrust into her.

"Griffin," she breathed. The delicious intensity built even as he filled her completely, once, several times. "Yes!" And then she let out a sharp cry as her orgasm rocked her, making her squeeze around him. It seemed to go on and on. She went limp against the sofa. *So good . . .*

His fingers dug into her hips as he plunged deep into her.

"Ahh . . ." It was almost too much. He was so thick and hard. A lock of her hair fell in her face, and she flicked it away. In the next moment, he bent over her to gather up her hair and toss it over the opposite shoulder. Considerate, for a man who had her bent over her sofa.

The naughtiness of the position added to her pleasure as he drove into her with sure, even strokes. He caressed her ass, and she raised one foot off the floor to rub against the back of his calf, not being able to touch him in any other way from this angle. But he could do anything he wanted to her. He reached around to cup her in front again without pausing in his rhythm. The welcome friction made her let out a little shriek.

"Does that please you, my cinnamon?" His baritone voice seemed to rumble through her body.

"Ahh . . ." He surely didn't expect a coherent answer at this point.

He pulled almost all the way out, moving his hand to her hip. *Fuck*. She restrained herself from actually grinding against the back of the sofa.

"I asked, does that please you?" His voice was dark, deep velvet.

Oh. He *did* expect an answer. "Yes! Griffin, please . . ."

She pushed back into him, but he caught her hips in his hands to prevent her, still only barely inside her. So it was going to be like that. She swallowed. It was easy to imagine him enjoying her helpless agitation.

"Call me the other thing." His voice was quieter, but no less deep and no less devastating.

Oh God, what other thing? "Sweetheart," she begged. He rubbed her ass again, in a slow circle. What? . . . *Oh*. "My lord, *please*."

With a gravelly sound in the back of his throat, he drove into her again.

"Ah!" she cried out in relief. "Yes . . ."

His hand found its place again, teasing her clit as he, well, swived her. He coaxed a few more *pleases* out of her, and even another *my lord*, and then—

"Yes!" Okay, maybe that *was* a scream, but it was his fault. She went limp on the sofa as the aftershocks of the climax shuddered through her. Nothing had ever felt that good in her *life*.

He gripped her hips with both hands and pounded into her with a madman's frenzy. His intensity left her gasping. He growled a word or two she couldn't make out . . . French? With a wordless shout, he climaxed, pumping into her.

Oh, wow. Stunned, she stretched her hand back toward him, touching his thigh as he pulled out of her.

He reached down for her, his panting breath warm on her skin, and gathered her up into a standing position against him. His arms were wrapped around her, and he pressed fervent kisses on her neck, her cheek, her hair. With her back against his chest, she could feel his ragged breaths. She moved to turn and face him, and he loosened his grip at once to permit her, then embraced her again and let his forehead come to rest on hers.

He raised his hand to caress her cheek. "My dearest lady."

She gave an unsteady laugh. The ardor in his tone wasn't exactly what she'd expected after him drilling her like a jackhammer. She thought dizzily, a knight in the streets, a freak in the . . . well, living room. He did *not* need much instruction, though he could have as much practice as he liked.

"I need to sit down," she realized aloud. She went around to the front of the sofa and wrapped herself up in the throw before curling up.

He sat next to her, frowning. "Is anything amiss?"

"What? No!" She'd had, hands down—literally hands down, on the sofa cushions—the best sex of her life. "My legs were just shaky."

"I was too rough," he guessed.

"No!" She laughed and kissed him on the cheek. "That was *fantastic*. In case you didn't gather that from my, you know, loud orgasms."

He nodded. "In my mind's eye I had seen us doing these things. 'Twas your wicked tongue that emboldened me."

"Now wait a minute," she said, laughing. "You like my wicked tongue."

He groaned. "That I do, my lady, more than I can say."

Twenty-One

On Tuesday morning, Emily left Café Libre, the place Laurie had recommended, with a to-go tray in her hand. She wanted to get on Laurie's and Terrence's good side—or at least, Laurie's *less* bad side—even if it meant going out of her way to a hipster coffeehouse.

As she walked to the museum, she took a sip of her own dark roast. *Hmm.* It really was less bitter . . . and to her annoyance and amusement, she *did* like it better. Maybe because she was no longer bitter herself.

She set it back in the tray, fished her phone out of her bag, and called Griffin.

"Good morning, my lady," he answered immediately. "I am in the Uber."

She smiled to herself. That was exactly what she'd wanted to know. "Great."

Earlier that morning, it had taken her over an hour to get the ride hailing app set up on his phone with his name and her credit card. She'd spent even longer teaching him how to use it.

"I have my card, too," he added, meaning his driver's license.

"Then you're all set! Do you feel ready?" The faint strains of a blues song mingled with the morning traffic, and she pressed the phone harder to her ear.

"Aye, my lady. I am eager to join Medieval Legends."

"You're their dream knight!" she gushed. The smells of freshly baked bread and buttercream hit her as she passed the bakery, quickly followed by a blast of diesel exhaust from the bus pulling away from the curb. "You already know how to ride a horse and handle a sword and do *everything*. Plus, you're so handsome, and they'll like the long hair." She turned onto Michigan Avenue and approached the musicians who often performed on that corner: a Black guy playing the keyboard and a foot-operated drum kit while singing, and a white guy playing electric guitar.

"Just be sure to be nice to everyone," she added to Griffin.

"I am always nice, unless anyone offers insult."

"Right. I'm just saying . . . if it *seems* like someone's offering insult, they might not be." She stepped around a middle-aged man with a backpack who had stopped on the sidewalk to dance, not surprisingly—those guys were good. As always, they displayed a corrugated cardboard sign with their Venmo account; she made a mental note to send them something, which she'd done once before. She told Griffin, "And just do what you're told. I mean *exactly*."

"I fought a war, my dove. I know there are times when one must follow orders."

"Of course. They're going to *love* you."

In the office, Terrence was especially appreciative of the coffee. He'd worked very late the night before finishing the Bruges window. Emily and Laurie both went to his worktable to admire the completed piece. In a scene of brilliant colors—ruby, cobalt, aquamarine, and violet—Sir Morien of the Round Table, recognizable for his ebony complexion and armor, was being knighted by King Arthur.

Emily went to her scheduled meeting with Jason in his office. Although she had fleeting thoughts of being fired on the spot, or perhaps even being turned over to the feds, her nerves settled as they had a perfectly normal discussion about her symposium presentation, *Dating Medieval Sculpture.*

Then Jason said, "You've probably been wondering about whether this contract will lead to full-time work."

Emily managed a smile. "It would be a dream come true to continue. But I know the circumstances have made it weird." She hadn't even gotten to prove herself, since her main project had gallivanted out the door.

Jason nodded. "I've made the case for another head count, but two people on the board are against it, for obvious reasons. It's on the agenda for tomorrow."

She suddenly felt shaky. "Is there anything I can do?"

He shook his head. "Everyone knows that nothing showed up on the security camera footage, and it's pretty clear the FBI couldn't find any incriminating evidence in the labs. I've been making the case all along that the employees are the victims here."

That was good of him, but still, her spirits fell to the floor. "Do *all* of them think I'm an art thief?" she asked, because she really had nothing else to lose.

"None of them are convinced of it. For one thing, the press hasn't been able to find any ties between you and organized crime." It was the first she'd heard of anyone pointing out reasons she might be innocent, and it made her feel a tiny bit better. "A few of the board members like the Russian theory, actually."

"I haven't heard about that one." She dared to ask, "What theory do *you* like?"

He paused and glanced up at the door. It was closed, though glass windows made his office visible to the rest of the office.

"I'm usually a fan of Occam's razor," he said. "You know what that is, right?"

"Of course. The simplest explanation is most often correct."

The hairs rose on the back of her neck. *Did he know?* Were they going to talk about this?

He said, "I want to ask you about something, and I promise I'll keep it completely confidential."

"Sure," she said quickly. It would be such a relief to talk to him about it.

"Was there anything strange about that sculpture?"

She'd been hoping for a more specific question, along the lines of, *Did that sculpture happen to come to life?*

What would he do if she told him this? He might think she was out of her mind. She couldn't have that. At the very least, she wanted to use him for a reference.

"It wasn't a normal sculpture," she said. "I mean, it had this energy . . ." She felt like she was betraying Griffin, calling him an *it*. "He felt like a real person, trapped in stone."

Jason nodded slowly. "And what theory do *you* like about it disappearing?"

In a light tone, as if it were a joke, she answered, "Oh, I think it just walked away."

Laurie appeared at the glass window and gave a wave. They'd run overtime and her regular one-on-one with Jason was next. Emily stood up, Jason told her to be fifteen minutes early for the symposium talk for a sound check, and then she went back to her desk.

There were other museums in Chicago, she reminded herself. This could just be a temporary setback. She'd worked at Bath and Body Works before, so she could do something like that again in the meantime. Or with her chemistry degree, she might be able to get a lab assistant job, as her father had suggested. Medieval Legends was almost certainly going to hire Griffin. Between the two of them, they'd get by.

Unless she went to jail, of course.

There's no evidence, she reminded herself for the thousandth time. None whatsoever. Yes, she looked suspicious, having worked on the sculpture and having kissed a knight in shining armor in the gallery . . . but the lawyer had said that his audition was a *slightly* plausible explanation for his wearing armor.

She really hoped the audition went well. Medieval Legends was the only job she could think of that wouldn't require him to mask his old-world speech and courtly manners. If he worked there, so many things would make more sense.

D eep in the suburbs, Griffin got out of the Uber and, before he forgot, fiddled with the buttons to pay the driver the extra money he was owed. He looked up at the large castle of pale, smooth stone. Across the front, large letters spelled out **MEDIEVAL LEGENDS**. A shiver went through his nerves.

Yes, he knew how to ride and how to fight, but that had been centuries ago. They probably did everything differently here. *Do exactly what you're told*, Emily had said . . . but did she even realize how much he still struggled with their modern English? How he sometimes nodded and smiled while having no idea what he'd been told?

His heart kicked into a gallop, enraging him. He'd fought in deadly battles, and now he feared this? He had been the lord of a manor—his father's property, by law, but his in practice—and the honored heir at the earl's even grander hall, a castle in all but name. He had once dined at the king's table! He wouldn't allow himself to be cowed.

He considered calling his new friend, Aaron, who would surely bolster his confidence. Griffin hadn't found the chance to tell

Emily yet that he'd confided in Aaron about the truth of his existence; how he'd been cursed and turned into stone, and how he'd come to life again. Aaron had been so amiable and so interested in the statue, and as he seemed to be a worthy gentleman, Griffin had wanted him to know about Rose's part in this miracle.

Aaron had expressed no doubt in his story whatsoever. Once Emily learned this, she wouldn't mind that Griffin had talked about it. Aaron had put his name and number in Griffin's phone, and had put Griffin's in his own, saying they must talk more soon.

Car doors slammed behind Griffin and he turned. Two men, one wiry with long black hair, and one shorter and stouter, with light brown hair and the beginnings of a beard, approached, walking toward the front door.

"I gotta say, this is pretty cringe," the shorter one was saying.

"All actors have embarrassing early gigs," his companion said.

What were actors doing here? Maybe this establishment also employed them as jesters. Griffin pretended to stare at his phone so he could keep listening.

The shorter one went on to say, "There's paying your dues, and then there's pretending to sword fight for a bunch of kids."

"It's not going to be *all* kids."

Emily hadn't told him that the knights of Medieval Legends were *actors*, and she hadn't said it was for an audience of children. Why hadn't she?

Because if he'd known, he would've refused.

"If I get in, I'm not telling my dad," the shorter one said as they walked past Griffin. "He'd be humiliated."

The image of his own father's face, with an all-too-familiar expression of disapproval, came into Griffin's mind. Heat rose on the back of his neck. This was not a respectable exhibition of sparring, but some kind of foolish play. He followed the two men to keep listening.

"Yeah, for actors, this is kind of the lowest of the low," the taller fellow agreed. "Unless you get to play the king or queen."

The ragged traveling troupes of actors in his time had loved playing kings and queens, too, in order to mock them, even though they were sometimes arrested for it. As part of the performance, they'd pretend to piss or shit, let out very real farts, or pantomime swiving the servants or donkeys, inspiring vulgar cries and hoots of laughter from the commoners who gathered.

These were the roles the men aspired to?

The first man snorted. "I hear you have to be a squire for two years before you can even be a knight."

Thunderstruck, Griffin stopped short and stared after them.

Was it possible that he, at thirty years old, would be asked to be a *squire*? No, not even that, though he had not been one since he was seventeen, but to *play* one as a degenerate actor?

What could've been more humiliating? Mucking out stalls? No, that would've been dignified by comparison. Catching rats? How could she have put him up to this?

The insult coursed through his veins as he took out his phone again and called for another driver. Another man walked past him, giving him a nod of greeting. There for the trials, too, Griffin supposed. What had the world come to, that men would compete for the chance to be an actor?

He stood in the middle of the parking lot waiting, feeling forsaken, his heart broken. Did she think so little of him that she thought this was the best he could do?

When Emily let herself into the apartment that evening, Andy bounded over to her as always, but Griffin sat on the sofa and looked up to her, unsmiling. Her heart sank.

All day, she'd been imagining him doing well at the auditions.

When she'd called him in the middle of the afternoon, he hadn't picked up. She'd told herself that was a good sign—he hadn't been sent home after a first cut or something like that—and had ignored the apprehension coiling in her gut.

"Hey," she said weakly. "How's it going?"

He just stared at her. What in the world? Frustration mingled with her disappointment. She came over to the sofa.

"How were the tryouts?" She didn't want to assume the worst.

"I did not go."

"*What?*"

She hadn't meant to, but she'd raised her voice in shock. Forcing herself to speak more normally, she said, "Did the driver not come? You were supposed to call me . . . Oh no, did your phone run out of minutes?"

"The driver came, and I rode to the castle." His gaze on her was flat. "I did not go in."

Ugh! There went their whole story of why he'd been cavorting in the museum in his armor on the day of the supposed theft. It still would've been a huge coincidence, but it was at least an *explanation*. One that she'd already given to the lawyer. Basically, she was going to look like a liar.

Emily wrapped her arms tightly around her midsection, as if it could pull in her frustration and bewilderment. "Why didn't you do it? You got nervous?"

"No!" The anger in his tone made her jump. "You think I would be fearful of that?"

How *dare* he yell at her? If anyone should be mad, it should be her. He was the one who was supposed to go and get a job.

"So you took a car all the way out there and then just . . . took a car home again?"

His jaw was locked. "Yes."

"Griffin, that cost more than a hundred dollars!" All this expense, and he wasn't even apologizing to her about it. Not to mention she'd spent a lot of time teaching him how to use the app. "Why didn't you audition? We talked about this a bunch of times!"

"It is beneath me."

Emily's blood heated. "Oh, I've heard that one before," she muttered.

Griffin got to his feet. "Do you compare me to that of a former husband of yours?"

There was a desperate sheen in his eyes, warning her that this could get out of hand, but she didn't know how to lower the tension. "No! I'm just saying that job is literally perfect for you!"

His face flushed with anger. "Think you so? Then you see me the lowest of the low. And what is worse, you did not even tell me! I have trusted you with all my heart, to my folly."

Whatever he was talking about, it was a mean thing to say. From the time he'd visited her in his dream, she'd done everything she could to help him.

He went on to proclaim, "Yet you urged me on my way to this false castle without once saying that they were *actors*."

"They're not actors!" She threw her hands up in the air. "They're jousters and riders . . . I mean, yeah, I guess they're actors, but they're doing all the things you're good at!"

His jaw was set in a rigid way she'd never seen before. "Two men there said it was the lowest rung of acting."

"Oh my God," she said helplessly. "It's not Hollywood, but it looked like a fun job. And you said before that you would do *any* labor."

"I did not say *any*."

It was true. He'd said something about his dignity. But could he stop thinking about his precious dignity for a moment and think about her?

She locked her hands and put them on top of her head. "In your time, did you have the expression *beggars can't be choosers*?"

"You admit that you see me as a beggar." His voice had dropped lower. "I am a learned man, and the son of an earl besides."

"Which means *nothing* now."

He flinched. *Good.* Because it was true. She was worried about losing her job, worried that he'd made a liar of her to a lawyer, and okay, she hadn't exactly talked to him about these things, but that was because she hadn't wanted to worry him, and was it too much to ask for him to try to get a job he was actually very qualified for?

He stood up and walked to the window, as if he couldn't stand to be closer to her.

"You are sorely provoking me," he said.

She stared at his back disbelievingly. "How are *you* angry with *me*? After all I've done for you?"

A horrible dread rolled over her. She'd sacrificed everything for Tom, and it hadn't meant anything to him.

"Ugh," she muttered. "I am so done with this." She hadn't been put on this earth to support men who didn't even appreciate it.

After Tom, all she'd wanted was a stable, sensible man. One who kept his commitments. Griffin was the exact opposite of stable and sensible. And she still hadn't minded, as long as he said pretty words to her and swept her off her feet. Right now, he wasn't doing that, either. He'd let her down, and he was being a jerk about it.

She'd suspected all along that his infatuation with her would wear off. It had always been too good to be true. Had suspected, in fact, that it wasn't real in the first place, but just a by-product, first of desperation, and then of the general excitement over being alive again. Maybe now the bloom was off the rose.

Griffin still stared out the window. "You do not respect me," he said in a cold voice that stung her to the core. She'd never thought he would talk to her like that.

Her emotions had gotten out of control, and his, too. She'd been in enough fights with Tom to know that there was no point continuing when they were both so upset. It broke her heart that she was fighting like this with Griffin, too.

"We need to take a break," she said sadly. "I'm going out." She could get some fresh air, have a little cry, and cool down. Maybe she'd go to the café a few blocks away and read over her presentation. The symposium was tomorrow, and although she had a finished draft, at least, she hadn't even edited it. The work would clear her head.

"Very well," he said, his voice rough.

This was so unlike him. Or was it? She hadn't known him long, after all. She grabbed her purse and coat, then paused by the door, hoping he'd meet her gaze, hoping he'd say *something* that would make her think they weren't in for a long round of fighting. If they could avoid that, she'd rather stay.

Nothing. He wouldn't even look at her.

She walked out the door.

Twenty-Two

Take a break. Griffin understood what that meant, for the other night, Aaron had said, *My wife and I broke up.*

Emily no longer wished to be with him.

What was the point of being alive in the world if he was going to be completely alone, with no one to care about him? At least as a figure of stone, indifference had not been personal. To be alive, to move, to speak, and to be rejected, by the very person who'd brought him to life . . . it was too much.

He had so overstayed his welcome that it had soured and curdled into contempt—which explained why she thought he was no better than an actor—and then rejection. He would start over, completely, from nothing, like Adam in the Garden before there was an Eve, lonely but not damned.

No, she was not the only person in the world. He could meet others. But would any of them ensorcell his heart the way she had done? She'd always thought they would, and he'd always said she was wrong.

It was a question for another time.

Maybe he should leave all the things she'd given him, the phone, toothbrush, the razor, and the clothes that she and Rose had given him as though he were a beggar. But she had no use for them, so he packed them up in one of the thin bags she used to clean up after her dog. He was pitying himself, yes, but he didn't care.

He would take his armor with him, too, but there was no way to carry it in his arms. What did it matter if no one else here wore it? It was his, and God knew in this new world, he needed all the protection he could get.

He stripped off his jeans and T-shirt. She'd washed his tunic and hose and gambeson, and folded them between layers of thin colorful paper, in a drawer. The care she'd taken tugged at his emotions, but he pushed it away; he'd dealt with enough emotions already.

As he bent to fasten his greaves, he remembered Emily helping him before as a squire would have done. Could he really bear leaving her? But he had no other choice. Their quarrel had caught fire so quickly he could hardly remember what had been said, but she'd wanted him to take the lowliest of jobs, and then she'd wanted to be done with him. He picked up the breastplate and worked on attaching it next. It couldn't protect his heart, which had already been pierced as though by a lance.

And yet he was not sorry to wear the armor again.

Emily had given him some money the day he'd spent at the museum while she worked. He'd bought ice cream, but he hadn't spent all of it; he'd left the paper and coins in the bathroom, in a basket among small bottles and tubes. After a minute's hesitation, he tucked it into his gauntlet.

When he walked toward the door, clanking slightly, Andy trotted alongside him and gave a soft whine. Maybe he was wondering where his mistress had gone in such a hurry. Or maybe he was hoping to be taken for a walk. It was hard to leave him. But Emily would be back soon, and dogs did not have long memories, did they? Before long, the hound would forget he'd ever lived here.

Still, as Griffin patted him on the head, he felt a tightness in his throat. "You are a fine dog, Andy War-Howl."

He left, closed the door behind him, and felt he was making another new start. Except now, instead of being filled with gratitude, hope, joy, and adoration for his lady, he felt loneliness, confusion, and sorrow.

The streetlights under the deep violet sky buzzed, and long shadows loomed across his path. The cool air carried the sound of traffic, like the roar of a distant ocean. Another dog on another block, barking. The honk of a horn.

It was still better to be alive.

He took a few steps down the sidewalk. *Ah.* He would go to the restaurant down the street, the one that was open all night. Emily had said such a place had allowed her to stay for hours, filling her coffee cup again and again. There he could ponder what to do next.

At the end of the block, he turned right onto the large street and saw the glowing pink sign that read **CORNER CAFÉ**. When he entered the restaurant, only a few tables were occupied, and a stout woman stood at the kitchen counter talking to a cook. She was maybe sixty, with very short silver hair and brown skin, and she wore a blue apron.

"Sit wherever you want," she called out as she turned around, and then she laid eyes on him. *"Oh."*

"Thank you, my lady," Griffin said, inclining his head to her, and she raised her eyebrows. Then she smiled.

He sat in one of the red leather booths near the large windows, and she brought him a large, glossy menu. The tag on her lapel read *Christine.*

"Here you go, hon. Can I get you some coffee?"

Coffee. That was the key to being allowed to stay all night. "Yes, if you please."

"Cream or sugar?"

"A great deal of both, please." He'd learned what sugar was, a powder sweet as honey, and it would go a long way to making the coffee fit to drink.

She chuckled. "All right. I'll be right back."

The menu included color pictures of all the choices, which Griffin appreciated. Christine returned with the coffee, and two large bowls, one filled with little white cups, and one filled with paper packets. "You know what you want?"

"The Hot Roast Turkey Dinner, my lady."

"Hmmph. Don't get too many orders for that this time of year," she said, scribbling on a notepad. "It's good, though. You need anything else?"

A friend.

"No, thank you," he said, and she retreated.

He figured out how to open the packets and the little cups and dumped the contents of four of each into his half-full mug and stirred it. When he took a drink, he found that the cream and sugar had done much to ease the bitterness of the coffee, just as friendly conversation might have eased his bitter spirit.

In his own time, if his spirits had been low, he would've confided in someone. In his sister, in Mordrain before he'd destroyed their friendship, or in another friend. He could hardly talk to Rose, since she was much more Emily's friend than his. At that very moment, Emily might've been describing all his faults to Rose, and Rose might be echoing her outrage, as such ladies who were friends were wont to do.

Aaron. The man courting Rose, the one whom Griffin had entrusted with the truth about his life. When Aaron had put his number in Griffin's phone, he'd said, *Call me any time.*

Griffin touched Aaron's name, the only one in the phone besides Emily.

After a few rings, a voice said, "Griffin! Hey, I've been wanting to talk to you." The friendliness in Aaron's voice was like sunshine through the clouds. "How's it going?"

"Very ill indeed," he confessed. "It is as though my very heart has been ripped from my chest. I am utterly bereft in the world and know not where to turn."

A moment's pause. "Uh . . . wow, man, sorry to hear that. Are you at Emily's?"

"Nay, and I am not like to go back." He couldn't keep the mournful tone out of his voice.

"*Oh*. Where are you now?"

"An inn. The Corner Café, on Broadway Road."

"Griffin, I'd like to stop by and talk to you. Can you stay there awhile?"

Griffin gave a short laugh. "I will stay all night, for I have no-where else to go."

Aaron didn't respond.

"My friend, are you still there?"

Nothing. Griffin took the phone from his ear, hung up, and tried calling again. The phone had run out of minutes. Emily had said this might happen soon. She'd meant to get him another one, but he supposed she'd forgotten. She'd never been very conscientious about phones. He sighed, got up, and tossed it in a nearby trash can.

Soon, Christine brought him a steaming plate, and he thanked her again. He tried to eat the roast turkey, mashed potatoes, and carrots slowly, but by the time Aaron walked through the door, he'd just taken his last bite.

Aaron wore a light jacket over a T-shirt and jeans, and when he spotted Griffin, his eyebrows rose. Griffin stood as Aaron drew up to him.

"Hey, man," Aaron said, reaching out, pausing, and then awkwardly embracing him. Having taken off his gauntlets to eat, Griffin slapped him on the back.

Aaron stepped back to look him over and gave a low whistle. "Beautiful suit of armor."

"Thank you." Griffin gestured for him to sit and did the same.

Aaron took his phone out and placed it on the table before setting the jacket next to him on the seat. "Do you mind if I record our conversation?"

Presumably, there was a device on the phone that would do so with no effort. Why would Aaron want to do so, though? Someday, Griffin would understand all the new social customs.

He shrugged. "Not at all, if you wish to."

Aaron nodded and touched a button on the phone. His gaze landed on the pile of empty cream cups and sugar packets. "I take it you two broke up."

He nodded. "She has withdrawn her love. But I loved her with a fierceness, and although she offended me greatly, I love her still."

Aaron shook his head. "I'm sorry. How are you holding up? I tell myself I'm over my wife, but . . ." He shook his head. "What did you fight about?"

The back of Griffin's neck burned. "She wanted me to do a job that, at the last moment, I could not do. It was beneath my pride as a man . . . and she was sore enraged."

Aaron nodded slowly. "The job was her idea in the first place?"

"Aye, it was. You can well imagine the kind of job she wished me to do." He raised his arms, indicating what he wore. There was only one place now where men donned suits of armor for work. Aaron would know that.

"Yeah, I can. I'm glad you decided to talk to me about this. Who else was involved?"

Griffin shrugged. "Rose. It required a great act of deception, though I am sure you will not hold that against her." Aaron would know all about identification cards, too.

"Right. And no one else was helping you?"

"Rose's brother," Griffin said. Though Griffin had yet to meet the man, he'd given Griffin his first clothes in this new world.

"She told me about her brother," Aaron said. "He's been in prison for theft, and now he works at a moving company. Right?"

"Aye, and that has been a great good fortune for him." Rose had said so.

"I'll bet. So will you be doing the same thing as before? Creating a diversion?"

Griffin understood none of this question but was too proud to say so. "Aye, as you say," he answered vaguely.

Christine came up to their table. "Hey there," she said to Aaron. "You need a menu?"

"You have apple pie?" She nodded. "Black coffee and apple pie." Aaron pointed at Griffin. "Let's get you a piece, too." He turned back to Christine again. "One check, I've got it."

As a boy in church, Griffin had learned, *It is more blessed to give than receive*, but he'd never truly believed it. He did now. Would he ever give rather than receive again?

Aaron gazed at Griffin sympathetically.

"Listen, Griff. I'm proud of you for not going through with the job."

"But I have disappointed the woman I love."

Aaron's brow furrowed. "If she really loved *you*, would she ask you to do this?"

"She wanted a man whose word she could trust," he recalled aloud. It was one of the things she'd said in the beginning, when answering those questions about suitors. How could he have been so stupid? She'd trusted him to do what he said he would do, and he had not. "And she wanted a man who didn't think himself too good to do a job."

"You did the right thing. You're better than a common thief," Aaron pointed out. It was strange that he said *thief* and not *actor*, but then again, the two often went hand in hand. "Most men think they're above *some* kinds of jobs."

"Exactly! It confused me . . . and now she curses my pride, and there will be love and affection between us no more. And I have no money, and do not know what to do."

"I'm sorry about the money problem. Is the job still going down without you?" Griffin frowned, uncomprehending, and Aaron added, "Are they still doing it?"

"Aye, of course." Why would people who played at being servants and knights and queens cease their performances, just because he would not join them? They didn't even know who he was.

"What more can you tell me about it?"

Aaron was strangely curious about this theatre. "I know nothing else. 'Tis no affair of mine."

Christine returned, setting a slice of pie in front of each of them. They both thanked her, and as she retreated, Griffin picked up a fork and tried a bite.

"This is excellent. Thank you," Griffin said. Aaron was a good friend. He at least had that.

"No problem. And the sculpture—that was Emily's job, too?"

Griffin frowned. "Aye, as you know." Emily had told him herself she'd been restoring it.

Aaron gave a small smile. "I just wanted to confirm it. You and she did that together?"

"Aye." Griffin let out a sigh. He didn't want to be rude to the only friend he had in the world, but he'd already told him the story of how he'd come to life. His friend was behaving strangely, asking questions for which he already knew the answers.

"Were Terrence or Laurie involved with the sculpture job?"

"Nay, not at all."

"Thank you." Aaron touched the screen of the phone again and hit a few more buttons before looking up again.

"Here's what I don't understand. This whole bit with you wearing armor, pretending to be from the fifteenth century. Why choose that for a diversion? Was that her idea, too?"

What?

Griffin set down his fork. "You think I am dissembling?" Frustration boiled up in him. Why did everyone expect him to be a vile actor? "I have told you the truth, and I thought you believed it."

Aaron raised his hands. "Whoa, I'm just saying—"

"You seem so gracious, and then call me a liar!"

Christine straightened where she stood at the counter. Griffin knew that look on her face, for he'd seen it on many a female innkeeper. He couldn't get himself thrown out. He had nowhere else to go. Raising his hands in a gesture of truce, he leaned back in his seat, but resentment burned in him.

Aaron set the phone back on the table again and said quietly, "You're telling me two different stories here. You really believe you were turned into stone and came to life again?"

"I do not believe it, sir," Griffin said coldly. "I *know.* And I thought you believed me, too." He stabbed the pie with his fork and took another bite.

"And this is your original suit of armor."

"Aye."

Aaron sighed. "You know, it's weird, because they have security camera footage of you running right out of the photography room in the conservator offices, wearing that armor, and it fits the time-line exactly."

"How did you know this?"

"I heard about it on a podcast," Aaron said with a dismissive wave of his hand. "And nobody has any record of you at all. The police, the Internet, they can usually uncover someone's history. Not with you." He met Griffin's eyes.

Griffin gave a huff of disgust. "They would have to search in the dusty annals of ages past. I have explained all this, sirrah."

"*Sirrah*," Aaron repeated. "You never break character." He frowned and took a sip of his coffee. "But you *just* told me that Emily stole the sculpture."

He'd said no such thing! Griffin's temper rose again; he struggled to contain it. What had he said, that had been so misconstrued?

Aaron went on. "But why the sculpture? *Anything* would've been easier to steal. Is this some feminist performance art thing? Because if it is, it's impressive." Griffin stared at him, bewildered.

"If you returned the sculpture, neither of you would do any time," Aaron added. "You'd be famous, and there would be a lot of ways to profit from it."

"She did not steal a sculpture. She is no thief! I will speak with you no more." He felt betrayed—again.

Aaron picked up his phone and typed something in. "So you're still saying you're a real knight."

"I swear by the blood of Christ, I am," Griffin said, knowing it was wrong to make such an oath. "I was knighted by Sir Baudwin, in the chapel at my father's house."

The time he'd been a squire, from when he was fourteen to the time he was seventeen, and thanks to the detestable man he served, Sir Baudwin, it had been the most miserable time of his life . . . un-til, of course, he'd been turned to stone, and that agony had eclipsed other sorrows.

After his knighting there had been a great feast, and a mock tournament. It would've been a sorry thing, if a young man were sore wounded or killed, on the very day of his knighthood, with all those who loved him in attendance. It had been like a pageant. A celebration of prowess and courage.

Like Medieval Legends.

There had been no shame at all in the mock tournament. It had been a joyful entertainment between friends . . . between lords.

Why had he not thought of that time before? And he'd known, even before going to Medieval Legends, that the tournaments were playacting. It was only when he'd been there, and had heard other men speak of it disparagingly, and say things that reminded him of the basest street entertainments, that his pride had been pricked.

His damnable pride. How had he been through so much and still allowed it to rule him?

"Although 'tis shameful to be an actor," he mused aloud, "there are worse things one could do."

Aaron stiffened slightly. "Why do you think I'm an actor?"

"I do not." How strange this man was, truly . . . but he was in no position to judge. "Anyone can see you are too rich to be an actor."

Aaron shook his head. "Uh . . . you do know that some actors are *very* rich, right?"

"No!" Was the man teasing him?

Aaron nodded. "Not most of them, but the A-list actors in Hollywood. They've got huge houses, and everybody wants to be them . . . They're like our royalty."

Griffin's mouth fell open. He could hardly imagine such a thing. And then he remembered the flimsy book he'd perused near the river. *Hollywood's Handsomest Bachelors!* They were rich and famous, Emily had said. These must've been the kinds of actors Aaron was talking about.

Maybe even being at the bottom rung of acting wasn't as low as he'd thought. Her expecting him to do it was not such a gross insult. And the plays he'd seen on TV weren't crass affairs but great adventures. The people were often beautiful, and they played their roles so convincingly that Griffin could hardly remember the characters weren't real people.

"It was very different in my time," he muttered.

Aaron picked up the check, and after a quick glance at it, he dug out his wallet, drew out a few bills, and laid them on the table.

"You said you were going to stay here all night," he said. "Do you really have nowhere else to go?"

"Nay, I do not."

"Looks like you're coming home with me, then." He pointed at the table. "Don't forget your money. Or your metal gloves."

Griffin put on his gauntlets and tucked the bills back into one of them. They both stood up. As they walked out, Aaron raised a hand to Christine. "Thanks. Have a good night." They stepped outside, and he pointed. "I parked down the block."

The night had grown quieter and colder. If Aaron hadn't met him, his loneliness might've overwhelmed him.

"You are generous to offer me hospitality."

"You might want to reserve judgment on that," Aaron said with a tight smile. When Griffin shot him a curious look, he added, "I'm just staying at a hotel right now."

"Hotel . . . like a *hostel*? The French word for an inn?"

Aaron stepped around to one side of a silver car. "You speak French, too?"

"Aye, I do," Griffin said. He walked around to the other side of the car and got in.

After Aaron had done the same, he said, "But *hotel* is a French word, too. *L'hotel*?"

Griffin shook his head. "Not in my time."

They got in the car and Aaron pulled the car away from the curb. After a minute, Griffin asked, "May I ask why you stay at an inn? You said you lived in this city."

"I do. But I'm rehabbing my condo. It's a construction site right now." As he merged onto a larger road, he said, "The hotel is actually near the museum."

"I do not know whether I am glad or dismayed to hear that I will be so close to Emily." As he stared at the signs and buildings rolling past them in the night, the shifting lights from other cars, his heart ached within him again. "My pride once led to my doom, and now, I wonder if it has done so a second time. Mayhap I am the biggest fool this world has ever known. Should I have taken the work, or at least endeavored to do so?"

"No," Aaron said irritably. "It's a crime."

Griffin swiveled his head to regard Aaron. "I am sure 'tis not."

Aaron cast an incredulous look in his direction. "Of course it is."

"To playact, and ride horses, and pretend to do battle, for the amusement of anyone who pays?" Griffin shook his head. "They openly conduct their performances, and the Medieval Legends castle stands there for all to see."

Aaron's eyes widened. The car drifted to the right and something rumbled under the wheels. He quickly corrected his course.

"*That's* the job you two fought about? *Medieval Legends*?"

"Aye . . ."

"Shit." In a moment, he repeated, *"Shit."* Then, in a louder tone, he said, "Call Brian."

The ringing of a phone sounded through the car—three times, four. "Come on, pick up," Aaron muttered. Then a voice said, "This is Brian. Leave a message."

"Brian, it's Aaron, I'm on speaker." He spoke loudly, with a flexed jaw. "Don't do *anything* else. Just call me back as soon as you can—I'm fine," he added and touched a button on the steering wheel.

Griffin peered at Aaron. What accounted for this sudden shift in mood? Had he suddenly remembered something important?

"Hey, speaking of ale," Aaron asked in a lighter tone that sounded a bit forced. "Do you want to stop and get some?"

"Aye, I do." It would be even more welcome after the coffee. The cream and sugar had made it drinkable but not enjoyable. He needed an evening of drinking and talking with a friend.

After stopping at a liquor store, Aaron took them to his hotel. He led Griffin to a back entrance rather than going through the front lobby, and they took a large elevator up. When they got off on a high floor, Aaron held up a hand to detain Griffin and peered up and down the hallway before they walked down it to his chamber. He double bolted the door behind them. Despite Aaron's dismissive words, his quarters at the hotel were more than a single room. One held a couch, a desk, and a large TV.

"Go ahead and get out of that armor, if you want to," Aaron said, kicking off his shoes. He sat down at the desk, took his laptop computer out of his bag, and then tapped on the keyboard.

Griffin removed it all and piled it in the closet, which made him miss Emily, because she'd put the armor in *her* closet. Everything made him miss Emily. He left his linen tunic on but stripped off his hose and pulled on a pair of underwear he'd stuffed in the thin bag.

When he walked over, Aaron offered him a bottle of beer. Griffin sat down on the sofa and Aaron turned around in his desk chair.

"Bet it feels good to get out of that," he said.

"Aye, it does," Griffin said slowly. He took a swig of the ale and looked at the bottle. "Bitterly do I regret leaving the Medieval Legends, for meseems it was not so shameful a place as I believed."

"Not shameful at all," Aaron said. "I went there once with my nephew. It's a good time."

"But do the actors pretend to do vulgar acts?"

Aaron's face screwed up with confusion. "What? No! It's more like the King Arthur and the Round Table books."

Oh.

"I would have greatly enjoyed such sport, and pleased Emily, too, had I not ruined everything again with my detestable pride."

Aaron leaned forward, his elbows on his knees. "It wasn't just pride. You were also confused. You can't blame yourself for that."

"There is a second day of trials tomorrow, but they will not want me back."

"Why not? Did you even talk to the people in charge?"

Griffin shook his head.

"Then it's no problem. I'll take you."

"But I was expected the day before."

Aaron shrugged. "I'll tell you what to say about that."

So Aaron had more than some skill at lying. Perhaps that should've caused Griffin some alarm, but he could not deny that it was a useful talent.

"Gramercy for your kindness," he said. "I must learn to ride the train and bus to get to where I want to go, and mayhap one day I will learn to drive a car, but I have no wish to risk getting lost on a day that might determine my destiny."

Aaron opened his mouth as though to say something, then shut it again. Griffin took another drink. Should he visit her in her dreams tonight? Was that even something he could still do? But the last time he'd visited her like that, she hadn't gotten any sleep, and tomorrow she would give a lecture to her fellow scholars. She wouldn't thank him if she was weary. He'd been cast into a centuries-long hell for challenging an exhausted man; if nothing else, he'd learned the importance of being well rested.

If he ruined his chance to make amends, he'd carry that sorrow forever. That aside, no matter what, he wanted her to do well. He wanted her to conquer.

"All will be well," he said, trying to encourage himself. "Emily has made a break with me, but perhaps when her ire cools, I will be able to tell her that I have gone to Medieval Legends, after all, and I have succeeded."

Twenty-Three

In the morning, Griffin woke up in the unfamiliar bed and stared at the window that framed the tops of buildings. His gaze swept across the room and landed on Aaron, sitting at the desk, hunched over a laptop computer, typing furiously. He wore earbuds plugged into his phone.

They'd stayed up late talking. Mostly, Griffin had talked, telling Aaron all about his life in the Before Times. Griffin had drunk three beers, which had felt to him much more like six. The base of his skull ached.

Emily. Griffin thought of her and the fight they'd had. Now his whole being seemed to ache.

If they hadn't fought, he could've kissed her before she walked to the train station. She would've called him afterward and told him about her lecture, for he had no doubt the whole event would be a success, leaving her colleagues wide-eyed with admiration.

He sat up, swung his feet onto the floor, and walked to the bathroom. Aaron didn't even look up, and as Griffin passed him, he muttered, "Yes. Unbelievable."

Griffin spent a few extra minutes washing up and splashing his face with cold water. When he emerged, he walked over to Aaron and tapped him on the shoulder. Aaron jumped, a full-body spasm, and then looked up at Griffin sheepishly. He took out the earbuds.

Griffin said, "Good morning." He silently congratulated himself on remembering to say *good morning* and not *good morrow*, given his sore and groggy head. "Did you not sleep this night past?"

"No, I didn't."

Aaron's usually easygoing manner had been replaced by gloom. Griffin asked, "What troubles you, my friend?"

"Eh . . ." He looked at his phone on the desk and shook his head. "Have you ever been in a situation where you're supposed to be working with someone, but they don't want to talk with you because they want to be in charge?"

"I have," Griffin said. "At the battle at Avranches, the man who commanded the archers did not want to confer with me, who led the horsemen. It nearly led to defeat, though we prevailed in the end."

Aaron snapped his fingers. "That's the other thing keeping me up. *Everything* you told me last night about a past life checks out. The battles at Avranches and Verneuil-sur-Avre . . . There's actually a record of a Griffin de Beauford at Verneuil-sur-Avre. And that French thing. Yes, *l'hotel* is modern French, but it didn't exist in middle French."

Griffin shrugged. He'd told the man as much.

"The inn you talked about last night, the Seven Bells," Aaron went on. "Sir Baudwin what's his name—" He looked at the document on his screen. "Yeah, Sir Baudwin de la Pole, who you squired for. I couldn't verify everything, but . . . I found your cousins' names, for Christ's sake."

Griffin was impressed. Although so much had been lost, it was remarkable how much remained, for anyone who knew where to look.

Alyse. Hope ached in his chest like an old wound.

He attempted to keep his voice light. "Did you happen across news of my sister, Alyse?"

Aaron let out a huff of disbelief. "Yeah, I did. Hang on . . ." He clicked on another screen. "Married to Jonathan Grey, the Earl of Kent."

"Jack!" Lightness filled Griffin's chest.

Aaron quirked a skeptical glance at him. "Friend of yours?"

"Aye, and a brother in arms." All amazement, Griffin strode over to the computer. "At the time I was cursed, he'd met Alyse but once, at a Martinmas feast at Hedingham Castle."

Aaron stared up at Griffin as though attempting to see right through him. "See, if you're delusional, why do you know so much? And it would be extreme commitment to the bit. And for what?"

The words made no sense to Griffin, and he didn't care. His mind reeled with this new information. "My sister was the Countess of Kent!" He waved at the computer screen. "Are there pictures of her?" Emily could find pictures of almost anyone or anything.

"I haven't come across any."

"Did she have children?" His gaze landed on the information he wanted and let out a delighted laugh. "Seven! Seven children! See, I have . . . four nieces and three nephews!"

"Mazel tov," Aaron quipped.

"Or had," Griffin corrected himself, staring at the page. Alyse had lived to be seventy-four—*praise God*. One of her daughters had died at the age of thirty-two, which must have grieved his poor sister. How he wished he could've been there to comfort her . . . and how he wished he could've met these babes, all long gone, and dandled them on his knee, and could've witnessed Alyse's wedding to Jack. But here were signs of a long and prosperous life, and that settled something in his soul.

Griffin stepped back and sat on the edge of the bed. "Is there any way to see her children's children?"

Aaron turned around in the chair to face him. "It would take a lot of time, but probably."

Did he detect a note of impatience in Aaron's voice? "You have already told me so much, and for that, I thank you. You must be a prodigious scholar, for not even Emily could unearth these things."

"I have access to more databases."

More mystifying words. Griffin shrugged. "As you say."

Aaron heaved a sigh. "Griffin," he said seriously, "why don't I think you're lying?"

Griffin felt a grin tug at his lips. "Because I am not."

Aaron held up a hand. "No, see, part of my job is knowing when people are lying. And I'm *very good* at my job."

"What job might that be?"

"I can't tell you that," he said, with what sounded like genuine regret. Then he glanced back at the screen. "Get dressed. We need to leave soon for Medieval Legends."

On the long drive to the false castle, Griffin asked Aaron, "Why are you helping me?"

"Because I like you." After a moment, he added, "And after I talk to my friends, I may have more questions for you."

"Very well."

Aaron gave him a sidelong glance. "Would you know what it meant if I said you've been a person of interest for a while?"

"Yes," Griffin said, pleased that Aaron found him interesting. "Thank you. You are also a man of interest."

"Okay," Aaron muttered to himself.

The pleasant conversation distracted Griffin from the anxiety of the trial ahead, but when they pulled up to Medieval Legends, that anxiety crashed down like an iron gate.

As Aaron parked, Griffin warned him, "This may take hours." Or much less time, he supposed, if they decided right away that they had no use for him.

"That's fine. I'll be right out here. Hopefully, I can talk with these people I'm working with. And then I'm going to catch up on my sleep."

Behind a desk inside the building, a young woman with pink-streaked fair hair greeted Griffin and then pulled up his application and photo, noting that he'd been scheduled for the day before. He used the excuse Aaron had coached him on—an abscessed tooth, emergency dental work—and she winced.

"Oh, that's the *worst*. Is it better now?"

He nodded.

"It's no problem. Good luck."

This time, he waited patiently with the other men, eleven in all, who had arrived for the auditions. All but one, he guessed, were younger than him. Would anyone laugh at him for desiring such an opportunity at his age? Would they secretly pity him?

Forget your pride, he told himself sternly. He was hundreds of years old; he would always be older than everyone else, regardless. He smiled and nodded as they discussed other acting jobs they'd done, and who had grown up in Chicago and who had not.

"I am American, but I was raised in Foula," Griffin said, when one of the men asked him directly. He was young, twenty at most, with thick hair in tight curls. "'Tis a tiny island between Scotland and Norway. There are only thirty-six people there."

Emily had come up with that story, and as he told it, he ached for her again. Would they both do well in their challenges today; her with her lecture, and him with whatever transpired here? Christ, that they might face the trials of life together, hand in hand. It was all he wanted, and he would count himself fortunate, no matter how great those trials might be.

"Oh, for real? Wow," one of the men said.

"They're going to love that," another added. He was closer to Griffin's age, pale, with brown hair pulled back in a ponytail. "And they're going to love your accent."

The envy in the man's voice encouraged Griffin, but he couldn't allow his hopes to rise too high.

"One never knows what will come to pass," he said. "We are all subject to Fortune's fickle wheel."

Two men appeared at the door. One carried a clipboard and wore a T-shirt with jeans. The other was dressed much the same, except that his T-shirt was printed with a green and brown pattern that reminded Griffin of a forest.

"Good morning, everybody, I'm Dan Leahy, the show manager and head knight here at Medieval Legends, and this is Marcus Johnson, another knight who will be helping with this audition. Let's go into the great hall."

As they walked, Dan said, "You don't need to have any fighting skills or experience going into this. We train people how to look like they really know what they're doing with a sword."

Griffin bit his tongue. It wouldn't help his chances, he was sure, to say that he very much knew what he was doing with a sword, yet it took almost intolerable forbearance to remain silent.

Forget your pride.

They filed into a large tournament ground, surrounded by rows and rows of seats. A tingle went up Griffin's spine. It was unlike the tournaments he'd known, yet similar enough that he felt an uncanny sense of returning to a place after a very, very long time. The other men took seats as instructed, but another man led a horse out to the edge of the ring, and Griffin stopped in his tracks, staring at the

magnificent beast. Its black coat shone, and its magnificent mane
was crimped from recent braiding.

"A Friesian," he said aloud. There was no mistaking it. He was
one of the warhorses bred in the north, though larger than the one
Griffin had once rode.

Dan raised his eyebrows. "You know horses?"

Griffin could not help the smile that came to his lips. "Aye, that
I do, my lord," he said, then mentally kicked himself as several of
the men chuckled. He wasn't supposed to say *my lord*.

But Dan only smiled himself. "All right, you're already in character."

He *liked* the way Griffin spoke. In that case, Griffin would just
be himself. That would be so much easier.

"Not too many people have heard of this breed," Dan went on
to say. "They almost died out. But now they're back again."

As am I. Griffin's throat ached to think of the near loss of the
magnificent beasts.

God help him—tears were threatening, and that would never
do. Men did not often cry in this modern world, he'd already
learned, though there had been no shame in tears in his time. No
less than the legendary Lancelot had wept frequently. What exactly
men were supposed to do with their grief and sorrow and the ex-
cesses of joy, Griffin had no idea.

He cleared his throat. "I have not seen one in a long while."

"They had those where you were from?" the pale man with the
ponytail asked.

"Aye, they did, and I owned one." He wanted to stride over and
ride this one right now. He'd missed horses even more than he'd
realized.

Dan asked, "Does anyone else have any experience with horses?"

A man with auburn hair raised his hand. A few of the others
looked down at the floor.

"It's fine if you haven't," Dan said. "We teach people that, too. But let's see you two ride."

Yes. To ride a horse again, especially a steed like this one, would be a joy. But eagerness lit the red-haired man's eyes, and to clamor to be first would be childish.

Griffin gestured with a hand. "Proceed, good sir." He took a seat.

As the other man strode over to the horse, Griffin considered how to make the most of his brief riding exhibition. Would it be too arrogant to ride standing on one stirrup, to the side of the horse? The horse might not be accustomed to such tricks, and Griffin had not ridden in, well, centuries . . . though in his time, it had commonly been said that one could never forget how to ride a horse.

The other man mounted with no effort—and Griffin saw fleeting tension in the horse, more subtle than a flinch. Not unusual, perhaps, as a reaction to a stranger. As the rider nudged him into a trot, Griffin watched closely.

He sucked in a breath. Something was wrong.

"Stop!" he called out as he launched from his seat and strode across the ring.

"Hey! What are you doing?" Dan demanded.

"Get off," Griffin ordered the red-haired man firmly, but not so loudly as to spook an already distressed horse. "He's hurt."

The rider gave him a look of disbelief but brought the steed to a halt and dismounted. "He's fine," he complained as Dan and the person who'd led the horse in both jogged over.

"Sit down," Dan said to Griffin, at the same time that the man who'd led the beast into the ring—the stable master, Griffin supposed—said, "We take good care of these horses."

"Aye, you do, my good sir, but when did he last see a farrier?"

The specific question made the stable master frown. "Maybe six weeks ago. He got sick. But he'll be here next Monday."

Griffin could not order them. He held out a hand and said humbly, "Please, if I may."

Dan raised one hand in a gesture that Griffin interpreted to mean, *Go ahead and waste all our time, then, you Jack-fool.*

Griffin approached the horse, murmuring, "Hello, my handsome fellow." He stroked the solid shoulder. The steed turned his head to sniff, easy tempered now that he was unburdened and standing still. Griffin crouched as he ran his hand down the length of the horse's leg. The stable master got down on his haunches, too, squinting over Griffin's shoulder.

Griffin didn't have to pick up the hoof to find the problem. "Here," he said, pointing. "'Tis but a small crack that troubles him."

"He shouldn't be worked until it's treated, though," the stable master said as they both straightened to their feet again. He regarded Griffin with new appreciation.

Griffin stroked the beauty's neck. "In a few more moments, you all would've seen it, too."

The stable master looked to Dan. "I'll take him back and bring out one of the quarter horses."

"We can get started with the sparring," Dan said.

He and Marcus gave them all practice swords and led them through basic thrusts, sweeps, and parries. Griffin's pride roared to life again, threatening to revolt against the child's play. He steadily ignored it, copying the moves exactly, even the ones that would have no place in a true battle.

The man next to him was struggling, aware he was doing a thrust wrong but unable to correct it. He gave a harsh sigh. Griffin hazarded a quick glance at Dan and then said quietly to the man, "Extend your arms more." He demonstrated.

"Right, thanks," the man muttered, bringing his upper arms away from his body in a more proper stance.

"Good," Griffin said in an undertone. The other man was his

rival, he supposed, but Griffin still remembered what it was like to feel awkward with a sword in one's hands.

Dan's gaze locked on Griffin. "You've done this before?"

"Aye, my lord, I have fought on foot and on horse."

Dan shuffled the papers in his folder. "Ren Faire?"

"No, Griffin Beauford."

Dan narrowed his eyes at him. "Come up to the front." He gestured. When Griffin did, Dan said, "Marcus and I are going to demonstrate a short, staged fight. Watch all my moves. When we're done, I want you to take my place and do as many of the same moves as you can. Got it?"

Griffin nodded and concentrated on the staged action. They moved too slowly and deliberately for soldiers. After ten minutes of demonstration, Dan beckoned Griffin to square off against Marcus.

Marcus asked, "Any questions before you start?"

"Might we go faster? Like the speed of a battle."

Dan raised his eyebrows. "We're going slowly so you can understand the choreography." He looked to Marcus and shrugged. "But sure. Try taking it up to speed."

Marcus stepped forward with the sweeping, two-handed blow that looked as though he wanted to cleave Griffin's head in two. Griffin parried it and counterattacked as Dan had done, picking up the pace even more. They went through each move of the false battle. Steel sang against steel, and Griffin's spirits rose with every clash. As they came to the end of the sequence, which had no victory or defeat, Griffin invented one by allowing the sword to be knocked from his hand. He stretched his arms out wide.

He cried out, "Though you may kill me, you vermin will never take our lands!"

Marcus stifled a laugh. In a voice not unlike Griffin's own accent, he said, "Pick up your sword, sirrah, for I will allow you to die with a blade in your hand!"

Griffin quickly replaced his delighted grin with a grim look as he scrambled for the sword and feigned a new attack, being obvious about the move so that Marcus could quickly block it. One of the other men watching let out a whoop. They sparred without a plan now. Marcus favored large, dramatic motions, and Griffin tried to do the same: a two-handed cleaving stroke above his head, a low sweep. Sparks shot off the clanging blades. He met Marcus's gaze, saw the light of enjoyment in them, and knew it was reflected in his own.

Marcus tilted his head and looked at the ground, and Griffin understood. He lifted his sword high, leaving himself wide open for a feigned thrust to his chest. He let out a strangled cry—like one he'd heard too often on the battlefield, but it brought him no guilt or grief now, because it was all in sport.

He fell to his knees. At the same time, Marcus took a step forward, sword lowered, an expression of alarm on his face. But when Griffin cried out, "Curse you and all French devils!" Marcus laughed.

The other men applauded. "That was realistic," Marcus said as he extended a hand to help him up.

Griffin had made a friend in Aaron, and now, maybe he was making a friend in Marcus, too. Of a surety, they would hire him, and he could be friends with Dan, too, and the stable master, who'd seemed a good fellow, and whichever of these men who also came to work for the castle . . . Hope bloomed in his chest.

And maybe, on top of such friendship, he would win Emily's affection again.

"Go ahead and sit down," Marcus said with a smile. He turned to the rest. "Okay, who wants to be next?"

"Uhh, nobody?" the man with the curly hair said, and the others laughed.

"Like I said, we usually teach people everything. Don't worry about it at all."

Griffin watched the rest of the men being put through their paces. When they brought out a chestnut horse, nearly as beautiful as the Friesian—a quarter horse, they called it, though it was large—both Griffin and the red-haired man took a turn riding.

Marcus put a blunted jousting pole in Griffin's hand and set him to the challenge of spearing metal rings he held up as Griffin rode past at a gallop. Griffin had never played such a game before; it should've been simple, but after so long out of the saddle, he still was unsure how it would go. Spurring his horse to a high speed, he supposed he'd do his best. He was embarrassed at how pleased he was with himself when he managed to spear the iron ring three times in a row.

At the end of the exercises, Dan told them all, "Good job, everyone. Thanks for coming out, and we'll call you about our decisions."

Griffin thanked Dan and Marcus and took steps to the door with the rest. Then something horrible occurred to him. They wouldn't be able to call him. He no longer had a phone.

He turned and walked back to the arena. It was empty now. Panic rose in him. Had the triumphs of the morning been for naught? He headed out another side entrance of the arena and relief flooded through him as he spotted them down a hallway, standing in close conversation.

"Messires!" he called out, raising a hand, and they both looked over. "I mean, guys!"

"Griffin!" Dan said. "Glad you're still here."

Griffin took long strides to reach them. "Forgive me for the trouble, but I no longer have the phone that I had before."

Dan said, "We were just talking . . ." He cast a meaningful look at Marcus, who frowned.

"The thing is," Marcus said, "like we said, we usually train guys from scratch. You're a squire for a couple of years, you learn how to do things the way we do them, and then you become a knight. We kind of have a process here."

Griffin's heart fell. Was he being rejected? Rejected for already knowing how to ride and to fight?

"It's not going to make any sense for you to go through all that," Dan said.

"But I am willing," Griffin protested.

"We appreciate that, but—"

"I will undergo all of it with a glad heart, and I shall never challenge your orders or authority."

"Griffin," Marcus said, "what we're saying is, we'd like to go ahead and cast you as a knight."

It took Griffin a moment. "You are making me a knight," he repeated, to make certain. "Not a squire?"

"Exactly."

"It's not many shows yet," Dan said, glancing down at his clipboard. "But one of our guys wants to cut back at the end of the summer because his girlfriend is pregnant. So once you learn the show, you could play the Green Knight on Saturdays—"

"The Green Knight!" Griffin exclaimed with joy. "I will be the Green Knight again!"

Dan squinted at him. "Were you at another Medieval Legends? You didn't say—"

"Nay, I was not. Forgive me. It is just that I am exceedingly glad to wear the colors of the Green Knight, with the black griffin upon it."

"Yeah, it's cool, it matches your name," Marcus said.

Griffin touched his fist to his chest. "I thank you both with all my heart for this invitation and for your courtesy. I accept it with all gratitude and"—he had to smile—"and indeed, with pride."

Dan cleared his throat. "Okay, great. So, um . . . you'll be working forty or more hours a week to get trained for the show. In terms of pay, it's not a lot." He quoted an hourly rate. Griffin mentally multiplied it by forty but had no idea how much it would buy. "You do get a medical and dental plan and a 4-oh-1-K. HR can answer all your questions about that." Griffin supposed that when he met HR, whoever he was, he could ask him what 4-oh-1-K meant.

Marcus opened his mouth to speak, hesitated, and then said, "And you have to be professional about it, obviously, but . . . it *does* make you pretty popular with the ladies."

Griffin's mood dimmed. "In truth, there is only one lady whose attentions I desire, and I know not whether I can win her over again."

Marcus grimaced. "Sorry, bro. Good luck with that."

Twenty-Four

Emily was supposed to meet Rose and another person at eleven thirty at the Nichols Board of Trustees Suite at the museum. They were going to have a tech check with her PowerPoint and the microphone before the symposium, where she'd deliver her presentation. But Emily arrived a little after eleven, wearing a silky top, a black skirt, and pumps, with a twenty-ounce cup of French roast in her hand. She'd put her hair up because it needed washing, and because she didn't want to keep pushing it out of her face while she was reading from her PowerPoint. The top was black, to hide any accidental coffee spills, and the pumps had low heels, so she wouldn't trip in the short distance from one of the tables to the podium. She wasn't usually clumsy, but anyone could have an accident when they were operating on zero sleep.

When she'd come back to the apartment the night before, still frustrated, but with a cooler head, Griffin hadn't been there. She figured he'd taken a walk himself. But after an hour had passed, she'd started to worry, and she hadn't stopped. At three or four in the morning, she'd called the police, even though they were the last people she wanted to talk to. They'd told her that a grown man staying out all night wasn't something they needed to investigate.

Now, she was beginning to droop. Maybe the concealer she'd practically applied with a trowel was hiding the dark circles under her eyes.

She'd half expected to find the room still locked, but she opened the door and found it empty, with a couple dozen tables draped with white tablecloths. It was, of course, the first time she'd been there. Guests could only access it by a private elevator; it was reserved for special events like this symposium. All these people who knew about art were coming to hear her speak, and she wished they weren't.

She wandered over to the floor-to-ceiling windows that offered dazzling views of Millennium Park and the glass and steel skyscrapers beyond, sparkling in the morning sunlight. Griffin was wandering somewhere out there in the city. The knots of anxiety and regret in her stomach tightened. What was she even doing here, going through the motions, when he was lost . . . or maybe in trouble?

"Hey! You're here early."

Emily turned around at the sound of Rose's voice. Her friend had a big purse slung over her shoulder and was carrying a tripod in one hand.

"Are you excited about your presentation today?"

Excited was about the last word Emily would've used. She felt weighed down by dread.

"I think I'm going to cancel." As soon she said it, she was sure it was the right thing to do.

"*What?* What's going on?"

"Griffin and I had a fight last night, and he left." Rose's eyes widened in alarm, doing nothing to assuage Emily's own fears. "I mean, I left and went to a café, and when I came back, he was gone." She wondered, for the hundredth time, if she'd been clear enough about the fact that she was just taking a breather because she didn't want them to yell each other.

"Oh my Goddess." Rose plunked the tripod down on the floor and came closer. "He's been out all night? Did you try calling him?"

"Of course I did!" Her voice came out sharper than she'd intended. "Sorry. Yes. I think that burner phone I gave him is out of minutes." Emily sat down in one of the chairs and pinched the bridge of her nose, as if that might squeeze some new solution into her brain.

"Okay, let's stay calm." Rose sat next to Emily. "It's not like he's a lost baby deer. He's a big, strong guy."

"Especially because he's wearing his armor," Emily mumbled. "Or at least, it's not at the apartment."

"See, that's good! The man invaded France, Emily. He knows how to handle himself."

"Right. But do you think . . . Is he coming back?" As she asked, she felt a stab of hopelessness.

"Of course he is! He's crazy about you. He probably just needed to think some things through. He's gone through so much . . . God, he's probably traumatized."

"He *is*," Emily said, almost in a wail. "And I got mad at him for not going through with the Medieval Legends audition!"

"He didn't *go*? Why?"

"He decided it was beneath his dignity." Rose rolled her eyes, and Emily continued, "He hadn't really thought about it as an acting job before yesterday—I mean, I hadn't really, either—and I think he has a really bad opinion of actors."

Rose's face screwed up. "Why?"

"Because they were basically the lowest of the low then. I guess I'd read something about that before, but I don't know . . . I didn't think about it. I mean, he loves movies, and St. George's feast day where they show off their armor . . ." Rose narrowed her eyes in confusion, but didn't interrupt. "I was reading more about it last night, and they didn't even let actors into churches, and they were always putting them in the stocks . . ." Emily sagged back in her chair. "I'm such an idiot."

"You are so not an idiot. You can't remember everything about medieval life, all the time." Rose squeezed Emily's shoulder. "And you've had a lot on your mind."

"What if I never see him again?"

"You're going to," Rose insisted. "I promise."

Emily looked hopelessly at all the empty tables. "We can cancel this, right?"

"No! There's nothing you can do about Griffin right now."

"But if he calls—"

"You can give me your phone. I'll put it on silent, and if a call comes through, I'll step out and take it. Once we're recording, I don't have to do anything."

"Okay, but—"

"You've worked on your presentation for *weeks*. And if you flake at the last minute, you're going to embarrass Jason."

"I don't want to do that," Emily admitted. Even though Jason always seemed as chill as a Chicago winter, the supposed sculpture theft had to have been a nightmare. "But I'm going to embarrass him either way, right? Standing up here talking about medieval sculpture, when a lot of people think I *stole* one?"

"But that's the thing," Rose said. "If you're a no-show, everyone's going to say it's because you're guilty. You can't let these bastards get you down."

"*Ugh.* You're right." Emily straightened in her chair and took a fortifying swig of her giant coffee. Then she stood up. "I should practice."

She stood up at the lectern and went over her introduction while Rose adjusted her iPhone on the tripod near the back of the room.

The tech guy arrived and then the other two speakers; a guy about her age and a woman several years older.

"Hi," Emily said to them both. "I'm Emily Porter. I'm an art conservator here."

They exchanged an incredulous glance, even though Emily hadn't gotten the impression that they'd met before. It was only a moment, and then they introduced themselves, too, but it told her that they'd heard of her—because they thought she was an art thief.

Emily sat down next to Rose at one of the tables as the tech guy fiddled with the microphone. Then he opened the door to the room.

A crowd of people stood on the other side. They flooded in— two hundred of them at least. Did these things usually attract so many people?

"Break a leg," Rose whispered and took her place behind the tripod.

Jason sat down next to Emily and they exchanged good mornings. Terrence and people she didn't know immediately joined them at the table, so she wasn't going to have the opportunity to continue her conversation with Jason from the other day. She'd been convinced after their talk that Jason knew Griffin was the sculpture come to life. But hours later, she'd convinced herself of the opposite: that Jason would never believe such a thing, because he was a sane, rational person.

There weren't enough seats for everyone who'd arrived, and people staked out places along the walls to sit or lean. At twelve o'clock sharp, Jason strode to the podium at the front, welcomed everyone, and mentioned how excited they were about the new medieval exhibit. Emily had been sure her boss would say something about the so-called theft. How could he ignore it, when it had made front-page headlines, and when probably half the crowd was here to gawk at her as a result? But he merely gave her a gracious introduction.

She was sick of feeling embarrassed. And guilty. She'd rescued a man from eternal punishment, and even though none of them would understand that, *she* knew who she was. That was enough reason to hold her head up high.

"Good morning," she said and then gave them all a bright smile. Some of them were probably podcasters. The hell with them. "I'm so excited to talk to you about how to date medieval sculpture."

The PowerPoint slides advanced smoothly on the screen. She'd included a few new bits of information: things she'd learned from Griffin. When she discussed codpieces, the audience really perked up.

"We never think of people wearing codpieces before 1475, and they weren't a part of the armor," she noted. "But if you take a look at this bas-relief panel from Normandy, and this effigy in St. Peter's church in Lowick that dates to the early 1400s, you can see the padding. I imagine this was for protection in battle, rather than vanity." A few people in the crowd smiled.

At the end of the presentation, the group applauded. Jason had a gleam of approval in his eyes. Emily's face flushed again—but now, it was with pride.

"Thank you," she said. "I'd be happy to answer any questions—"

"FBI. Everyone stay where you are," a loud baritone voice boomed from the back.

Every person in the room swiveled around to look. The two FBI agents Emily had seen before, both wearing dark suits, strode into the room, followed by two other guys in navy T-shirts.

Emily froze at the podium, staring. What was happening? They were coming straight toward her. Her legs were shaking. That was so strange. Really, she was perfectly calm. Wasn't she? She grabbed onto the podium for support.

The man said, "Emily Porter, you're under arrest for the theft of a major artwork." One guy in a navy T-shirt with gold letters that spelled out *FBI*, like a name tag, walked right past her . . . No, he was behind her; he took her wrist and clicked a cold steel cuff around it, and then the other one.

I'm dreaming. This isn't happening.

But it was. He ushered her past Jason and Terrence, who both looked aghast, past audience members taking photos with their phones, and said, "You have the right to remain silent . . . Anything you say can and will be used against you in a court of law."

"This is *bullshit*!" Rose's voice rang out, followed by a chorus of gasps. She took two long strides toward the officers.

Emily snapped out of her nauseated daze. "Rose, don't!" The last thing she needed was her friend to get in trouble, too. "If he calls, tell him what happened, and tell him I'm sorry!"

Rose nodded, her face flushed, her eyes filled with tears. "Don't say anything!"

The big guy who'd put handcuffs on Emily let go of her arm as they stepped out into the hall. Why had they sent *four* people to arrest her? Did these people seriously think she was a threat? It was a very good thing Griffin wasn't here. He would've lost his mind.

She spiraled even deeper into despair. Where *was* he? Would she ever see him again?

This was crazy. The FBI couldn't possibly have any actual evidence against her. What had changed? Why now? As they marched her down the stairs, they attracted the stunned attention of museumgoers.

"I gotta admit, I'm impressed," said the other guy in a T-shirt, speaking for the first time. "It took a genius to get that sculpture out of here."

He wanted her to tell them how she'd done it. Because they still didn't exactly know. Anger rose up in her.

"Rose was right," she said as they passed the Chagall windows. "This is bullshit."

The woman in the dark suit said, "In that case, do you want to tell us what happened?"

"No, I want to call my lawyer."

"You can call them once we get you processed."

"Probably a good idea, if you're guilty," her partner added.

He was goading her, and she knew it. But she'd had it.

As they headed to the side entrance, she said, "You know what, though? I'll tell you *exactly* what happened."

All four of them looked to her.

"The sculpture was actually a medieval knight who had been turned to stone by a sorcerer," she said.

"All right, very funny," the man in the suit said.

"You wanted to hear this," she said as they went out the side doors where a black van was parked. "He visited me telepathically in my dreams, and then I broke the spell with a kiss, so now there's no statue."

As one of the guys in T-shirts slid the van door open, the woman in the dark suit said kindly, "Listen. You've been through a rough divorce, you've got no record, you clearly love medieval art. The most you're going to get is a slap on the wrist. You might want to think about telling us the truth."

A new shudder of fear went through Emily, but she pushed it away. "I already did. That's my story, and I'm sticking to it."

Twenty-Five

The men at Medieval Legends gave Griffin a time to come back and fill out paperwork. When he emerged from the building, the sun was peeking through the clouds, echoing his tentative hopes about reconciling with Emily.

He reached Aaron's car and tried to get in, but the door was locked. Aaron, wearing his sunglasses, had pushed his seat all the way back and appeared to be sleeping soundly. When Griffin pounded on the door, Aaron jumped. He unlocked the door, pulling his seat back up as Griffin got in.

Aaron glanced at the dashboard clock and muttered, "Shit." Then he asked Griffin, "So? How'd it go?"

Griffin squared his shoulders. "I am now the Green Knight. At least part of the time."

"Congratulations. You've been restored."

Despite his worries about Emily, Griffin had to grin. When he'd first been brought to the museum, they'd spoken of restoring him, but no one could've imagined him coming to life again—and, at least in one sense, becoming a knight again.

This knighthood would have none of the horrors of his old one, and all the reasons he'd wanted to become a knight. Camaraderie. Gallantry. And, yes . . . a little bit of showing off. But he wouldn't have been completely himself again without an opportunity to do that.

"Let me try these guys one more time," Aaron said, getting out his phone. He called three numbers, but was only able to leave short messages, saying he'd try again in a couple of hours.

He took Griffin to a late lunch with several TV screens on the walls, playing without sound.

"They are talking about the Cubs," Griffin said, pointing at one of them.

Aaron grinned. "You're a Cubs fan already? I'm a Cardinals fan, myself." He scanned the room, looking for more agreeable entertainment, Griffin supposed. Then he straightened and his face flushed purple. "What the *fuck*?"

Griffin followed his gaze to another TV. A blond woman in a bright red dress was speaking, and a banner below read:

FBI ARRESTS MUSEUM EMPLOYEE FOR ART THEFT

The TV cut to a scene, blurred at first and then in focus, of men and one woman leading Emily out the door that she'd once led him through, when he'd first found his freedom. Her hands were clearly bound behind her back.

"*No!*" Griffin roared, leaping to his feet and startling a server badly enough that she dropped the two plates in her hands. They crashed into pieces on the floor. He didn't care.

"Fuck!" Aaron said again behind him. Griffin's eyes fixed on the screen. The woman was talking again, but he wanted to see more of Emily and make sure that she hadn't been harmed, and he wanted to memorize the faces of the people who'd arrested her.

"I'm going to have to ask you gentlemen to leave."

Griffin turned back. A man with glasses stood facing Aaron, who'd already gotten to his feet.

"We're going," Aaron said grimly. "Griffin, come on."

It was not unlike the way a lord might order a servant or a faithful hound, for that matter, but Griffin had no care for his pride. Aaron would know what to do.

Once they'd gotten in Aaron's car, Griffin asked, "Can you take me to her?"

"Yes." He pulled away sharply from the curb and barked, "Call Brian."

After a ring, a man's tenor voice said, "Aaron. Hey—"

"What the *fuck*, Brian?"

Aaron's tone took Griffin by surprise. The man had been mild and courteous before. But under the circumstances, Aaron's anger seemed only fitting.

"We get to make the arrest, not you," Brian said.

Griffin's blood beat so hard, it pounded in the artery in his neck. This was the man responsible for Emily's arrest?

"Is that why you weren't returning my calls? Why you rushed this? So the Art Crimes division wouldn't get the credit?" They approached a yellow light, and Aaron accelerated, zooming through the intersection. "I left a second message saying not to do anything!"

"I know, but Chicago FBI has jurisdiction here—"

"And you didn't have enough to make the arrest!"

"The hell are you talking about? You patched us through to the confession. Her boyfriend admitted she's a thief."

Griffin yelled, "I said no such thing, varlet!"

"Let me do the talking," Aaron muttered at the same time Brian said, "He's with you?"

"Yeah, we're coming in. This is what I wanted to tell you. The conversation you heard was *out of context*."

"You have offended and wronged my lady Emily," Griffin said, "and for that you must answer with your—"

"Brian!" Aaron interrupted. "Stay on the line." He touched a button on the dashboard and shot a glare at Griffin before returning his eyes to the road. "If you want Emily to be okay, you need to stop interrupting."

Griffin swallowed. "I understand. But they are festering canker-blossoms for putting my lady in chains!"

"Sure." Aaron touched the dashboard again. "Brian, still there?"

"Yeah. What job was he talking about, if it wasn't the sculpture?"

"He tried out for Medieval Legends."

After a moment of silence, Brian said, "*What?*"

"Listen to the second recording I sent you!" Aaron glanced at Griffin again. "And get Emily Porter out of handcuffs if you know what's good for you. You don't want a civil suit on your hands."

After Aaron hung up, Griffin said slowly, "You are a sheriff."

"Special agent, FBI, Art Crimes division, D.C. Brian heads up the FBI here in Chicago, but let's just say the field offices don't always like it when the experts like me get involved." Griffin must've looked confounded because he added, "Basically a sheriff."

"My lady Rose will be much vexed by your deception."

Aaron's mouth tightened. "Yeah, I know."

They reached the city limits but went in a different direction than Griffin expected, heading south. They reached a tall glass building, though not even close to as tall as the ones near the museum.

After Aaron parked, Griffin reached for the car door handle, but Aaron grabbed his sleeve to stop him.

"Listen very carefully. These are serious guys. They're being dumbasses, but they're serious. If you assault one of them, they *will* shoot you dead, and that'll ruin my day. Understand?"

Griffin took a deep breath and nodded, even though rage made him feel like the blood in his veins had been replaced by fire. "I will school myself to restraint."

"Good man."

When they walked in, Aaron told the woman behind the desk, "He's with me."

The woman asked to see Griffin's driver's license, and Griffin noticed Aaron peering closely at it. She returned it and directed them to pass through an archway. Aaron led Griffin to an office not completely unlike the place where Emily worked, with computers and desks.

A ruddy-faced man in a dark suit approached them. This had to be Brian, Griffin thought. He muttered under his breath, "Infected arse-boil."

Aaron gave Griffin a sharp look and then said to the man in the suit, "Take us to her."

Brian gave a surly incline of his head, and as they began to follow him, he said, "You know, this wouldn't have happened if—"

"We're not doing that now," Aaron said in a tone that brooked no arguments.

Griffin's heart pounded in his chest. Would Emily still be angry with him for being such a fool . . . and now, for being the cause of her rude treatment and public humiliation, besides? All he could do was beg her forgiveness.

They went into a room with bright lights overhead and the shutters on the windows closed tight. Around a table sat one woman in a suit, two strong-looking men in T-shirts, and . . .

"Griffin!" Emily jumped out of her seat, almost knocking it over, and rushed over to him saying, "I was so worried about you!"

She wore bright lipstick, and she'd arranged her dark brown hair up on her head, but a few locks had come loose, sweeping against the tender curve of her neck. Flinging her arms around him, she demanded, "Are you all right?"

He pulled her closer, his heart filled with relief and adoration. "Aye, my cinnamon." He cleared his throat against the hoarseness of his voice.

She pulled back and then blinked. "Aaron? What are you . . ." Understanding dawned in her eyes. "Ohhhh."

He gave a little nod of confirmation. "Aaron Coleman, FBI Art Crimes."

Griffin took her hands. "My dearest love, I most sincerely and bitterly regret my churlishness and my stupid pride." His gaze hung on hers.

"You were confused." She shook her head. "I'm the one who's sorry. I think you had the wrong idea about actors—"

"Aye, I did, but Aaron has explained all."

"I shouldn't have gotten so angry." Regret filled her brown eyes. "I was worried about a lot of different things, but—"

"Nay, 'twas more than just, my sweet cinnamon, after all you have done for me." He swallowed. "Small wonder that you wanted to leave me, but dare I hope that you have changed your mind?"

"I . . . What? No!" Horror washed across her face. "I didn't want to leave you! I mean, I *left* you, but I was just going to be out for an hour or two, to calm down . . . I didn't want us to yell at each other."

His heart filled with gratitude and relief. He added tenderly, "These scabrous miscreants have done you no harm?" He raised her hands and turned them over to examine her for marks or bruises, relieved to see nothing but a faint line where the cuffs had been. He lowered his lips to one of her wrists, closing his eyes and treasuring the sensation of the delicate skin beneath his lips, the pulse there . . . the life that meant more to him than anything.

"I'm fine, now that you're here," she murmured.

He couldn't resist kissing her any longer. A sweet kiss, not the kind that led quickly to swiving, out of respect for her modesty in front of strangers, but it still roused his soul.

"Awww," the woman in the dark suit said. When her men in T-shirts gave her dubious looks, she added, "What? We listened to the second conversation. There's no evidence pointing to them."

Griffin asked Emily, "How was your speech?"

She gave a short laugh. "Good, actually. You helped with some things." She looked around the room, her bright lips tightening into a thin line. "But then these guys had me arrested in a room in front of my boss, my coworkers, and my peers."

Griffin's blood heated again.

Brian put his hands on his hips. "We're dropping the charges. We already told her she's free to go."

"After you got her face plastered all over national news," Aaron said. Emily gave a little gasp of dismay. "We're going to make it right." He swept a steely gaze across the room.

"Shouldn't we take this guy to the mental hospital, though?" one of the guys in the T-shirts suggested. "He thinks he's a freaking knight!"

Brian rubbed his face. "Under Illinois law, we can't. He's not a danger to himself or anyone else." He sounded disappointed.

"Excuse me." At the new female voice, they all looked over. The woman in uniform stood next to a perturbed-looking man of middle age who was wearing a dark suit and carrying a case in one hand. "It's Ms. Porter's lawyer . . . ?"

"Ah, shit," Brian muttered.

Griffin's eyebrows raised. He knew that word, *lawyer*; did Emily's family keep one in their employ?

Aaron strode over to the stranger and extended his hand with a smile. "Aaron Coleman, FBI Art Crimes. There's been a bit of a misunderstanding."

This lawyer, as soon as he heard of the wrongful arrest, began using the same phrase Aaron had used earlier—*civil suit*. Griffin asked Emily what it meant, and she explained to him that maybe the Jack-fools who had arrested and humiliated her would have to pay her a lot of money in recompense. Emily demanded her phone, which was speedily returned to her, and she called her parents and assured them that she was being set free.

Emily, Griffin, and the lawyer—his name was Steve—walked outside the doors of the brick building into the sunlight. Steve arranged for a time to speak with Emily about the experience, and Griffin told the man that he hoped he would make the whoresons pay. Steve offered to drive them back to their apartment, but Emily declined, saying they'd call an Uber.

Once Steve had shaken hands with them and was headed back to the parking lot, Emily looked up at Griffin, who was squinting in the bright sun. "I just wanted a few minutes alone with you."

His heart melted. "Aye, sit with me in the grass, under this tall tree." He gestured. Emily kicked off her shoes and took his hand, and they walked over to the oak.

He looked her up and down as she settled herself next to him, sitting on her heels with her knees together, in her short, narrow skirt. "Are you sure you are well, after all this, my heart's queen?"

"I'm fine. Promise. Just a little dazed."

He brushed back a strand of hair that had fallen across her cheek. "I did not know you had a lawyer."

She shook her head. "I only met him once before. My parents wanted me to talk to him in case I got in trouble."

"Why did you not tell me?"

"Because I didn't want to worry you." She plucked a fuzzy-headed dandelion near her knee. "And I told him you were wearing armor in the museum that day because you were going to try out for Medieval Legends."

"Ah. And when I did not go, you did not want a man of the law to think you were a liar."

"Yeah, that was bothering me, too. Though it really wouldn't have made a difference."

Griffin gently touched two fingers under her chin, so she would look him in the eye.

"You must not try to shield me from your worries and concerns." He gave a wry chuckle. "Indeed, I am more accustomed to protecting than being protected."

"You're right," she admitted. "It made things worse. It's just that I think I was not enough fun around Tom, so I don't want to be like that again, and—"

"*Tom*," Griffin repeated with disgust. "I am not a man for only one season, but here for the storms as well as the sun."

Her eyes glossed over with unshed tears. "It's just that you've been through so much."

"Aye, perhaps so I might be here with you." He leaned down and blew on the fuzzy dandelion in her hand, sending the seeds free on the breeze.

She kissed him and then said, "Oops," and wiped at his mouth. Some of her lipstick must've come off on him. He didn't mind.

"You have to promise me something, too," she said. "You're still getting used to the modern world. If there's something that doesn't make sense—like me expecting you to be a filthy actor . . ." They shared a smile at this. "Try to not get all upset until we can talk it through, okay?"

"Aye, you are right," he admitted. "So many things are unfamiliar to me, and I am not used to being nobody . . . I am ashamed to admit that my pride was pricked as soon as I arrived at that false castle."

"You can tell me when you're frustrated, or scared, okay? We'll both be honest with each other."

He took her earnest face gently between his palms and kissed her, as the breeze rustled the green leaves above them and lifted the ends of their hair. The summer, he thought, had just that instant begun.

"And you're not nobody, my lord," she whispered when they parted. "To me, you will always be a noble knight."

Oh. In all the clamor of the day, he had not told her his good news yet. He sat taller.

"Soon no one may dispute that I am a knight, for I will be one at Medieval Legends."

It gave him great satisfaction to see Emily's mouth fall open. "*What?* Wait . . . you tried out, after all?"

"Aye, I did this very morn, and I will be no squire, but the Green Knight."

"Oh my *gosh*!" She threw her arms around him and squeezed him tightly, then pulled back to look up at him. "That's amazing!"

The pride shining in her eyes was all the admiration he'd ever need in life.

Twenty-Six

On the way home, in the back seat of the Uber, Emily scrolled through approximately one hundred texts from Rose, alternating between supportive, vindictive, and despondent. Emily called her, putting her on speakerphone so Griffin could hear; if the Uber driver had a podcast, she supposed, he could have the scoop. Rose was thrilled to hear that Emily had been released, with the charges dropped, but unsurprisingly, she was pissed at Aaron.

"He lied to my face! And he got me to tell him all these personal things!"

"My lady Rose," Griffin said quietly, "for what it is worth, I believe he sincerely likes you."

"Too bad I don't date cops *or* liars," she shot back.

"No, I get that," Emily admitted, feeling for her. Rose deserved a guy who treated her right and listened to her and flattered her. It sucked that the lovely night at Cindy's hadn't been real—or completely real, anyway.

Once Emily and Griffin were inside the apartment, Emily

wished she could whisk him into the bedroom, but Andy needed to get out first. She loved the dog, and he deserved plenty of walks and visits to parks . . . but still, it *would've* been nice, now and again, to be able to open a back door and let him out into a yard. Griffin went with her on the walk, recounting his evening with Aaron, and telling her what he'd learned about his sister.

As they approached the apartment building again, Emily said, "I should call Jason."

"I don't believe you need to."

Emily peered up at him. "Why not?"

"You can talk to him now." He nodded ahead at the front gate.

She'd vaguely noticed the man lingering there, but she hadn't recognized him. Her boss, whom she'd only ever seen in a suit, was wearing sunglasses, a gray T-shirt, loose black basketball shorts, and dirty white sneakers. What was he *doing* here?

"Hi, Emily," he said as they approached, and nodded to Griffin. "I just heard about your release on the news."

"Yeah." That was fast.

"Sorry to bother you at home, but we need to talk." Andy responded first, with one of his trademark bellows. "Jesus," Jason muttered under his breath.

"Sure," Emily said. "Come on in."

Andy licked Jason's knee as she keyed in the code for the gate. "That's Andy War-Howl," she told him.

Jason didn't smile at the name, as she'd expected. In fact, he'd barely taken his eyes off Griffin. She added, "And this is my boyfriend, Griffin Beauford." She mentally added, *You might know him from TikTok, security camera footage, or the national news.*

"How's it going?" Griffin said, as she'd taught him to do.

Jason said, "Yes, I believe we've met."

Griffin's eyebrows shot up. He exchanged a shocked glance with Emily.

Did he mean . . . ?

"Have you known all this time?" she asked quietly, pausing in the hallway. "That Griffin used to be a statue?"

Jason frowned. "I mean . . . yeah, I had my suspicions."

"We should go inside," Emily said. Once she'd closed the door behind them, she asked, "Can I get you anything? Would you like a beer?" She glanced up at the clock. Well, it was *almost* five.

"I think we could all use one," Jason said.

As she opened two beers for Griffin and Jason and poured a generous glass of rosé for herself, she heard Jason compliment the apartment and ask Griffin if he lived there, and he told her boss yes. She came back out into the living room and handed Jason a bottle.

"How did you know? I mean, I know there was footage of Griffin in the office, but . . . ?"

"There were a couple of strange accounts about the sculpture, over the centuries," Jason explained. "A maid's diary said it talked to her in her dreams, and Richard Burke the First said the same thing in the original version of his will. He didn't want it to be sold off." Jason shrugged. "I thought it was going to be haunted."

Emily shook her head in disbelief. "But you acquired it anyway?"

He pursed his lips. "Can we keep some secrets here?"

She nodded. Griffin said, "If you keep ours, we shall return the favor."

"I acquired it *because* I thought it was haunted." He paused. "Some of my colleagues and I are interested in studying art and artifacts with supernatural qualities."

"Some of your colleagues at the Art Institute?" she asked.

"Uh, no, although there are a few pieces there rumored to have certain . . . properties." While Emily took that in, he said, "I'm talking about colleagues at various museums around the world."

She shook her head. "So what, you're like in some kind of secret society?"

"No, it's more of a . . . private association."

Which was different from a secret society, *how*?

Griffin said, "This is why you were at the Burke estate years ago."

Jason flashed a grin. "Exactly. I was at the MFA in Boston then. That's the other museum in the US where we, uh . . . collect."

"Wait," Emily said. "Where are the other ones?"

"I really shouldn't say."

"Oh no. After all I've been through, you owe me."

He looked reluctant. "There are a dozen of them in all. The Egyptian Museum in Cairo and the Kunsthistorisches in Vienna are two of the major ones."

Emily shook her head. "I . . . Why are you doing this, though? What's your goal?"

"Have other people been turned to stone?" Griffin demanded. *Good question.* She hadn't even gotten to that yet.

"*No*, this is unprecedented," Jason said, gesturing with the beer bottle in his hand. "It's incredibly exciting." At Griffin's glower, he added quickly, "I mean, it's horrific, what happened to you. But it's fantastic that you're alive again."

"It is," Griffin said, seeming mollified. "And I daresay I would not be, had you not brought the statue here, so that I might meet my lady." He cast an ardent look Emily's way.

Emily asked, "So you want to . . . interview him and stuff?" She had an awful thought. "You're not going to take him anywhere, are you?" He better not try, or Griffin wouldn't be the only one fighting him.

"No! I mean yes, I would like to interview him. Both of you, actually. He can stay right here, or wherever he wants." He took a sip of the beer. "In fact, we can help him get settled. We've done that kind of thing before."

What? If no other statues had come to life, then what exactly was he talking about?

Before Emily could ask, Jason said to Griffin, "I'm guessing it hasn't been easy, adjusting to the modern world."

"It has been a great effort," Griffin admitted.

"First things first. You'll need a social security number and a birth certificate."

"Exactly," Emily said, her attention swinging on the problems at hand. "We got a fake driver's license, but that's it."

"Send a photo of that to me. We'll create a provenance for Griffin."

"Can you really do that?" she asked. "That's amazing."

"I know people who can." He looked back to Griffin. "We can create a provenance for that armor of yours, too, and get it auctioned at Christie's."

"Oh, he won't sell it," Emily said.

A wide smile crossed Griffin's face. "No, I will."

"Seriously?" Her voice came out a squeak.

He shrugged. "I no longer need a fine suit of armor to remind me of happiness or to know my own worth."

Her heart melted.

Jason said, "Emily, we may need to fake a little bit of patina on the armor, though."

She nodded. "I can figure something out."

"And I can't make any promises, but I'll see what we can do about the head count. I might be able to muster up some sympathy, now that you've been falsely accused and released. In the meantime, of course, you're still a temporary employee."

"Thanks." She wasn't going to get her hopes up there. She was just grateful to be free and with Griffin.

"I'm sorry you went through all this," Jason said. "And Terrence and Laurie, too, and your friend in social media. It doesn't make up for it, but I've gotten you all invited to the opening gala."

"Oh, wow. Thank you." She'd almost forgotten about the museum's high-dollar fundraiser with the sneak peek of the exhibition.

It would be, hands down, the fanciest and most lavish party she'd ever attended. "That's going to be so much fun!"

"It's the least I can do." He took out his phone and glanced at the screen. "I should get going."

Emily felt a twinge of exasperation. She had a lot of questions about this secret society thing . . . Although, somehow, she suspected she wouldn't be getting a lot of answers.

Jason turned back at the door. "Oh, and Emily. Great presentation today."

"Thanks." She took Griffin's hand. "I had a little help."

Twenty-Seven

A few weeks later, Griffin arrived with Emily at the museum for the Masterpiece Ball.

The sight of Emily in her new, floor-length emerald gown had nearly stolen his breath. It was immodest in the modern fashion, baring her arms, neck, and décolletage. He was bedeviled by thoughts of kissing her all over, and especially at that tender place beneath her ear that made her give a little moan, but he took satisfaction in knowing he would be able to do that later that night or the next morning, and again and again in the coming days and years.

He himself wore a special black outfit, a *tux*. It had seemed strange to him to rent garments for a special occasion, but Emily had assured him this was a common practice, and they had purchased gleaming black shoes to go with it. She had very much approved of his appearance, too, and he held his head high as he strolled in with her on his arm.

The stark Modern Art wing had been transformed into a magical space with gold and magenta lights, and filled with guests—mostly older, but some in their twenties and thirties, milling around with drinks in their hands before dinner. Flickering candles and arrangements of creamy camellias decorated the tables draped in white.

They found Rose, who'd brought her brother, Ryan. Griffin was glad to meet the man in person and thank him for the clothes he'd donated when Griffin had first come back to life. Terrence arrived with Scott—who, with his red beard, indeed looked like a Scot. Griffin was glad to no longer count the Scots, whom he had battled in his day, as enemies. Nor did he judge that the men were married to each other, which Emily had explained. It was strange to him but not the strangest thing he'd encountered in this new era. Having suffered so much, he couldn't think ill of anything that brought joy and did no harm.

"You are a professor of law, I hear," Griffin said to Scott, shaking his hand. "I am sure your Latin is far better than mine."

Scott laughed. "I wouldn't bet on it."

"I've never been to such a fancy party," Emily confessed to the group, looking around.

"Nor have I," Griffin said, "except for the one after the coronation." It did remind him of the feast after the crowning of Henry V, when he'd still been but a squire. He'd always been proud to tell people he'd been in attendance . . . but when Emily shot him a quizzical look, he realized his error.

"I am joking!" he assured them. "I was not invited to the last coronation."

"Me neither," Ryan deadpanned. "I don't know what I did to piss those guys off."

Rose said, "After all the drama lately, it's nice to just relax and have a good time."

"There's Jason," Terrence said with a nod. "Working the room."

Griffin turned to see the man, in a midnight blue tux, moving from one little group of people to the next. He shook hands with one and then patted another on the shoulder, saying something that made them laugh.

"He's good at that," Emily said.

"Oh, yeah," Terrence agreed. "He's pretty active at getting donations, too."

Griffin supposed Jason had to be, since he, along with his secret friends, were acquiring art with magical powers. Who *were* those colleagues? How had Jason gotten involved in it? He'd interviewed both Griffin and Emily, but whenever she asked a question, Jason had managed to distract her, turning the focus back onto them.

A few minutes later, when Emily and Griffin left the group briefly to go back to the bar, Jason intercepted them.

"My contact sent Christie's some initial photos of the armor," he said quietly. "She's very excited. She wants to put it in an auction in a few months called *Made in Britain*."

Griffin sighed. "Must we wait so long?"

Jason quirked a smile. "This isn't like putting a couch on Craigslist."

Griffin supposed this Craig was a merchant and was about to say that perhaps they should talk to him, but Emily told him, "A few months isn't long." She asked Jason, "Is the auction here in Chicago? I always wanted to go to one of those."

"*Made in Britain*? It's in London."

"Right, duh. Shoot," Emily said. "I wish we could afford to go."

Jason said, "Well, listen—"

"I wish that, too, sweeting," Griffin said and kissed her temple. "It would be a great pleasure to see that city again and marvel at how it has changed."

"We'll go someday," Emily promised.

Jason gave an impatient shake of his head. "They're starting the bidding at one million pounds."

"Oh my God!" Emily exclaimed, loudly enough that nearby

partygoers looked over. Griffin didn't know what a pound could buy, but her reaction was encouraging, and a million of anything was probably a lot. In a quieter voice, Emily asked, "Is that too high?"

"No. They think they're going to break the record for an armor auction. There's literally nothing like it on earth."

After a dinner that included roasted halibut and colorful little pastries called macarons, but before the mystery musical performance outside in the giant tent pavilion, Jason gave a brief speech thanking the donors and the organizers of the event and inviting them to get a sneak peek of the *Medieval Might* exhibition.

Among a few hundred other guests, Emily and Griffin made their way through the museum to the gallery. They admired the intricately carved Aztec club, edged with obsidian blades, and the samurai helmet and breastplate. When they reached the Essex armor, Griffin froze, and his blood chilled in his veins.

The helmet had been cleaned, the gilding reapplied, and now he could see the etching of the jackdaw with its baleful staring eye— the death-bird, the emblem of Mordrain's house. When he'd seen the armor before, he'd been exulting in his newfound life, and he'd been too distracted to notice that the shoulder plate was missing.

"I still get the worst feeling about it," Emily said quietly, staring along with him.

Griffin pointed at the place where a round disk should be. "This piece broke off in the tournament when I knocked him from his horse, and it was trampled underfoot." He turned to her. "This is Mordrain's armor."

She paled. "Seriously? Are you sure?"

"That is not his sword, though," Griffin added.

"No, we just gave him that." She said to the armor, "Fuck you, bastard." A nearby couple exchanged judgmental glances and stepped away. Griffin knew that was vulgar language, which Emily rarely used, but because she used it to address his enemy, albeit posthumously, it sounded sweet to his ears. "Fuck you and your magic."

Griffin surprised himself by letting out a hearty laugh. "What does it matter now?" His voice rose along with his sense of triumph. "He is dead, and I am alive!"

Emily clutched his arm with a little gasp. He looked down at her, then followed her shocked gaze. The sword arm of the suit of armor raised slowly.

Mordrain! Or his ghost . . .

With a wild swing, the armor wrested itself free of the stand, which crashed to the floor.

As it took two steps toward Griffin, he shoved Emily to the side and behind him, so hard she stumbled right into a man whose back was turned. "What the hell," the man said sharply, but it was almost lost in the exclamations of the crowd.

Jason's voice carried over the excitement. "Oh, shit."

The armor—no, *Mordrain*—raised his sword with both hands over his head. Griffin took several steps back as a shriek tore from Emily's lips, reverberating with other screams from the crowd.

"A sword! I need a sword!" Griffin shouted at no one in particular as Mordrain advanced. He brought his blade down in the direction of Griffin's skull.

Griffin dodged it completely, picked up the Aztec battle club, and fended off another blow. That weapon hadn't been designed to deal with armor, though, and while the sword in Mordrain's hand was dull, it was steel, and heavy. Griffin could only survive for so long without a proper weapon . . .

Then Emily was at his side, holding the elegant Ethiopian sword. Griffin released the club to grab its hilt without missing a beat. "Run!" he shouted at her.

She darted away just in time to avoid Mordrain's sword thrust.

Griffin blocked the next one, albeit awkwardly—he wasn't used to the slim curved blade. For once, Mordrain had the advantage.

"What are they *doing*?!" a woman shrieked as Griffin and Mordrain exchanged two more blows. "They're going to damage those!"

"Yeah, this isn't cute," someone else said.

Mordrain's spirit had probably been enraged to hear Griffin crowing about being alive. Maybe he'd been angry, too, to see Griffin with an adoring woman on his arm. All this time in Chicago, while Griffin had been enjoying life to the fullest, Mordrain had been frozen in rage . . .

Griffin knew what that was like. It was hell.

Time slowed down for him, as it always had in the heat of battle, his vision and hearing sharpening, as he noticed every movement, the sound of his own breath, the pounding of his heart. He and Mordrain circled each other, trading blows, trying to get past each other's defenses. They neared the Bruges window—and Terrence planted himself in front of it, his hands balled into fists, clearly willing to risk life and limb to defend his handiwork.

"Put down that sword *right now*!" Laurie yelled from somewhere in the crowd, in a tone she'd probably perfected as a mother.

Behind Mordrain, Emily darted forward, the Aztec club in her hand. Griffin's heart lurched. He let his gaze slide right over her, not allowing his expression to change, so Mordrain wouldn't turn around, but he wanted to shout at her. She didn't know what she was doing. The weapon was too heavy for her. She ran toward Mordrain's back—

And tripped on the edge of her gown.

Mordrain spun around as she fell to her knees almost at his feet. *No!*

Mordrain raised his blade over her. Almost blinded by terror, Griffin rushed forward and grasped Mordrain's sword arm.

At the same time, Emily smashed the club into the groin of the armor.

God's bones. Mordrain dropped the sword and hunched forward. Griffin tackled him from behind, getting his left arm around his neck in a choke hold, as Emily, to his relief, scurried out of reach.

But there was no breath in Mordrain to choke out. The spectral warrior twisted and spasmed with a ferocious strength. He managed to knock the blade out of Griffin's other hand with his dull sword. Griffin cursed himself for his lapse in focus. He couldn't pick the sword up without loosing his hold on Mordrain.

How could Griffin win a fight with a ghost? If he disarmed Mordrain and smashed the armor to bits, Mordrain wouldn't be able to inhabit it. But might he still haunt the museum where Emily worked every day? There had to be a better way.

"Mordrain, listen to me." A hush fell over the crowd, but Mordrain still struggled like a fish on a hook. "You've already taken more revenge than any man has ever taken on another. But now I am free, and you are still a prisoner—frozen like stone, in your own anger."

Mordrain stilled.

"We were like brothers, once," Griffin said much more quietly, for Mordrain's ears alone. "Were we not happier then, roaming the village and the meadows, before pride and ambition poisoned our souls? We were told that our worth lay in our riches and our might. We both suckled on the venom of these lies."

He never would've guessed he'd be able to speak to Mordrain like this. He should want the man to suffer at least a fraction of what he'd suffered. But could there be no end to violence and revenge? Jason had made his way to the front of the crowd, and he silently picked up the sword Mordrain had knocked to the floor, never taking his eyes off the suit of armor.

"I know what it is to be trapped," Griffin said softly. "There is no worse torment. But only you can set yourself free."

Warily, he loosed his grip. Mordrain took a step back and turned to face him.

He raised his sword.

Jason and Emily lunged forward, though Emily was empty-handed—

But Mordrain let the sword fall to the floor with a clang.

The suit of armor collapsed into a heap after it, and the heaviness in the air evaporated.

The crowd gasped. Griffin stared at the inert pile of steel, his heart still hammering in his chest. Emily was alive, Griffin himself was alive, and the age of enmity was past.

Emily ran over to Griffin and hugged him. Ah, God, she felt good. He almost squeezed the breath out of her. A few people applauded and cheered. In Emily's peripheral vision, Jason sidled over to casually set the shotel back in place.

Jason said loudly to the guests, "I hope you all enjoyed the performance. And I hope you're ready for the next one!" He announced the mystery musical guest and then flashed an apologetic grimace in Emily and Griffin's direction. The crowd broke out in excited chatter.

Jason slipped over to join Griffin and Emily. "You guys all right?" he asked in an undertone. "I had *no* idea that thing was going to be violent. Obviously."

"It did have a bad vibe, though," Emily said.

He raised an eyebrow. "Next time tell me if something has a bad vibe."

Emily crossed her arms. "Next time, you and your friends be more careful." Jason tilted his head, as though to acknowledge this was fair. "But yeah, if anything else creeps me out, I'll let you know."

Griffin wrapped his arm around Emily's waist. "It is truly finished now."

Jason nodded. "I, uh, I've got to go." He jerked a thumb in the direction of the dispersing crowd. They were headed back to the Modern Art wing, where they could exit the museum to the outdoor tent pavilion for the show.

"I have the most chaotic boss," Emily murmured, staring after Jason. Then she shook her head. "Let's go out the front doors. I could use a minute."

She showed her ID to the security guard, who let them out the front entrance. They stood at the top of the steps, and the cool evening air touched their faces. The bronze lions stood guard below, as if ready to protect them from any further threats.

"I've never seen you fight before," she commented, taking his hand. "It was pretty impressive."

An incredulous huff escaped him. "You were supposed to run. When I saw Mordrain lift his sword over you, my soul nearly left my body."

She shook her head. "Sorry, but we're a team." The museum's outdoor lights, illuminating the pillars behind them, were bright enough for him to see her mischievous expression. "Anyone who fights you, fights me, too."

He couldn't help but chuckle. "Then woe betide any challenger. That was a mighty blow, and you were very brave." He pulled her closer and brushed his lips across hers.

"You've been brave all along," she said softly. "I know it's been scary sometimes, being stuck in a new world."

Griffin looked around them. Cars filled Michigan Avenue, and the skyscrapers glittered like promises.

"I was stuck for centuries, but I am not stuck now. If I could be anywhere, at any time, I would be here."

"In Chicago?"

He turned to her. "Nay, my heart's queen. By your side."

The adoration in her eyes made him feel like a king. "I want that forever. I love you so much."

He gathered her in his arms and kissed her deeply. Their kiss spoke of months, years, and decades of joy and sorrow to come, but mostly joy. Crackling and popping distracted them, and they looked up to see the sparkling fireworks shot off from nearby Navy Pier, reflecting in the dark waters of the lake and turning it into a second sky, filled with stars for a thousand wishes coming true.

Epilogue

Six Months Later

This is such a cute house!" Rose said as she stepped inside. "Thank you!" Emily said. "I mean, it's really Griffin's." They'd just moved in a few weeks before.

Andy greeted Rose in his usual fashion, by putting his paws up on her legs. "I bet you like it here, too," Rose said, giving him some ear scritches.

"He's so happy to have a big yard!"

That had been a plus, but they'd chosen the house almost completely based on location. It was just a few miles to the train station that took her downtown to her full-time job as an Objects Conservator at the Art Institute of Chicago. It was also close to her parents, and even closer to Medieval Legends; to the amazement of his coworkers, Griffin walked to work. Emily's dad had given Griffin a couple of driving lessons, early in the morning when there was no traffic in the suburbs, and while it hadn't gone especially well, they all figured he'd get the hang of it eventually.

Rose dug into her purse. "Here, I made you two a blessing ball." She held out a clear glass globe, like a large Christmas ornament, filled with crystals and dried plants and hanging from a loop of jute rope. As Emily took it from her and held it up to the light, Rose said, "It's got black tourmaline to absorb negative energy, obviously, and selenite to cleanse the space, and sage and bay and St. John's wort."

"I love it," Emily said and gave her a big hug. "I'm going to hang it in a window." For the time being, she set it on a high bookshelf, out of Andy's reach.

Rose peered around the corner into the kitchen. "Can I get a little tour?"

"Sure! But I still haven't unpacked all my boxes."

Griffin had been able to buy the house outright. Though it was a midcentury brick ranch, she'd given it a few old-world touches, like the replica of the fifteenth-century tapestry on the wall in the living room.

She expected to do a little more decorating once she got the settlement money for her wrongful arrest from the Chicago FBI. That had taken a lot of time, but her lawyer, Steve, said they were hammering out the final details. In the absence of clues or leads, the headlines about the art theft had dwindled to almost nothing.

"I love the desk," Rose said when Emily showed her the office.

"Yeah, look. It has griffins." Emily pointed to the carved legs. "I wanted him to have a good desk for studying." Griffin was taking two courses at the nearby community college.

"How is that going?"

"It's a lot on top of work, but he likes it. He can read modern books really well now. He's thinking about becoming a high school history teacher."

"He would be amazing!"

They finished the tour and headed out to the front porch. As Emily was locking the door behind them, she said, "I'm kind of surprised you wanted to go to Medieval Legends a second time."

Rose grinned. "It's a great show."

Soon after, they were sitting in their front-row seats in the Green Knight section, wearing gold cardboard crowns and eating roast chicken with their fingers. Children in the crowd waved glowing plastic swords; parents, dating couples, and groups of girlfriends chatted and drank colorful cocktails.

A recorded trumpet fanfare filled the arena. Griffin's friend Dan, who had recently been promoted to the Lord Chancellor role, emerged on his horse, shouting a welcome to all the lords and ladies. Everyone cheered. He told them it was time to introduce the brave knights who would fight in the great tournament.

Emily told Rose, "Griffin's going to be the third one."

Dan hollered, "Are you ready to face the talons of the griffin?"

Emily laughed. "Never mind! I guess he's first today!"

Dan raised his arm. "Give it up for the Green Knight!"

Their section exploded into cheering and banner-waving. Through a cloud of dry ice mist, Griffin emerged on a galloping black steed, holding a banner aloft, his golden hair flowing behind him.

As he slowed to a stop in the middle of the ring, Emily realized she'd been holding her breath. It was her fourth time at the show, but she was *never* going to get used to that dramatic entrance. The first time, she'd actually gotten dizzy.

"And next," Dan said, "get ready to meet the—"

"Stop!" Griffin yelled. His voice seemed to echo from the rafters.

Dan turned to him. "Green Knight, why dost thou . . . interrupt our ceremonies?"

Oh no. Emily's heart was in her throat. In the first few weeks that he'd had the job, she'd worried that he might go off script. He seemed to be doing that now.

"Forgive me, Lord Chancellor, and all my lords and ladies!"

Griffin said. Wait . . . he had a microphone! Everything was all right. This was just a new bit.

"Before I face this deadly battle, there is one thing I must do," Griffin went on.

"And what might that be, O Green Knight?" Dan asked.

"I must ask the lady I love to be my wife!"

"Oh my *God*," Emily said as the crowd cheered. She turned to Rose, who was bouncing in her seat and squealing. *She knew!*

Griffin tossed his banner to Dan, who caught it easily, and rode over to their section. The other knights on their horses emerged from the wings. Griffin dismounted, strode over to Emily, and got down on one knee.

"My lady Emily Porter, when first I met you, it was as if I was in a dream." Emily gave a choked laugh and covered her mouth with both hands. "And the first time we kissed, I felt as though I had come to life again."

"That's so *romantic*," a woman sitting behind Emily moaned.

Love shone in Griffin's eyes as he gazed up at Emily. "Your kindness, wisdom, and beauty are without parallel, and to you only would I be steadfast, loyal, and true. Will you do me the great honor of being my wife?"

"Yes!" In case they couldn't hear her in the back rows, she lifted her arms in the air and shouted it again at the top of her lungs. "Yes!"

Cheers rocked the arena. Griffin stood, and she leaned over the railing and kissed him.

"I love you," she whispered, and he wiped away one of her tears with his thumb. She kissed him again, her heart overflowing with joy. How was it possible that not so long ago, she'd thought this kind of romance was as fake as the cardboard crown on her head? Dreams did come true, lives did start anew, and right in Chicago, she'd found her very own knight in shining armor.

AUTHOR'S NOTE

I originally wrote *Her Knight at the Museum* to bring myself joy in a difficult time. I know many of us, at some point in our lives, have felt trapped or overlooked, like Griffin . . . or have felt the sting of betrayal or regret, like Emily. I love writing and reading romance novels because they remind us that a better chapter may be ahead.

For the sake of the story, I've taken some poetic license with the organizational structure and operations of the museum. I've also taken liberties with Griffin's speech patterns, because if he really spoke like someone from the early 1400s, he and Emily would struggle even more to understand one another. The first song Griffin sings at the clinic is "La Mule," an old French folk song, and the lyrics really are that strange.

Thank you so much for reading my book. I hope you enjoyed it, and if you did, I'd be so grateful if you'd take the time to leave an online review. I look forward to sharing more stories with you!

ACKNOWLEDGMENTS

I have so many people to thank for helping me bring this book to life.

My blog readers read some excerpts of this story when it was a work in progress. Their encouragement kept me going! Pamela Donovan, Jenifer Boles, and Jennifer Fujita were beta readers. I can't thank them enough for their insightful feedback and support.

I would like to thank Kristin MacDonough and Daisy Wong for kindly taking the time to talk with me about their work and experiences at the Art Institute of Chicago.

I am so fortunate to have the wonderful Julie Gwinn at Seymour Agency as my agent and Berkley as my publisher for this story. My diligent and gifted editor, Sarah Blumenstock, believed in this story and made it shine, and I am so grateful. It was truly a pleasure to work with her, Liz Sellers, and the whole Berkley team.

Thank you to all my family and friends, including the Chicago-North Romance Writers, for being so supportive in my author journey. Thank you to my husband, Gill Donovan, for all his help and his unwavering belief in me. I love you.

Author photo copyright © *Maia Rosenfeld Photography LLC*

Bryn Donovan is the author of several romance novels. She's also written nonfiction books for writers and the story treatments for two Hallmark Channel movies. Her work has appeared in *McSweeney's, Writer's Digest,* and many literary journals. A former executive editor in publishing, she earned her MFA in creative writing from the University of Arizona. She's a voracious reader, a rescue dog lover, and a hopeless romantic who lives in the Chicago area and blogs about writing and positivity.

VISIT BRYN DONOVAN ONLINE

BrynDonovan.com

BrynDonovanAuthor

BrynDonovan

AuthorBrynDonovan

Ready to find
your next great read?

Let us help.

Visit prh.com/nextread

Penguin
Random
House